THE BLEEDING

After losing at a poker game, Leo Aikin heads home in the freezing Connecticut rain to the home he shares with his wife, Judith, and her sister Paula—the Runyon girls. But they're not there, and Leo begins to worry. A search of the area turns up their car, but not the sisters. Soon, his nerve-wracking search leads to New York, where he begins to turn up a hidden history of failed theatrical careers, burlesque houses, and a possible murder. Shadowed by an affable private detective named Florian Singleton, Leo delves into a past that is now beginning to overshadow the present. His only lead is a handsome man seen talking to his wife the day of her disappearance—and a bloody nightmare image of death!

THE EVIL DAYS

Caleb Dawson lives in the suburbs and works for a New York publisher. Every day he takes the train into the city. But today is different. Today he learns that his wife Sally has found a lost bag of jewels which the TV reporters are announcing belong to the wife of the owner of his publishing company. Sally does not intend to give up the jewels—she wants more than Caleb's salary can provide. Then Caleb discovers the murdered body of a local poet whose latest collection of unsaleable poetry the owner of the publishing company had just asked Caleb to accept. But nothing prepares him for the shady characters who come looking for the jewels—or the sneaking suspicion that there is more to the poet's death than mere coincidence.

BRUNO FISCHER BIBLIOGRAPHY
(1908-1992)

Novels
Ben Helm Series
The Dead Men Grin (1945)
More Deaths Than One (1947)
The Restless Hands (1949)
The Angels Fell (1950; reprinted in pb as The Flesh Was Cold, 1951)
The Silent Dust (1950)
The Paper Circle (1951; reprinted in pb as Stripped for Murder, 1953)

Unrelated Novels
So Much Blood (1939; reprinted in pb as Stairway to Death, 1951)
The Hornets' Nest (1944)
Quoth the Raven (1944; reprinted in the UK as Croaked the Raven, 1947; in U.S. pb as The Fingered Man, 1953)
Kill to Fit (1946)
The Pigskin Bag (1946)
The Spider Lily (1946)
The Bleeding Scissors (1948; reprinted in the UK as The Scarlet Scissors, 1950)

House of Flesh (1950)
The Lustful Ape (1950; originally pub as by Russell Gray; reprinted as by Fischer, 1959)
Fools Walk In (1951)
The Lady Kills (1951)
Run for Your Life (1953)
So Wicked My Love (1954)
Knee-deep in Death (1956)
Murder in the Raw (1957)
The Fast Buck (1958)
Second-Hand Nude (1959)
The Girl Between (1960)
The Evil Days (1974)

Collections
A Mate for Murder: And Other Tales from the Pulps (1992)

As Jason F. Storm
Domination (1970)

The Bleeding Scissors
• • •
The Evil Days

Two novels by Bruno Fischer
INTRODUCTION BY GARY LOVISI

STARK HOUSE

Stark House Press • Eureka California

THE BLEEDING SCISSORS / THE EVIL DAYS

Published by Stark House Press
1315 H Street
Eureka, CA 95501, USA
griffinskye3@sbcglobal.net
www.starkhousepress.com

THE BLEEDING SCISSORS
Originally published by Ziff-Davis Publishing, Chicago, and copyright ©
1948 by Bruno Fischer.
Copyright © renewed Nov. 10, 1975 by Bruno Fischer.

THE EVIL DAYS
Originally published by Random House, New York, and copyright © 1973 by
Bruno Fischer.

Reprinted by permission of the Estate of Bruno Fischer. All rights reserved
under International and Pan-American Copyright Conventions.

"Rediscovering Bruno Fischer" copyright © 2015 by Gary Lovisi.

ISBN: 1-933586-80-x
ISBN: 978-1-933586-80-9

Book design by Mark Shepard, shepgraphics.com
Cover art by Robert Maguire, one of the designs for the original paperback
edition of *The Bleeding Scissors*, used by permission of Lynn Maguire.

PUBLISHER'S NOTE:
This is a work of fiction. Names, characters, places and incidents are either the
products of the author's imagination or used fictionally, and any resemblance
to actual persons, living or dead, events or locales, is entirely coincidental.
Without limiting the rights under copyright reserved above, no part of this
publication may be reproduced, stored, or introduced into a retrieval system
or transmitted in any form or by any means (electronic, mechanical,
photocopying, recording or otherwise) without the prior written permission of
both the copyright owner and the above publisher of the book.

First Stark House Press Edition: August 2015

7
Rediscovering Bruno Fischer
by Gary Lovisi

11
The Bleeding Scissors
by Bruno Fischer

147
The Evil Days
by Bruno Fischer

Rediscovering Bruno Fischer
by Gary Lovisi

Bruno Fischer wrote 25 mystery novels that have sold over 10 million copies and have been translated into 12 languages. That's the cold hard facts of his writing career but it tells you nothing about the real man. The real man was neither cold nor hard, but a wonderful writer and the most decent of gentleman. I met Bruno and got to know him during the last years of his life and was privileged to have him as a guest at my annual book show in New York City. He was a joy to be around, with a winning smile and a mischievous twinkle to his eyes — even though he was almost blind from a life of writing and editing. He was very kind and generous and we became friends — a friendship I treasure to this day. Bruno was a special person I will never forget. He generously allowed me to reprint some of his short crime stories in my magazine *Hardboiled*, and eventually I published a collection of his horror / terror pulp tales, *A Mate For Murder* under my Gryphon Books imprint in 1992. Sadly, before that book appeared Bruno passed away from a stroke on March 16, 1992 while vacationing in Mexico with his wife, Ruth. It was a terrible time and as the years passed Bruno's books went out of print and were only available in old rare hardcover editions, or yellowing vintage paperbacks from the 1940s and 50s. Bruno Fischer was becoming a forgotten author, but he was never forgotten by serious crime noir fans who knew the "good stuff."

Bruno's work is the good stuff! It is time to rediscover Bruno Fischer and his classic crime fiction, and the perfect place to begin is with the two outstanding suspense thrillers that make up this new edition from Stark House Press.

Bruno Fischer was a master storyteller who conjured his magic with words as he learned his craft in the pulp magazines of the 1930s. Under his own name, and a plethora of pseudonyms, most notably Russell Gray and Adam Train, he wrote pulp suspense noir tales that were dark stories of tension, thrills and train-wreck intensity. In each tale he piled on the tension and suspense until it grew to a pulse-pounding crescendo. These stories became hits with the reading public of the era and were beloved by editors of the pulps who always asked him for more. These stories are still great fun to read today. In some cases Bruno wrote most (if not all) the stories in some issues of those pulp magazines. This training ground in the pulps enabled him to hone his talent to a sharp precision, and as that talent grew it transformed him into one of the best crime suspense authors in the pulp magazine field.

Later, through a series of hardcover crime novels published in the 1940s (all of which were reprinted in paperback by Dell and Pocket Books in the 1940s and 1950s), as well as some outstanding crime noir paperback originals done for Gold Medal Books throughout the 1950s, Bruno Fischer eventually became one of the best and most popular crime authors of the era.

The two novels that make up this special Stark House Press edition: *The Bleeding Scissors* (1948), and *The Evil Days* (1973), are examples of Bruno's best work. They highlight his wonderful plotting and creativity, mixed with his trademark suspense and tension, all building with every page you read. Reading these novels is a pulse-pounding experience as each scene piles on the stress and tension to dizzying heights.

In *The Bleeding Scissors*, Leo Aikens is caught up in a seemingly hum-drum normal domestic life, until his wife, Judith, turns up missing. Has she run off? Or is it something worse? Evidence points to conflicting answers — of which the police have none — but the tension and plot twists come fast and furious. Leo soon realizes that he must seek out the truth himself so he begins his own investigation to find out exactly what happened to his wife — and his wife's sister — who is also missing. The two women are missing and there seem to be no clues. No reason. However, the young women have a local reputation among some in town as the "wild" Runyon Sisters. Leo grows concerned over those rumors, but he knows Judith and is sure she is in danger and that she has not just run off with some "mysterious young man" as the cops and neighbors tell him.

Leo's investigation leads him into a complex case full of sinister characters, back-stabbing motives, blind greed, and heart-pounding excitement. The reader follows Leo with nail-biting tension as he gets closer to the truth and discovers answers he does not want to face. This novel is a fine noir, full of memorable characters such as Leo's enigmatic wife, Judith, and a charming fellow known as Singleton — both of whom's motives are suspect. Bruno Fischer keeps the twists and turns racing right up to the end as he piles on grand doses of tension and suspense. This is a most memorable noir crime thriller, an enjoyable read of the type they just don't write anymore. It is a classic!

Then in the 1960s Bruno took on a job as editor of Macmillan's Collier Books, a paperback outfit, as well as education editor of the Arco Publishing Company. He had been an editor in his younger days, editing *The Socialist Call* in the 1930s, but then left to write crime stories full-time for the pulps. In his ten years as editor at Collier Books he was responsible for publishing many fine books. However his editing work cut severely into his writing output so it was not until ten years later, in 1973, that he published his 25th and last novel, *The Evil Days*. This one is outstanding!

In *The Evil Days*, we are introduced to Caleb Dawson, solid citizen, along with his very nice wife Sally, contemporary suburbanites on a tight budget, trying to eke out their life with two young kids. He is an editor at a big New York publishing house — much as Bruno was himself at the time. And here Bruno includes much fascinating and rather cynical but pinpoint truth about the publishing business and the writing game.

In one cynical scene that most likely came from Bruno's own experience in the business, he has his hero Caleb talking with another editor about the publication process in their office:

"Caleb, are you there?" he called over the partition.
"Yes."
"Last night I spent a little time on that Carlton novel you asked me to look over. By all means take it on."
"Don't tell me you liked it!"
"What's that got to do with it? It's up to his usual standard — incredibly bad. What's to the point is that he sells."
"I know. That's why I hesitate to turn it down. If only he knew a bit about writing."
"If he learned how to write, he'd rise to mediocrity and lose his public."

Caleb and his wife are soon thrust into a whirlwind of dire circumstances when she finds a treasure trove of priceless jewelry in a strip mall parking lot. Instantly their life changes as they see this windfall as the answer to all their financial woes. The jewelry is said to be worth more than a quarter of a million bucks. Caleb and Sally's plan is to keep the jewels and sell them for cash — instead of returning them to the rightful owner. That decision leads them into dark deception and danger as their moral standards collapse in the lust for riches. Of course in any good noir, these things never work out very well and the plot piles on the stress and tension, while including devious twists and turns that make this novel an experience you will never forget. The book takes place in just one week, one chapter per day, it begins on a Wednesday and the pace roars like an out of control locomotive.

By day seven, a Tuesday, Caleb puts together the many pieces of this convoluted puzzle and it is a real shocker. You are in for a terrific mind-blasting conclusion where all the known — and some surprising, but fair to the reader, unknown — knots of this complex noir puzzle are revealed.

The Evil Days is Bruno Fischer's masterpiece. It is a little known sleeper of a noir that has until now escaped detection by more astute critics — other than Ed Gorman, who has praised it highly. Now you can experience this fine novel yourself. Greg Shepard and Stark House Press have done a great service for all crime and noir fans by bringing out this attractive new edition of *The Bleeding Scissors* and *The Evil Days* for a whole new generation of fans and readers — all of whom can now rediscover the outstanding noir crime fiction of Bruno Fischer. I'd like to say now *relax* and enjoy these two stories, but I've read them and I know better! *You won't be able to relax!*

Gary Lovisi
Brooklyn, New York
March, 2015

The Bleeding Scissors
By Bruno Fischer

1. The Empty House

I paused at the foot of the porch steps to adjust the buckles of my arctics. In that freezing rain the others didn't stop to wait for me.

"George, I have to go back for a minute," I called.

The four men had reached the three cars parked on what was either the semicircular driveway or the lawn. It was impossible to tell. The layer of ice-covered snow made all of that flat area between the house and the road a crumpled, gray-white blanket, slit by the tire ruts of the three cars.

"Okay, Leo," George Kloe said. He ducked into his car, out of the rain.

I went back up the porch steps. The front door was unlocked. I pushed it open without ringing, and from the center hall I turned right to the dining room where we had played stud poker at the big round table. Bernard Terhune was gathering up the cards.

"Forget something, Leo?" he asked.

"Mind holding till payday the check I gave you?"

The check was still on the table. Terhune sat down and picked it up and stretched it between his long fingers. "One hundred and twenty-three dollars," he read aloud as if I didn't know the amount. "Your pay check won't quite cover it."

Bernard Terhune was owner of Jorberg Plastics, which made him my boss. He was a rangy, square-shouldered, unsmiling man who'd been a crisp-speaking army captain during the war, and acted in his plant as if he were still running a battalion. I'd met him when I'd been attached to his Chemical Warfare battalion a few weeks after the invasion of France. A year after the war ended he'd written me at the testing laboratory of a Chicago department store, where I worked at the time, and had offered me a better job with him. That hadn't been a favor for past acquaintanceship. He'd needed a good chemist and knew that I was one.

"All I ask you to do is hold the check for a few days," I said stiffly. "Let me worry about covering it."

"You owe me fourteen hundred dollars already," he reminded me dryly. Probably the reason he'd advanced me the money on my pay was so that he could keep reminding me of it. Then he added in the crisp lecturing manner he'd learned as an officer, "You had no business playing tonight."

"You were the one who forced it up to dollar-limit stud," I retorted. "It started off as a quarter game."

"If it comes to that, you can't even afford to play penny ante."

I sunk my hands deep into my overcoat pockets. "Oh, hell!" I said and swung to the door.

"Just a minute, Leo."

I turned. Terhune was tearing up the check. He tore it into eight precise pieces and piled them on top of an overflowing ash tray.

It wasn't a gracious gesture the way he did it, and then his words made it just plain mean. "Pay me when you can," he said, "but remember that's the last you're clipping me for."

I found that I was huddling in my overcoat like a cringing beggar receiving a handout. I jerked myself erect.

"I'll give you another check on pay day," I said, fumbling for my pride. Though how I'd manage to cover that check I didn't know.

"Your trouble, Leo, is those irresponsible Runyon sisters." He pushed aside the ash tray and started to lay out cards for solitaire. "Having Judith for a wife was enough of a problem, but Paula had to move in on you, too. They were always wild."

"Just what do you mean by that?" I hadn't cared for the implication in his tone.

Carefully Terhune straightened out the rows of cards. "Specifically, I'm referring to the way they throw away your money."

"Is that any of your business?" I'd had to take a lot from him in the army because a sergeant was supposed to from a captain, but I didn't have to from an employer.

Terhune raised his eyes from the cards. Their pale blueness was as bleak as a frozen pond on a windy day. "Maybe it isn't my business what you do with the money I lend you. But Paula is my business. After all these years — "

His jaw snapped shut. Abruptly he was wholly occupied with his solitaire game. He regretted having let his guard down long enough to reveal to me a lonely, bitter man who had only what money could buy.

Vaguely I had known that Terhune used to go out with my sister-in-law Paula. That hadn't meant anything in particular because, from what I'd heard, there had been scarcely a young man in Jorberg who hadn't been her boy friend at one time or another. But now I understood why the most eligible bachelor in town lived alone in this oversized house with a widowed sister. The fact that Paula was also still unmarried, that evidently she preferred no man at all to him, wouldn't be easy for a man like him to take.

I felt a little sorry for him then, and a little smug too because my life was working out so much better than his. I had a few debts, but I had a real home and Judith in it.

Terhune was rejecting my presence in the room by not again looking up at me from the cards. In the army he would merely have dismissed me; here he was doing the same by ignoring me.

"Good night," I said briskly.

He muttered something which may have been good night, but sounded like nothing at all.

George Kloe was listening to the one o'clock news on his car radio.

"A miracle," he said when I got in beside him. "We actually quit before one."

"It's a weekday night," I pointed out, "and we promised each other we'd quit early."

"Sure, but we always do. This is the first time we stuck to it."

George backed the car out to the road. As soon as we hit the road we were in trouble.

It was the kind of weather you'll get in early March in Connecticut. All day a sticky, mushy snow had fallen. At eight o'clock it had stopped after leaving three or four inches. Snowplows had gone through, clearing the roads, but that had been a mistake because at around ten-thirty a freezing rain had started. It was still coming down, covering the cleared roads with a murderous layer of ice.

We lived only half a mile away, but when George pulled up in front of my house he was exhausted. He lit a cigarette, and I remained in his car for another minute to light one too.

"How's Edna Runyon?" he asked suddenly.

He meant Judith's and Paula's aunt who'd been in the hospital for two months and would not leave alive.

"It may be any day now," I told him.

"Much pain?"

"Not yet, but the doctor expects it."

"Tough," he said. "I suppose you're footing the bills."

"There's nobody else."

I opened the car door.

"You lost a lot of money tonight," George said. "I never saw such lousy luck."

I paused with one foot through the door. The dash light showed his heavy face watching me solemnly. He was a big man; in his shaggy brown coat he looked like a bear hunched over the wheel. I wondered if he was going to offer to lend me money. I'd never thought of him as a particularly close friend. Up to this moment he'd been only the next door neighbor from whom you borrowed tools and with whom you played poker and whom you sometimes invited to a party with his wife when there were a lot of other people. He was a salesman for display signs, and doing very well, I'd heard. He could afford to let me have a loan.

As soon as the thought crossed my mind, I hated myself for it.

"Your expenses must be plenty heavy, just getting married and buying a house and the hospital bills," George said.

Was he working up to offering me a few hundred? I got out of the car before he did, or before I weakened and asked him for it.

"I manage pretty well," I told him. "Thanks for the lift. So long."

His car crawled toward his driveway a few hundred feet ahead. He skidded as he made the sharp turn, but not much. My feet broke through the crust of ice over the snow as I walked up the flagged path to my house.

I'd bought that house eight months ago, when Judith and I were married. It spread out on a single floor; it had a sundeck over one bedroom and an eating terrace off the dinette and lots of big windows. Very modern. The scene I walked up to could have been picked off the cover of a magazine for middle-class homeowners. A piece of moon showed up the tan stucco house sentimentally against the snow and the background of snow-laden trees covered with a sheen of ice.

What was most important about that house was that Judith was in it. All the lights were out, which meant that she was asleep, but she would wake when I entered the room and would turn her head on the pillow for my kiss. Let Terhune feel superior because he had money.

I got rid of my hat and coat and arctics in the foyer and headed straight for our bedroom. In darkness I groped around the foot of the bed to the night table and turned on the night lamp.

Judith wasn't in bed.

I crossed the hall to Paula's room. Her bed was also empty.

Judith hadn't told me that she was going out tonight. At eight-thirty I'd left her and Paula settled for the evening. They must have decided to go out after I left, and Judith wasn't in a hurry to return home because she expected the poker game to last as late as usual. So that was all right, but I hoped they weren't out in the car on a night like this.

They were. The sedan wasn't in the attached garage.

Still no reason to worry particularly. During the day I'd put the chains on the tires. Though they weren't much use on ice, they would help a little, and Judith was a good driver. She'd have sense enough to go downgrade in low gear.

I went back into the bedroom and hung my jacket in the closet and draped my necktie over the rack on the closet door and got into my slippers. Then I sat down in the living room to wait with a magazine.

At one-thirty I stood at a window looking out at the road. It was too late to be visiting friends in Jorberg on a Tuesday night. What must have happened was that they'd left before the freezing rain started and now were afraid to drive back. But even if the rain stopped at once, the roads wouldn't thaw out until morning, if then. She should have phoned me before this, at Terhune's if not here.

I turned my head to the window on my right and saw that a couple of upstairs windows in the house next door showed light. George was probably in bed by now, but there was a phone extension in their room. I went into the dinette where we kept the phone and dialed the Kloe number. George answered after the first ring.

"George," I said, "has Mabel any idea where Judith and Paula went?"

"Went when?"

"Tonight. They aren't home yet. Maybe Mabel knows."

"Just a second, Leo." A muttering came over the wire, then George said into the mouthpiece, "Mabel saw them leave in the car tonight. At around eleven."

"That late?"

"Well, Mabel — Just a second, she'll talk to you herself."

Mabel Kloe came on the wire. "I was getting undressed for bed when I heard a car. I looked out of the window and saw the light on in your driveway and your car pulling out of the garage."

"Were Judith and Paula together?"

"Yes. Judith got out of the car to close the garage door and turn off the floodlight, and I heard her talk to Paula who was in the car."

"At eleven?" I said. "That was after the rain started."

"Everything was already covered by ice. I remember worrying about George having to drive home. Leo, are you sure they didn't go to the hospital?"

I uttered a relieved sigh. "That's it, of course. Their Aunt Edna must have taken a turn for the worse and they rushed to the hospital."

"That occurred to me as soon as I saw them leave that late in such weather. I suppose she'd be better off if the end came quickly."

"Much better off," I said. "Sorry I disturbed you. Good night."

I phoned the hospital. Edna Runyon, I was told, was resting comfortably. No, Miss Runyon's nieces had not visited her tonight, and no call had been put in for them to come.

I remained seated at the phone table and tried to be rational about it. If they were stuck somewhere or afraid to drive home over these roads, Judith would phone me at Terhune's and there she would learn that I was home. But not if she thought she could still beat me home from the game without worrying me. All I had to do was wait.

I waited.

The picture started to come. There were variations of it, but basically it was always the same: a car off the road and near it two shapes in the snow. The car was on its side or upside down or crumpled or burning, and the shapes moaned or stirred in agony or were motionless. And the rain spread ice over snow and macadam and metal and flesh.

At twenty minutes after two I phoned the police station. Cory White, one of Chief Middle's force of five policemen, answered drowsily. If I knew our cops, and White in particular, he'd probably been dozing at his desk. I asked him if there had been an auto accident that night.

"Well, Bob Johnston skidded on Maple Lane and his head hit the window and he knocked himself out cold," he drawled.

"You haven't heard that my wife was in an accident?"

"Nope. She out in a car, Mr. Aikin? I've never seen the roads as bad as tonight."

"If you hear anything, please call me at once."

"Sure thing," he said. "Anybody's crazy for taking a car out tonight."

I went into the living room and looked out of the window some more. Then I returned to the dinette and started to phone Judith's friends in town. I dragged a lot of people out of bed and didn't care.

Every call drew a blank.

I'd known it would. Even in good weather Judith and Paula wouldn't have gone out at eleven at night to pay a social call. But the answer to where they'd gone and why wasn't nearly as important as why they weren't home.

At ten minutes to three there was nobody else to call. Almost four hours since they had left, and all the tragedy in the world could happen in a lot less time.

Again I phoned the house next door. This time it took much longer for George Kloe to answer.

"Sorry to wake you," I said, "but I'd like to borrow your car."

"Who's this — Leo? What's that you want?"

"Your car. I know it's a big favor. I might wreck it on a night like this, but they haven't come home yet."

Suddenly George was wide awake. "Didn't they go to the hospital?"

"No."

"And they didn't phone?"

"No."

He spoke to Mabel. Then he said to me, "Sure, you can have the car."

When I hung up, I sat at the table for a few moments longer. I had never known that there could be such terror in an empty house.

2. The Abandoned Car

George Floe kept me waiting on his porch for a couple of minutes after I rang his bell. When he came downstairs to let me into the house, he was fully dressed.

"I'm going with you," he told me.

"No," I said. "You're doing more than enough by lending me your car."

"Mabel says I shouldn't let you go alone. If we find — if there's been..." He concentrated on getting on his arctics. I wasn't the only one who had a picture in my mind.

"You know," I said, trying to talk away that picture, "when they come home and tell me why they left so late and where they've been, there'll be a simple reason for everything. That's the way these things always turn out."

"Sure, Leo," George said, getting into his overcoat.

"Judith and Paula never bother to answer letters or leave word of where they're going or call up when they're delayed," I went on. "They wouldn't hurt anybody for anything, but they're thoughtless about things like that. Paula more than Judith, but Judith learned it from her sister."

"Sure, Leo," George said. "Let's go."

We went out to the garage. We let half the air out of the rear tires to give them more traction; that and the chains should get us up and down almost any place.

"Leo," Mabel called me from the house.

I stepped out on the driveway. She had an upstairs window open, but was keeping her head inside, out of the rain.

"I just remembered something," Mabel said. "I told you I heard them talking while Judith was closing the garage door. I remember that Judith said, 'Are you sure it's Mill?' and Paula answered, 'Of course I'm sure.'"

"Mill Street?" I said.

"Well, I think she said Mill. Maybe she said the Mill, but I never heard of any such place around here. And there is a Mill Street."

George said from the garage, "How about somebody named Mill?"

The only Mill I'd ever known was Joel Mill who'd gone to high school with me two thousand miles away.

The coupé was backing out of the garage. I got in beside George. "It must be Mill Street," I told him.

Mill Street was a narrow, weaving tar road cutting Jorberg in two from north to south. We got on Mill Street in the northern hilly section where we lived and followed it south for a mile to the compact little business section fringed by the only real streets in the town. Then another half mile to the few small factories, including Jorberg Plastics, clustered around the railroad, and at the railroad station Mill Street ended.

Ordinarily I made it in five minutes. Tonight every downgrade was a hazard to be taken by almost motionless crawling in low gear, every upgrade an obstacle to be surmounted by weaving and skidding. And when we pulled up in front of the railroad station, George's big body settled back with easing tension and I closed eyes strained with peering.

Nowhere had we passed another car in motion. Several had been parked along the side of the road, probably stuck there for the night, but none had been mine.

"There's a phone booth in the station," George said. "Maybe they're home by now."

The station waiting room was deserted. I dialed my home number on the wall pay phone. After a full minute I hung up.

When I came out, George was across the road at the station parking lot. He was playing a flashlight over the four or five cars which had been left there overnight. He returned across the glass-smooth road as if walking on eggs.

"No answer?" he asked.

I shook my head.

He fished cigarettes out of his overcoat pocket. "Had an idea that what Mabel heard them say was that they were going down Mill Street to the station. But your car isn't parked in the lot."

"They wouldn't have to discuss how to reach the station," I said. "They've lived in Jorberg all their lives."

"I guess that's so."

He stood outside the car. The rain was gentle, as freezing rain usually is, and he got his cigarette lit at the first attempt.

"I still think they went to visit somebody named Mill," he said. "You sure you don't know anybody by that name?"

"I'm sure. There's more to Mill Street than we covered."

He sank his big body deeper in to his shaggy overcoat. "Nothing much at the other end of Mill Street." He'd had a taste of the roads, and I couldn't blame him for not being eager to risk his car or his neck. It wasn't his wife and sister-in-law.

We got into the car. But when we were back at our end of town, George didn't make the left turn to our houses. He kept going on Mill Street.

"Thanks, George," I said.

He said gruffly, "You'd do the same for me," and then for a long time we were silent as he concentrated on fighting the ice under the crawling wheels and I stared into a void glimmering wetly in our headlights.

Beyond the populated sections of Jorberg, Mill Street was even less of a street. It meandered emptily through rocky New England fields and patches of trees, scraggy in winter, until it lost itself after half a dozen miles in Route 6. At intervals we passed a dark, humped mass off the road, an isolated house asleep or deserted, but I'd never heard from Judith or Paula that they knew anybody who lived around here.

In the middle of nowhere in particular a sedan grew out of the darkness.

"That's it!" I yelled.

For an instant George forgot how deadly the road was. His feet came down on brake and clutch pedals. The car slewed slowly to the left, glided broadside toward my sedan, then nudged the snowbank at the shoulder of the road and came to rest.

I flung the door open. My feet hit the ground and gave way under me. I sat down. I pushed myself up by my hands and this time took mincing steps.

There was nobody inside or outside my car.

"Funny." George came around his coupe. "Doesn't look like an accident or anything."

He sprayed the beam of his flashlight over the sedan. There wasn't a sign of damage. And the car was parked as nearly to the right of the road as it could get without mounting the snowbank which the snowplow had piled up.

"So that's the answer," George said. "They got stuck here and decided to walk home."

I should have felt relieved. Here was the car safe enough, and that meant that they couldn't have been hurt. All the same, the tight knot in the pit of my stomach didn't loosen.

I opened the left front door and leaned in to switch on the lights. The key was in the ignition lock. I got behind the wheel and pressed the starter. Without hesitation, the motor caught. I released the hand brake, shifted into gear, and sent the car forward a few feet. I pulled up the brake and turned off the motor.

George's face was framed by the window on my left. Through the glass we looked at each other.

"Nothing wrong with the car," I muttered.

"But plenty with the roads. What happened is simple. They didn't want to risk driving any more, so they left the car here and started to walk home."

"And left the key in the ignition?"

"You know how women are with cars."

I opened the door, but didn't get out. "What time is it?"

He pulled back his coat sleeve to look at his wrist watch. "Three-forty."

"The car's pointing away from Jorberg," I said. "That means they left this spot shortly after they left home. Nearly five hours ago. It shouldn't have taken them more than an hour to walk home. Say two hours, and there are still nearly three left over."

"Maybe they were cold and tired and stopped off at a house on the way."

"And didn't phone me?"

It was as if we were debating for points. I was trying to prove that something was wrong and George was trying to beat down my arguments.

"Lots of houses don't have phones," George said. "Or they phoned you when you weren't in and figure you're still at the poker game."

I got out of the car. I said, "Let's have the light," and took it from his hand and played the beam off one side of the road and then the other. Everywhere past the snowbanks white snow was crushed by smooth, unbroken ice. Even a small animal would have left a trail.

"What makes you think they'd walk off into the fields?" George asked.

"I don't know."

"They're home or safe somewhere else," he said impatiently. He wiped rain off his face. "It stands to reason that they're okay if the car is."

Did it? Well, sure. I was letting my imagination substitute for unknown facts; I was scaring myself with ghosts the way people always did when they were worried. That was all it was. I merely didn't know the facts.

I told George I'd follow his car in mine. But before I started I took the long jack handle out of my car trunk and stuck it in the snowbank.

"What's the idea?" George stood outside the door of his own car, watching me in the rain.

"Maybe I'll want to find this spot again," I said.

I wasn't quite sure why I would want to. Maybe I was still looking for ghosts.

We crawled back, my car behind George's, and for company I had the clanking of the tire chains and swishing of the windshield wipers. And when we reached my house, it was as dark as when we had left it.

I sat behind the wheel of my car. The motor continued to run. I thought of shutting it off, but I didn't. I just sat there.

George came over from his car parked in front of mine.

"They might have gone to bed. We were away quite a while."

I nodded. I shut off the motor and together we walked up to the house. The door was locked on the spring lock. As I fumbled to get the key in, George was a hulking shadow leaning against the wall. Like myself, he was listening to the silence of the house.

Inside the house, I headed straight for the bedroom, switching on lights as I went. Then I was in the bedroom, with George behind me, and we were both staring at the unoccupied bed and the undisturbed green bedspread.

George said, "Like I said, they stopped off somewhere. Maybe they tried to phone you while you were out."

There was something pink on the floor between the foot of the bed and Judith's dresser. I looked at it a long time, trying to understand it. I moved forward and picked it up. It was one of Judith's silk slips.

"Listen," I said hoarsely. "This wasn't on the floor when I left the house."

"What wasn't?"

I held up the slip. "I went to that night table to put on the light. I couldn't have passed without stepping on the slip. When I went to the table, there was no light, but when I came back I would have seen it, and I would have seen it when I went back later to turn out that light."

George frowned. "So what?"

I turned to Judith's dresser. The middle drawer was partly open. I pulled it all the way out and saw that it was practically empty. I opened the other two drawers. There was stuff in them, but not nearly as much as there should have been.

George was at my side. "My God, Leo, you look green around the gills!"

I straightened up. The tense knot was gone from my stomach. Only emptiness was left. I heard myself say, "The other day Judith complained that she didn't have enough drawer space."

George started to say something and changed his mind.

I brushed past him and went to the closet. It had been too small for both of us, but there was plenty of room now.

"Her clothes are gone too," I said. "Her tweed suit, her red dress, her velvet —" My voice choked off. An inventory wasn't necessary.

"That's lousy, Leo," he murmured sympathetically. "What about Paula?"

We went into Paula's room. There were underthings in her dresser and dresses in her closet, but not enough. They'd gone off together.

Our luggage was kept in the large hall closet. There had been a valise and two matched bags and a small week-end case. Only the valise was left.

I stood holding onto the edge of the closet door. I tried to think. I had to think straighter and clearer than ever before in my life, but nothing was straight or clear.

"Leo," George said gently. His hand dropped on my arm. He led me into the living room. Still in my wet hat and coat, I sat down on the couch.

George must have left the room, for when I looked up he was coming out of the dinette with a bottle of bourbon and two pony glasses. "I guess we can both use a drink, Leo." He filled the glasses at the coffee table and handed me one and sat down opposite me on the club chair.

"Well," he said in the soft, quiet tones you use to somebody in a sickbed, "at least you know they're safe and sound."

My head came up so quickly that my chin nicked the glass and spilled a little of the bourbon on my coat. "Don't you get it?" I said. "Those clothes were taken in the last hour, while I was in the car with you."

He rolled the rim of the glass against his lower lip. He looked sorry for me.

"Look," I said. "I told you Judith's slip wasn't on the floor when I came home from the poker game. And her clothes were still in the closet. I hung my jacket in the closet and I took it out again when I dressed to go to your house. I would've noticed if that many of her dresses were missing."

"You mean they came back here while we were looking for them?" He studied his bourbon as if for an answer. "Could be. They went out to meet somebody" — he paused delicately — "and then they must have left their car on Mill Street because they didn't need two. Then they decided to go away with — " He struggled to ease the blow. "So they came back here for their clothes," he ended it up feebly.

"That's a damn lie!" I said.

The vehemence of my tone startled him. He looked into his glass again and decided that its contents belonged down his throat. Then he sighed heavily. "Those Runyon girls!"

"Damn you!" I said. "Judith didn't walk out on me. Can't you see that she wouldn't have done it this way, sneaking away in the middle of the night without a word to me?"

He couldn't see it, but he didn't say so. He refilled his glass. I hadn't touched mine. Later maybe I'd want to get drunk, but not right now. I sat holding the glass and George sat opposite me, both of us in our damp hats and coats and wet arctics, George a great bear of a man crowding the armchair, staying on with me the way a man will stay with a friend who has been badly hurt.

"Somebody else came for their clothes," I said suddenly. "To make it look as if they left home willingly."

My mind was too dull and tired and bruised to understand the full implication of my words until they were out. Then I looked back at what I had said and my hand trembled and a little more of the bourbon sloshed out.

"Easy, Leo," George said. "It's bad enough she walked out on you with another man."

He had lost his delicacy. He had said it — *with another man*. Because not the worst of what could have happened was that she had left me for somebody else.

I drank the bourbon then. It was like water. "No," I said. "She'd never do it like that, if she did it at all."

"You don't know those Runyon girls, Leo. You married one and the other lived with you, but you don't know them."

Maybe at other times I would have swung at a man who said that. At least I would have kicked him out of my house. Now all I did was turn away from the pity in his heavy-lidded eyes.

In the bedroom the electric clock made its whirring noise. Something was wrong with it; it had done that for a month, but I'd become so used to the sound that I'd stopped hearing it. Now I heard nothing else.

"Have another drink, Leo."

George was standing over me, the bottle in his hand. I shook my head and stood up and went to a window.

I was looking for them to come up the walk from the street. Judith would be walking with that buoyant grace of hers, hardly able to keep herself down to Paula's more languid movement, the bright, young freshness of the two sisters a sight for any man's eyes. And when they came in shaking out their wet hair and their brown eyes glowing and both of them calling me darling and perhaps Paula kissing me too as she sometimes did, they would have a perfectly ridiculous and irresponsible explanation for everything.

All I saw through the window was that the rain had stopped.

3. The Runyon Girl

Dawn was bright and cloudless, with a hint in the air of the spring which was officially only ten days off. The roads were already turning to slush under the slanting rays of the rising sun.

Chief of Police Mort Middle and one of his cops were with me. We stood where I had left the jack handle in the snow-bank and peered across the craggy white fields on either side of Mill Street. We walked a short distance north of the jack handle and then south. It wasn't necessary to leave the road to see that nobody had gone into the fields after the snow had stopped at eight o'clock last night.

"One thing's sure," Chief Middle said. "They weren't dragged out of the car and into the fields."

"Let's go farther up the road," I urged.

Middle rubbed his jowls. He was a thick-set, slow-moving man whom everybody in town called Mort. He started to say something and changed his mind and nodded. He was humoring me because I was a taxpayer and a solid citizen.

Slowly we drove all the way to the highway at which Mill Street ended. The cop was at the wheel; Middle and I sat in the back seat of the police sedan. Once I yelled for the driver to stop. I dove out of the car and in among a sparse growth of trees. The ice crust made small crunching sounds as my feet broke through it. But what I'd seen were only the prints made by an animal, probably a large dog. That was good news, for if they had been taken into the fields it would have been more terrible than anything else that could have happened to them.

We turned at the highway and returned down Mill Street. At the jack handle the driver stopped the car. I got out to fetch the jack handle.

"Well, that's that," Middle said as we moved again. "There's no law says two grown women can't go away from home if they want to."

"But what about the abandoned car?" I protested.

He shrugged. "So what does it mean? Now if there was a sign of anything, violence or tracks in the snow, I'd say it was police business. You say you heard Mrs. Kloe say they were going to Mill Street. We know by where you found the car that's just what they did. Looks like they had a date to meet somebody in another car, likely a couple of men, and went with them." He held up a hand when I opened my mouth. "You're going to say why didn't the men call for them at the house. Maybe they figured you'd come home early before the roads got too dangerous. Fact is, they packed their clothes and took them along, so it was plain they'd made up their minds to go away with somebody."

"But I told you they came back for their clothes hours later, while George Kloe and I were looking for them."

"How does that change anything — if that's what they did? All it means, they made up their minds later to go away with those men."

"Why do you keep saying they went with men?" I yelled at him. My hands were clenched in my overcoat pockets: I wanted to hit somebody — anybody.

"They went with somebody because there had to be another car."

"Not Judith," I said. "Not like that."

Middle shifted uneasily in the seat and turned his face to the window. I saw the cop who was driving look at me through his mirror. They were sorry for me, the way George Kloe had been a few hours ago when we had discovered that their clothes were gone.

"It's not the first time the Runyon girls ran away," Middle muttered, keeping the back of his head to me.

It always came to that — the Runyon girls.

I grabbed his arm. "Judith didn't walk out on me. There was no reason for it. Everything was fine. And she wouldn't do it that way, sneaking off without a word. She'd tell me to my face. She'd — " My voice caught. I cleared my throat. "She'd at least leave a note."

"Maybe she'll write you," he said placatingly.

We were back in the village. The sedan turned toward my house and stopped behind my car which I'd left parked at the curb.

"Are you going to let it go at that?" I said. "Aren't you going to make an attempt to find them?"

Middle patted my shoulder — soft-soap for an irate and unreasonable citizen. "Maybe you'll hear from her soon, or she'll change her mind and come back."

I got out of the car. When he said good-bye to me, I slammed the door in his face.

I was still outside the house when I heard the phone ring. By the time I reached the dinette, the ringing had stopped. The operator said sorry, my party had hung up.

Judith? I stood beside the phone, waiting for it to ring again. My legs were caving in on me. My coat was weighing me down in the warm house. I removed it and my hat and my arctics, but the load was still on me. I took an orange from the bowl on the table and peeled it with my fingers and ate it, all the while listening to the silence. I went into the kitchen and started to make coffee.

The phone rang. My heart bounced with the sound. I rushed into the dinette; I was clumsy getting the handset off its cradle.

It was only Bernard Terhune. I hated him because he wasn't Judith.

"What's this I hear about Judith having left you?" he said. It was only eight o'clock, but already the town had heard it that way. I told him that it wasn't that at all, that something else must have happened.

"I met Mort Middle," he said. "He claims that they packed up their belongings and beat it. She and Paula both."

There was no point arguing with him. He wasn't even a cop who ought to do something about it. I said, "Did you phone me a few minutes ago?"

"About fifteen minutes ago. I hung up when there was no answer."

The coffee maker had been in my hand when the phone had rung, and it was still in my hand. The lower glass bowl had water in it, the upper bowl coffee grounds; the whole thing shook in my hand.

The wire was silent. I hadn't anything to say to him, and Terhune wasn't one to put into words the real purpose of his call. He didn't give a damn about Judith being gone, for whatever reason. He was thinking of Paula — of the woman he had again lost without ever having had.

"Are you coming to work today?" he asked crisply when the silence became ridiculous.

"I doubt it," I said. "Good-bye."

I went into the gleaming, super-duper kitchen that had set me back fifteen hundred dollars and placed the coffee maker on the electric range. Right at this moment I needed coffee desperately, black and strong. For a while I watched the clear water in the lower bowl refuse to come to a boil. A sense of futility weighed down on me — about hearing from Judith, about the coffee boiling, about everything. I dragged myself into the living room and sank into the club chair.

The Runyon girls, I thought. One of them was Mrs. Leo Aikin, but to the town Judith remained one of the two Runyon girls. They had become a tradition in Jorberg; anything they did could be explained by a smile and shrug, by the fact that they were the Runyon girls. You couldn't think of them apart.

Not that they were much alike physically except for brown hair and brown eyes. Judith was taller, full-bodied, buoyant, her irrepressible enthusiasms out in the open; Paula was slender, sleek, languid, her irrepressible enthusiasms under the surface. When those two enthusiasms came together, as they nearly always did, the result was exciting and breathtaking and bewildering. It had led them into all sorts of escapades when they were younger, though harmless and innocent enough from what I'd heard. It had led them to an obstinate and unsuccessful assault on the Broadway stage. It had led them in the last few months to furnishing this house with the abandon of drunken sailors.

The joke went around town that when I married Judith Runyon, I also married Paula Runyon. The fact was that Paula had been in our house more than in her own, and a couple of months ago she had moved in with us and become part of the household. Living with Judith was wonderful. Living with both of them was somewhat exhausting.

I didn't mind too much. Even my feelings for Judith were tied up with Paula. I loved my wife; I was immensely fond of my sister-in-law.

No, you couldn't think of them apart. Even when they disappeared, they disappeared together.

Sitting in the armchair and waiting for the coffee to boil, I closed my eyes, groping for a clue to tell me why they were gone. In spite of the unpleasantness about the rug, which I'd insisted go back, Judith's kiss hadn't lacked its usual ardor last night when I'd left the house for Terhune's poker game. It had to be something else, maybe going far back, and it struck me that I probably knew less about the Runyon girls than almost anybody in Jorberg. Less than Bernard Terhune or George Kloe or Chief of Police Middle. I only happened to be the husband of one of the Runyon girls.

In the kitchen the coffee boiled madly.

One cup of it I poured black and scalding down my throat. It put new life into me. I was making toast to eat with a second cup of coffee when through the window over the combination sink and dishwasher I saw Chief Mort Middle leave the house next door. I watched him walk down the porch steps. When he reached the sidewalk, he didn't turn toward my house. He got into his car and drove off.

The second cup of coffee I had with milk and sugar and four slices of buttered toast. I couldn't think about what Middle had been after in the Kloe house. I was concentrating on the silence, waiting for the phone to break it.

When I finished breakfast, I gave up waiting. I put on my hat and coat and went to the house next door.

Mabel Kloe came to the door. At the moment she was a flabby, washed-out blonde, sloppy in a thin housecoat over a white nightgown which hung shapelessly to her ankles. That was because I'd caught her so early in the morning. When she was painted and held together by whatever women with her build wore under their clothes, she looked pretty good in a buxom way.

"Oh, Leo, I'm so sorry," she said.

Sorry for what specifically? That sentence was vague enough not to express an opinion on what had happened last night. Whatever had become of Judith and Paula, it was proper to be sorry for me.

George came out to the hall. He wore pajamas and slippers and a bathrobe I could have fitted into twice. "How about some breakfast?" he offered, trying to sound hearty. "We just had ours, but there's coffee left."

I said, "No, thanks," and we drifted into the living room. I dropped hat and coat on the couch and sat down. They didn't seem to know what to say to me.

"What was Mort Middle doing here?" I asked.

Mabel sat in a straight-backed chair. She glanced at George who was leaning against the wall.

George gave me the answer. "He wanted to know what happened last night."

"I'd told him everything," I said. "Didn't he believe me?"

"The usual police routine," George assured me. "You want him to investigate, don't you?"

Mabel said, "He asked if I'd seen anybody go into your house last night after you and George had driven off to look for the girls. I couldn't help him out. I fell asleep shortly after George left with you and didn't wake till he came home."

I nodded to myself. Chief Middle was attending to business. I should have thought of asking her that question when I'd come home and found their clothes gone.

"Leo ought to know about that guy, honey," George was saying.

I lifted my head. "What guy?"

Mabel pulled together her housecoat over her prominent bosom. "It was somebody who visited your house early yesterday afternoon when I was there. I'd gone to talk to Judith about the Red Cross drive when he came in. I thought at the time that it was odd that he didn't ring the bell. He just walked in like it was his own house."

"Who was he?"

"I'm sure I never saw him before," Mabel said. "Later when he drove off I saw his car. It had a New York license plate. The letter Y on it; that means he was from Manhattan. I know because I was once a New Yorker myself."

"What did he look like?"

Mabel ran a pink tongue over her lips. Probably she would have enjoyed gossiping about it with other women, but telling it to me wasn't easy.

"He wasn't more than thirty. Very handsome. A beautiful tall figure. They knew each other well because he called her Judy. It struck me at the time that I'd never heard her called Judy around here. She called him Eat."

"Eat?"

"Maybe short for Eaton," George suggested. "Know him, Leo?"

"No." I kept my voice steady. "Go on, Mabel."

"As I said, he walked in without ringing. Judith acted very strange; she didn't introduce me. She seemed nervous. She asked him if he had driven and he said yes. That kind of thing, words which didn't mean anything. I stood there being ignored by both of them. It was clear, of course, that I wasn't wanted, so I said good-bye and left."

She was letting me have it gently, only the bare outlines, but it was there. While I was at work, a handsome young man from New York had walked into my house as if he belonged in it, and Judith had been rude to a neighbor because she had been too upset or cautious to introduce him to anybody who knew me.

"Was Paula at home?" I asked.

"Not when he arrived. From my window I saw her arrive about thirty minutes later. Then shortly after that he left."

I sat with my hands on my knees and looked straight at Mabel and then at George. "It's not what you think," I said. "Judith would never do anything like that."

"Sure, Leo," George said. "I told Mabel that he'd come to call on Paula."

She glanced sharply at her husband. He hadn't said anything of the kind when she'd handed him that juicy bit of scandal yesterday. "But, George, why would Judith be so uncomfortable and not introduce me and — "

"Hell, honey!" George said.

She clamped her mouth shut; the toes of one slipper fumbled at the heel of the other slipper.

I stood up and put on my coat. "I suppose you told that story to Middle?"

"Well, sure, Leo," George said. "We can't hide anything from the police. Besides, there was no reason to, was there?"

"No." At the door I stopped. I rolled my hat in my hands. "Look. I think I know less about Judith and Paula than almost anybody in town. I mean, I didn't grow up with them. You did, George."

He didn't seem to care about it. He stubbed out his cigarette before he replied. "I was older than the crowd they ran around with."

"What about later?" I said. "When they were both on the stage. You're in New York a lot on business. You told me you see nearly every show on Broadway."

He was busy lighting a fresh cigarette. "They weren't such big-shot actresses, neither of them."

"But they were home-town girls whom you knew. You'd make it a point to see anything they were in."

"What's that got to do with anything, Leo?"

Mabel was listening to us with her face tight.

"It can't be coincidence that a stranger from New York showed up yesterday a few hours before they disappeared," I said. "I think that what happened to them may be tied up with their actress days in New York. I'm looking for a lead. Maybe a producer on the chance that they've gone back to acting."

George's mouth twisted. "Well, I never saw them on the stage."

He was a bad liar. I could see it all over him, and I could see by the tight way

Mabel kept her face that she knew the truth too, whatever it was. And they didn't ask what should have been an inevitable question: how it was that I, Judith's husband, didn't know any details of her acting career.

"George, for God's sake!" I said. "Why lie to me about a small thing like this?"

He said stiffly, "If you think I'm lying, why keep asking me?"

I stopped rolling my hat. I put it on my head. What was the matter with me? Because a man hadn't seen my wife act on the stage I called him a liar.

"I'm sorry, George," I told him. "You were swell last night. I didn't know what I was saying."

"That's all right, Leo. My nerves would be haywire too if I were going through what you are." He gave my shoulder a comradely thump. "You ought to go home and get some sleep."

I said good-bye to Mabel. I was so tired that I could hardly lift my feet. It wasn't only because I needed sleep.

4. The Nightmare Past

Morning visiting hours were from ten to twelve for private patients. I had a forty-minute wait, and I dozed off in the hospital lobby. The nurse at the desk woke me. I walked up the corridor to Edna Runyon's room.

There wasn't much left of her. What I could see of her — hand limp on the cover, long throat exposed, narrow face on the raised pillow — was beyond thinness. But her eyes retained their brightness, and she could still call up an inner warmth for her smile.

"How nice, Leo," she said. "Are the girls with you?"

"No, Aunt Edna. I took a few minutes off from work to run in to see you."

I sat down on the chair beside the bed.

Her fleshless hand moved out to pat my knee. "I wish Paula would marry a man like you. Then I'd be sure both girls were being taken care of when I'm gone."

I said the usual things about her having a good many years of life left. She didn't seem to hear me. She lay very still.

"Aunt Edna," I said. "What caused Judith to have a nervous breakdown shortly before I met her?"

"I wouldn't say it was a nervous breakdown. She came back from New York very ill."

"It was something mental, though, wasn't it?"

Her face turned against the pillow. Her sunken eyes, duller suddenly, studied me. "Leo, Judith isn't ill again?"

"No, no. She's fine. But I've got to thinking. Why doesn't she ever want to talk about the stage?"

She was still looking at me, but no longer seeing me. Her voice became remote too. "It was my fault. I should have been firmer with them from the beginning, but I knew little about children when my brother died and his two little girls, Paula eight and Judith six, came to live with me. They were so pretty, so bright, and I suppose I was the adoring aunt."

That didn't seem to be an answer to my question, but maybe it was. Maybe only the far past could answer it.

"You were wonderful to them, Aunt Edna," I said.

"No. I was too lenient for their good. When they grew older, I found that I could not control them. It was one thing to let young girls enjoy themselves; it was another thing not to restrain them at all. Don't think they were bad. They were high-spirited, independent, impulsive, but never really bad."

She paused to peer through the years. "Impulsive and thoughtless too. Like the time Paula left home without a word, without a message. You can imagine how frantic Judith and I were, and how sensationally the newspapers treated the mysterious disappearance of an attractive twenty-year-old girl. It was almost two weeks before a letter arrived from her. She was in Hollywood, where she had gone to try to get into pictures. She hadn't let me know that she was going because she was afraid that I would object. I received only two or three letters from her in the next few months, each of them a request for money. Don't think she was deliberately cruel; it was only that she seldom got around to writing. Then one day Paula returned home, as suddenly and with as little warning as she had left."

"What had happened in Hollywood?"

"She simply hadn't made out. In Jorberg she was the town beauty. In Hollywood she was only one of thousands of beautiful girls."

Her blue-veined eyelids closed. She lay so still that I thought she was asleep or too tired to go on speaking. I should have let her alone. I couldn't.

"But the next time Paula left home, she let you know she was leaving," I prompted her.

Aunt Edna returned to the subject with a weary snort. "She told me the morning she left, if that was letting me know, and in the afternoon she took the train to New York. She'd been restless during the year since she'd returned from Hollywood, and I wasn't surprised when she left again. This time she was going to be an actress on the legitimate stage."

So far there was nothing I hadn't known. I sat and listened.

"Then Judith wanted to follow Paula," she went on. "Judith was twenty, and the restlessness was in her too, and the yearning for the glamor and excitement that couldn't be found in Jorberg. She had had some experience in high school theatricals; she thought she could act, and she certainly had the face and figure. But there was another reason why she went. She'd always worshipped her older sister. Where Paula led, she followed. If Paula was on the stage, that was where she belonged."

That hadn't changed, I reflected. Paula was a guest in her sister's home, but

Paula ran the home.

"I fought to keep Judith with me," Aunt Edna was saying. "I couldn't bear to be alone. Besides, I didn't consider that a life for a young girl. But years before that I had lost control over her as well as over Paula. One morning I looked into Judith's room and found that her bed had not been slept in. There was a note on her dresser telling me that she had gone to join her sister."

She had left her aunt a note. Wouldn't she have left me one last night?

"I had Paula's address. The next day I went to New York. The girls were living in a room hardly larger than my pantry. They were very sweet and affectionate, as always, and as always their minds were set. For three days I stayed near them at a hotel. Then I came home."

"Didn't you ever see them act?" I asked.

Aunt Edna lay silent a long minute before she found the strength to go on speaking.

"I doubt that they got many parts. In the next two years I visited them three or four times, but each time it seemed that a play had just closed or that they were rehearsing for a new play. They couldn't fool me. They would have starved if I hadn't sent them money now and then."

"But they must have mentioned the plays they were in?" I persisted.

"If they did, I don't remember the names. I was never interested in the theater. Perhaps I am old-fashioned, but I consider it somewhat indecent — at least for nieces of mine to display themselves in public, and like as not without enough clothes on." Her tiring eyes regarded me. "Why don't you ask Judith?"

I fished cigarettes out of my pocket; I stuck the pack back without taking one out.

"You may smoke, Leo. I don't mind."

I lit a cigarette. "Aunt Edna, you know they don't speak of their experiences in the theater. I think it's my right to know what happened."

Her eyes closed. "Happened?" she echoed softly.

"According to Judith, the struggle to make a success on the stage became too much for her. She says talking about it still upsets her, so that's one subject that's barred in our house. I was always puzzled how a girl with as much vigor and health as Judith would go to pieces because she didn't at once become the toast of Broadway."

"Judith had great resiliency," Aunt Edna said without opening her eyes. "She recovered completely in a few months."

"Then why does she refuse to talk about it even now to me, her husband? And why does Paula avoid the subject too, even when Judith isn't around? I never thought much about it, but now I'm pretty sure I never got all the facts."

"I'm afraid, Leo, that you don't know how a sensitive girl reacts to a shattered career."

Her voice faded to a whisper at the end of that sentence. She became very quiet. In the war I had seen dead men and women who looked less dead than she. I leaned over her bed. Her breathing was low, but regular. She appeared to have fallen asleep.

What did I have? One definite fact: that a handsome young man from New York had called on Judith, or maybe Paula, yesterday afternoon, and that Judith hadn't cared to introduce him to Mabel Kloe. One uncertain idea: that something had happened during Judith's stay in New York that she didn't want to tell me about. One nebulous feeling: that George Kloe had lied to me about not having seen Judith or Paula or both on the stage.

That wasn't enough to add up to anything, and nothing was coming of my hope that Aunt Edna could give me more.

When she spoke again, her voice was scarcely audible. Her eyes remained closed; she might have been talking to herself.

"Paula brought Judith all the way home from New York in a taxi. Paula wasn't well either. She didn't stay in bed for three weeks the way Judith did, but they had both changed. They were apathetic — Paula too, and Judith even after she had recovered. It was frightening to see girls like that, who had always been so energetic, always going places and doing things, now uninterested in anything. The party at which you met Judith, Leo, was almost the first she had gone to since her return home." Her face turned to me. "What helped Judith most was falling in love with you. That was when she really became her old self again."

"Shock?" I asked myself aloud. I leaned closer to the bed. "It was shock, wasn't it, Aunt Edna?"

Her bony fingers plucked at the cover. "I don't know what to do."

"Aunt Edna, I'm her husband."

"Yes," she whispered. "It's your right. But I don't really know, Leo. It's only what I learned from Judith's nightmares those first few days she was back. One night she screamed in her sleep. When I rushed into her room, I heard her say words in her sleep. 'Blood!' she shrieked. 'It's pouring out of his throat!' "

I dragged cigarette smoke into my lungs. "There was an accident. An auto accident."

"No, Leo." Under the cover her torso twisted toward me. "She spoke of scissors. Blood and scissors. 'The scissors in his throat!' she said. 'Blood spurting past the scissors in his throat!' she said. There I was standing in her room and Paula had come in too, standing behind me barefooted and in her nightgown, and Judith was writhing on her bed in sleep and holding her hands over her face. And speaking of a man lurching toward her, staggering, blood spurting past the scissors in his throat."

Aunt Edna sank back exhausted.

I should not have let her go on like that; her agitation was deadly for her. But I had to be ruthless for the sake of the healthy living. All that I could spare her was the knowledge that her nieces had disappeared.

I said, "People often see blood in nightmares."

"Paula woke her up," Aunt Edna said hoarsely, not answering my statement, or perhaps working indirectly toward an answer. "Judith sat up in bed and wept hysterically. After a while I went back to my room, but Paula stayed with her all night. Two nights later it happened again. When Judith's screams brought me into her room, she was out of bed, but still asleep. She was cowering against the dresser. She was shrieking, 'Oh, God, don't come near me! The blood! The blood!' Paula rushed past me. When she tried to take Judith by the shoulders, Judith fought her. She must have thought Paula was the man in the dream. 'Don't touch me!' she said wildly. 'You're dead! I killed you!' she said. She —"

The door opened.

"What's going on?" a nurse demanded. "Was that you yelling, Miss Runyon?"

Aunt Edna forced a smile to her bloodless lips. "I'm afraid I spoke too loudly," she said with surprising calmness. "I was trying to persuade my nephew to take me home."

"It was my fault," I told the nurse. "I'll see that she's quiet."

The nurse said, "If there's any more of that, you'll have to leave, Mr. Aikin," and went out.

I stood up and crushed my cigarette out in the ash tray on the dresser. In the mirror I saw that Aunt Edna again appeared to be asleep. Blood wouldn't gush like that from a throat, especially not if the weapon more or less plugged up the wound. I was a chemist, not a doctor, but I was sure that there weren't any veins in the throat large enough to make blood spurt. Which meant that the dream was just a dream.

I returned to the bedside. Aunt Edna opened her eyes and rested them solemnly on my face. As if there hadn't been a break, she took up the story where she'd left off, speaking quietly now.

"After we calmed Judith down and got her back into bed, I had a talk with Paula in the hall. She insisted that what Judith had said were only the senseless, meaningless words people say in nightmares. I wanted desperately to believe that, but neither of the girls had ever lied to me, and I knew that Paula was lying then. She was too perturbed over the simple fact that her sister had had several nightmares; she was evasive and refused to meet my eyes. And there was the point you raised a few minutes ago, Leo: I couldn't believe that mere failure as an actress would have caused Judith's illness."

I said hollowly, "But if her nightmares were based on fact, that explained her nervous breakdown."

"Yes, Leo." She paused for strength before she went on. "Paula returned to Judith's room and got into bed with her. After that Paula slept with her every night for weeks. If Judith had another nightmare, Paula must have awakened her before I could hear anything. That was something else: Paula made sure that I would hear no more of Judith's ravings. I never again mentioned the subject.

You see if I wasn't told definitely, I could pretend that there really hadn't been anything."

I couldn't sit. I walked to the door and back. People were always saying throat when they meant neck, I thought. The scissors could have protruded from the front side of the neck or slanted in from the throat — in either case, what they had punctured or severed must have been one of the great arteries of the neck. That would send blood spurting like a fountain.

"You're sure Judith said that she killed him?" I asked.

"I'm sure, Leo. I haven't repeated all that she said in the two nightmares. I don't remember all, but there was no doubt. I called a psychiatrist in for her, a Dr. Meerbaum. He used long words that meant nothing to me. And they should have, Leo; I'm not an illiterate. It seemed to me that Dr. Meerbaum was hiding something too — that he had promised Judith that whatever she told him would be in confidence."

Her head lifted from the pillow. "Leo, this doesn't make you feel any differently toward Judith?"

"Did you think it would, Aunt Edna?"

She sank back. "Perhaps I should have told you before. She's a good girl. Whatever she did, Leo, it wasn't vicious or underhanded or mean."

"I know."

She reached for my hand. It was like holding hands with a skeleton.

"She has you to watch over her, Leo. She's been a good wife to you — sweet and loving and devoted. She is making you a fine home."

"Yes, Aunt Edna."

"If only Paula would settle down too. Bernard Terhune would marry her in a minute. He has been in love with her for years."

"Evidently Paula doesn't love him."

"I suppose not." She released my hand. "Leo, I haven't long to live."

"Nonsense, Aunt Edna."

"I'm not as naïve as you think. It's cancer, isn't it?"

"Whatever gave you that absurd notion?"

She smiled rather wistfully. "I hardly expect anybody to tell me, but I know. Paula will be alone. I never could control her or Judith, but now Judith has settled down with you and I'm no longer worried about her. But there's Paula. She thinks the world of you, Leo. You'll watch over her too, won't you?"

"Of course, Aunt Edna." The words almost stuck in my throat.

"I'm leaving them in your hands, Leo." Her smile came back. "It won't be easy. I spoiled them too much."

"They're fine women," I said.

"We know they are, don't we, Leo? Whatever may have happened."

There was little left to her voice. It came from too deep in her, forced past her lips like a bated breath.

I said I had to hurry back to the office and leaned over the bed and kissed her brow. As I was straightening up, she patted my cheek.

"Tell the girls to come more often," she said. "They weren't here yesterday."

I tried not to gulp. "I'm not sure they can make it today. Probably tomorrow." I picked up my hat and coat. "Good-bye, Aunt Edna."

She lifted the hand from the cover and dropped it limply.

5. The Kirman Rug

A light delivery truck was parked in front of my house. I pulled my car up to within three feet of the truck's rear double doors on which faded letters read: "McCABE's NEW AND USED FURNITURE."

Ed McCabe was ringing my doorbell. He turned when he heard me come up the walk. "Here's the rug, Mr. Aikin," he said, thumping the long, rounded, paper-wrapped object which leaned against the door.

"The same one you brought yesterday?" I asked.

"Sure. How many genuine Kirmans do you think I get my hands on?"

I went up the three flagged steps to the small square terrace. "I told you yesterday I didn't want it."

"What's going on here?" McCabe scowled. "Last night Paula Runyon phoned me to bring it back first thing in the morning."

Since last night the world had completely lost its reason. This was a minor bit of madness compared to the rest, but it was all of one piece.

The details of yesterday's argument over the rug were clear enough in my mind. When I had come home from work, I had found Ed McCabe in the living room with Judith and Paula, the three of them admiring a bright red rug on the floor.

"What's that?" I had demanded.

Judith had stepped across to kiss me and then had stood hugging my arm. It was the way she generally greeted me, but I had had a feeling that this time I was receiving special treatment to soften me up.

"We've always needed a rug for this room, darling," Judith said. "Paula saw this perfectly stunning Persian rug in McCabe's store and ordered it right away. Off course it's a used rug; that's why it's so cheap."

"How much?"

"It's a genuine Kirman, darling," Paula put in brightly. Every man whom she called by his first name was darling to her; that was her theatrical background. "It will make the room look twice as smart."

"How much?"

Judith hugged my arm tighter. Her short, loose hair was against my cheek. "Remember it's a genuine Persian Kirman, darling."

I appealed to McCabe as one man to another. "How much?"

"A bargain at two hundred seventeen dollars," he told me. "I bet I could get four hundred for it."

"Then why don't you?"

"Darling, Mr. McCabe is being very generous," Paula said in that honeyed tone that was calculated to override all obstacles. "He says you won't have to pay for it for several months."

"Sixty days," McCabe corrected her. "Plus carrying charges."

I should at least have waited until McCabe was gone, but this was the culmination of all the other times I had come home to find still another piece of furniture for which I had no money. So I hit the ceiling.

What I said was what husbands say under such circumstances. Paula listened in that favorite pose of hers when something wasn't going her way — hands clasped, slim shoulders back, a long-suffering expression on her very attractive face. Judith kept tugging at my arm, saying please, darling, control yourself, of course the rug would go back.

But I had my say; I poured it out of myself. McCabe had started to roll up the rug while I was still talking. Suddenly I felt embarrassed at carrying on like that in front of a stranger. I shut up in the middle of a sentence.

"It's okay with me, Mr. Aikin," McCabe said as he tied the wrapping paper around the rug. "I got a customer will pay spot cash for it."

There was silence until McCabe carried the rug out. Then Paula sighed. "What a pity!"

This time I retained self-control, but it wasn't easy. I went to the bathroom to wash up.

Nothing more was said about the rug during the meal and after. But I had a feeling that Judith had withdrawn from me, closer to her sister than to me, the two of them against me. For once I had triumphed in a matter of money, but without a word they made me feel that I had done something mean and unfair to them. I found myself wishing that Paula would get the hell out of my house and let Judith and me live our own lives. I didn't say it, of course; I liked Paula too much. But I was burned up, and that was the real reason I didn't object when that night at the poker game Terhune raised the stakes. There was no sense trying to hang onto money, which I didn't have to begin with, against the competition of my wife and her sister.

Now here next morning was the rug back again, and McCabe was saying irritably, "I'm a busy man, Mr. Aikin. You think I got nothing to do but lug this rug back and forth?"

"Listen," I said. "Did you say that my sister-in-law phoned you last night to bring this rug back?"

"Called me around nine last night. She said she wanted to make sure I didn't sell it to nobody else and I should bring it first thing in the morning."

"You're sure it was my sister-in-law's voice on the phone?"

"I know Paula Runyon since the day she was born. I lived only a block away from Pete Runyon on Batterman Drive. You don't believe she called me, go ask her."

The town was slowing down. Everybody in it hadn't yet heard of their disappearance.

"She's not in," I muttered.

McCabe pulled the rug away from the door and held it with one end resting solidly on the terrace. "You want it or don't you?"

I said wearily, "All right, bring it in."

I didn't know why I said that, except perhaps because Judith was gone and it would be a pleasant surprise when she came home and saw it on the floor. But it wouldn't be a surprise, I told myself as I unlocked the door. She had expected it; she and Paula had agreed to buy it in spite of my abjection.

If they ever did come home.

"So long, Mr. Aikin," Ed McCabe said.

The door closed. I dropped into a chair. Outside McCabe was having trouble starting his truck. The motor coughed, sputtered, died, followed by the ominous sound of a starter whirring impotently. The fool flooded his carburetor, I thought dully, my mind on trivial matters because the other thing was too much for it. Suddenly the motor gave out a roar like an exultant cry of triumph. I lost interest. My eyes closed. Without particularly wanting to, I fell asleep.

I awoke in a sweat. I sat panting; my hands clutched the arms of the chair.

The dream had been too real. There had been blood over Judith's face, over her dress. Not her own blood. It gushed at her from the throat of a man staggering toward her. I had never seen the man, but somehow, in the fantastic way of dreams, he had been familiar, a handsome young man, and I had known that he was the one who had called on Judith Tuesday afternoon. Paula had been in the dream too, but already the details were fading from my memory, and I could not recall how or in what role. But Paula had belonged in it as much as Judith and the handsome young man and the man with the scissors in his throat or neck.

There had been something else in the dream I should remember. Sitting there in a cold sweat, I tried to bring back details. Abruptly, it came to me. Judith and the dying man, and perhaps Paula too, had been standing on a rug, and it had been the one McCabe had brought back this morning.

It was all mixed up, of course. It had happened at least fifteen months ago, and none of us had seen the rug before yesterday, and, of course, the man who had called on her yesterday couldn't be the one who had been killed many months ago. It was wacky, but like all dreams a thin line of truth ran through it.

In this case, a thin red line.

I roused myself. I went into the kitchen for a sharp knife and cut the cords which bound the rug. My act had no significance. I told myself that as long as I had the rug I might as well get it out of the way by spreading it on the floor.

When the rug was down, it didn't look like much. It scarcely covered half the living room floor, and whoever had owned it before had used it long and hard. But it was a genuine handmade Persian Kirman, wasn't it? Two hundred and seventeen bucks.

It had a bilious green border, which was bad enough. What gave me the shivers was the pomegranate red inside the border. Like the color of fresh blood, I thought.

6. The Unexcited Cop

Chief of Police Mort Middle was digging a sandwich out of a paper bag when I entered his office.

"Got no time to go home for lunch," he complained. "Steve Gale is sick with a cold, so that leaves nobody but me to answer the phone. Heard from your wife yet?"

"No." I unbuttoned my overcoat and sat in the rush-bottomed chair near his desk. I told him about the Persian rug.

While I talked, Middle unhinged his jaw for a pumpernickel and cheese sandwich not more than two inches thick. Every few bites he washed down with a vast gulp of milk from a quart bottle.

"So you see," I said, "at nine o'clock last night they had no intention of leaving for good. Otherwise Paula wouldn't have phoned Ed McCabe to bring the rug back today."

"Maybe they didn't leave for good," Middle said through a mouthful of pumpernickel. "How do you know they won't be back in a few days?"

My frown said that I didn't follow him.

He cleared his mouth with milk. "You're pretty broke, aren't you, Mr. Aikin?"

"What's that got to do with it?"

"Well, let's see," Middle said. "You came to Jorberg last March. You got a pretty good job with Bernie Terhune. You bought yourself a brand-new car, and paid Mrs. Gregory twenty-five a week for her best room and bath and board. You lived pretty good."

"Why not?"

"Sure, why not? A single man with a good job. Had a nice bank account too — better than four thousand dollars. Then you got married to Judith Runyon and bought the Hotchkiss house. Paid seventeen thousand. Real estate prices are terrific these days and you paid twice what the house was worth before the war, but that was a good buy and you hadn't any trouble swinging it because you got a G.I. loan and mortgage. Only you didn't figure on the way the Runyon girls like to do things. What your wife couldn't think of to do to that house, her sister Paula did. They pulled the kitchen apart and bought a new one for fifteen hundred bucks. They had every room redecorated. They made Ed

McCabe rich buying furniture from him. They — "

"What's going on?" I cut in. "If you're trying to show how much you know of everybody's private affairs, save it for some other time."

"Now's a good time." Middle filled his mouth with pumpernickel, but it didn't completely impede his speech. "I keep my eyes and ears open. It's my job. This morning I did a little extra checking up. Like I was saying, those Runyon girls kept spending your money like it was water. They were always like that — never knew what a dollar meant. They'd gone through their aunt's money before that. Time was Edna Runyon was well off. Then a couple of months ago she got sick and was taken to the hospital. It took lots of money for the nurses and operation and all that. Paula sold her aunt's house, but there was so much mortgage and taxes due that less than two thousand was left, and right off that went to pay doctor and hospital and nurse bills. Paula moved in with you, and you had to support her too, and keep paying the hospital besides. You owe everybody in town, but that didn't stop the Runyon girls from buying a secondhand rug from Ed McCabe for two hundred and seventeen dollars."

"Pretty good," I said sourly. "Now that you've shown me you're up on what's none of your business, let's get back to your business, which is finding my wife and sister-in-law."

"Fact is, I think it's all part of the same business," Middle told me comfortably. "I knew all about that rug an hour ago. Ed McCabe came to me when he heard the Runyon girls were missing. Seems you didn't tell me you had a terrific battle yesterday with your wife and sister-in-law about that rug."

"We had an argument. Didn't you ever argue with your wife?"

"Sure. And if she disappeared right after, I wouldn't blame the police for wondering about that argument." Heartily he pushed what remained of his sandwich into his mouth.

"Wait a minute," I said. "Do you think that I — that..."

Chief Middle nodded amiably. "A cop's got to think of everything. Like I said, it was an hour ago Ed McCabe told me about that battle you had with your wife, but early this morning, when you took me out to Mill Street where you said you found your car, I already started thinking. Say a man wanted to get rid of a couple of women. Say he figured he was clever as hell. He could dispose of the bodies somewhere and then leave his car abandoned on the road and then come back and find it there. Just to confuse the police, sort of."

I gaped at him. He dug a second sandwich out of the paper bag. He seemed very pleased with himself.

"So that's why you were at the Kloe house this morning?" I said. "You were checking up on me."

"Among other things."

"But I was in a poker game at Terhune's till one in the morning."

"And then had two hours between then and the time you and George Kloe went out to look for the women." He set to work on the second sandwich.

"Don't get the idea I'm accusing you, Mr. Aikin. I just want to show you I'm on my toes."

"All right, you're on your toes," I conceded. "Now tell me what happened to Judith and Paula."

"Money," he said breezily. "The root of all evils. You hadn't any more. You were a mean, cruel guy to them; you wouldn't even let them have a worn-out, secondhand rug for only two hundred and seventeen bucks. So they went to where there was money."

I pulled out my cigarettes. My fingers had trouble working one out of the pack; I had more trouble lighting it. Chief Middle chewed his sandwich as placidly as a cow chewing her cud and watching me with a half-amused, half-pitying expression.

"Not Judith," I said when I had a light.

"Those Runyon girls!" He shrugged elaborately. "When they want something, they go after it. I remember the first time Paula Runyon ran off. Us police were looking everywhere for a body, till one day her Aunt Edna came in with a letter from her. Seemed Paula was in Hollywood. Then a year or so later she went off again, and then Judith went off. Those Runyon girls were always going off."

"Judith left her aunt a note that time," I said. "She would have left me at least that."

Middle finished the last of the milk and set the bottle down on the floor. "Now we come to the guy who called on your wife yesterday afternoon. Young and very handsome, Mabel Kloe says. You know about him?"

"Only what Mabel told me this morning."

"Yeah. The way your wife acted when he came in, I wouldn't be surprised if he was an old boy friend from New York. Judith and Paula made a date to meet him somewhere that night — him alone or maybe he had another guy with him."

"At eleven at night?"

"Why not? You were at a poker game. Say he had plenty of dough. They figured here was where they could get money for rugs and such. Paula was afraid McCabe would sell the rug to somebody else, so she phoned McCabe to make sure he'd bring it next day. Then they went out to keep the date. Could be their first idea was just to hit him up for dough for old time's sake, but he wouldn't play that way. He says: Come with me — or with me and my pal here — and you can have a wad of dough. The roads were terrible, so they took only one car — his car — to come back to the house for their clothes. And off they went."

I stood up and went to his desk. I wasn't going to hit him, but he must have thought so, for he threw his hands in front of his face.

"Now don't get sore, Mr. Aikin. You don't want to kid yourself, do you?"

"You're the one who's kidding himself." My hands were flat on his desk. My voice quavered. "You don't know Judith and Paula. They may be impulsive, but they'd never hurt anybody. I don't say Paula wouldn't go off with a man. She's unmarried; she has no ties. But she wouldn't do it by sneaking away. And she wouldn't go with him unless she cared for him, and never for money. And Judith..."

"Take it easy, Mr. Aikin. Sit down."

I returned to my chair. I sat forward.

"Judith is my wife," I said. "She loves me and I love her. That should be enough answer. If you need another, there's this: if she'd gone willingly, no matter where or why, she would have let me know. And if she left me for another man, she'd tell me to my face. She'd say: It's no go with you; there's somebody else I prefer. And she'd move out openly. That's Judith."

Middle seemed to have lost his appetite for the second half of his second sandwich. He pushed it to one side of his desk. "What about the guy who called on her yesterday?"

I said, "If a detective came here from New York, would you know about it?"

His shaggy brows arched. "You think he was a detective, Mr. Aikin?" he asked softly.

I shouldn't have brought that up just then in just that way. Now I was in a corner. I couldn't say to him: Perhaps they ran away because a detective came up from New York in connection with a murder.

"I'm asking you," I hedged.

"You think they got into some kind of trouble when they were in New York?"

"I don't think anything," I retorted. "You seem to know everybody's business. This is just an idea I'm kicking around."

Middle handed me a superior smile. "There's nothing in that one. To begin with, if the New York police are interested in anybody in Jorberg, they'd let me know right away. A New York detective wouldn't work on his own here; he hasn't got jurisdiction. He'd come to see me as soon as he hit town. If he wanted somebody arrested, I or one of my boys would do it, and we'd let you know. We got no secret police in this country."

He had talked me out of the corner and had answered my question. The man from New York wasn't a detective, and they hadn't run away from him.

"Got any other ideas kicking around?" Middle's voice was pleasanter than his grin.

I leaned back and crossed my legs. I wasn't relaxing; I was taking my time answering. I had to be careful not to say too much.

"Something like this," I told him. "Last night, while they were in the car, they were stopped on Mill Street by another car and abducted."

"Kidnaped?" Middle clucked his tongue. I seemed to be entertaining him. "Then the girls told the kidnapers they wouldn't have a thing to wear while they were being held, and the kidnapers were good guys and let them go home and get their clothes."

"The kidnapers could get the house key from either girl's handbag. One of them went for their clothes to make it look as if Judith and Paula had left of their own free will."

"And then the kidnapers left your car parked right on Mill Street where it would be found next day and show that the girls hadn't driven off in it."

"If there was only one kidnaper, perhaps the man from New York, he couldn't handle more than one car."

"Then why bother getting their clothes? The car had to be gone too to make it look like they'd driven off. And why were they driving out in the middle of the night in that kind of weather if it wasn't to meet somebody they knew?"

"They could have known the kidnaper without knowing that he was going to kidnap them."

Sighing, Middle shook his head. "The difference between the way I look at it and you look at it is that my way makes sense. Use your head, Mr. Aikin. Why would anybody want to kidnap them? Do you have money you can pay to get them back?"

I couldn't answer that. I couldn't tell the Chief of Police that, fifteen or more months ago, my wife had stuck a pair of scissors into a man's throat. And if I told him, how could it be tied up with their disappearance? The fact remained that any way you looked at it, through his eyes or through mine, what facts we knew didn't form any sort of convincing pattern.

"What about the rug?" I said. "If nothing else, it proves that they intended to be home today."

"Could be they changed their plans when they met somebody after eleven last night."

This wasn't getting anywhere.

"So you're going to sit here and do nothing?" I said bitterly.

"We'll send out the regular missing persons circular. I remember we sent one out when Paula Runyon ran away to Hollywood."

I buttoned my coat and put on my hat. He spoke again when I was at the door.

"I'm not forgetting, Mr. Aikin, that yesterday you had a battle with them, and that between one and three this morning you had a lot of time on your hands." He said that negligently, as if even the possibility that he had a murderer in his office didn't excite him.

I turned at the door. "Make up your mind. Did my wife run out on me or did I murder her?"

"Maybe you know best," he said placidly. He stretched out a beefy hand for the remnants of his second sandwich. "I'm watching all angles, that's all. I'm no dope."

I said, "Aren't you?" and left.

7. The Virgin Mistress

I reached for her cozy warmth and felt only the cool sheet. "Judith?" I whispered drowsily.

My eyes opened. The night lamp was not on and the hall beyond the open bedroom was also dark; the house was too silent.

"Judith!" I called.

There was a sickening gush of remembrance. I lay flat on my back, staring into darkness, and in the room with me were all the tender intimacies of eight months of marriage. The first month, before we had a chance to furnish the entire house, Judith had brought her bedroom furniture from Aunt Edna's house. When we were buying our bedroom set, Paula, who was, of course, with us, recommended twin beds for a modern home; but Judith said what was the good of having a husband you loved if you couldn't snuggle up to him at night.

Lying alone in the double bed became unbearable. I left it and sat in the living room club chair. At dawn I fell asleep. The phone woke me. My eyelids were sticky as I rushed into the dinette. And still it wasn't Judith at the other end of the wire.

"Gale at police headquarters," a voice said.

"Yes?" I said tensely.

"You got a picture of your wife and Paula Runyon? We're getting out a circular on them."

"You mean to say you didn't do that yesterday?"

"Well, we're pretty busy here, Mr. Aikin. Besides, we need pictures."

Somebody came up the walk. The mailbox outside the door rattled; the mailman gave an indifferent toot on his whistle. A letter mailed yesterday in Connecticut or New York would arrive this morning.

"I'll bring over the photos in a little while," I said and started to hang up.

"We'll need descriptions too," Gale said placidly, as if no letters were waiting in the mailbox. "You know — height, weight, color of eyes, all that."

"Yes, yes," I said and hung up and rushed out to the mailbox.

There was a single letter, a bill from the hospital for Aunt Edna's private room. Past due, of course.

When I was back in the living room, I crumpled the bill and flung it furiously at the fireplace. It hit the lower edge of the mantel and bounced to the green border of the Kirman rug. I kicked it under a chair. That didn't make me feel any better. I shaved and dressed and made myself a breakfast of fried eggs and toast and coffee. Just before I left I went into Paula's room for the photos.

They were in an oak veneer, double standing frame on her dresser, the five-by-seven photo of Judith on the left and the one of Paula on the right. They were sleek, theatrical jobs, the kind actresses have made of themselves by the gross, though as far as I knew these were the only two in the house. For my taste, the photographer had gone in too heavily for brittle glamour. The faces were lacquered and there was too much sexy emphasis on bare shoulders. Judith looked so vivacious that it produced a somewhat wanton effect, which wasn't at all like her, and Paula looked unnaturally hard.

Even in photos they were together, and I could not gaze at the woman I loved in the double frame without also seeing her sister. "I'm leaving them in your hands, Leo," Aunt Edna had said yesterday morning. What had I done since then but wait for a phone call and kick a bill from the hospital because it was not a letter from my wife?

I removed the photos from the frame and drove to police headquarters in the Municipal Building.

Steve Gale was at the high desk behind the gate. He smirked at the photos.

"Boy, are they lookers! Usually when one sister's pretty, the other is a pie-face. But not the Runyon girls."

I said dryly, "Are you still interested in their descriptions?"

He wrote as I dictated. Judith Aikin: age, 23; height, 5 feet, 7 inches; weight, 128; hair, brown; eyes, brown; complexion, fair; identifying marks, a birthmark the size and shape of a dime on the left thigh. Paula Runyon: age, 25; height, 5 feet, 4 inches; weight, 112; hair, brown; eyes, brown; complexion, fair; identifying marks, none that I knew of.

My next stop was Jorberg Plastics, Inc. Through force of habit I parked my car as close as I could to the outside door of my laboratory, but I didn't go in there. I walked along the side of the low, sprawling, cinder-brick building to the office entrance. I said good morning to the two women in the office without checking my stride to the frosted glass door.

Bernard Terhune sat in his red leather chair behind his bleached oak desk. He said briskly, "I wondered if you'd come in to work today."

"I didn't come to work. I want a leave of absence."

He flung an arm over the high back of his chair. "For how long?"

"A few days or a few weeks. I can't tell."

"Don't tell me you've a crazy idea to look for Judith and try to make her come back to you?"

"It may seem crazy to you. It doesn't to me."

"Very well," he said in his crisp, business manner. "I can't keep my employees from making damn fools of themselves. Where do you propose to look for her?"

"I'll start in New York. I wonder if you can help me."

"I?"

I said, "There isn't anywhere I can even start. Did you ever see them act?"

"You ought to remember that I was in the war. You were with me."

"They were on the stage for a year after you returned to this country. You had a crush on Paula. You'd make it your business to look her up. You'd at least want to see her act."

"I would," he agreed, "if she had been acting. But the couple of times I saw her in New York, she and Judith were hanging around doing nothing. Like most actresses, they were waiting for something to turn up."

"You must have met some of their friends in New York."

Terhune smiled sourly. "Paula didn't take me around. It's not a thing a man likes to say, but I think the only reason she went out with me was that she couldn't quite brush me off. I took her twice to night clubs, and on both occasions Judith was with us."

"With a man?"

"No. I escorted both girls." Bitterness touched his voice. "Judith was our chaperon. Evidently Paula didn't care to be alone with me, even in public."

"There must have been conversation. Actresses always speak about the plays they've been in."

"Not these actresses. I wouldn't want to bet that they'd ever been behind footlights."

"Damn it!" I said. "They were two years on Broadway. They must have got somewhere in that time. In fact, I think George Kloe saw them on the stage — at least one of them."

Terhune looked interested. "Did he? In what?"

"He denies that he saw them, but I believe he's lying."

His long fingers picked up a pen, but he didn't do anything with it. "Why would George lie about a thing like that?"

"I don't know. Maybe you're lying too."

Terhune looked at me from under a brow corrugated by a frown. "You're not yourself, Leo. I can understand that. But what could you expect, marrying one of the Runyon girls?"

"You'd like to be married to the other one," I flung at him.

"Yes." His mouth twisted sardonically. "They get under your skin, don't they, Leo? If Paula were married to me and walked out on me, I'd tear hell apart to get her back."

I said what I'd said so often since early Wednesday morning, that they hadn't left of their own free will, and I told him of the rug and how their clothes had been taken after they'd left and how there hadn't been a note from Judith telling me that she was going away.

"I know all that," Terhune said when I finished. "I had a long talk with Mort Middle last night. If I were in your shoes, perhaps I'd also prefer to believe that almost anything happened to my wife except that she left me."

"All right," I said wearily, tired of arguing. "Whether they left willingly or not, I'm going after them."

He opened the middle drawer of his desk and took out a checkbook. "I know how broke you are, Leo. What's the minimum amount of expense money you think you'll need?"

His tone was again crisp. He was trying to make a generous gesture, but he didn't know how to do it decently.

I said, "All I want is the pay due me."

He couldn't resist a sneer. "The Runyon girls go away and give you a chance to regain your pride on money matters. How will you pay your expenses?"

"Not with your money."

His pen made random marks on the inside cover of the checkbook. "This money is for Paula. Give me a chance to do something for her." His head dipped; he spoke without looking at me. "For more years than I care to remember, before the war and during and after, I mooned over her like a lovesick schoolboy. There was a time, just before the war, when she seemed to care for me. In fact, the gossip in town was that she was my mistress. Not for any particular reason except that we were together so much and Paula inspired that kind of gossip because she didn't care what people said. If they only knew Paula. She can be a mistress and at the same time a virgin."

"You mean she accepted money from you?"

"It wasn't necessary in those days. Her Aunt Edna was supporting her." As he spoke, he wrote the date and then my name on the check. "Then I went into the army, and when I came back it was different. I was like a stranger to her. Take money from me! Listen. I looked her up in New York. I saw how poor she and Judith were, living in a flea-bitten boarding house. When I said good-bye, I handed her a check. She didn't even look at the amount. She said, 'Thanks, Bernie, but we're not desperate.' Not desperate! She wasn't desperate enough to accept money from me, but shortly afterward she and Judith were so desperate that they...''

His voice faded in the middle of the sentence. He made another mark on the check.

"They what?" I demanded.

He lifted his head. "Huh?"

"What did they do because they were desperate?"

"I meant that Paula would starve trying to get on the stage," Terhune said quietly, "but she wouldn't take a cent from me."

"Damn it!" I said. "What are you hiding from me?"

"Hiding?" He laughed sardonically. "Didn't I just dangle my soul naked before you? Don't be a sap, Leo. Let me do this one thing for Paula. Take five hundred dollars. You need it."

"No."

"Suit yourself." He wrote out the rest of the check. "Here's your pay." And he added characteristically, "I must have that handbag formula by next week."

"Marty can work it out from my notes."

"He's a kid. If you're not back by next week, I'll have to hire another chemist."

He handed me the check and went to the window which covered an entire wall of his private office. He'd become the hard-bitten boss again, I thought, to cover up for having poured out to me something of his frustrated love-life. It embarrassed him to have been for even a little while a human being.

The amount of that check was for exactly two-fifths of a week's salary, representing the two days I'd worked; almost any other boss would have given me a full week's salary. That was the way he was. Tuesday night he had torn up my check for my poker losses to humble me, and he had just offered to finance my search because it was an investment that might get Paula back, at least to the same town in which he lived. I put the check in my wallet and said good-bye.

Terhune didn't shake my hand or wish me luck. He mumbled something with his back to me and continued to stare out of the window — looking over the years he had loved Paula, I thought. I wasn't at all sorry that he wasn't my brother-in-law.

I drove home. When I passed George Kloe's house, I didn't see his car parked outside, which meant that he hadn't yet come home for lunch. He almost always did when he wasn't on the road selling neon signs. From my own house I called the Kloe number and asked Mabel to tell George to come over to see me as soon as he got in. I explained that I had a good used car for his brother Al if the deal was made at once.

After I hung up, I didn't know what to do. I had four hours to pack and eat before the 4:37 train left Jorberg for New York. And when I reached New York, what?

Yesterday, I had ransacked the house, trying to find a physical clue to the past. It was an easy house to search because we hadn't lived in it long enough to accumulate junk. In the storeroom Paula's old trunk had contained only a few old dresses and a motheaten cloth coat. In the third bedroom, which was a combination study and guest room and repository for furniture which didn't fit elsewhere, there was a secretary stuffed with odds and ends; I had found old bills and circulars and wish-you-were-here cards, but nothing written to either woman from New York, nothing from people I didn't know, nothing from a man whose name could be shortened to Eat. All I'd got out of my bedroom and Judith's had been memories that had hurt. Paula's room had produced the same result, without the memories.

It was wrong, of course. Mementoes pile up among people's possessions, and actresses would have accumulated more than most people. There should be photos, clippings, contracts, union cards, letters, at least programs of the shows in which they had appeared. But there was nothing. Because, I wondered, a pair of scissors in a man's throat made any tangible remnant of the past dangerous?

I roused myself and searched the house again because it was easier than doing nothing. When I reached Paula's closet a second time, I not only peeped into the cardboard hatbox on the top shelf, but I removed the hat, which I did not remember ever having seen her wear. Under the hat was a brown leather writing case with Paula's name stamped on it in gold.

The case contained a writing pad without pages, a few blank envelopes of assorted shape, a letter written three years ago by Aunt Edna to "Dear Girls," and beginning: "I am sorry that I cannot spare more than this very small amount because taxes and mortgage..." And a smaller print of the same photo of Paula I had removed from the frame on her dresser. And a frayed theater program.

Something at last. Excitedly I fumed the pages of the program.

The name of the show was *The Virgin Mistress*. The date was three years ago last fall. Produced by Herbert Seller, directed by Luther Hadman. My eyes skipped the rest, ran down the cast. "*Gladys — Paula Runyon.*" Her name was next to last of a cast of at least fifteen.

This was the first concrete evidence I had that Paula had appeared in at least a minor role in a Broadway production. Maybe that was the only show she had been in during those two years, and Judith had been in none. Or maybe because Paula hadn't used that writing case in years she had overlooked the program when she and Judith had destroyed everything else which linked them to the stage. Whatever the reason...

Wait! What was it Terhune had said in his office an hour ago? "Paula can be a mistress and at the same time a virgin." A virgin mistress! Had he made a cynical play of words on the title of a show in which he knew she had appeared? Maybe. That was all any of my questions came to — one maybe strung out after another. I had no definite answer to anything.

Except this now, the title of a play, the first break since their disappearance. Not much of a break, probably, but at least a starting point.

The doorbell rang. I put the program and Paula's photo on my dresser to make sure that I packed them with my clothes, and then I answered the bell.

George came in without a hat or coat. "Who's selling a car, Leo?"

"I am," I said.

He followed me into the living room and sat down. "Thought so. You need money that badly?"

"Yes."

"Al can't afford to pay more than eight hundred for a car."

Mine was only a year old and worth thirteen hundred. But I hadn't the time to shop around. "I'll take a thousand if I can get a check before the bank closes," I said.

George studied me solemnly. He seemed to be weighing how cheaply he could get the car for his brother, but I didn't think that was it. "You going somewhere, Leo?"

"To New York."

"You heard Judith is there?"

"No. I've heard nothing. But I've got to start somewhere. I'm up against a blank wall. Maybe I can work my way behind it from the past."

He said nothing. He had discovered the Kirman rug and was brooding down at it.

"Did you ever see a play called *The Virgin Mistress*?" I asked him casually.

"What?"

"*The Virgin Mistress.* It ran about two years ago at the Bandstand Theater on Forty-fourth Street."
"Never heard of it."
"Paula was in it," I said.
"That so?" George didn't seem particularly interested.
I burst out, "For God's sake, George, why do you refuse to help me?"
The toe of one shoe ran a few inches along the border of the rug and then back. An embarrassed child would have done something like that. "I don't see all the shows on Broadway. I'm in New York maybe two weeks every six months."
"All right, you didn't see *The Virgin Mistress.* But you're hiding something from me."
His tongue flicked over his lips. I could see another lie coming. Instead he hedged. "Maybe it's none of my business, Leo, but Judith has hurt you enough. Suppose you find her. You'll be hurt more than you are already if you find her with another guy." His jaw jutted. "Go on, get sore, but I'm telling you."
I was too fed-up to get sore at him. "If you have to tell me anything, tell me what you're keeping from me."
His gaze went back to the rug. "Why should I keep anything from you?"
I could beg him on bended knees. I could threaten to kill him. I could do nothing.
"The hell with you!" I said. "Your brother can have the car for a thousand dollars if I get the check before two o'clock."
George thought it over. "I guess he'll go that high for a good buy." He brightened considerably now that the subject was changed. "Tell you what I'll do. I'll give you my personal check right now for a thousand and get it back from Al tonight."
"Fine."
He wrote out the check and I wrote out the transfer of ownership. I went with him to the door.
"George," I said. "No matter what Judith did, it wouldn't make any difference to me."
"Sure." He walked to the edge of the terrace and stopped. "Let it lay, Leo. If she loves you, she'll come back."
I said stiffly, "You're a hell of a pal," and returned to the house and packed my clothes in the one bag left in the hall closet.

8. The Patient Actors

What I stepped out to from the elevator must once have been a corridor. Now it was a narrow reception room. The floor was covered by dark-gray carpeting and the walls by portrait photos, no doubt of famous actors and actresses, though I wouldn't know. Against the wall opposite the elevator stood a small, round mahogany table bearing a copper jug converted into a lamp. On the left of the table was a plush-covered bench, on the right three plush-covered chairs.

A pretty dark-eyed girl and a prettier blond man sat on the bench as far apart as they could. The girl looked up at me from a magazine, the man looked up at me from his fingernails, and within a moment both lost interest in me. A sleekly turned out woman in her late forties sat in the center chair; her knees were crossed and a cigarette dangled rakishly from a very red mouth. When I passed her chair, she tossed me an impersonal smile. It was the first smile anybody had given me in New York. I smiled back.

There was a door in the left wall, but that would be for those privileged to enter directly into the inner offices of Herbert Seller Productions, Inc. For me the first stop was a small window panel in the right wall.

Through the window I saw a piece of a switchboard, a head of hair so glaringly platinum that even I knew its owner hadn't been born that way, and under the hair a round doll face. Fingers tipped by paint the color of raw steak were rummaging through a box of candy.

I tapped on the glass. She twisted her round little chin to her hunched left shoulder, and she may or may not have seen me, though she looked directly at me. She resumed her hunt in the candy box. Presently she reached a decision. She popped something covered with chocolate into her mouth, chewed thoughtfully, turned her face again to me, reached out a hand, slid the glass panel open.

"Yes?" she said.

"I'd like to see Mr. Herbert Seller, please."

"You got an appointment?"

"No, but it's important."

She chewed contemplatively. A thought struck her. "What's your name?"

"Leo Aikin."

She wrote my name on a pad and pushed it aside to make room for the candy box directly in front of her. Before she could make a second selection, a light flashed on the switchboard. She pulled a plug out and pushed another in and dug deep into the box. Suddenly she became aware of a foreign presence and turned her head quickly and stared at me disapprovingly.

"Sit down and wait," she ordered.

I went away from the window, but I didn't sit down. That would show her. I stood between the table and the elevator door and lit a cigarette.

The pretty boy on the bench again looked up from his nails. This time he kept his eyes on me longer — very bored eyes. His wavy blond hair glistened. So did his lips. He wore a pale-blue shirt with a flowing collar and a dark-blue necktie with a knot nearly as big as my fist and a tweed jacket as shaggy as a lawn and with a pound of padding in each shoulder. I was pretty sure that he didn't care for my conservative gray double-breasted suit.

The elevator door opened, and as if at a signal everybody's attention switched to it. A tall man strode out. He wore no hat, no coat. He looked as if he belonged on the other side of the door, but he wheeled right to the window panel. He said something to the platinum blonde, and I heard her giggle. But evidently a wisecrack wasn't enough, because after a half minute he came away from the window and arranged himself in a chair beside the middle-aged woman. So he was only another actor trying to get to see somebody in a producer's office.

Often during their two years on Broadway Judith and Paula must have waited like this.

Casting those four actors would be simple. Dark Eyes was obviously the love interest. Pretty Boy wouldn't be my choice for the hero; women mightn't agree, but a man would prefer him a villain. The middle-aged woman was a natural as Dark Eyes' ultrasophisticated mother. That left the newcomer as the hero, which was all right with me because men preferred that rugged face, that lean whipcord build, that likeable awkwardness of movement.

The hell with play acting! I looked at my watch. Twenty minutes since I'd arrived and nothing had happened. I couldn't be sure that anybody but the platinum blonde existed beyond the wall.

"How long do you generally have to wait?" I asked nobody in particular.

All four looked at me as if I had advocated violent revolution. Actors didn't question eternal waiting.

"By now I have squatter's right to this bench," Dark Eyes said without emotion and returned to her magazine.

"Does anybody ever get to see Herbert Seller?" I persisted.

The middle-aged woman flicked ashes on the carpet. "If you're waiting for Herb Seller, you'd better sit down. He's on the Coast."

"What coast?"

The rugged man grinned. "Brother, you're not in this racket. There's only one coast — the West Coast. And the West Coast consists of California, and California consists of Hollywood."

I strode to the window and rapped on it. The blonde frowned at me, did things with switchboard plugs, frowned at me again, and slid open the panel.

"Yes?" she said.

"Why didn't you tell me that Mr. Seller isn't in town?"

"Mr. Knobel is here."

"Who's Mr. Knobel?"

"He's Mr. Seller's secretary. He's the same as Mr. Seller when Mr. Seller is on the Coast."

"All right," I said, "I'd like to see Mr. Knobel."

"What's your name?"

"I told you twenty minutes ago. Leo Aikin."

She wrote it down on her pad. "Please sit down and wait."

I didn't sit down, but I waited.

The idea came to me thirty minutes late. It should have occurred to me at once that these actors and actresses would know lots of others in their profession. Out of my inside jacket pocket I took the two photos, the one of Paula I'd found in her writing case and a snapshot of Judith. The snapshot had been taken last summer on Long Island Sound and showed her in a revealing two-piece bathing suit. I would have preferred one which displayed less of her, but it was the clearest picture in the house of her face.

I tried the photos first on the middle-aged woman on the assumption that she had been around longest. "They were on the stage until a year ago last November," I explained. "This one is Judith Aikin — I mean Judith Runyon — and this one is Paula Runyon. They're sisters."

The rugged man leaned sidewise for a look at the photos. "Neat build on that one," he commented, nodding at Judith's photo. "I'd remember her if I ever saw her." He settled back in his chair.

The woman said she did not know them and returned the photos.

I took the photos over to Pretty Boy and Dark Eyes. Pretty Boy shrugged padded shoulders. Dark Eyes said, "Runyon? The name is familiar." That was as far as I got with her. She raised her magazine.

I kept plugging, speaking to all of them. "Paula Runyon was in a play called *The Virgin Mistress*. It was produced over two years ago by Herbert Seller and ran at the Bandstand Theater."

"A Seller production?" the middle-aged woman said. "I thought I knew them all, but I never heard of that one."

Pretty Boy spoke for the first time. "A turkey. One of Hadman's turkeys. He directed it."

"What's Luther Hadman doing now?" the rugged man asked him.

Pretty Boy laughed nastily. "Hitting the bottle like always, only more so."

I asked, "Where can I find Hadman?"

Nobody knew. Pretty Boy suggested maybe in a gutter. Then they all subsided. We five waited.

The window panel opened. Every head turned toward it expectantly. "Miss Montgomery," the platinum blonde called.

Dark Eyes went to the window. There was a brief mumbled conversation, then Dark Eyes returned to the bench for her handbag and crossed to the elevator and pressed the button. Her face was empty. The elevator came and took her away. We four waited.

I wasn't an actor, so I didn't have to stand for this. I banged on the window. This time the platinum blonde slid the panel open in a hurry.

"Say, you trying to break the glass?"

"Does anybody get to see anybody in this place?"

"Let's see, you're — " She consulted the pad. There were a number of scrawls on it. She didn't seem able to make any of them out.

"Leo Aikin," I told her. "You've already written it down twice. I want to see Mr. Knobel."

"Oh, yes. Mr. Knobel's secretary wants to know what about."

"I thought Mr. Knobel was Mr. Seller's secretary."
"Of course, but Mr. Knobel has to have a secretary. Will you please state your business?"
"I'm investigating something. I'm not an actor, so stop pushing me around. Do I see him or don't I?"
I assumed that it was my manner that made the change come over her. She said almost civilly, "Just a minute," and plugged in a wire. "Kate, tell Mr. Knobel — " I heard her begin. Then she looked up at me and slid the panel shut and whispered the rest into the mouthpiece.

It was magic. Sixty seconds later a wisp of a man came out of the door on the left. "Mr. Aikin?" he threw into the room. He waited just outside the door.

I went over to him.

"I'm Knobel," he said so low that I was the only one in the room that could hear him. "Are you a city detective?"

"Nothing like that. I'm looking for my wife."

His pinched face stiffened. "You told Miss Pease you were a detective."

"I told her I was investigating. She jumped to the wrong conclusion." The two men and the woman were watching us; they could hear now what we were saying. I said, "Can't we go somewhere and talk?"

Knobel looked at his watch.

"All I ask is a minute of your time," I urged him. "I'd like some information about Paula Runyon."

"Who?"

I repeated her name. I showed him her photo; he barely glanced at it.

"I'm sorry I can't help you out." He turned to the door which was only a couple of feet away.

I grabbed his arm. "Paula Runyon was in a Seller production — *The Virgin Mistress.*" My free hand dug out the theater program. "Look, here's her name — Paula Runyon."

"I'm sorry, but I never heard of your wife."

"She's not my wife. She's my sister-in-law."

A corner of his mouth lifted in a grimace of annoyance. "You told me she was your wife."

"I'm trying to get a line on both sisters, my wife, Judith Runyon, and her sister, Paula Runyon. Judith Runyon was an actress also. Maybe you know her."

I released him and got out the snapshot.

He let his eyes rest on it for an instant. That was mere courtesy; he very much wasn't interested. "I wish I knew what you wanted. You tell Miss Pease you're a detective and then you tell me your wife is your sister-in-law."

"Oh, hell!" I said. "All right, we'll concentrate on Paula Runyon who acted in *The Virgin Mistress.*"

"I was on the Coast during the production of *The Mistress.*"

"Is anybody else here who had anything to do with that show?"

"There was Reggie Levine, but he's on the Coast with Mr. Seller."

Damn the Coast!

Knobel was looking at his watch again. In a moment I would lose him.

"What about Luther Hadman?" I said.

He snorted. "I assure you that Hadman will never again direct a Herbert Seller production."

"Do you know where I can find him?"

"I assure you that I am not interested in the whereabouts of Luther Hadman. Would you mind removing your hand from my sleeve?"

I removed my hand. I hadn't been aware that I had grabbed his arm a second time.

Knobel jerked down his jacket. He was physically too insignificant to look haughty, but he tried it. His eyes swept over the bench and the chairs. Pretty Boy turned his face slightly to display his profile. The woman smiled sweetly. The rugged man grinned like a small boy trying to please. Knobel made a half-turn, glanced back at me, nodded briskly, disappeared into the inner sanctum.

I stood with the photos and program clutched in my hand. I looked down and saw that I was breaking the back of the larger photo and crumpling the program. I loosened my grip.

"Why don't you give *Variety* a ring?" the woman suggested.

I took several steps toward her. "That's a theatrical magazine, isn't it?"

"You dear boy," she said. "Don't you know anything? It's our bible. They'll know where Luther Hadman is, if anybody does. The other day I heard that he was looking for angels."

Pretty Boy said tonelessly, "Angels meaning spirits. Spirits meaning what comes in bottles." And he smiled tiredly.

The woman burst into laughter. The rugged man's grin broadened.

I turned to the elevator and punched the button viciously.

9. The Wingless Angel

The building was so narrow that it had only three windows on each floor facing the street, and it looked as if it would collapse if it weren't held up on one side by a down-at-the-heel hotel and on the other side by a garage constructed vertically. The cramped lobby was dim, musty; nothing on the walls indicated that there were offices upstairs. But this was still the theatrical section, and the address was the one somebody at *Variety* had given me over the phone.

There was no elevator. I walked up unwashed tile stairs to the first floor. Five doors faced the hall. One door announced direct mail promotion and another a theatrical agency. Three doors were blank.

I went up to the second floor. The name hit me as soon as I entered the hall. Black and gilt letters on a glazed door proclaimed: *"Luther Hadman."* Nothing besides the name, as if that were enough to tell the world. I opened the door.

The office was a single small, cluttered room with a single window. There were two desks. At the nearest, barely far enough from the door to permit it to open, sat a young woman too attractive and too polished for those surroundings. Her hair was blue-black and as precisely arranged as if she were in an evening gown. She wore a tight green sweater which she filled with blatant lushness. Everything that could be done to a feminine face had been done to hers, including plucked eyebrows and artificial lashes. Her sensuous lips were painted purple, and her fingernails were long enough to be weapons and were also purple.

I wondered how she could type without breaking those nails, how she could do anything in that place without getting messed up. Maybe her job was simply to sit there and fill the eyes of whoever entered. At the moment she was reading a newspaper. She did not immediately look up when I closed the door.

The side of the second desk was some ten feet away, against the window. A flabby man sat behind it. He turned his head from the window to give me a brief, blank stare, then resumed concentration on whatever was outside the window.

"Luther Hadman?" I said.

The young woman tore her eyes from the newspaper and appraised me apathetically.

"What can I do for you?"

"I'd like to see Luther Hadman."

She turned her head. "Luther, this gentleman wants to see you."

The flabby man reluctantly shifted his gaze from the window. "Who is he, Dacia, sweetheart?"

Dacia asked me who I was. I told her my name and that I would like to see Luther Hadman. They began to get the idea.

"A playwright?" he asked me distastefully. "Perhaps an actor?"

I kept my temper. In the Seller office I had learned that in this neighborhood a straight line wasn't the shortest distance between two points.

"I'm a chemist," I said. "So what? I'd like to have a talk with you."

"Ah, a business man." His face broke into a hungry smile. He rose. "Come in, Mr. — ah —"

"Aikin." I came in by walking around Dacia's desk. In only two minutes after I entered the office I had managed to get close enough to Luther Hadman to smell the whiskey on his breath.

I smelled it when he shook my hand. His hand was as loose and boneless as his face. His small, colorless eyes, sunk deep under beetling brows, were crisscrossed by thin red veins. His nose was lost between puffy, pasty cheeks. His fleshy mouth was so slack that it gave an impression of jaw muscles not functioning properly.

"Sit down," he said expansively, waving to a chair in front of his desk.

I looked down at a disordered pile of magazines and newspapers on the chair. Then I smelled perfume. It came from Dacia's hair. She sidled between me and the wall, scooped up the magazines and newspapers, dumped them on the floor, returned to her desk. A tweed skirt went with her green sweater. She was slimmer than I had gathered from the upper-half view of her behind the desk.

I sat down. Luther Hadman sat down. The surface of his desk was invisible under a chaos of scattered letters and manuscripts bound with blue paper folders.

"Plays," Hadman said, thumping one of the folders. "The foremost playwrights in the nation are deluging me with their creative output. They know what Luther Hadman direction means to a play. Now here is one" — he dug into the mess — "ah, yes, *My Bed for Sale*, by Thomas M. Garrison. You may never have heard of Garrison, but I assure you — "

"I'm interested in somebody who acted in *The Virgin Mistress*," I said testily.

His face writhed. "Please don't remind me of *The Mistress*." His hand reached out for a paper cup near the edge of the desk. From where I sat the cup looked empty. He contemplated the inside of it for a moment, then brought it quickly to his mouth. There obviously wasn't enough for a decent gulp; disappointedly he let the cup fall to the floor. "Medicine," he explained to me. "One spoonful in water every three hours."

I said, "The reason I'm here is that there was an actress in *The Virgin Mistress* — "

"Don't talk to me about that stinker," he cut me off. "Was it my fault? Always they give me lousy scripts. Like Herb Seller. I read *The Mistress*. 'Herb,' I said, 'this will stink even worse than your other shows,' I said. 'Luther,' he said, 'if anybody can make a play out of this, you can,' he said. You see how it is? They think all they need is a great director. But even Luther Hadman needs a script. Dacia, sweetheart, tell this gentleman what a stinking script *The Mistress* was."

"Darling," Dacia said without looking up from her newspaper, "it's always the script and you're the world's greatest director."

"Don't be bitter, sweetheart," he said. "God Himself couldn't make an actress out of you." He picked up a script and waved it at me. "But now Luther Hadman picks his own scripts. He not only directs them; he produces them. This writer Garrison has put everything into his play — humor, pathos, punch, suspense, sex. I don't know what your business is, but you never invested a cent that will return you one-tenth as much as — "

"Look, Mr. Hadman," I cut in desperately. "All I want is some information about an actress named Paula Runyon who had a part in *The Virgin Mistress*."

Slowly he put down the script. The loose folds of his face hardened. "Paula Runyon, did you say? What has she to do with me?"

"She played the part of Gladys in *The Virgin Mistress*. You must remember."

He looked out of the window. I looked also. There was an alley and on the other side of it the blank wall of the garage.

"So many plays, so many actresses," he murmured. "They come and go."

I took out the two photos and placed them in front of him. I smelled perfume and raised my head to see Dacia standing beside my chair. She leaned across the desk to look at the photos. Without a word, she straightened up and returned to her desk.

Hadman looked at her and then at me. His red-veined eyes were almost hidden by narrowed lids.

"What do you want?" he demanded suspiciously.

"Paula Runyon is my sister-in-law. She disappeared a couple of days ago. I'm trying to get a line on her."

"These are pictures of two different girls."

"The one in the bathing suit is Judith Runyon. She's Paula's sister and my wife. She was also an actress. You may have known her too."

"Your wife?" A gradual smile appeared on his slack mouth. Suddenly he was a different man, hearty, my pal. "Well, well, this calls for celebration. Judith Runyon is married!" He opened a lower drawer and came up with a bottle and several paper cups. "We'll have a drink on it."

Perhaps he was looking for an easy excuse to have a drink, but I didn't think that was all of it. His change of manner had been too abrupt.

"Not for me, thanks," I said, repressing a shudder. I couldn't imagine anything coming out of that bottle I'd care to have inside me.

He half filled two paper cups anyway, replaced the bottle, and tossed off the contents of one cup without pausing for a deep breath. Then he shuddered and sighed, crumpled the cup, let it fall from his fingers.

"Ah, yes, I remember Paula Runyon very well indeed," he told me, running the back of a hand across his mouth. "I must say that I have an eye for an attractive face and figure."

"You old goat," Dacia said angrily from her desk.

"Dacia resents any female who is not built as top-heavy as she is," Hadman said placidly to me. "I am afraid that Paula was less than a superb actress, but she was very decorative on the stage. I like to decorate my stage with sex appeal. It is worth money at the box office." He leaned forward and considered the second cup of whiskey.

"You said you also knew Judith Runyon," I prompted him.

"An extremely decorative girl." He tapped her snapshot with a forefinger. "A splendid figure. I was casting *Sing Softly*. A stinking script. Whenever Herb Seller had a stinking script, be brought it to me and said, 'Luther, you're the only director I knew who can do anything with this.' And would you believe it, I whipped that stinker into a play that ran eight months and sold to Hollywood for one hundred and seventy thousand dollars. In all modesty I can say that if anybody but Luther Hadman had directed..."

Two of his fingers touched the paper cup. He blew out his cheeks and withdrew the fingers an inch.

"I like to take my people with me," he went on. "I had a part for Paula in *Sing Softly*. Nothing sensational, but somewhat fatter than she'd had in *The Mistress*. Perhaps she was not worthy of it, but I am afraid that I am a sucker for an attractive female, Mr. Runyon."

"Aikin."

"Yes, Aikin, and Judith Runyon is your wife. A lovely creature. I recall that Paula brought her to me and introduced her as her sister and asked me to give her a part. I tried her out." His small, deep eyes gave me a swift, searching glance. "I do not know what version she gave you of the incident."

"She never mentioned it to me."

"Ah, yes. She would prefer not to." He scowled darkly. "She could not act and her voice had limited carrying powers. After all, I do not direct burlesque shows. An actress must be more than decorative. So, reluctantly I told her that I was sorry. As a result, her sister Paula attempted to blackmail me."

Dacia uttered a small sound, but didn't say anything.

"Blackmail?" I said.

"Blackmail. The crudest sort. Paula dared say to me, 'Give my sister a part or I will walk out of *Sing Softly*.' It was ridiculous. On occasion a director must give way to pressure from a producer or an angel or even a star, but from a minor actress of limited ability it was an outrageous affront. Needless to say, my reply was that as far as I was concerned she had already walked out of the part and that neither she nor her sister would ever again appear in any play in which Luther Hadman had the slightest concern. I never again saw either girl."

He dove for the second cup of whiskey and poured it into himself. He shuddered and grunted and wiped his mouth with the back of a hand.

I turned in my chair to look at Dacia. Her back remained toward us, but she was no longer reading the paper.

There was a thump on the desk. Luther Hadman had a palm flat on a script. He leaned toward me, leering unsteadily. "This play by Garrison has just the role for her," he said thickly.

"For whom?"

"For your wife, naturally." He beamed at me. "The lead, nothing less. And a fat part for Paula too."

Dacia said, "I thought they were lousy actresses."

"Sweetheart, you don't know anything about the stage," he told her haughtily. "Luther Hadman can make any decorative woman into a great actress." He burped gently at me. "This is the opportunity of a lifetime for you and your wife. Let bygones be bygones. You make a fortune and your wife has a role worthy of her beauty and talent. And the extraordinary part of it is that *My Bed for Sale* can be produced for a pittance. Why? Because there is only one set, a bedroom scene, and a cast of only four — the husband, the wife, the lover, the mistress.

Think of it — twenty-five per cent of a smash hit for a mere ten thousand dollars."

"I haven't the money," I said, "and if I had I wouldn't be interested."

Incredulity completely unhinged his jaw. "You don't want your wife to be a star?"

"All I want is to find her."

Hadman sighed in the direction of the desk drawer which contained the bottle. He'd had at least one of those oversized drinks before I entered, and most other men would already be flat on their faces. Hadman merely had a coat on his tongue and a film over his eyes.

Dacia asked me from her desk, "Didn't you say it was Paula who disappeared?"

"Both of them did at the same time," I told her. "Did you know either of them?"

"No," she said.

"What do you mean, disappeared?" Hadman mumbled. He seemed to be trying to think, probably to work out a different approach to selling me the play. He didn't take seriously my insistence that I didn't have the money; no doubt in his experience everybody who married an actress was rich.

"They left home or were taken from home Tuesday night," I said.

"Is that all?" He dismissed the whole thing with a wave of his hand. "Let her know that you have the lead for her in a Luther Hadman production and she'll come running back to you."

I'd drawn a blank. I'd found out a little about their past, but so little that it didn't mean anything. I tried once more; I asked if he knew a man named Eat.

"Eat what?" Hadman mumbled. His attention had returned to the blank wall of the garage beyond the window.

"Possibly short for Eaton. A first or second name. That's all I know about him."

I didn't get an answer from either of them. I gathered up the two photos from the littered desk.

"Thanks for giving me your time, Mr. Hadman."

He roused himself for a final effort. "I'll tell you what I will do. For five thousand dollars I will give you a fifteen per cent piece of the show and your wife can still have the lead. What can be fairer?"

"Lay off, Luther," Dacia said disgustedly. "He's no angel. Can't you see he hasn't any wings?"

"Is that true?" Hadman demanded. "Haven't you actually got any money?"

"Not a cent."

He snorted. He regretted having wasted his time, though he appeared to have nothing else to do with it.

When I passed Dacia's desk, she rose and accompanied me the couple of steps to the door.

"Good-bye, Mr. Hadman," I said.

An angel without wings wasn't worth his effort to turn from the window.

Dacia opened the door for me. Her other hand touched my palm. I felt paper against my skin and closed my fingers over it. Then I was out in the hall and she had shut the door between us.

I walked halfway down the stairs before I unfolded the paper. Two of its edges were ragged; it had been torn from a larger sheet. On it there was a four word message, "Come at eight tonight," and under it was her name, Dacia Wilmot, and an address on East Twenty-first Street.

It was now twenty minutes to five.

10. The Genial Detective

I ate in an underground restaurant on Forty-seventh Street. My table faced the entrance, and I saw him come in.

He stopped at the bar, leaned negligently against it, gave the waiter his rugged-faced grin. Though it was overcoat weather, he was still without hat or coat. I wondered if he had waited until now to try to see somebody beyond the waiting room of Herbert Seller Productions, Inc.

A waiter brought a glass of beer to my table. Twenty minutes ago I had ordered it along with my dinner, and its appearance was the first indication that I wasn't being completely ignored. The world-wide belief that New York did everything in a breathless rush must have been started by tourists who had nothing to do with their time. It was twenty to seven, and I began to worry that I wouldn't be through with dinner in time to keep my eight o'clock date with Dacia Wilmot.

"Any luck?" a voice asked.

The rugged man stood at my table. A glass was in his hand.

"Hello," I said. "I saw you come in and wondered how long you stayed at the Seller place."

"Till five-thirty when they closed the joint down. Mind if I sit down?"

"I'd like company," I said, meaning it.

He sat down opposite me. "My name's Singleton."

"I'm Aikin."

"I know. I heard you tell the blonde at Seller's." Across the table we shook hands. I drank my beer and he drank the yellow stuff in his glass.

"You get anywhere in your case?" he asked casually.

"Case?"

"You're an agency man, aren't you? New at it, too. Trouble is you tried to be too subtle. You were all right when you told the blonde you were an investigator, but you shouldn't have tried to take it back when Knobel came out. Why didn't you flash your buzzer all over the place? People respect buzzers, even the

Boy Scout ones they give private investigators in this state. A look at your buzzer and Knobel would've opened up without horsing around."

I let him finish the speech without interruption because I was trying to make out what he was talking about. I said, "Believe it or not, everything you said is pure gibberish to me."

"Come off it, Aikin," he said affably. "I know you're not a city copper because you didn't throw your weight around at Seller's. That leaves you an agency legman."

I saw light. "You think I'm a private detective?"

"What then?"

I laughed. "I suppose I'm trying to be a detective, but I'm strictly an amateur. I really am looking for my wife and sister-in-law."

Singleton rolled his glass between powerful-looking hands and gave me a long, half-amused stare. "You know, Aikin, I believe you. No professional would be as corny as you were up there."

"I guess I'm pretty bad at it," I agreed. "Maybe you can help me out. You're an actor. You must know the ins and outs of — "

"Me an actor!" The notion seemed to entertain him vastly. "I'm what I figured you to be." He dug out a wallet and showed me a star-shaped badge and placed a card beside my beer glass. The card said: *"Florian Singleton, Confidential Investigations."* He grinned. "Blame my mother for the Florian. I had to fight my way through school because of it."

I fingered the card. "I spotted you as just another actor waiting to see somebody at Seller's."

"That's what I wanted everybody up there to think. I was hanging around to see if a certain lady came up to visit Wilbur Knobel. She's another man's wife."

"Not Knobel!"

"Doesn't it beat all hell what the ladies go for? And she's twice his size, too. Her husband wants evidence. This morning he overheard her on the phone making a date to meet a man this afternoon. He thought it was Knobel, but wasn't sure. By the time he got me to try to find out, the missus had left the house, so I had to work it from the Knobel end. It didn't pan out. She didn't come to his office and he didn't leave till five-thirty."

A detective, I thought. Here I was playing at detective, but he was the real thing.

He finished his drink. "A Scotch sour. Ever had one?"

"Plenty of whiskey sours, but I never heard of a Scotch sour."

"Let me buy you one."

He went to the bar. I picked up his card and put it down and watched him stand in that loose-jointed, indolent position of his at the bar. An experienced detective wouldn't run up and down blind alleys the way I'd been doing. He would know where to look and what to do when he got there.

Florian Singleton returned to the table with two glasses and set one down before me. I sipped the Scotch sour. It was very good.

"Two or three years is going pretty far back to look for a wife," he said.

The beginning of my dinner arrived. As I ate onion soup, I started to give him a brief outline, but it got away from me and details piled up through the roast beef. Singleton hadn't ordered food. He nursed his drink and listened, now and then frowning slightly, but he didn't comment until I reached the part where the man named Eat came to the house.

"This lad Eat is the first definite lead," he said. "How did Mrs. Kloe describe him?"

"She said he was very handsome and had an athletic build and was around thirty years old. Brown hair and she wasn't sure of the color of his eyes. Nothing to go on, you see. It would describe you and me both except for the very handsome part."

"I bet your wife thinks you're handsome as the devil," he said with an open-faced smile. "And women don't always find me repulsive. It shows how right you are — it's no description. Was Eat the only name the lad had?"

"That's all Mabel Kloe heard. I'd say it was short for Eaton."

"You never heard your wife or sister-in-law mention him?"

"No. They'd cut themselves off completely from that part of their past."

Singleton swished the liquid in his glass. "I wonder why?"

I said I had no idea. I wasn't going to tell him about Judith's breakdown and her dreams. But there were other things it was all right to talk about, the rest of what had happened that night and after.

"Dacia Wilmot," he mused, when I got to where she slipped me the note. "She told you she never heard of your wife and sister-in-law, but she wants to see you tonight."

"Do you know her?"

"Who around this part of town doesn't? A showgirl on occasion, with ambitions to be a dramatic actress. I can't imagine her tied down to an office desk. And if she is, what's she doing working for a broken-down elbow-bender like Luther Hadman?"

"That puzzled me."

"Maybe she's trying to make you," he suggested with an amiable leer.

"That's crazy."

"Don't be modest. You look like a lad a girl can go for. If she had anything to tell you, why didn't she do it then and there in the office?"

"I'll find out soon enough." I pushed aside my plate. "You haven't given me your opinion. Do you think my wife ran out on me?"

Singleton shrugged. "What's the difference? I saw her picture. If I had a wife like that, I'd want to find her no matter why she disappeared."

"That's just about it," I agreed.

The waiter asked me what I'd like for desert. I ordered apple pie and coffee. When the waiter was gone, Singleton said, "I'd start off the way you're doing, working your way from the past to the present. There's no choice. The trouble with you is that you've had no training. You don't organize the search. For instance, you've done practically no research."

"I plan to do that tomorrow. I'll look through the theater sections of newspapers covering the period when they were in New York."

"That's a start, but there's *Variety* and *Billboard* and other publications that deal with the stage. And don't overlook Equity."

"What's Equity?"

"The actors union. They both belonged to it if they were on the stage at all. In one day one of my boys could uncover more than you could in a month."

"In other words," I said, "you're trying to drum up business for yourself."

Singleton gave me half of his grin. "A private investigator is like a lawyer or an insurance agent, always alert for a client. I've a small agency, only four men working for me, but in all modesty I can say we're very good at certain specialized jobs. You might prefer one of the big agencies, but my advice is to get yourself professional help."

If I wanted to hire a private detective, he would be my choice. In the short time I'd known him, I felt that he was my friend. Maybe that was just salesmanship on his part, but it wasn't the hearty, nauseating kind. He sounded smart and looked as if he could be as tough as the toughest if it became necessary, and at the same time his grin was as frank and open as a boy's. I liked him.

"I told you I had no money," I said.

"You wouldn't need much. Two hundred bucks tops; maybe a lot less."

It wasn't so much the money. I was afraid of what a professional investigator might dig up.

"My rate is twenty-five dollars a day and expenses," he said. "There should be few expenses."

The waiter brought pie and coffee. I ate and drank in silence. He watched me without trying to sell himself to me. He gave an impression of wanting the job simply because it fascinated him.

But if he did too good a job and found out about a pair of scissors in a man's throat, what then? If he were honest, he'd take the information to the police. If he were a crook, he might use it to blackmail me; I didn't have cash, but I did own a house. The fact remained that I couldn't afford to have him come in.

"What's the problem?" Singleton asked after a while. "It can't be the dough if your wife means that much to you."

"It's not the money."

"What then?"

I left the pie half-eaten and fished change out of my pocket for the tip. "I'd rather try it myself for a little while longer. Thanks a lot for your advice."

"I think you're making a mistake, but that's your business. Where are you staying?"

"The Mammoth." I looked at my watch. "I've got a date in twenty-five minutes."

"Watch out for her sex appeal." His grin came on full blast. "Unless you don't want to watch out. You could do worse."

"Are you speaking from experience?"

"Not with Dacia, unfortunately."

We left the restaurant together. In the street we shook hands and Florian Singleton walked off hatless and coatless into a biting wind. I felt very much alone as I headed toward the Lexington Avenue subway.

11. The Business Woman

The room was a living room, a bedroom, a dinette, depending on which wall you were nearest. When she opened the door to admit me, I found myself at the edge of the dinette. A partially opened closet door revealed a combination refrigerator and gas range and a toy sink. There was another closet which held a bathroom and a third for clothes. The whole affair was approximately half the size of my living room in Jorberg, and was called an apartment.

Dacia Wilmot greeted me with a languorous handshake and a purple-mouthed smile. Paint was so fresh on her face that it glistened. She wore a quilted silk housecoat, and though it covered her as effectively as a blanket, I thought of Florian Singleton's suggestion that maybe she was trying to make me. I had read enough fiction to know that there was only one plot when a woman invited a man to her apartment and received him in a robe.

She placed a hand lightly on my arm and conducted me past the bed to the living room sector. She waved me to a carved, spindly Victorian chair and sat down opposite me on a matching settee and pulled her legs under her. One white knee showed. Casually she tugged a piece of the housecoat over it and lit a cigarette. All the same, I wondered if sooner or later I was expected to join her on the settee.

"Did you or didn't you know them?" I said.

"Paul and Judy Runyon were my dearest friends."

Paul and Judy. According to Mabel Kloe, the man named Eat had also called her Judy, but to everybody in Jorberg they were always Paula and Judith. Singleton would call that a clue.

"In Hadman's office you told me you had never heard of them," I reminded her.

"That was in the office." Dacia Wilmot didn't go on to explain why it had been necessary to lie in the office. "You're wondering what I'm doing working for Luther Hadman."

I didn't see where it mattered to me, but I didn't say so.

"Luther is really a genius," she said. "He hits the bottle hard, but so do lots of others who're still up on top. The main thing wrong with Luther is that he's had a run of hard luck. For a while everything he touched on Broadway turned sour for one reason or another. Then he went to Hollywood and tried too hard to be arty and was just dull. So word got around that he'd lost his touch, and that's the worst thing can happen to a director."

I tried to look patient as I listened.

The sharp point of a purple fingernail removed a fleck of tobacco from a purple lip. "A girl has to think of all the angles in this lousy racket. She's got to grab hold of somebody's coattails and ride with him. Luther has the stuff. He'll make a comeback and then little Dacia will be sitting pretty. I'll be able to have any role I want in any show he directs."

"That's fine," I said. "But what I want to know is what I'm doing here?"

"I got the impression you're after information."

"I am."

Dacia blew smoke at me and looked at me through it. "Who you working for?"

"I'm an industrial chemist."

"You don't say?"

I couldn't understand why there was a mocking inflection in her tone. I said, "If you were a close friend of theirs, as you say, you must know a lot about their history in New York."

The cigarette tilted upward as she smiled. She put her head against the high back of the settee.

"You want a sales talk?" she said. "Okay, I'll sketch my qualifications. I met Paul and Judy after they'd been in New York close to a year. We were all doing the same thing, hanging around agents' and producers' offices, joining the mob scenes at tryouts, not even praying any more for the big break a girl always gets in the stories, but praying for any little part, anything at all to get behind footlights and receive a pay check. They were living in a two-room apartment near here on Third Avenue — a walk-up dump on the third floor, all they could find in the housing shortage and better than they could afford. Practically their only income was a check now and then from an aunt in the Connecticut tanktown they came from."

"Jorberg."

"That's it. Well, we got very friendly. I was living in a crummy rooming house, and when they asked me to move in with them, I jumped at the chance. I was on my uppers myself until I landed a spot in the chorus of *Don't Kid Yourself*. Then for a while I paid all the rent. That's how close we were to each other."

"Didn't Judith get anything on the stage?"

"I got her the first job she had, with me on the chorus line of *Don't Kid Yourself*. I had some influence and one of the girls got sick and dropped out, and Judy looked very good behind footlights, especially with no more clothes on than you could put in your vest pocket. Things started getting better for all of us. Even Paul stopped her run of bad luck. She'd had a couple of walk-on parts in a couple of turkeys. Then she got a dozen lines in *The Virgin Mistress*; not a fat part, but the fattest she'd ever had, and Luther Hadman liked her and took her along when he cast *Sing Softly*. She had a good chance to go places. But that's just where the trouble started."

Dacia paused to light a fresh cigarette. "Judy had her heart set on being a dramatic actress. She said she didn't come to New York to kick her legs at a lot of leering faces. So Paul introduced her to Luther Hadman and he tried her out. Luther didn't think she was so hot as an actress, but he thought she was plenty hot as a female. There's more than acting ability gets you places in this racket, so he gave her a small part in which she hardly had to open her mouth, but it was a beginning just the same."

"That's not the way Hadman told it," I said. "You heard him say in the office this afternoon that he hadn't wanted to use Judith at all and that Paula had threatened to quit if he didn't."

"Nuts! Paul had more sense; she knew she didn't pull enough weight for a stunt like that. Luther gave Judy a part for his own reason. She quit *Don't Kid Yourself* and started rehearsing *Sing Softly*. She rehearsed three days and was flattered because the great director paid so much attention to her. The kid didn't know the score and I didn't want to tell her. She'd find out soon enough. She did when Luther took her out to dinner the evening of the third day. He tried to sell her a bill of goods. He told her that if she put herself into his hands he'd make a star out of her. Maybe he would have eventually; he could make an actress out of a stick of wood. But Judy didn't know that by putting herself into his hands he meant putting herself into his arms."

I had become as rigid as the chair on which I sat.

"They were funny girls, both of them," Dacia said reflectively. "They never got it into their heads what a girl had to do to get places in this lousy racket. Even later..."

She gave me a furtive glance and expelled smoke through her nostrils. "Anyway, after Luther got through telling Judy what he'd do for her, he took her home. I was working and Paul was on a date, so the apartment was empty. She invited him in, just being innocently sociable, but that old goat had other ideas of what was social. He was ready for his first installment. He put his arms around her and tried to kiss her. She pushed him away. Luther wasn't discouraged. She'd made a deal with him, hadn't she? At least that was what he thought, so he persisted, and Judy took a sock at him. Then Luther was definitely discouraged. He left."

She chuckled. "Judy is a girl who can sock. For a week Luther had to tell people that a door hit him in the eye."

I relaxed. I smiled to myself.

"So Judy was out of *Sing Softly*. So was Paul. When she heard the story from Judy, she walked out of the show. Not that she would've lasted anyway; Luther would've got rid of her for being Judy's sister." She shook her head. "They were dopes, Judy especially. She could've got plenty out of Luther. He was a big-shot director in those days, and lots of girls would've given their right arms for her chance. How could Judy and Paula hope to get anywhere in this racket if they refused to be realistic?"

"Are you realistic?"

When the words were out, I was sorry I'd said them, but Dacia wasn't offended. She smiled slowly.

"Sometimes," she said, "but I never got a chance to with somebody as important as Luther was in those days. The trouble with those two girls was they refused to accept the fact that men are men. That's the main reason they never got anywhere in the big time."

"In that case, how did they manage to get what parts they did?"

Dacia shrugged quilted shoulders. "That was small stuff. I was talking about really going places, like a director taking a personal interest in you. Judy tried to get back on the chorus of *Don't Kid Yourself*, but of course her spot was filled. So there were Paul and Judy making the rounds again. It was almost summer and there was little doing and the checks from their aunt started getting smaller and the girls..." She drew deeply on her cigarette and scratched a bare ankle.

"And then?" I prompted.

"That's all for free, mister."

"For free?" I echoed, frowning.

Dacia pushed her legs out from under her. One of her furry mules dropped off a bare foot, and I saw that her toenails were painted the same color as her fingernails. She looked me over calculatingly. "You'll never get on the stage, mister."

"What makes you think I want to?" I said, trying to follow her.

"Don't ever want to. You're a rotten actor. Five minutes after you walked into the office this afternoon I knew you were a cop."

I laughed sourly. "You're the second one today to mistake me for a detective. The other one is a private detective himself. I suppose anybody who tries to trace missing people acts like a cop."

"The point is that you acted like a cop trying not to act like one. You're not a city cop; they like to throw their weight around. You're a private snoop hired by somebody."

"I'm Judith's husband."

"She never told me of a husband."

"We were married eight months ago." I leaned toward her with my hands clasped. It was as if I were begging her, and maybe I was. "I think they were kidnaped Tuesday night. Probably a man named Eat had something to do with it."

Dacia bent over to pick up her mule from the floor. "What do you know about Eat?" she said to her bare ankle.

"Nothing. I'm hoping you can tell me."

She straightened up and tucked her feet under her. "Maybe I can help you a lot. But why should I?"

"You'll be helping Judith and Paula."

"Don't change the subject. I want to know what I'll get out of it."

"Why should you want to get anything out of it?"

She looked at me through a screen of artificial eyelashes. "Still acting the dumb hick. Okay, I'll draw you a diagram. It may be news to you, but this is a world where you get nothing for nothing. When a woman wants something from a man, she has to pay for it in the only currency she has — the currency Luther wanted from Judy. When a man wants something from a woman, she prefers her payment in the green stuff she can go out and buy food and clothes with. Catch on?"

"Cheap cynicism," I said angrily.

"I'm cynical, he says!" she declaimed to the ceiling. "What do you think of that, little Dacia has been turned into a nasty cynic because she looked the world in the face and saw what a rotten, low-down job it is?" She put her eyes back to my face. "Let's can the moralizing. Let's say I'm a business woman."

"How much?" I asked her.

"One thousand dollars."

After I had paid some of my most urgent bills, I had five hundred dollars left from the sale of my car.

"A thousand dollars for a small thing like that?" I said.

Only her purple lips smiled. "Is it small?"

I sat very still. She knew about a pair of scissors in a man's throat. Only that kind of information would be worth a thousand dollars.

I said, "It's a deal for a hundred dollars."

"Don't waste your breath trying to bargain."

"How do I know what you'll tell me will be worth the money?"

"That's the chance you take. There's no money-back guarantee."

I kept trying. "If you'll give me a hint of what you have, maybe we can do business."

"Cagey lad, aren't you?" She plucked tobacco from her lip. "If you're completely in the dark, a hint will give you the lead you're looking for."

I drew in my breath and plunged. "Is it about somebody who died?"

"Yeah, died very dead, if you want to be cute about it." She swung her feet to the floor. She looked angry. "If you know that much, maybe you know everything and don't need anything from me." She stood up. "I've a date for nine o'clock."

I stood also. "Does your friendship for Judith and Paula mean so little to you that you want money to do anything for them?"

"You're asking me to do something for you."

"For Judith's husband."

She twisted her torso in annoyance. "I don't give a hoot if you're a snooper or Judy's husband. You're a man, and there's only one thing I want from a man, just like there's only one thing any man ever wanted from me." She touched the cord of her housecoat. "Would you mind giving me a chance to get dressed? Among other things, this happens to be my bedroom."

"I honestly haven't more than a couple of hundred dollars."

"That's too bad. Good night, mister. Aikin you called yourself, didn't you?"

"Leo Aikin," I said. "You can get in touch with me at the Mammoth."

She stepped around me and took six steps to the bathroom door. She turned her head, and her painted face was expressionless. "You're the one who will want to get in touch with me. And don't bother if you don't bring along a grand in cash."

Dacia went into the bathroom. The door closed and I heard the lock turn.

12. The Policeman's Voice

I spent the following morning, Saturday, in the New York *Courier-Express* building. They were very cooperative. A young man settled me at a table and brought me bound copies of the newspaper.

I started at the approximate date when Judith and Paula had returned to Jorberg and from there I worked back. I went back three months and then forward a couple of months. The *Courier-Express* liked to dig its teeth into a murder, especially if a picture of a photogenic woman went with it, but there was no photo of Judith, no mention of her name. I had hardly expected to find anything like that, for almost any big-town newspaper publicity about a Jorberg girl would have reached her home town. But neither was there a line about a man having been killed with scissors or found mysteriously murdered with a wound in his throat or neck.

After three hours of that I returned to my hotel. Florian Singleton was waiting for me in the lobby. He shook my hand heartily and asked if I'd dug anything up since last night.

"Very little," I said.

He handed me a neatly typewritten sheet of paper. "I had one of my boys do a little research this morning. Thought you'd like to see it."

According to the report, Paula had appeared in three shows, *The Virgin Mistress* having been the last. There were the dates when each show had opened and closed and the name of each character she had portrayed. Judith was mentioned only once; for a period of eleven days she had been in the chorus of *Don't Kid Yourself*.

I returned the report to him. "There isn't anything in this I didn't learn last night from Dacia Wilmot."

"That right, you had a date with her. Learn anything else from her?"

I hesitated. If I wasn't going to hire him, it was none of his business. He was watching me curiously, with only half of a grin on his rugged face.

"All she told me so far is what's in that report," I said.

"Why couldn't she have told you that in Hadman's office?"

He was questioning me as if I were actually his client, and he had assigned a man to spend a morning on my case.

"I didn't hire you," I reminded him pointedly.

"That report is a sample of the kind of job my agency can do. Of course it's very preliminary. For a retainer we go on from there."

It didn't sound right. I asked him how long he had been waiting in the hotel lobby for me.

"Maybe an hour," he replied.

"I'm not a complete dope," I said. "Does the head of a detective agency spend his time and the time of an employee on the remote chance of landing a client who has told you he has very little money?"

"Let's say your case fascinates me."

"Not to that extent. Being a detective is a business with you, not a hobby."

His ingratiating grin spread all over his face. "You win, Aikin. The truth is that I haven't an agency. There's only myself. I had one measly case, the one I told you about yesterday, and this morning that folded. The husband took it to a big agency. He was right; a lone wolf like myself can't handle a shadowing job. Frankly, I can use anything thrown my way. That can't be called a recommendation, but I believe your job is up my alley."

And maybe the alley would lead where I didn't want it to. Because it always came back to that: I wasn't sure I could afford to have anybody probe too deeply into Judith's past. Was I doing the right thing? How could I know when I knew so little, when I was groping blindly through a fog and afraid of what would be revealed if the fog lifted?

"No job for me, eh?" Singleton said.

I would have another try at Dacia Wilmot this afternoon. Maybe I could get her down to five hundred. She'd take it if I convinced her that it was a choice between that sum and nothing.

"Sorry," I said. "No job."

He didn't look particularly disappointed, but you couldn't tell with him. His grin covered everything else in his face. "If you change your mind, you've got my card." We shook hands and he left.

I stopped at the desk. Immediately after I had registered at this hotel Thursday night I had called up George Kloe long distance and told him where he could get in touch with me in case Judith and Paula returned home. Living next door, he and Mabel would be the first to know. I asked the desk clerk if a phone call had come in for me.

His answer was the same as every answer since early Wednesday morning: nothing.

I went up to my room and wrote a letter.

DEAR AUNT EDNA:

Thursday Bernard Terhune sent me to New York on business for the company. When I went home to pack, Judith and Paula insisted on going along and making a holiday of it. We had to leave in such a hurry to make the train that it wasn't possible to stop off at the hospital to say goodbye to you.

I had assumed that one of the girls would write you, but this morning I learned that neither one had. You know how they never get around to writing letters, so I'm doing it for them.

The girls are fine. We went to a musical comedy last night and today the girls are making the rounds of the department stores. I hope they'll leave enough money for carfare home.

I don't know how long we'll stay. I'll write you every day.

Love from the three of us and may you be up and about when we return home.

LEO

That should keep Aunt Edna from worrying about her nieces not visiting her at the hospital. The explanation of why they didn't write themselves was convincing; she'd had more experience than I of their resistance to letter writing.

And thinking of that, it struck me that for all I knew a letter from Judith might be waiting for me at home. That would be one letter she would write — if she were able to. I could ask George or Mabel Kloe to go next door and look in my mailbox.

The phone was at my elbow. I called the Kloe number. No answer. I scowled at the phone and then called my own number in Jorberg. No answer, as expected.

Perhaps the Kloes were gone for the day or even longer, and if Judith and Paula had returned home they wouldn't know where to get in touch with me. I couldn't raise any hope that that had happened, but I couldn't overlook any possibility. I called Jorberg Plastics and spoke to Miss Townsend, our combination switchboard operator and typist.

"Mr. Terhune isn't in," she said. "He left this morning with the police and told me he'd be gone all day."

Something squeezed my stomach. "The police?"

"Mort Middle was here at ten-thirty. He spoke to Mr. Terhune for a few minutes in his office and then they both left."

"What was it about?"

"I have no idea," Miss Townsend said. "Mr. Terhune seemed very upset when he left with Mort Middle. They drove away in a police car." Her voice dropped to a confidential whisper. "Everybody in the place is talking about it. You don't think it has anything to do with the plant?"

I didn't answer that. I said good-bye and hung up briefly and then asked the operator to get me the Jorberg, Connecticut, police.

"Police headquarters," Steve Gale announced cheerfully.

"This is Leo Aikin."

Abruptly his tone became solemn. "You in New York, Mr. Aikin?"

"Yes."

"We tried to get you all morning. They said at the Hotel Martha that you weren't registered there."

"I'm at the Mammoth."

"That's funny. Mrs. Kloe said you were staying at the Hotel Martha."

"What happened?"

"It's a hell of a note, Mr. Aikin. The Chief heard from the Hartford police late last night. They weren't dead sure of the identity, so the Chief was anxious for you to meet him in Hartford. He waited till after ten this morning, and then when he couldn't get in touch with you — "

"In heaven's name, what happened?"

"It's Paula Runyon, Mr. Aikin. She's dead."

All I felt was a vast, dull fatigue. It was as if I had known it since early Wednesday morning, but had refused to face it.

"Hello, Mr. Aikin?" Steve Gale said.

My voice didn't sound like my own. "What about my wife?"

"We don't know a thing about her. Just Paula Runyon. A state trooper found her on Route 6, near Hartford. She was dead when he found her."

"Murdered?"

"They're not sure. Maybe a hit-run accident. That's one of the things the Chief went there to find out. And the identification. Fact is, they aren't absolutely sure it's Paula Runyon."

"You mean she was — her face was battered?"

"Not so much, the way I heard it. You remember those two pictures you gave me Thursday? Well, we put them on a circular and sent them out. The state trooper who found the body saw the pictures and went to the morgue in Hartford where the body is and the body measured up to the description. But that's not positive identification."

"Is that why Terhune went with Middle?"

"How do you know that if you're in New York?" He sounded suspicious.

"I called the plant."

"Well, you not being here, the Chief had to scout around for others to drive to Hartford with him and identify the body. He figured Terhune knew her as good as anybody in Jorberg. He took Mrs. Kloe along too because, being a woman and a neighbor, she'd maybe be able to identify the clothes. But they'll need you there, Mr. Aikin, you being the closest relative around."

"How long will they be in Hartford?"

"Guess they didn't get there before an hour ago. I can phone the Chief and tell him to wait for you."

"Just a minute." I opened my bag and dug out the New York, New Haven, and Hartford timetable and returned to the phone. "I can make the 1:30. It reaches Hartford at 4:15. Ask Middle to have somebody meet me at the station."

"Sure thing." Steve Gale paused and then said, "I guess you were right after all, Mr. Aikin. Something did happen to them. To one of them, anyway."

I said good-bye and hung up.

I picked up the letter I had written to Aunt Edna. Because tomorrow was Sunday, she wouldn't receive it until Monday. I started to tear it up and changed my mind. I wrote Special Delivery across the envelope, pasted on the stamps, and mailed it on the way to Grand Central.

13. The Dead Face

Bernard Terhune met me at the station. "I'm sorry, Leo," he said, putting a hand on my arm.

The hard shell of him had cracked and permitted gentleness to soften his voice, genuine emotion to crumple the controlled severity of his face, loneliness to melt the ice in his eyes. At that moment — and for the first time in the years we had known each other in war and peace — we were friends.

"So there's no doubt that it's Paula?" I said.

"No doubt, Leo." With his hand still on my arm, he led me out of the station to a parked sedan. "I borrowed Mort Middle's car. I wanted to meet you alone. I don't know how much you've heard."

"That Paula was killed, but not how."

He didn't reply until the car was moving. "The police believe that she was struck by a car. But why would she be walking on the road near Hartford so late at night?"

My fingernails dug into my palms. "And Judith?"

"No sign of her. No word from her. Yet Tuesday night they left the house together and a few hours later Paula was killed."

For a while we drove in silence.

Suddenly Terhune slammed his right hand on the steering wheel. "You at least had almost a year of Judith. I never had a real minute of Paula. And now I never will."

So that was all his grief amounted to: he was sorry for himself.

I didn't speak. I didn't look out at the streets of Hartford passing by. Presently the car stopped. We got out and I walked at Terhune's side, and then we were in a small room and Mort Middle and Mabel Kloe were there, and a state police sergeant and a man in plain clothes I later learned was a Hartford detective.

Mabel's plump face had the frozen set of people in the presence of death. She looked up from where she sat in a wooden chair, said, "Oh, Leo!" and brought a handkerchief up to her nose.

"Why didn't you tell the police I was staying at the Mammoth?" I asked her. On the train that had bothered me, perhaps because a minor unimportant question blocked out the maddening larger questions.

"The Mammoth?" she said through her handkerchief. "Wasn't it the Hotel Martha?"

"I told George it was the Mammoth when I phoned him Thursday night and I left him the phone number."

"Oh, I'm so sorry, Leo," Mabel took the handkerchief from her face. "George left yesterday afternoon on a selling trip. I was sure he told me you were staying at the Hotel Martha. I'd stayed there once with George and the names are so much alike that I must have got them mixed up in my mind. And this morning I couldn't find where he'd left the phone number of your hotel. I feel terrible, Leo."

"Well, I'm here," I said.

There was a wooden table against a wall and a woman's clothes spread out on it. I stared at the clothes.

"That's everything she had on when she was killed," Mort Middle told me. "I guess the identification is definite enough, but you'll have to make it final and claim the body and the police here would like a statement."

A black fur coat covered half the table. The rest consisted of a brown dress, panties, brassiere, nylon hose, open-toed black shoes, arctics, a scarf she often wore instead of a hat.

I said, "The coat looks like hers and the dress and scarf are familiar, but I can't say about the rest."

"That brown wool dress was certainly hers," Mabel spoke up, "I saw her wear it several times. And she's had that Persian lamb coat since I've known her."

The sight of the underwear hurt me particularly. It seemed to me somehow indecent to display the brassiere and panties like that. I turned away from the table.

Chief Middle planted his thick body at my side. "I guess you want to know just what happened, Mr. Aikin. We don't know ourselves, exactly. Sergeant Billings here was driving west along Route 6, just inside the Hartford city limits. It was Wednesday morning at around three o'clock when — "

"It was 3:18 A.M.," the state police sergeant said. He looked like any other state cop I'd ever seen — burly and erect.

"All right, 3:18 A.M.," Middle conceded. "He was crawling along. You remember how bad the roads were. There was a freezing rain."

"Worst night in years," the Sergeant said. "The roads were like glass. I wasn't doing more than ten miles an hour."

"Then Sergeant Billings saw her on the road," Middle went on. "He found that she was — "

"I didn't know right off it was a woman," the Sergeant said.

Middle sighed and gave up. "All right, you tell it your way, Sergeant."

The Sergeant stepped to the middle of the room, like an actor seeking the front of the stage for his best lines.

"The only thing my headlights showed was something dark at the side of the road. The rain froze on my windows except where the windshield wipers wiped it off and I couldn't see so good. I thought it was a log or a long rock. My headlights were practically past it when I saw something white on it, like it might be a face. I got out and investigated and sure enough it was a woman. There was a mean wound on her left temple; it must've bled plenty, but there wasn't so much blood then. I guess the rain must've washed off some of the blood. Funny the way her face looked, like it was wax or covered by glass. After her body cooled off, the rain froze on her face, covered it with a layer of ice, and covered the rest of her too. She was dead, all right. I called in on my radio and then started looking for a wreck. There wasn't a thing, just that woman lying there off the road. It figured like a plain case of hit-and-run. She was crossing the road and walked along it, and a car hit her and knocked her clean off the road. There wasn't a thing on her to identify her."

"There's no handbag of hers on the table," Middle told me. He turned to Mabel Kloe. "Would a woman go out without a handbag?"

"She might," Mabel said. "She had pockets in that coat."

"There wasn't a thing in the pockets."

"Then I can't imagine her not taking a handbag."

Terhune swung from the window through which he had been staring. "You think that her handbag was removed to obscure her identity? But why would a hit-and-run driver do that?"

Middle rubbed his jowls. "Makes you think, doesn't it?"

"There was no way to identify the body," the Sergeant repeated stolidly. "No laundry marks even. Guess she washed her underwear and stockings herself, and the scarf was hand-knitted and the dress had never been dry-cleaned and no label was in her coat."

"The label was ripped out?" Terhune asked.

The Sergeant shook his head. "They can tell in the laboratory if a label's been ripped out. Maybe she'd had her coat relined, like my wife did last year. Well, so the body was here in Hartford in the morgue. She was found in the city limits, so it was Hartford's case. Then yesterday I saw the circular sent out by Jorberg. The picture of one of the two women, Paula Runyon, looked like the one I'd found, though that's not much to go on because dead people look a lot alike. But they'd disappeared in the direction of Hartford only a few hours before 3:18 A.M. Wednesday, so it looked like it could add up. I went to the morgue and her description and weight and measurement matched close enough to be a good chance it was the same woman."

Middle cleared his throat, but said nothing. Terhune was looking out of the window. Mabel Kloe fumbled in her handbag for a cigarette.

"Can't an autopsy tell if she was hit by a car?" I asked.

The detective spoke for the first time. He had been standing against a wall — a wiry man with a pipe which was practically part of his mouth. "Well, now, that's not so easy. It was the blow on the head killed her."

"Wouldn't a car have hit her lower down before it could do anything to her head?" I persisted.

"There are contusions all along her left side, from shoulder to knee, but they're only contusions. Maybe she was crossing the road and saw a car coming and slipped on the ice when she tried to get out of the way and was struck on the head as she was falling." The detective put a match to his pipe. "Maybe she was struck with a blunt instrument and got the contusions when she fell on the frozen ground. I'll take a bet either way."

They were all silent then. Mabel had trouble lighting her cigarette. At the window Terhune's back was to me, but I saw that his one visible hand was clenched.

"She was murdered," I said.

My words hung in the air for a brittle second and died without response from any of them.

"It's getting late," the detective told Middle. "Let's finish up with Aikin."

Terhune and Mabel stayed behind. The three policemen and I walked up a corridor, past closed doors, and then one door was opened and we were in with the chemical smells of the dead. In a wall there were drawers to hold once human flesh and there were white tables, all bare but one. We gathered around the table on which something lay covered by a sheet.

The detective uncovered the face.

Paula's face, but no longer Paula. It was just a dead face.

And where was Judith's face? On another table in another morgue, waiting to be identified? Or... or... God in heaven, or what?

"Do you identify this woman as Paula Runyon?" the detective asked as if reading from a printed form.

"Yes."

He grasped the end of the sheet as if to cover the face. "You asked me about marks on the body." His hand moved the wrong way, toward the foot of the table, and she was uncovered to the waist.

All her clothes were on that table in the other room. Even in death she had the right to the privacy of her body.

"Damn you!" I said. "Cover her!"

"What the hell, she wouldn't mind now."

"Cover her!"

"Okay, okay, but I wanted to show you her wrists." The detective worked the limp hands over the sheet and pulled the sheet up to the throat. He picked up the left hand. "See these abrasions on the wrist?"

I bent over the table. There was a faint bluish mark on the left side of the wrist, a fainter mark on the right side.

"The post-mortem report made a special point of these marks." The detective walked to the other side of the table and lifted the right hand. "The same thing on this wrist, only this time more pronounced on the right side."

He pulled the sheet all the way up, but it needed more than a cover over that dead face to block it out from my vision. I thought that I would never be able to recall her beauty, her languid smile, the way she stood and spoke and moved, the smoldering charm that had made me so immensely fond of her. I would never recall anything of her but the obscene caricature on a white table.

I walked halfway to the door and stopped.

"Rope made those marks," I said. "Is that it? She was found with her hands tied."

The Sergeant was a step or two ahead of me. Resentfully he twisted his head to me. "If her hands were tied, you think I would've figured it as a hit-run accident?"

The detective came up to me and leaned against one of the bare tables. "Rope would've bit deeper and the abrasions would form a complete ring around each wrist. I've got a theory." He lit a match for his pipe, making us wait for his theory. A nice bit of dramatic suspense. "I've seen marks like that on the wrists of a man who was fighting a pair of bracelets."

The chemical smell of death was overpowering. I moved on toward the door and the policeman moved with me.

When I was in the corridor, I said, "You mean handcuffs?"

"It's just a theory," the detective replied. "But I'd back it with even money."

My legs were wobbling. I leaned against the corridor wall.

"The girls were tied up in the car," I said. "If there was only one man, he had to keep them quiet and helpless when he drove to the house for their clothes. Don't you remember, Chief, that's what I told you from the first?"

"I guess you did, Mr. Aiken. Even if he didn't go back for their clothes, he'd tie them so they couldn't interfere with his driving. So why not handcuffs?"

"And gags," I muttered.

"Tied and gagged, that's the routine," the detective said. "I asked the doc if he could tell if she'd been gagged, but he couldn't. That doesn't mean she wasn't. A thick handkerchief stuffed in the mouth and then a wide strip of cloth — say, like her scarf — tied around the face to hold the gag in, and no marks would necessarily be made. There's just no telling. I wouldn't want either end of that bet."

"Judith!" I heard myself say hoarsely. "What did he do to her after he killed Paula?"

The detective lit a match for his pipe and for a long moment held it suspended over the bowl. Then he used it and said, "Chief Middle gave us the dope, but we'll need your statement, Aikin."

I was led into an office. I was offered a chair; I sat deep in it and spoke. A male stenographer took down everything I said directly on a typewriter. For the first time since I'd started telling the story I didn't leave out a single thing. I told them about Judith's nightmares.

"You think she'd murdered somebody in New York?" the detective broke in sharply.

"I don't know any more than I told you."

Middle said resentfully, "You didn't tell me about those dreams."

I sat with my hands on my knees and said nothing.

The detective came around to the front of my chair where he had the psychological advantage of looking down at me. "So you tried to cover your wife, Aikin? That's human; we'd all do the same for our own wives. But after what happened to her sister, you're afraid that worse can happen to her than being caught up with on an old killing."

I didn't say anything.

"So you might as well give us the whole thing," the detective urged. "You've more to go on than a dream."

"No. Only what her aunt told me she'd heard Judith say in those nightmares."

"Then what made you so sure that Paula Runyon was murdered?"

"You're sure, too," I said.

The detective sucked on his pipe and smiled.

"Did you hear me mention murder?" he said. "I'm not sure of anything, not even that those marks on her wrists were made by handcuffs. We've got a little of this and a little of that, but no neat column of figures that add up. For instance, Tuesday night they left the house on a nasty night to meet somebody on Mill Street. You don't go out to meet your kidnapers to make it easier for them to snatch you. And if Paula Runyon was slated to be killed, would the killer tie her up and after driving quite a while with her stop to kill her when he could've done it easier on Mill Street?"

"If her body had been found on Mill Street," I argued, "she would have been identified immediately."

"Then why didn't he drive her a lot farther from Jorberg than Hartford? It was either too close or too far away. And if he killed one sister, why not the other instead of leaving her alive to be a witness against him?"

Middle said heavily, "We don't know that Judith wasn't killed too."

I felt myself sink into myself.

The detective's pipe stem ran in and out of his mouth. "Then why not kill both of them at the same time? If I'd just knocked off a woman, I wouldn't want to keep driving with her sister who can put the finger of murder on me. Not even if she was tied and gagged. Too dangerous. Unless" — another dramatic pause while he lit a match — "unless she didn't care that her sister was murdered."

Middle sighed.

I stared up at the detective. "What are you trying to say?"

"I'm saying, Aikin, that those sisters went willingly to meet somebody on Mill Street. Maybe one sister got in the way and showed that she was in the way while they were driving and so she had to be got rid of by the other sister and the man."

I opened my mouth and let it hang open a long moment without saying anything. He was trying to be clever, to shock me into saying something I might not otherwise say. I held onto myself.

"Make up your mind," I told him. "Was Paula murdered or wasn't she?"

"Let's say I'm trying out variations on a theme, like the musicians do. We can try another variation. The sisters went willingly with a man or men. On the way Paula Runyon got sore at them and insisted on getting out of the car then and there and while she was walking along the icy road another car came along and smacked her. The odds are —"

"You and your bets," the Sergeant cut in. He hadn't spoken for a long time. "Some day somebody will take you up and you'll lose your shirt. It's a homicide either way you look at it: she was killed by a club or she was killed by a hit-run driver. We want the guy who did it."

"Right!" the detective agreed. "We also want to know what happened to the other sister and why. Can a dream tell us anything? Can we say that on top of one killing there's another way back because a woman had a dream a year or two ago, and that both of them are connected?"

"We can kick this around all night," Middle complained. "It's after six. I'd like to get home for supper."

I went on with my statement. The detective interrupted me again when I reached the part about Eat calling at the house Tuesday afternoon. He wanted more information about him.

I said that so did I, and that Mabel Kloe, from whom I'd learned what little I knew about him, was in the other room.

"She described him, but it's like most descriptions," the detective said. "Tall, but she couldn't tell if very tall or just above average height. A very handsome guy, but no details. Try to describe somebody you spent an evening with. If you're like most people, I'll bet even money you wouldn't even know the color of his eyes. Mrs. Kloe didn't see this Eat guy for more than a few minutes."

I dictated the rest of it. I told them about Dacia Wilmot and her offer to sell me information for a thousand dollars.

"Maybe we'll get something from her," the detective said skeptically, "but I'll lay long odds all she wanted to sell you was some scandal. Actresses are always getting messed up in scandals."

I signed the statement. I signed other papers — identifying the body, claiming her clothes, accepting release of the body to me. Then I was back in the other room with Mort Middle, and Bernard Terhune and Mabel Kloe were putting on their coats. We went out to Middle's car.

"I'm taking the 7:22 back to New York," I told them when we reached the car.

Mabel was already in the back seat, and Terhune, following her, paused with his hand on the open door. Middle, sitting behind the wheel, stuck his head out.

"What are you going to do in New York?" the police chief demanded.

"What I've been doing — look for Judith."

"The police all over the East will be looking for her. What do you think you can do they can't?"

"I don't know," I said, "but I can't just stay home and wait. Bernie, will you do something for me?"

I had never before called him by his first name. In the army he had been captain or sir, and in Jorberg, both at work and in our social life, I had avoided addressing him by name at all. But Paula's death had brought us closer together than I had ever thought anything would.

"Anything you want, Leo," he said.

"I'd appreciate it if you'll take care of the funeral arrangements. Use Bergman's Funeral Parlor. Tell Bergman I'll take care of the bill right after the funeral."

"I'll pay for everything, Leo."

"No."

"Damn you!" Terhune clung to the car door with one hand and raised the other as if to hit me with it. "I'll pay for the funeral. Can't you let me do anything for her, even now?"

Middle, half in the car and half out, watched us curiously. Mabel leaned toward us.

"All right, Bernie," I said. I tried not to let it sound like a favor from me to him, but that was what it was all the same. "If you'll call me at the Mammoth as soon as you know when the funeral will take place, I'll come in for it."

Terhune started to get into the car, then turned back to me. He put a hand intimately on my arm, the way he had when he had met me at the station. "Luck, Leo."

I said good-bye and stepped back from the curb and the car drove away. I looked at the building out of which I had come. There was a song about a girl lying in a morgue — "so stark, so white, so bare." I tried to think of the name of the song, and I realized that I was doing it again, concentrating on other things because it hurt so much to think of the dead and the living.

14. The Long Night

At 10:30 P.M. I was back in New York. From Grand Central Terminal I took the Lexington Avenue subway down to Twenty-third Street and walked two blocks south and a block and a half east to Dacia Wilmot's apartment.

There was going to be no bargaining for information. I would say to Dacia: Paula has been murdered and God knows what happened to Judith. It's gone past the stage where you can do business on your past friendship with them, or where you'll want to if you really were their friend. Now give.

That would open her up.

In the lobby of the building a man sat on an upholstered bench. The upper half of him was covered by a newspaper he held spread out before his face. I crossed the lobby to the automatic elevator and pressed a button. Behind me paper rustled. Instinctively I looked around. The newspaper had dipped, but it was going up again; I glimpsed a black slouch hat and nothing else from the waist up.

Dacia Wilmot lived on the third floor. When the elevator door slid open, I heard radio music and laughter and boisterous voices pour into the hall from the direction of her apartment. A party, I thought, and I resented that almost more than anything she had done. In that one-room apartment filled with people it would be impossible to get her off by herself short of bringing her out here in the hall where there would be hardly more privacy. And she'd probably be drunk. By the sound of that party, everybody at it was drunk.

But when I reached her door, I found that the party was in the apartment to the left of hers. There was no response to my knock. I put my ear against the door panel, but the party blocked out any other sound on that floor. I turned the knob. Locked.

Well, I should have expected her not to be in. An attractive young woman wouldn't be sitting home on a Saturday night. There was somebody else I also wanted to see tonight, and after I saw him I'd be back.

Florian Singleton's business card was in my pocket. The address was on West Eleventh Street, in the heart of Greenwich Village. I took the elevator down to the lobby.

The man reading the newspaper in the lobby hadn't changed his position in the least, as if he'd been frozen in it. This time I was facing him when I crossed the lobby to the street door, and this time I saw the paper come away from his face. But only from part of his face. Only enough to reveal that black hat, the tip of an uptilted cigar, two black eyes resting on me for no more than a second before the paper again rose all the way.

It was, I thought, an odd way for a man to be reading a newspaper. But by the time I reached the street, he and his paper were out of my mind.

The night was crisp, good for walking, so I walked. It took me half an hour to reach the address on Singleton's card. It was a three-story apartment building, which meant that his home was also his office. Hardly a sign of a prosperous private detective business, but all the same I had confidence in him. Maybe it was only his charm that made me believe that he could do a job as good as any man in his profession, but it wasn't a phoney charm. At any rate, I'd have nothing to lose but the fee I'd pay him.

He wasn't in either. I shouldn't have expected anybody in New York to be in on a Saturday night except people who were throwing parties.

Leaning against the hall wall, I wrote a note to him in my address book and took the sheet out and slipped it under his door. The note consisted of one line:

"Get in touch with me as soon as possible at the Mammoth — Leo Aikin."

From there I walked north to Fourteenth Street, then east until I came to a restaurant on Union Square. Since breakfast at eight that morning I hadn't had more to eat than a couple of sandwiches and coffee. Now I had a complete steak dinner, not rushing because I wanted to give Dacia plenty of time to get home. It was past one o'clock when I returned to her building.

The man who had been reading a newspaper on the bench was still in the lobby. He was standing now, staring at a huge potted rubber plant at the side of the entrance. The rolled-up newspaper stuck out of a pocket of his black overcoat. I still couldn't see his face.

He was a man who liked to hold a pose for a long time. He held his pose with his back to me, not moving a muscle, this time evidently not interested in who had entered. While I waited for the elevator to come down, I glanced quickly around. The rubber plant continued to hold his attention.

The party was as noisy as it had been two hours ago. And Dacia hadn't returned.

"Looking for somebody?" a quiet voice asked.

I swung from Dacia's door. He had come up the fire stairs. Everything about him was black, except his shirt which was gray and his skin which was swarthy — black hat and necktie and suit and coat and shoes, and what I could see of his hair was curly black and his eyes glittered like wet coal in sunlight.

He wasn't anybody I'd ever seen.

"What's that your business?" I said.

He came over to where I stood at Dacia's door. His hand went into the coat pocket which didn't contain the newspaper and came out with a badge. The police hadn't wasted any time.

I told him my name.

His intense black eyes looked me over. He removed his cigar. "Can you prove it?"

I showed him my driver's license. He returned it and asked me where I was staying in New York.

"At the Mammoth."

He nodded. "It checks with what Hartford told me on the phone. You're Paula Runyon's brother-in-law and the guy Dacia Wilmot wanted to sell information to for a grand."

"You're not a Hartford detective?"

"I'm Hubbard, a precinct detective. We're doing a job for Hartford, and maybe our own job too if Judith Aikin came to New York or was brought here. Your wife, that is."

"Yes," I said, "my wife."

The black eyes never left my face. "Why'd you come here? Don't you think the police can handle the Wilmot dame?"

"Maybe not," I said. "You cops might rub her the wrong way or scare her, and in either case she might deny knowing anything."

"I get it. You brought the dough for her."

"No. She'll talk to me for nothing when she hears that Paula is dead."

"Sure you didn't want to get to her before the police?"

I frowned as if I didn't understand, but of course I did. He hadn't been so far wrong.

"In case she told you something you didn't want anybody else to know," Hubbard explained. But he didn't make anything further of it. He looked up and down the hall. "Might be a long wait. A dame like this won't hurry home on a Saturday night."

The door of the apartment next door flew open. A. woman squealed, "God, I need air!" but she didn't come out to the hall for it. The door banged shut.

"Maybe Dacia's in there," I suggested.

"Nope. First thing I did was try that party. How about going downstairs? They got a bench."

We went downstairs. We sat side by side on the bench. Hubbard opened his newspaper and held it before his face.

"Why don't you want to be seen waiting here?" I asked him.

He looked at me in surprise. "Come again?"

"You were keeping your face covered by that paper the first time I came in. The second time you had your back turned so that nobody coming or going could see your face." He chuckled softly. "You got your ideas of detectives out of story books. Would I be so corny? I always read a paper that way." And he proceeded to do so.

People left the building and people entered it, but not Dacia. I felt my eyelids become heavy.

Suddenly I was wide awake. I had dozed off. My watch said ten minutes to three.

"Why don't you go to bed?" Hubbard said. "I'm not sure I'll let you hang around when I talk to her, so why punish yourself?"

"Will you let me know what you learn from her?"

"We'll want to have a talk with you after that anyway. Match up with you what she has to say, or confront her with you if she denies having anything to say. Go on home." I said good night and walked up to Twenty-third Street where I caught a cab.

At my hotel, the desk clerk plucked a letter out of my box. The envelope had no stamp and only my name was written on it. Inside the envelope a sheet of hotel stationery was covered on both sides by a thin, compressed script and signed by Dacia Wilmot.

Standing beside the desk, I read:

Saturday, 4 P.M.

LEO AIKIN:

> I feel like a heel.
>
> Last night I tabbed you as a detective of some kind so why should I give you anything for nothing or if you weren't a detective and you were really Judy's husband she'd run out on you and if you wanted dirt on her past you'd have to pay money for it.
>
> Even for the grand I wouldn't have told you much anyway except what's more or less public knowledge but I didn't know then what had happened to Paul.

I sat down in a nearby leather couch and in my hat and coat continued to read the letter.

> Earlier this afternoon I made up my mind to check up on you if you were really Judy's husband and if Judy and Paul had really disappeared like you said so I made a long-distance phone call to the Jorberg police.
>
> The Jorberg cop I spoke to sounded awfully suspicious but I softened him up by saying I'd been a pal of Paul and Judy in New York and I met you on the street and you told me something had happened to them and then the cop told me that Paul had been killed in Hartford but he didn't tell me how.
>
> Killed means murdered doesn't it? She was murdered wasn't she?
>
> I was a heel last night. I care an awful lot for those two girls but last night I didn't realize how serious it was and I thought you were just another guy I could get something out of.
>
> Maybe what I can tell you hasn't anything to do with what happened to Paul and with helping find Judy if she's still alive but now I have to tell you because I'd do anything for those two girls and it won't cost you a cent.
>
> I waited here at your hotel for an hour and now I can't wait any more.
>
> Perhaps you went back to Jorberg when you heard Paul was killed but they told me at the desk that you didn't check out so I guess you'll be back soon so I'm writing you this here in the lobby.
>
> What I have to tell you is too long to write in a letter and anyway I wouldn't want to write it down.
>
> I'm going home from here and I'll be home all evening and night and as far as I know tomorrow too so please come as soon as you get this.
>
> I'm sorry for the way I acted last night.
>
>   Sincerely yours,
>   DACIA WILMOT

I read the letter again and then just sat there. I knew that I should get up and do something, but at the moment I couldn't make the effort.

A coatless and hatless man came in through the revolving door. He headed jauntily toward the desk, checked himself when he saw me, brought his grin to his rugged face, came over to the couch.

"I got home thirty minutes ago and found your note under my door," Florian Singleton said. "It sounded urgent, so I came right over in spite of the late hour."

"I want you to work on the case," I told him. I sounded listless to myself, as if I didn't care if he did or didn't. But that wasn't it. I was crushed by the weight of accumulating terror.

"I was hoping that was what you wanted." Singleton sat down beside me and glanced at the letter in my hand and then looked searchingly into my face. "What's up? You look like a man who's lost his best — " He broke that off abruptly. "Anything new come up?"

I said, "Paula is dead."

He leaned back against the arm of the couch and stretched his long legs. His face got that empty look when his grin vanished.

"Dead how?" he said.

I told him.

"Screwy," he commented when I finished. "Nothing adds up."

"That's what the Hartford detective said."

"To begin with, why snatch your wife? You kidnap somebody to hold for ransom, to get something in return for their release, but what have you got? Besides, no demands were made on you. Or you kidnap somebody to murder in private, away from witnesses, like your sister-in-law was. Though what's wrong with that is that the street where they were snatched was a lot more private than the outskirts of Hartford. But say for some reason it was decided to murder her after they'd driven a while, or say that she left the car alive and unharmed and was killed by a hit-run driver — in either case, what happened to your wife? Why would she drive on if she were alone, or why would she be driven on by the kidnapers after they'd released or killed her sister? Unless..."

He treated that one word as if it were a complete sentence, a complete thought.

I burst out savagely, "Unless Judith murdered her sister or condoned it. Is that what you mean?"

Singleton stared at me. I cringed inside my overcoat. I shouldn't have said it. I hadn't even thought it, consciously; it had come out by itself, stark and naked and intolerably ugly.

"Take it easy," Singleton said gently. "We don't know anything yet. If you're going to be my client, I ought to know about Dacia Wilmot, if there's anything. What'd she want to see you about last night?"

I handed him the letter.

His grin returned as he read it. "What are we sitting around here for? Let's drag her out of bed if necessary."

"I went to her apartment as soon as I got home. I was there at a quarter to eleven and she wasn't in. A New York detective had arrived before that. I waited with him until almost three and then came here and found this letter from Dacia."

Singleton neatly folded the letter in three and returned it to me.

"So what?" he said musingly. "She's a girl who likes dates. Say a date came up the last minute and she couldn't resist it." He twisted his head to the big clock on the wall. "Five to four. Even Dacia ought to be getting home by now. Let's go."

We got into a cab parked in front of the hotel.

Detective Hubbard rose from the bench in the lobby when we entered. He and Singleton said hello, calling each other by name. I showed him the letter.

Hubbard read slowly, without a line changing in his swarthy face. When he finished, he said, "Any objection if I hang onto this?"

"No."

He unbuttoned his coat, stuck the letter into his inside jacket pocket, buttoned his coat — a methodical, unhurried man. Then he put his black eyes on Singleton.

"Aikin your client?"

"Any objection?" Singleton said affably.

The black eyes shifted to me. "What d'you want to hire a private investigator for? There are plenty of real cops working on this."

"The more the better," I said.

Hubbard blew smoke at the ceiling and then without another word went away from us. He disappeared down the ground-floor hall.

In five minutes he was back with a hulking man who was buttoning his shirt. They went to the elevator and Hubbard pressed the button. Singleton and I entered the elevator with them. Hubbard didn't say anything; he seemed to be ignoring us.

The only sound of the party when we reached the third floor was radio music. The hulking man took a key ring out of a pocket and unlocked the door and stepped aside. Hubbard entered first, then Singleton. I hung back for a moment; my legs were turning to water. I locked my teeth and went in.

Hubbard was already at the bathroom door and looking inside. Singleton had the closet door open. From where I stood I could look into the kitchenette.

"That's that," Hubbard said, turning from the bathroom.

"Plenty of clothes in the closet." Singleton crossed over to the bedroom section and opened each of the three dresser drawers. "Drawers more or less filled. She didn't pull out."

"Why would she after she'd written Aikin that letter?" Hubbard said.

Singleton shrugged and looked under the bed.

Hubbard went to the hulking man who was watching us drowsily from the hall. "When was the last time you saw Miss Wilmot?"

"Who knows?" the hulking man said. "I'm the superintendent. It ain't my business to see tenants unless there's a complaint."

"Okay, I'll bring the keys down to you," Hubbard said.

The superintendent padded off without a sound. He was wearing slippers. Hubbard came back into the apartment. "You two beat it."

Singleton started to say something and decided not to. He and I went down to the lobby and sat on the bench.

"What's he going to look for — clues?" I said.

"Anything there is to be found. Maybe what she wanted to sell you is in writing." Singleton pushed out his legs. "Hubbard is a good egg. We're pretty friendly, but official police don't like private detectives around when they're working."

Hubbard was up there for forty minutes. When he came out of the elevator, he headed down the hall to return the key. We heard him say good night to the superintendent and then he came into the lobby and stood in front of the bench with his legs apart.

"Anything?" Singleton asked him.

"A stack of sexy letters written to her in the last few months by a guy named Tommy. No second name. No return address. Either of you know a Tommy who knew her?"

Neither of us did.

"Nothing else useful." The corners of Hubbard's mouth lifted. "I didn't search her room. She mightn't like it when she comes back and thinks I searched her room without a warrant."

"Sure you didn't," Singleton said.

I stood up, walked to the door, returned to the two men. "When she comes back!" I said shrilly. "Do you expect her to?"

Hubbard took his black cigar out of his mouth and spoke to it. "A girl likes to go out with a man Saturday night. Letter or no letter."

"Maybe a week-end date," Singleton suggested.

"Sure, likely with that guy Tommy. It wouldn't be the first time. I read the letters" — he smiled — "unofficially."

Why not that? They were trained investigators; they kept their feet on the ground, examined all possibilities; they hadn't had their nerves twisted and torn until no notion was too wild.

"What are you going to do?" I asked Hubbard.

"Wait for her."

We three waited. I didn't sit down again. I stood here. I stood there. I prowled the lobby.

Hubbard was worrying about where his wife and children would spend the summer. Seashore summer rentals were too expensive these days for a cop and rates in the country weren't much lower. "You still got that place upstate?" he asked Singleton. "Croton, isn't it?"

"Near Croton. It's just a shack. I don't use it much."

"You don't want to rent it for the summer?"

"For your wife and kids? It's got no running water and only two rooms."

"Well, look, Singleton, maybe it's better than a summer in the city. How much would you want for it for two months?"

"I wasn't thinking of renting, but..."

This went on and on. They slipped into a discussion of high summer rents and then the places where they each had spent summers and how New York was no place for kids when the weather got hot — until I couldn't stand any more and went out to the street.

I watched the dawn come up.

At seven in the morning another detective arrived to relieve Hubbard. They conferred in whispers, then Hubbard came over to Singleton and me.

"I'm going home to bed," he said. "Why don't you guys do the same?"

Singleton yawned and said it was a good idea. We three left the building.

"Are you police going to do nothing but hang around here?" I said angrily, not sure what I was angry about.

"Believe it or not, we know our business. Be seeing you." Hubbard walked east.

Singleton and I walked west, looking for a cab. When we found one, Singleton showed the deference due a client and insisted that I take it uptown to my hotel.

15. The Palace Theater

The phone jarred me out of sleep. My watch said a few minutes to nine, not much more than an hour since I had hit the pillow. The phone rang again. The police, I thought, and suddenly I was very wide awake.

But it was Bernard Terhune calling me from Jorberg. The funeral would be at three o'clock that afternoon.

"We had to rush it," Terhune said somewhat apologetically. "After all, she's been dead quite a few days."

I could just about make it. I showered and shaved in a rush, got to Grand Central with ten minutes to spare, used half of that time to snatch part of a breakfast.

Terhune met me in his car at the Jorberg railroad station and drove me to Bergman's Funeral Parlor. From there, shortly after, the procession left for the cemetery. There had been little time to make elaborate arrangements, but there were at least thirty cars in the line, and when we reached the cemetery others were already there. These were people who had known Paula most of their lives. They were young men and women just beginning to live, to set up homes of their own and rear children. And Paula was dead.

And Judith...

I stood off alone with Terhune. I was afraid that if I spoke to any of the others Judith's name would come up, and I would not be able to endure that while earth was thumping down on Paula.

It was over. We were straggling back to the cars when Mabel Kloe came up to me. A handkerchief was held to her nose.

"Leo, can I see you for a minute?"

Terhune glanced sideways at her and hurried ahead. Mabel's shoulder brushed mine as we walked very slowly.

"Leo," she said, "do you remember when you asked George if he had ever seen Judith and Paula on the stage?"

"And he lied to me," I said.

"He didn't lie. He just didn't want to..." She sniffled into her handkerchief. "George is on the road. He'd tell you now that — that Paula's dead and nobody knows what happened to Judith and she's been missing so long and... and... " She sniffled again and made a fresh start. "George saw them act in a theater in Coast City, New Jersey."

Dacia Wilmot hadn't told me that they had acted in New Jersey and Singleton's report hadn't mentioned it.

"Both of them?" I said.

"Yes. It was at the Palace Theater. I'm sure George said it was the Palace because once, when I went along with George on a selling trip, we stopped overnight in Coast City and he took me to the Palace."

"When was this?"

"About four years ago when George and I were first married."

"I mean when George saw Judith and Paula act?"

"As I remember, it was only a few weeks before they returned to Jorberg and Judith was so very sick. When George came home from that trip, he told me about having seen them on the stage."

We came to within thirty feet of Terhune's car. He was standing beside it, talking to a couple of men. Mabel and I stopped walking.

"Go on," I said.

"That's all I know. I told you everything George told me."

I looked at her. She raised the handkerchief to her eyes, but I doubted that it was so much to wipe them as to avoid meeting my gaze.

"Then why didn't he tell me when I asked him?" I said.

"I can't imagine." She was still a bad liar. "George won't be home for at least ten days. But I thought you ought to know."

"Why didn't you think I ought to know when I asked you Wednesday morning? What makes you think now it has anything to do with Paula's death?"

"I don't know," she said piteously. "I don't know, but it doesn't seem right to hold anything back from you after all the terrible things that have happened."

She was continuing to hold something back from me, but she had told me a lot. The Palace Theater in Coast City.

"Thanks, Mabel," I said.

She ducked away from me and I moved on to Terhune's car.

He drove me to my house. When he pulled up at the curb, I asked him if he would mind waiting for me five minutes and then drive me to the station.

"Rushing right back to New York, Leo?"

"Yes."

"I spoke to Mort Middle a while ago. He told me the New York police are looking for a woman who'd offered to sell you information and then disappeared. Do they think she was one of Judith's kidnapers?"

That was a new angle, but I couldn't see how that could lead anywhere. "Nobody knows yet," I said.

I went up to the house and opened the mailbox. There were lots of letters — business letters, bills, a cheery note from my brother in Denver, telling me that a new niece or nephew was six weeks on the way. But nothing from Judith or about Judith.

I entered the house. It was exactly the way I had left it, empty and terrifying. Back in the living room, I paused, looking down at the Persian rug under my feet. Paula and Judith had both wanted it very much, and now here it was. I hurried out.

At the railroad station Terhune and I shook hands.

"You've been swell, Bernie," I told him.

A corner of his hard mouth went crooked. "You don't really like me, Leo. You never have."

I supposed I didn't even now, but I liked him more than I ever had.

"You've been swell," I said again, evasively, and went into the station.

The New York train was due in thirteen minutes. I went into the phone booth and called the hospital. The nurse told me that Edna Runyon had spent a bad night, but that she was resting fairly comfortably now.

"I heard of her niece's death," the nurse said. "Of course Miss Runyon mustn't hear a word about it."

"The three of us are supposed to be in New York," I said. "Please tell her that I phoned from New York instead of writing her today. Tell her that Judith and Paula and I are fine and" — my voice got hoarse — "and having a swell time."

I was back in New York shortly before ten o'clock.

At Grand Central I called Florian Singleton's apartment. No answer. I called my hotel. No message for me. I dialed the operator and asked for police headquarters. I was connected with the central headquarters on Centre Street, which turned out to be the wrong place to get Detective Hubbard, but after hanging on for ten minutes or so I was put through to a precinct station and there spoke to a Detective Morganstern. He said that Hubbard wasn't in, but that he knew all about me and that as of thirty minutes ago Dacia Wilmot hadn't returned to her apartment.

I hung up and pushed the booth door open, but I didn't leave the stool. I sat smoking a cigarette. The smart thing to do would be to go to the Mammoth and make up the sleep I hadn't had last night and get a fresh start in the morning. A start to do what? Well, there was the Palace Theater in Coast City. Why not tonight? Coast City was just across the river; there wouldn't be a legitimate theater so close to New York, and any other kind, like a vaudeville theater, would be open on a Sunday night. It would be easy enough to find out.

I got the number out of a New Jersey directory.

"Palace," a woman's drawling voice said.

"How late will the theater be open?"

"The last show went on forty minutes ago."

"I want to know when it's over."

"Eleven-eighteen."

She hung up before I could ask her what kind of a theater it was. If it showed only movies, I would be wasting my time.

I took a cab crosstown to Pennsylvania Station. There I learned that I could reach Coast City at 11:05.

The train was seven minutes late getting there and a cab took another five minutes. The crowd was already pouring out of the theater and cabs and private cars jammed the street in front of it. My cab stopped half a block away.

I didn't stir from my seat. Through the windshield I could see a huge painted sign over the marquee. The sign bore only one word, "GIRLS," and on either side of the one word was a full-figure silhouette of a voluptuous nude-looking woman who appeared to be wearing only the vaguest sort of clothing, if any. In case that wasn't sufficiently convincing, flashing lights on the marquee announced: "60 BEAUTIFUL, GORGEOUS, CURVESOME GIRLS."

"This is the nearest I can get, mister," the driver said.

I put my hand on the door handle. "Is this the Palace?"

"Sure thing, mister. But you can see the show's over."

I got out and paid the driver and walked to the theater. The crowd coming out swirled around me. It looked like any other theater crowd, except that there was a higher proportion of men.

The box office was deserted. Bucking the stream of outgoing traffic, I worked my way into the outer lobby. Easel photos of women covered the side walls. The usual stuff — some wearing diaphanous colored veils over lavishly curved flesh, some covered by a G-string and their two coy hands. If they had been more subtle, this could have been the lobby of a night club or a musical show; less subtle and it could have been the midway of a world's fair. As it was — a burlesque theater.

Mabel Kloe had made a mistake. She had confused this theater with another, as yesterday she had confused my hotel with another.

All the same, I continued to move against the crowd.

16. The Refined Stripper

A pimply-faced young man was hooking open the last of four pairs of double doors. I shouldered my way crosscurrent to him and asked to see the manager.

He straightened up. "If you got a complaint..." He didn't bother to finish it; the way he looked me over made it obvious that complaints weren't wanted.

I had learned my lesson in New York — that if I wanted to play investigator I had to act as deviously as one.

"I'm from Herbert Seller," I said somewhat haughtily.

It was inspiration. He became practically obsequious. "You want Kip Trojan, the producer? I don't think he's left." He ducked into the theater.

In a matter of seconds he returned with a round little man. A pudgy, clammy hand thrust out at me. "Glad to see you, Mr. — " A bright little inquiring smile tilted up to me. "Aikin," I said.

"I'm Kip Trojan. So you're from Seller? Well, well, how's my old friend Herb?"

"He's on the Coast," I said.

"That so? You know, I haven't seen Ruby Whale around for a long time. What's he doing?"

I had never heard of Ruby Whale, but I knew the inevitable answer. "He's on the Coast."

A shoulder hit me in the small of the back and sent me swaying toward Trojan. We were directly in the line of traffic from the still emptying theater.

Trojan grabbed my arm. "What are we standing out here for? Come in my office."

He led me into the theater which smelled of stale tobacco smoke and rancid sweat. We went through a door next to the men's room and were in a tiny office containing an oversized desk, a couple of chairs, several filing cabinets, and four walls covered by photos of women in a variety of more or less nude poses. Trojan helped me off with my coat as if I weren't quite capable of getting out of it by myself, stuck a cigar into my mouth, held a light for me. It was pleasant to be considered important for a change.

"So you caught my show tonight?" Trojan had settled himself behind the desk. "High-class for burly, huh?"

"It was all right." My eyes were searching the photos on the walls.

"Let us not beat about the bush," he said. "Smelly Gor is what you liked. Is he a comic! A pantomime artist, y'know what I mean? A genius. Of course he's under contract to me, but for my good friend Herb Seller..." His waving cigar said that for his good friend Herb Seller no sacrifice was too great.

I hadn't been sure what I was supposed to be doing there, but now I knew. I was a talent scout.

I said, "To tell you the truth, Mr. Trojan —"

"Who calls me Mr. Trojan but the hired help at home? Kip's the name."

"All right, Kip. Frankly, I'm interested in a girl who once worked for you. Her name is Judith Runyon."

"Runyon?" He looked thoughtful. "How long ago?"

"Fifteen or sixteen months ago. Her sister also worked in this theater — Paula Runyon. At least I have reason to believe so, though I'm not absolutely sure about either."

Not sure? If I was sure of anything, it was that I was on the wrong track. What would they have done in a place like this?

"In the chorus?" he asked.

"I don't know."

He rolled his cigar between his lips. "I got a good memory for names. I don't remember a Runyon."

I nodded. I had expected that. But I had to be certain. I dug the two photos out of my pocket and placed the one of Paula in front of him.

Trojan studied it for a long moment. "Iris Opal," he muttered. "Maybe I'm wrong. I see lots of girls." His head came up. "You said there was a sister?"

I showed him the snapshot of Judith.

"Cherry Opal," he stated without hesitation. "So Runyon was their real name? Here they were Cherry and Iris Opal."

"Are you sure?" I said tightly.

"My God, will I ever forget Cherry?" He went to one of the standing files which was almost as tall as himself. After a long hunt he pulled out a photo and handed it to me and returned to the file to hunt some more.

It was a photo of Paula from the waist up. She wore a few silver beads and her smoldering smile. At the righthand corner of the photo was a name: Iris Opal.

I tossed it on the desk. Trojan stood over me with a second photo. I took it from him.

This one was of Judith, full length. She wore very high-heeled red shoes and a red veil. Her back was turned three-quarters to the camera and she was smiling out of the photo over her left shoulder. Her body looked richly tinted, as if it had been painted like her face. The name signed on the photo was in her handwriting: Cherry Opal.

"Some setup, y'know what I mean?" Trojan said.

I had never before heard that term used to describe a woman's figure, but I knew what he meant. I tossed that photo on top of the other one and fumbled out my cigarettes. I remembered that there was a cigar in my mouth and put the pack back.

Trojan had returned from behind his desk. "That's them all right, huh?"

"Yes," I said.

He looked at me speculatively, as if trying to make up his mind about something. "You ain't kidding me you're a Seller scout?"

He would talk to a talent scout where he might not to Judith's — or rather Cherry Opal's — husband. I said, "Both those sisters acted in Seller shows a couple of years ago. After that they were out of work for awhile, and I guess they took a fling at burlesque to fill in the time. Now Herb Seller has a spot for Judith Runyon — the girl you know as Cherry Opal. He needs a tall — uh — decorative brunette who has some acting ability, and he wired me from the Coast to look for her. I've traced her as far as you."

It didn't sound to me like a particularly convincing story, but it seemed to convince Trojan.

"Sure, sure, they told me they were hot from Broadway productions." He chuckled. "That's Herb, all right. Gets his mind on somebody and he won't take anybody else." He leaned confidentially over the desk. "You know, I'd outbid Herb Seller himself to get Cherry Opal back. Did you know her?"

"Yes," I said.

"That girl had something. What I could've made of her if it hadn't been for that trouble!"

"Trouble?"

He didn't appear to have heard me. He brooded at Judith's photo. "A stripper like you find once in a lifetime," he said wistfully.

I said through a frog in my throat, "She did a strip tease?"

"What a sweetheart! Cherry was built to peel, y'know what I mean?" He hunted on his desk for an ash tray, couldn't find one, flicked cigar ashes on the floor. "Those were funny girls, those Opal sisters. Refined, y'know what I mean?"

"Then why did they go into burlesque?" I said it to prod the story out of him, but I couldn't help saying it angrily.

"What's wrong with burly?" he retorted. "Just because it's for ordinary people who don't have the price of a night club or one of Seller's fancy productions you got to turn your nose up? Like those New York reformers who chased us out of New York and made us come across the river because seeing the form beautiful, like they say, is only for jerks with plenty of dough."

"All right," I said. "What do you mean they were refined?"

"It's a long story." Trojan arranged his round little body in his chair to tell a long story. "Iris Opal came direct to me for a job. I said see my stage manager, Ray Fahn. She said she didn't want a chorus job, she wanted a specialty number. Well, who doesn't? She looked good enough, but too small for a strip act, even if I'd take on a stripper cold. I asked her what could she do. She said she could act, she'd been on Broadway. I said, 'Honey, who wants an actress in burly? You want a chorus spot, I'll tell Ray Fahn to try you out.' So she said okay and Ray put her in the chorus. But her sister Cherry didn't come to me at all to ask for a specialty. I didn't know she was working in the Palace till I caught her a couple of days later."

"Who hired her if you didn't?"

"The stage manager hires the chorus. One day I was out in the wing taking a look at the curtain raiser. It was the first time I saw this Cherry and I didn't know till later she was Iris' sister. That's the way show business is — the wrong one of those sisters thought she was good enough for a specialty. One look at Cherry was enough for me. Ray had put her in a showgirl spot. She had height and a wonderful setup. Brother, was that a sweetheart!"

Trojan beamed at me. "That Ray Fahn, he was a stage manager from hunger. All he knew was lining up meat on the stage like in a butcher store. I got art in my soul, y'know what I mean? All a showgirl has to do is be a backdrop for the chorus and walk around a little, but that Cherry had something. I'm a psychologist, y'know what I mean? I watched the jerks."

"Jerks?"

"The audience. I watched them and they looked at Cherry more than anything else on the stage, though she wasn't doing a thing but standing there. She had personality, youth, freshness, something sweet, y'know what I mean? So about a week later I said to Ray Fahn that Cherry Opal was born to be a stripper. Ray said, 'Maybe she'll develop in a couple of years.' I said, 'She's got everything developed already. Give her a strip solo in next week's show.' Ray started to argue, but all at once he smiled and said okay. He was a big, ugly man who could scare children, so how could I know what he was smiling about? Later I knew."

He paused, contemplating his cigar.

"I wasn't surprised when she and her sister Iris came to see me. Actresses are screwy anyway, and this Cherry was a very sensitive soul. She wasn't sure she wanted to do a strip. Iris said was it all right if she did the act instead. Just like that. Can you dope it out?"

I muttered, "Paula — that is, Iris was always the sister who led and Cherry the sister who followed. I suppose the idea of that act was too much for Cherry, but not for Iris."

"I guess so. I said to Iris, 'Honey, you walk out of this show this minute and I can get a dozen like you tomorrow, but that sister of yours is one in a million.' I said to Cherry, 'Honey, this means a hundred bucks a week to you, and there's no telling how high a stripper can go — night clubs, Broadway, even Hollywood.' Cherry looked at Iris and Iris said, 'I'm not sure you ought to.' Cherry shoved out her jaw at her and said, 'If it would be all right for you to do it, it's all right for me.' And she gave me that smile of hers that lights up a whole room and said okay, she'd do it."

Sadly Trojan shook his head. "That Ray Fahn, not an ounce of art in his soul. He let Cherry come out in one of those skin-tight dresses covered all over with spangles and beads. Made her look like a tough, hot number, and that was all wrong. She wasn't the type, y'know what I mean? She sang a song. Didn't have a voice worth a damn, but what stripper has? It was the wrong number for her, one of those hot kind. Then she was all fingers when she started to peel. So awkward it hurt. She peeled halfway and then she couldn't do any more. The jerks started yelling and that scared her more and all of a sudden she ran off the stage. They nearly tore the house down, but she wouldn't come out again, not even to show her face."

Poor Judith, I thought. I hated Trojan and the unknown Ray Fahn and the anonymous audience.

"So Ray Fahn said to me, 'I told you it wouldn't work out, Kip.' I said, 'You're from hunger. How do you know what will work?' I went up to the dressing room and she and Iris were all dressed and ready to go. For good. Both walking out, quitting. Iris said, 'You've been very nice to us, Kip, but I guess we're not for burly.' Funny her talking like that, like both of them were one person. Iris was fine in the chorus, so why should she quit? But if one quit the other quit. I said to Cherry, 'Don't be a dope, honey. You stay and I'll raise your pay to one hundred twenty-five per week.' Cherry said she couldn't go out and face those jerks again. I'm a psychologist, y'know what I mean? I said, 'So you haven't got what it takes, honey? So you're a quitter?' Cherry's jaw started pushing out and so did Iris' jaw, so I knew I had something and kept talking. I told Cherry my idea. Iris said, 'Well, I don't know.' But this time Cherry made up her own mind. She said, 'I'm not a quitter. I don't care if it's a super-duper Broadway production or burlesque, I'm going to make a go of it.' And she did."

I opened my mouth and closed it. I didn't have anything to say.

"When I told Ray Fahn we'd try Cherry again in a specialty he thought I was crazy. He said, 'You're crazy, Kip.' I said, 'You're from hunger, Ray. You don't know human psychology. You saw the way the jerks nearly tore the house down when Cherry didn't peel off more than a society dame wears in the evening. That girl's got something, but you got to have art in your soul to bring it out.' Another cigar — eh — what'd you say your name is?"

"Aikin."

"First names are good enough for me."

"Leo."

"Another cigar, Leo?"

I had discarded mine less than half smoked. I had no taste for cigars or anything else.

"No, thanks," I said. "What happened then?"

"I worked on Cherry's act personally. A week later she was ready. This time she came out dressed like what she was, a clean, sweet, refined girl, like your own daughter or sister. She wore a simple white dress and a picture hat and flowers. No sexy stuff. Just walking out on the stage she had more real sex than the dames who throw it in your face, but it was the sweet, pure kind of sex you want in your own wife. Y'know what I mean?"

I knew what he meant.

"She came out on a bedroom set. Soft blue spot. Didn't sing or dance — nothing. Came on like she'd just come home from a date with a nice boy and was ready for bed. Took off her hat, shook out her hair, kicked off her shoes, peeled off her stockings — everything nice and slow, and kind of humming to herself. You catch on, Leo? The act was her getting into bed. No grinds, no bumps, no flashing of all she had. Just a refined young girl getting into bed, and the thing is she looked and acted the part to perfection because that was what she really was."

It didn't matter. But she should have told me.

"Would you believe it, there wasn't a sound during Cherry's act? But when she got in bed and pulled the covers over her and the curtain dropped, the applause and whistling and yelling shook the house. All she did was sit up in bed and throw kisses and then pull the cover up again to her neck, but no stripper ever got a hand like that by snapping her G-string. The funny thing is they saw less of her than they saw of any girl in the chorus. Even when she slipped on her nightgown she was sort of half behind a chair. I'm a psychologist. You know why Cherry's act got them so wild? It was like peeping in a bedroom window, though she didn't flash so much more than your own wife does on the beach. You got a wife, Leo?"

"Yes," I said, "I have a wife."

"So the jerks wouldn't look around if they saw Cherry walk along the beach wearing nothing but two tiny handkerchiefs, but Cherry peels down to the same thing on the stage and they eat it up. The jerks were sick of just meat. They came flocking to see her because she made them think of hearts and flowers mixed up with sex, y'know what I mean? In a week I raised her salary to one hundred and fifty per, and she was worth every cent."

George Kloe was a fool. What had he thought I would do if he told me that one night, while stopping over at Coast City, he had gone to a burlesque show and seen Paula in the chorus and Judith doing a strip tease? Had he expected that I would haul off and sock him? And this afternoon at the funeral Mabel, who had heard it all from George, had also been afraid to tell me more than that they had worked at the Palace Theater.

As if it could matter at all when so much more mattered.

Trojan was leaning back in his chair, watching me through cigar smoke. A happy expression was on his round face. He liked telling this story; it demonstrated his genius. No doubt he was a genius in his way.

"You mentioned trouble," I said. "Why didn't she last?"

"It was that Ray Fahn's fault." He sighed. "A few weeks later Cherry killed him."

I sat staring at him.

"It's no secret, though it was hushed up," he said. "I guess Ray asked for it. I didn't know what was going on till one day between shows Cherry came to my office. She wanted me to make Ray Fahn let her alone. I said, 'What's the matter, honey, that crazy stage manager want you to change your act? He doesn't know from anything, he's from hunger.' Cherry said, 'He lets my act alone, but he doesn't let me alone. He's been that way since the day I came here, and he's getting worse every day.' Well, I don't interfere in the private affairs of my people, but I knew Cherry — a sensitive soul, y'know what I mean? — so I spoke to Ray. I said, 'Keep your hands off her.' He said, 'I haven't put my hands on her yet, but how I'd like to.' I said, 'There's plenty of tramps around without you messing with a refined kid like Cherry.' Ray said, 'Sure, but who wants the tramps? That kid's got me crazy, Kip.' I said, 'You were born crazy. Let her alone.' But he didn't."

He hunted for an ash tray.

"And she killed him?" I whispered.

"Stuck a pair of scissors in him." He gave up looking for an ash tray and used the floor.

I said, "And the police?"

"They said Ray had it coming to him. The district attorney sent for me and I told him how she'd complained to me Ray wouldn't let her alone. The whole business was hushed up, y'know what I mean? Not even a trial."

"Where did it happen?"

"In Cherry's apartment. He went there one night after the show and made a dive for her. That's all I know. There wasn't even much in the papers." He sighed. "A stage manager like Ray Fahn I could pick up by the dozen in the gutter, but I never saw Cherry again. She was priceless, that girl. I made her what she was, y'know what I mean?"

I removed my coat from the filing cabinet over which Trojan had draped it.

He jumped up. "What's your rush, Leo? Sit down and talk about Smelly Gor."

I looked blankly at him. "Smelly Gor?"

"My God, didn't you catch Smelly Gor tonight? My comic. He's under contract to me, but for Herb Seller — "

I said wearily, "I didn't see your show. I'm only interested in Judith — Cherry Opal."

"So why don't you come tomorrow and catch Smelly Gor? Look at all the great comics that came out of burly. There's..."

I walked out of the office. His short legs pumped to keep pace with me as he recited the names of the great comics who had come out of burlesque.

In the lobby I shook Trojan's clammy hand and promised I'd catch his show tomorrow and walked out to the street. All the theater lights were out.

17. The Justifiable Homicide

I spent the night in a Coast City hotel because there was still something I had to do in that town and I wanted to get an early start doing it. Though I had slept hardly at all the night before, sleep took a long time coming, and then it was broken by strange, perverted, terrifying scenes inspired by what Kip Trojan had told me.

The last time I awoke it was eleven o'clock in the morning.

I was more tired than when I had gone to bed. Another day, Monday, and I was no nearer to Judith than I had been on Wednesday morning. I dressed without haste and ate breakfast at the same pace. Then I walked to the city hall.

I told the frozen-faced, elderly woman in the district attorney's office that I was Judith Runyon's husband. The name didn't mean anything to her. Would I please state my business?

"It's with the district attorney," I said. "My wife was known in this city as Cherry Opal. Does that help?"

It didn't. Perhaps if I came back in the afternoon an assistant district attorney might be able to spare me a minute.

So I had to let her have it. "My wife killed somebody in this town."

One eyebrow arched. She said, "Just a minute," and went through a door. Within thirty seconds she was back and told me to go right in.

District Attorney Harold Norman rose from behind his desk. "Leo Aikin?" he said.

I hadn't told the woman my name because I hadn't thought that it would mean anything to anybody there. For a moment I wondered how Norman knew it, and then I was shaking his hand across the desk. He looked the way voters would like a district attorney to look — tall and gray-haired and distinguished.

"So you are Cherry's husband?" he said conversationally when we were both seated. "Or should I say Judith? A charming young woman."

I went directly to the point. "I'd like to know what happened when — when Ray Fahn was killed."

He shrugged delicately. "We did not hold your wife responsible. I would not worry about the matter."

"As her husband, I think I'm entitled to the details."

"You can obtain them from your wife." He was watching me closely.

"She never talks about it."

Norman put the tips of his fingers together. "You are aware of her — ah — profession at that time?"

"She and her sister Paula worked at the Palace Theater."

"Ah, yes, Iris Opal — Paula Runyon. You must forgive me if I think of them as Cherry and Iris, though I soon learned their real names. The details are no secret. One evening after the show the two sisters had a small party in their apartment on Woodcock Street. At approximately one o'clock in the morning, Ray Fahn, who was the stage manager at the Palace, appeared at the apartment. He was obviously under the influence of liquor. At that time Cherry was in her bedroom, renewing her make-up. He saw Cherry through the open door and entered the room and locked the door behind him. Then he attempted to assault her. The others at the party could not come to her assistance because of the locked door. As Cherry struggled to defend herself, she snatched up a pair of scissors from the dresser and lashed out with them at her assailant. The scissors entered his neck and practically severed his carotid artery."

"Self-defense," I muttered.

"Self-defense beyond a shadow of doubt. There were the witnesses in the apartment to corroborate Cherry's story that Fahn had attempted to assault her. There were people at the theater to testify that since Cherry had started to work there Fahn had thrust his attentions on her and she had repeatedly rebuffed him. Finally, the post mortem revealed considerable quantities of liquor in his body, proving that he had been drunk at the time of death."

"But isn't there always a trial in such cases, no matter what the circumstances?" I asked.

"Certainly not. It is lawful for an individual to employ sufficient force to protect his or her life. I could see at once that Cherry Opal was a decent young woman in spite of — ah — her performance at the Palace Theater. Investigation revealed that she and her sister had gone into burlesque only recently and only through financial duress. And their background, we found, was highly respectable. Please do not infer that if she had been a different kind of woman she would have been treated differently, but at the same time a person's character and antecedents must be taken into consideration. Obviously, she was legally guiltless of homicide in any form, and nothing could be gained by undermining her reputation and character through public exhibition of her in connection with Ray Fahn's death."

"So her name was kept out of the papers?"

"To the best of my ability. Of course something did appear in the newspaper, but the press never learned that the woman who had killed Fahn in self-defense had any name but Cherry Opal." His smile was fatherly. "A district attorney often has unpleasant duties, but there are compensations when I can use what influence I have to maintain unsullied the name of a decent young woman who had an unfortunate experience through no fault of her own. I had become fond of Cherry; I had learned to admire and respect her during her ordeal. You should have no doubts concerning your wife because of that one — ah — lamentable incident."

So the scissors in a man's neck had been nothing to hide, nothing to endanger her with the police. It explained her nervous breakdown and her nightmares and why she and Paula had cut themselves off from memory of their days on the stage, but it didn't explain another thing.

"Who was at the party when it happened?"

"Come now, Mr. Aikin," Norman chided me gently. "I mentioned that I protected your wife's name. I can do no less for the others who were not even directly implicated."

"Respectable local citizens?"

His mouth thinned. He looked at me without saying anything.

"That's the real reason it was so completely hushed up," I said. "Because respectable local citizens were anxious to keep their names out of the papers. Can you tell me one thing? Was an actress named Dacia Wilmot at that party?"

His fingers started to drum on the edge of the desk. "What do you know of Dacia Wilmot?"

"She was a friend of theirs from New York," I said. "I don't see why you can't tell me in confidence whether she was at the party."

"She wasn't." Norman became aware of his fingers drumming on the desk; he withdrew his hand as if he had been touching something hot. "What are you hiding, Mr. Aikin?"

"Hiding?"

He merely smiled at me.

I got it then. He had known my name though I hadn't met Judith until months after Fahn's death and though I hadn't told it to the woman outside.

I said, "So you've heard what happened to Paula and Judith?"

"Yes, Mr. Aikin. And the real reason you are here is for information concerning Dacia Wilmot."

"I'm after information about anything that will help me find my wife. Dacia Wilmot wanted to sell me what she knew. She disappeared. The New York police are looking for her."

"Are they?"

I said, "Has she come back? Or..."

"Or what, Mr. Aikin?"

He watched me the way he would watch a prisoner he was questioning. His fingers again started to drum on the desk; he didn't seem to know what they were doing.

"Has Judith been — found?" I said tightly.

"As far as I know, she has not." Abruptly he stood up. "Come with me, Mr. Aikin."

He led me into a small room which contained a long, scarred table and half a dozen plain wooden chairs. "Wait here," Norman said crisply and left.

I was alone for less than a minute. A man came in. He had the mouth of a sullen ape and the eyes of a bored fish. Without a word or more than a glance at me, he sat down at the table. He didn't do anything at the table except to use it as a prop for his forearms. His fish-eyes were open, but for all they seemed to see he could have kept them closed.

After a while I said, "Are you also waiting?"

He discovered that I was in the room. "Waiting with you," he said in a voice as dull as his eyes.

I walked about the room. I stopped at the table. "Are you a detective?"

"Yeah."

"What would happen if I decided to leave this room?"

"Huh!" That probably meant: Try it and see what happens.

"Am I under arrest?"

He blew out his cheeks. I was making conversation, and conversation bored him. "I only work here, mister. Take a load off your feet and relax."

I sat down, but I didn't relax. I sat for a couple of hours.

18. The Elusive Eat

Florian Singleton and Detective Hubbard came into the room. I leaped up from my chair.

"What's going on?" I demanded.

Singleton turned on his grin. "You're the damnedest client. I have to spend half the night and all morning hunting for you."

For days I had been angry. I had been frightened and bitter and sick at heart, but mostly I had been angry. I said bitingly, "How about looking for my wife? The police don't seem to be particularly interested, but I hired you to be."

Hubbard pushed his black hat back from his brow. His swarthy face showed disgust. "Maybe this will surprise you, but the police can do a thing or two now and then, and do it quicker and better than a guy who thinks he's the only one who knows anything. It didn't take us long to find out that your wife and her sister once worked in a Coast City burlesque house, and that your wife was once involved in a killing. Early this morning I came to Coast City to get the dope on that killing from the D. A. I no sooner get back to New York than there's a call from Norman that he's holding you for us."

The local detective at the table was listening with his thick-lipped mouth open and his fish-eyes showing what practically amounted to animation.

"But why?" I said. "What did I do?"

"You asked questions about something Norman knew the New York police were interested in. Especially questions about Dacia Wilmot. When I was here this morning, I'd told Norman that she'd been knocked off and that we — "

"Murdered?" I blurted.

"Surprised?" Hubbard asked me sourly.

"No," I said slowly. "I guess not." I drew in my breath. "So that's why I'm under arrest? You suspect me."

Singleton answered that quickly, before Hubbard could get his mouth open. "You're in the clear. Naturally the New York police want to talk to you about it. I was with Hubbard when the call came from Norman that you were here, so I came along."

"Let's go," Hubbard said impatiently.

The detective at the table came to life. "Hey, wait! You got a release for him?"

"Nuts!" Hubbard said.

The three of us walked out.

They had driven to Coast City in Singleton's sedan. On the way back to New York I sat beside Singleton; Hubbard had the back seat to himself.

Singleton told me that Dacia Wilmot's body had been found early that morning amid the wreckage of slum houses being torn down for a new housing development on the East River. "She'd probably been there since Saturday night where the killer dumped her behind a pile of timbers. When the wreckers showed up for work this morning, they spotted the body. Because yesterday was Sunday, nobody'd been near the place since Saturday afternoon."

"Likely that was the idea," Hubbard observed from the back seat. "The longer it takes for a body to be found, the colder the clues get."

"Are there clues?" I asked.

Hubbard's answer was a savage grunt which meant that there weren't.

"Several things are known," Singleton told me. "She was murdered Saturday night. The medical examiner believes it was that long ago and the logic of events backs him up. She was wearing her hat and coat, and her handbag was found beside the body. She was hit over the head and then strangled."

"Conked on the head like Paula Runyon," Hubbard commented.

Singleton took his eyes from the road to glance back at Hubbard. "Paula Runyon was killed by the blow. The one Dacia received wasn't hard enough to more than knock her out."

"He didn't have room in the car to give her a sock that counted," Hubbard said, "so he finished the job by choking her with his bare hands while she was unconscious." His eyes turned to the window. "Or if a woman did it, she knocked Dacia out first so she could strangle her without trouble."

I twisted in the seat to face Hubbard. "Could she possibly have been murdered in her apartment?"

"Not a chance. A body couldn't be carried out of that building early Saturday evening without being seen — or later, for that matter, even if the building hadn't been watched from nine-thirty on."

"So probably she met somebody in a car," I muttered.

"We don't know where she was killed, but it's a safe bet a car was used to transport her body to where it was found behind the timbers."

I said, "The fact is she went out to meet her murderer. The way Judith and Paula went out to meet whoever killed Paula and kidnaped Judith."

Hubbard pushed his shoulders into the corner of the back seat. "I'll tell you the way I see it. The Wilmot dame had something to sell. You weren't buying; anyway, you hadn't the dough. Somebody else had — somebody she could pin murder on or kidnaping or both. So she made a date to do business with him. He picked her up in his car."

"Her letter to me said she'd be home waiting for me," I reminded him. "She'd had a change of heart."

Singleton chuckled dryly. "You don't know dames like Dacia."

"That's right," Hubbard said. "How much heart did she have in the first place to change? Maybe she was going to give you the dope. We'll never know. But she didn't see why she couldn't do a bit of business before that. Appease both her business sense and her conscience at the same time — sell it to him and give it to you. Only she was too smart. She got what blackmailers are always asking for."

We approached the entrance to the Holland Tunnel. Singleton fumbled in his pocket for change. I got out two quarters first and paid. Eventually I would have had to pay it anyway in the expense account.

"You haven't a thing to worry about, Leo," Singleton assured me as we entered the tunnel.

Now I was Leo to him. As if, having gone to New Jersey to fetch me, I had become more than a client to him — a friend. That was all right, but what would I call him? Florian sounded ridiculous and Flo more so.

"No, I haven't a thing to worry about," I said bitterly.

"I mean you're in the clear on this killing," he said. "You have the best alibi in the world. You were with the Hartford police Saturday afternoon, and right after the train got you back to New York you were at Dacia's building. Hubbard saw you arrive and was with you all night."

Hubbard said, "He was away for a couple of hours around midnight, but it's good enough."

There was a long silence as we rushed under the Hudson River. Hollowly I was thinking that everything had stopped, that everything that had happened since Tuesday night had taken Judith farther and farther away from me. The Hartford police had one murder to concern them and the New York police had another, but all that mattered to me was the living.

If she still lived.

"Eat," I said aloud.

Singleton glanced sideways at me and pushed his tongue against his right cheek.

"What's that?" Hubbard asked.

"Find this man Eat and you'll have all the answers," I said.

"Could be, but we haven't a thing to show that those two women went off with him. My bet is that if we find your wife we'll find everything we want." The back seat creaked as Hubbard shifted his weight. "Funny about that killing in Coast City."

"What's funny about it?" Singleton said. "Open and shut self-defense. Closed case. The D.A. gave you all the dope."

"Sure, but—" Hubbard paused and after a moment went on musingly, "You find an old killing and two fresh ones, and all three are tied up with the same people—all women, all three related or friends, all in show business. Can't see how it all connects, but it's funny just the same."

We emerged at the New York end of the tunnel. Singleton headed uptown. At the headquarters of the Homicide Squad on West Twentieth Street Hubbard and I left Singleton. That was as far as they would allow a private detective to come.

The police were very nice to me. There were no lights flashed in my face, no barking cops. The detective in charge of the case was a lieutenant with a trick mustache and thick-shelled eyeglasses and an amiable smile. His name was Joslyn. He wanted to know everything, though he must have had complete reports from Chief Middle and from the Hartford police. He interrupted me often with questions, and after a while I realized that the questions chiefly concerned Judith. He was doing the right thing. The living were more important than the dead; the main job was to find Judith.

But he was a homicide detective. Wouldn't kidnaping be under another department, even though it appeared to be related to the murder of Dacia Wilmot? And why would he want to know how strong Judith was physically? What did that have to do with anything?

Casually he was asking me if Judith could have carried one hundred and fifteen pounds of dead weight. That was when it hit me between the eyes.

"Listen," I said. "You don't think that Judith—that she..." Joslyn removed his glasses and stood holding them like a lecturer on a platform. "Would you mind answering my question, Mr. Aikin?"

"You're crazy," I said. "You're trying to show that Judith could have carried Dacia's body out of a car."

"I'm trying to get everything I can. Judith Aikin is a rather husky woman, isn't she?"

"Not husky."

"Well, hardly anemic." He replaced his glasses and watched me intently through them. "Yet not strong enough to strangle another woman without knocking her unconscious first."

It was technique. He was working on the possibility that I was holding something back and would blurt it out if I got sore enough.

I said testily, "And I suppose she also murdered her own sister?"

"We don't know her sister was murdered. According to the Hartford police, it could have been an accident. Say Judith let Paula out of the car at Hartford and while walking Paula got hit by another car."

"But Judith was kidnaped."

His glasses came off. "I've been over the reports and I've listened to you. There's a lot more that shows she left of her own will than that she was kidnaped."

I was back where I had been on Wednesday morning with Chief Mort Middle.

Hubbard spoke up. "I've been thinking, Lieutenant. Maybe that killing in Coast City wasn't self-defense after all."

Joslyn smiled. "The D.A. told you it was."

"He wouldn't be the first D.A. who was fooled. Or..." Hubbard left that in the air.

"Go on," Joslyn said. "Dacia knew that it had been cold-blooded, premeditated murder and had the proof to reopen the case against Judith Aikin."

"The trouble with that," Hubbard pointed out, "is that Judith didn't have blackmail money."

"We don't have to stick to the blackmail angle," Joslyn said. "Let's go back a week. Say Judith wanted to get rid of Paula. For the time being, we can play with the usual motive — Paula was having an affair with Judith's husband. So Judith gave her the business. I know, sisters, but it happens."

I told the lieutenant that he was raving mad.

He waved his glasses at me in a deprecating gesture and continued to speak to Hubbard. "Dacia was a pal of Paula's. When she heard Paula was murdered, she knew who'd done it and why. So she was ready to give out with the real facts behind the old killing in Coast City. But Judith got to her first and shut her up forever. It figures."

It figured in the fantastic game they were playing — for their amusement, or to get under my skin, or because that was the way cops worked, blundering about. And all I could do was to tell them again that they were crazy.

"It's an angle," Joslyn told me pleasantly. "We can't afford to overlook any angle."

"What about the man named Eat?" I yelled. "Isn't he an angle?"

"Maybe. We don't know. But if he is, he's only one. We've got to look at all of them. At that, could be Eat and your wife are the same angle — accomplices."

"You're crazy," I said for the third or tenth time.

He dropped the angles then and returned to questioning me about what facts I had. I went on to the end, which was when Hubbard and Singleton had called for me in Coast City. Then Lieutenant Joslyn thanked me very politely and said I could go.

Singleton was waiting for me downstairs. I hadn't eaten since breakfast; I suggested we have dinner together. We drove in his car down Seventh Avenue to a restaurant south of Fourteenth Street. He didn't ask me about my session with the police until we were settled at a table.

"One of their pet theories is that Judith did it," I said wearily.

Singleton toyed with his fork. He didn't seem to have any comment to make.

"My God, you don't think that too?" I said.

"Why should I kid you, Leo? It occurred to me, of course. There's probably nothing to it, but look at it from the police point of view. They can't afford to overlook any possibility."

My mouth was dry. I drank water.

"What the devil have you been doing since I hired you?" I demanded when I put down the glass.

"I'm only human, Leo. The police of two cities aren't doing any better."

"Then why should I pay you?"

"Maybe so you won't be too lonely. Maybe because you need one man who's all the way on your side."

His manner was so ingratiating that I felt like a heel for having taken out on him all that was going on inside me.

We ate. We were polishing off our shrimp salads when a woman swooped down on us. She was tall and raw-boned, and she rushed to our table with a mink coat flapping open.

"Eat, darling!" she shrieked joyously.

Singleton's long body came up straighter in his chair. He turned the full force of his grin on her. He said, "That's just what I'm doing, Hagar — eating."

"Your puns are deplorable, darling." She dropped a hand on his shoulder. "Where have you been keeping yourself? I don't think I've seen you since I was up at your place in Croton last summer."

I sat very still. My eyes shifted from Singleton to the woman and back to Singleton. His grin ignored her. It was fixed on me.

"What name did you call him?" It was my voice asking the woman that question, but it didn't sound like my voice.

She frowned at me. "Aren't you men together?"

"I'm his client," I said. "Did you call him Eat?"

She pressed a hip against his side. "Darling," she said to him, "does he expect me to call you Florian? What a horrible name!" She smiled at me. "His best friends call him Eat." She patted his shoulder. "I'm one of your best friends, darling, aren't I? At least I used to be."

I started to rise.

Without taking his eyes off me, Singleton stroked the woman's hand on his shoulder. "I've been very busy being a detective, Hagar. You see, all ready for a job."

His other hand flicked open his jacket. I saw part of a shoulder holster and a bit of the blue-black butt of a gun sticking out of it.

He wasn't showing it to her. He was showing it to me.

19. The Reciprocal Escape

The woman went away. I stood where I was, my thighs against the table in front of me, my calves against the chair behind me. From the other side of the table Singleton grinned at me. You had to look close to notice that the edges had worn off his grin. His jacket had fallen back over his shoulder holster, but his right hand was at his necktie. From necktie to holster was no more than ten inches.

It was only a few minutes after six o'clock. Less than a dozen people, including the waiters, were in the restaurant. That was enough. Just one witness was enough to prevent Singleton from doing anything but run for it.

He didn't run. He said, "Sit down, Leo."

I sat. There was one shrimp left in my bowl. I ate it, trying to act as casual as I sounded.

"Eat," I said. "That just about makes me the prize sucker of all time."

"Not short for Eaton," he told me, gently stroking his necktie. "A moniker like Florian Singleton cries out for a nickname. As a kid, I was terrifically hungry, always eating or wanting to eat, so in those days I came to be called Eat. Some of my particularly close friends still call me that."

"Was Judith one of your particularly close friends?"

For a brief moment he looked away from me. "What are you talking about?"

"Where is Judith?"

"That's what you're paying me to find out."

I kept looking at him.

He plucked a piece of lettuce out of his shrimp salad and nibbled on it. He used his left hand.

"Use your head, Leo," he said. "If I were that *Eat*, would I drag you around with me to places like this where somebody would know my nickname?"

"You couldn't help yourself. You had to stick close to me. As you said, very few people call you Eat, so you weren't taking much chance."

"How many men, most of them Eaton, are called Eat for short?"

Suddenly I wasn't sure. He had so much charm, so much confidence. But there was a final test.

"All right, I was wrong." I pushed my chair back. "I've an important phone call to make."

I was halfway up from my chair when he spoke. "Sit down, Leo."

I sat down and put my hands flat on the table and waited. Singleton's fingers tapped the knot of his necktie. "What do you think I am, Leo?"

"A murderer," I said.

Anybody in the place looking at us merely saw two men conversing in low tones over their dinner.

"I'm not," he said, "but if you believe I am, don't forget that a murderer would be desperate. They can't burn him in the chair for more than one killing."

A couple of men entered the restaurant. Slowly the place was filling up. It didn't matter how many people there were; he wouldn't dare do anything to me here.

Then Singleton was speaking to somebody else. "We haven't time to eat the rest of our dinner."

The waiter was standing at our table with a filled tray. "But, sir, you ordered two complete dinners."

"We'll pay for them," Singleton said. "Let's have the check right away. We're in a hurry."

When the waiter had written out the check and was gone, Singleton twisted his torso to the wall on his right. His right hand went to his left armpit. I felt myself tie up into a suffocating knot.

The gun did not appear. He slid it down inside his jacket and under the table. Then he stood up, and his right hand was in his jacket pocket. He could shoot me through the pocket without revealing the gun, without anybody in the restaurant realizing where the shot had come from.

"Let's go, Leo," he said. "Mind paying the check? I'm short of cash."

He had to do it this way — take me with him so I couldn't tell the police. And then what? Kill me where there were no witnesses.

I put on my hat and coat. Because he never wore either, he did not have to remove his hand from his pocket for an instant. He waited, standing beside the table, until I passed him, and then he fell in behind me. We went by the table at which the woman who had greeted him as Eat sat with another woman and a man. She waved to him, and he said, "Be seeing you, Hagar." Then I was at the counter, fumbling out my wallet to pay the check.

Through the street window I saw two men and two women stand outside the door as if debating whether to come in. I glanced back at Singleton. The left side of his body leaned negligently against the counter; his right hand was buried in his pocket.

"This is only a dollar bill," the cashier told me.

I had made the mistake deliberately. I fumbled some more in my wallet.

After a small eternity the two couples in the street made up their minds. They entered the restaurant. Between the cashier's counter and the first of the tables there was less than ten feet of space. The first woman, walking to the right of the man, would pass very close to me. I dropped a five dollar bill on the counter. I drew in my breath and leaped.

My hip clipped the woman's side as I went past her. I made a half-turn and thrust my hands against her back. With a startled cry, she stumbled toward Singleton.

The second couple was between me and the door. The man opened his mouth to say something, but he never got it out. I plunged between him and the woman, my body spreading them apart, and there was the street door which hadn't quite swung shut. I yanked it open.

It had happened so quickly that the shouting in the restaurant didn't start until I was outside. I glanced back through the window. People were bunched between the door and the counter. They were just people; I didn't pause long enough to see what one person in particular was doing. I ran up the street.

People on Seventh Avenue looked at me, but for all they knew I was merely running to catch up to somebody. I glanced back. There were people between me and the restaurant, blocking out my view of it, but I could see that nobody else was running.

I forced myself to slow down to a rapid walk. My wallet was still in my hand. I stuck it into my hip pocket.

On the next block I passed a cop. By then it was too late to ask him to go back with me and make an arrest. Singleton wouldn't hang around. By escaping from him I had let him escape from me.

I walked uptown until I reached a subway station. I rode two stops on a local and got out.

Lieutenant Joslyn wasn't at police headquarters, but I caught Detective Hubbard as he was leaving for his own precinct station. He led me into a large room filled with desks, and there he listened to what I had to tell him.

"Singleton?" he said skeptically, "I've known him a long time. Honest for a shamus, and as nice a guy as you'd want to meet."

"What if he's the king of Siam? He's the Eat we've been looking for."

"I never heard him called Eat."

"It's a nickname only his closest friends use. Don't you see why he was so anxious for me to become his client? He heard that I was coming to New York to dig into the girls' pasts and he picked up my trail. By working for me he could be on the inside, have an excuse to hang around me and the police and find out what was happening. It paid off. He learned from me that Dacia wanted to see me Friday night, and he reasoned that she was out to sell what she knew, so he murdered her."

Hubbard plucked at his cheek. "Mabel Kloe described that man Eat as very handsome. Singleton isn't a bad-looking guy, but would you call him very handsome?"

I said irritably, "To a lot of women a man doesn't have to be pretty to be handsome. Not to mature women like Mabel Kloe. They go for the rugged, virile type like Singleton."

"Okay, but just because he's not bad looking and somebody called him Eat—"

"My God!" I burst out. "Isn't it enough proof that he forced me to leave the restaurant at the point of a gun?"

Hubbard remained damnably calm. "Let's go over it," he said as if he had all the time in the world while Singleton was in flight. "A woman called him Eat.

It was a nickname he had as a kid. He denied to you that he's the Eat who visited your wife. He showed the woman his gun. Why shouldn't he carry a gun? He has a license for it, and he's on a job. He didn't threaten you with it."

"Not in words. But keeping his hand near it was a threat. So was transferring it to his pocket when he was ready to make me go with him."

"You don't know the gun was in his pocket. You only think so. You think he threatened you. You think you ran away from him. All you know is that somebody called him by a nickname that's the same as somebody else's. People get so nervous they build up things that don't exist. Like old maids imagining they see men peeping at them through bedroom windows."

I yelled, "What are you trying to do — protect him?"

"I'm trying to get the facts, if there are any. We'll pick Singleton up and let Mabel Kloe look at him. But don't hope for too much. Say she does identify him as the guy who called on your wife Tuesday afternoon. That wouldn't prove that he met her and her sister that night."

"You're wasting time," I said.

Hubbard's coal-black eyes rested gravely on me. Whatever was on his mind he didn't put into words. His head bobbed up and down once in what might have been a nod. Then he left the room to send somebody to pick Singleton up.

But Singleton, I thought dully, wouldn't be in his apartment or anywhere the police would look for him. He was already in hiding or in flight. Day after day it had been like that: you thought you had something, and it slipped away, leaving only terror and death and futility.

There was nothing left for me to do at police headquarters. I could sit in my hotel room or walk the streets or chew the floor. I sat where I was.

Croton.

Abruptly that name was in my head. Croton was the huge system of reservoirs which supplied New York City with water. Call it Croton-on-Hudson and it was a community in northern Westchester County, near the reservoir. Last summer Judith and I had driven there for a week end with a friend I had made in the army — an advertising writer who owned an ultramodern flat-roofed house overlooking the Hudson River.

I found myself shaking with excitement. I looked around, and there was Hubbard returning.

"Listen," I said. "Singleton has a summer place in Croton." Hubbard frowned at me.

"Saturday night you and Singleton talked about it in the lobby of Dacia Wilmot's building," I reminded him. "And the woman who called him Eat in the restaurant also mentioned it."

He sighed. "Singleton's no dope. That's the last place he'd go to hide out."

"I'm not thinking of that. Paula's body was found on Route U.S. 6. That's the way to Croton from Jorberg. Judith and I took the trip last summer — Route 6 through Danbury and to Peekskill and then a few miles south to Croton-on-

Hudson. In Hartford he stopped to murder Paula and then he drove on to his summer place with Judith."

Hubbard remained unimpressed. "Could be. But that was Wednesday morning. It's a summer shack, pretty uncomfortable at this time of the year. She wouldn't stay there longer than she had to."

"She'd have had nothing to say about it."

"Kidnaped, eh?" His tone practically mocked me. "Let me give it to you straight. I never could see the kidnap angle. And how would he keep her up there when he was in New York?"

"It's not far from here to Croton. He could drive up there at least once a day, and he could have somebody else staying with her."

"A gang?" The way he said that made it sound absurdly melodramatic. "What's in it for them? Ransom? It doesn't stand up any way you look at it."

I said bitterly, "It's at least an angle. Or do you police only go in for angles when they seem to implicate my wife?"

The corners of his mouth lifted. I'd scored a debating point, which was about all it appeared to mean to him.

"Oh, sure, we'll investigate," he told me. "We never pass up a possibility, even one as remote as this. Of course it's in another county, so I'll have to ask the state police up there to have a look."

I went back to where I had left my hat and coat. When I passed him again, he asked if he would be able to get in touch with me at the Mammoth.

"This evening I'll be in Croton," I said.

"Still think you can do more than the police?"

I said, "There's nothing else I have to do," and left.

At Grand Central a man at the information desk told me that the next train for Croton-on-Hudson wouldn't leave for another hour. But there was a 7:40 for Harmon, which, he said, was practically the same as Croton. It was leaving in less than two minutes.

I hurried to the gate.

20. The Mewling Cat

In fifty-one minutes I was in Harmon where northbound trains changed from electric to steam. Outside the station a cab driver, seeing me pause to look around, offered to drive me anywhere in Harmon or Croton for fifty cents. I asked him if he knew where Florian Singleton's summer bungalow was.

"Gav Rowan knows everybody," he said. "Hey, Gav."

A hatless, bald man stuck his head out of a parked cab. I went over to him.

"Singleton, the detective?" he said. "Sure. Summers he's always throwing parties and I'm always driving people out there from the station. Only it's not in Croton. Nearer Yorktown Heights, on Ritt Pond."

"All right, take me there."

Rowan leaned over the seat to open the back door. When I was inside, he remained turned to me.

"You sure he's there now?" he said. "Nobody stays overnight in those summer places this time of the year. Some of them start coming up for the day on Sundays, but it gets mighty cold at night with no insulation and no heat."

"I'll take the chance that he'll be there."

He looked me over speculatively. I could see that I was going to be clipped.

"Three dollars," he said. "That Ritt Pond road is murder this time of the year. A dollar more if you come back with me."

"All right, all right," I said. "Get going."

When, after a few miles, we reached the dirt road, it turned out to be a stretch of churned, half-frozen mud weaving through stark trees. The night was clear and crisp and moonless; a sky full of stars did little to dispel the blackness through which the headlights cut. I sat on the edge of the seat.

"Here it is," Rowan said suddenly.

I peered through the windshield. Past the headlights there was only the black wall of night. The car was still moving, very slowly, and that caricature of a road was still curving. Then the car stopped, and an edge of the left headlight touched a corner of a white bungalow.

A pinprick of light would have been a beacon in that darkness. There was nothing and there had been nothing. Because if the police had already come and found Judith, they would still be here. They had either come and found the place empty and left, or they had not yet arrived. In either case, another blank.

Something like a sob passed my lips.

"Like I thought," Rowan said. "Nobody there."

I got out of the cab and asked him if he had a flashlight.

"What do you think you're going to do?" he said suspiciously.

"I don't know," I said. "Maybe Singleton left a message for me. I was supposed to meet him here."

"Detective business, huh?" He nodded and handed me a flashlight. Detective business, like show business, seemed to explain anything.

I played the flashlight beam over the bungalow. Hardly a shack. It was long, larger than I had expected; the coat of white paint and green trim looked fresh. It would be very attractive in the summer.

I moved around to the front of the bungalow. There was a small, roofless porch. Nothing had been done with the grounds — stubble and rocks and mud except for a crude path of flat fieldstones running from the road to the steps. My eyes were becoming accustomed to the starlight, and now, not many feet away, I could see water. Ritt Pond. Nearby there would be other summer bungalows sitting as dark and silent and empty as this one.

The road ended here in a broad, flat area where cars could to be parked and turned. There was nowhere else to leave a car.

I returned to the cab. Rowan stood outside it, his hands deep in his overcoat pockets, his bald head tilted back.

"Smoke's coming out of the chimney," he said.

I peered for long moments before I could distinguish by starlight the steady stream of smoke rising from the fieldstone chimney. My heart started to pound.

"A fireplace?" I said.

"What else? But it doesn't mean anybody's inside. Must've left the fire burning when he went away."

But it meant that somebody had used the bungalow within the past hour or two. And it meant that we were too late. Singleton had come and taken Judith away.

Maybe. It was always maybe.

I returned to the bungalow. I peered into one of the side windows. Blackness. I went up to the porch. There was a door in the middle and a window on either side. I tried the door. Locked.

"Nobody home," Rowan said from his car. "I can't hang around here all night."

I turned from the door. I was putting my foot out to the top step when I heard a sound.

It was a thin, remote mewling, and it seemed to come from inside the bungalow. I went back to the door and put an ear against the panel. There it was again.

All right, so Singleton had shut up an animal, probably a cat, in the bungalow. He would have been in a sweat to get away; he wouldn't have had time to worry about leaving a cat shut up.

Inside the bungalow something creaked. It could have been the hinges of a door slowly opened or closed. Could have been. But so far there had been nothing that actually meant anything.

Abruptly the mewling stopped. The cat had settled down on something that creaked and was now content and silent.

I looked back at the cab. Rowan was leaning against a fender, watching me.

The cat mewled again. This time it stopped almost as soon as it started. It stopped too abruptly.

I banged on the door. When I paused, the silence was back, inside the bungalow and outside — silence so deep that I could hear my panting breath. I resumed banging. Let the bungalow be empty. This door was at least something for my fists to smash at. And I heard myself shout, "Open up or I'll break the door down!"

There were footsteps in the bungalow. I dropped my hands. Singleton? He would have his gun out. I had been a reckless fool. I heard the lock turn, and I stepped back.

It was too late to run, even if I wanted to. I stood facing the door, the beam of my flashlight covering it when it opened. A woman stood there.

She was not young, not quite middle-aged — nothing much except short and plump. She wore a heavy sweater which she filled excessively and corduroy slacks which were too tight at oversized hips. In her hand she held a fire poker.

"Yes?" she said, blinking into the flashlight.

I lowered the beam to her feet. Over her shoulder I saw a very large room. The entire bungalow seemed to consist of that room, though I couldn't be sure. The only light came from a blazing fireplace; it left most of the room in deep shadow.

"What do you want?" There was an edge to her voice. The poker shook a little in her hand.

"Why didn't you open the door as soon as I knocked?" I said.

"I'm a woman living way out here alone. I don't open the door to anybody at night." She lifted the poker. "That's why I picked up this when I heard you banging. What do you want?"

"Is Eat here?"

"I'm the only one lives here."

"At this time of the season?"

"I've got plenty of cut wood. Mr. Singleton lets me use this place because I got nowhere else to stay. Would you want his address in New York?"

Her short, broad body blocked the doorway. I glanced back to the road. Rowan had come to the foot of the porch steps and was listening to us.

"I'm supposed to meet Eat Singleton here," I said. "May I come in and wait for him?"

"I won't stay here alone at night with a strange man."

I couldn't see a cat. Cats are curious; they come to investigate visitors.

I said, "I heard something in here. Like a mewling."

"Mewling?" Over her shoulder she looked into the room, then back at me. "That's my cat."

"Listen," I said. "I'm going in."

"No!" The poker rose menacingly. Terror twisted her face. "You let me alone!"

I could take the poker away from her without trouble. I could force myself in. But there was Rowan. He wouldn't stand for anything like that. I'd have to get rid of him.

I said, "All right, I'll wait outside for Singleton."

The door slammed in my face. I heard the lock turn.

Rowan chuckled when I came down the porch steps. "It's the women you wouldn't touch with a ten-foot pole that are always afraid every man wants to jump them."

"You can't blame her for being nervous living alone here." I tried to make myself sound casual. "Singleton must have been delayed. I'll wait around for him."

"Suit yourself." We had reached his cab. He gave me that speculative look.

"You'll have to walk if Mr. Singleton doesn't show up. You need a flashlight."

I asked him how much he wanted for his dollar flashlight. "Five bucks," he said blandly. "And three for the trip is eight."

I didn't haggle. After I had paid him he drove to the parking area and turned. On the way back toward me his motor stalled, and in the interval before he started it again I heard the sound of another car. I snapped off my flashlight.

Rowan stopped his car where I stood at the side of the road. "Guess that's Mr. Singleton now."

"Yes," I said.

The headlights of the other car swung around the bend. Singleton had a gun and I didn't, but the darkness was on my side. I moved away from the road, over stubble and past thorn-studded blackberry bushes.

"Hi, Ted," I heard Rowan say.

The second car had stopped within a few feet of the cab. The driver got out, and when he passed the headlights of his car merging with those of the cab, I saw his uniform. He was as tall as Singleton, but twice as broad. All state policemen, in any state, were built the same way.

The New York state trooper spoke to Rowan through the cab window. Then he looked at the bungalow, then he said something else to Rowan, then he looked in my direction, though he couldn't see me. His hand dropped to the gun sagging along his left thigh.

"Here I am," I said loudly. I snapped on my flashlight and walked back to the road.

The trooper hooked his thumbs in his gun-belt and asked me who I was. I told him.

He hadn't heard of me. His orders, he said, had come on his car radio from zone headquarters at Hawthorne: he was to find out if a man named Florian Singleton and a woman named Judith Aikin were here, and if they were to hold them for the New York City police. He had adequate descriptions of both. He said he'd had a hell of a time finding this bungalow. They hadn't known in New York just where it was except in the general Croton area. He'd finally got the directions from the mailman at his home.

"You should've asked me," Rowan said. "I know everybody."

"Do you know the woman who's staying here?"

"Nope. Surprised to find anybody living here this time of the year."

She had put a light on in the bungalow. There was a thin line of it along one window where the shade did not wholly cover the opening.

I said irritably, "Are you going to stand here talking all night? She's hiding something or somebody in there."

"You sure?" the trooper asked.

"I'm not, but it's your job to make sure."

"I know my job," he said. "You come with me."

He didn't want me out of his sight because he had only my word as to who I was. That was all right with me; I was as anxious to go along as he was to have me come. Rowan got out of his cab and accompanied us.

The bungalow door opened as he ascended the porch steps. She stood short and broad and solid in the doorway, barring us. The trooper told her what he was after.

"I haven't seen Mr. Singleton in weeks," she said, the words coming out in a breathless gush. "My name is Mrs. Beatty. Last year Mr. Beatty died and left me without a cent and nowhere to live. You know how hard it is to find a place to live these days. Mr. Singleton was a friend of my husband, and he's been very kind to me and let me use this place till I can find something else."

"What about Judith Aikin?" the trooper asked.

"Nobody's come here. I've been all alone. It's not too warm, especially at night, and all the other houses on the pond are empty and it's very lonely. Sometimes I get nervous, like when this gentleman came to the door a while ago." Her lower lip trembled. "A widow like me who hasn't a place to live in can't be particular. I'm grateful Mr. Singleton lets me have a roof over my head."

She was talking too much, as if trying to tell us something. I could see that the trooper and Rowan were sorry for her. Even I was, a little, believing her and at the same time not believing her.

"Do you mind if we have a look inside, ma'am?" the trooper said.

Mrs. Beatty's hands folded. Her mouth got tight. "Have you a search warrant?"

"No, ma'am. People who have nothing to hide don't ask to see search warrants."

Her eyes shifted past the trooper and rested momentarily on me. Her hands unfolded. "Well, come in," she snapped. "It's cold enough inside without you keeping the door open."

The trooper and I advanced into the large room. Rowan went to the fire and extended his hands toward it.

The room was a good thirty feet long, and about two-thirds of it was twenty feet wide. A square section toward the rear was partitioned off with plyboard — doubtless the bedroom. Next to it, as a part of the living room, was the kitchen, containing a sink, an electric refrigerator, a couple of wooden cabinets. The furniture consisted of the odds and ends you usually find in summer places, and two divans and a couch, so that in that room alone a small party could spend the night.

"Black window shades," I commented, looking at one of the windows, "so light won't show through on the outside." I turned to Mrs. Beatty. "Why black shades?"

"How should I know? Everything was here when I came."

The trooper was in the kitchen part of the room. He opened one of the cabinets, though it wasn't large enough to hide anything important. I went into the bedroom. The light switch was at the side of the door. I clicked it.

It was just a bedroom — bed, dresser, small table, one wooden chair. A double-burner kerosene stove was lit, helping the fireplace in the other room to keep the March chill out of the uninsulated bungalow. Even in my overcoat I didn't feel particularly warm.

In one corner a closet was built out from the wall. All it held were two dresses and a cloth coat. Not Judith's. I looked in the dresser. One drawer contained a few articles of clothing, evidently belonging to Mrs. Beatty. The other drawers were empty.

The trooper came in. "Nothing in that other room. Any sign that a man or a young woman was staying here?"

I shook my head and looked down at the bed. The sheet was gray with dirt; two or three army blankets were a jumbled mess. I dropped down on my knees. All I saw under the bed was a couple of small valises thrust there to get them out of the way.

We returned to the other room. Rowan stood rubbing his hands at the fire. Mrs. Beatty gently rocked herself in a reed rocking chair.

"Are you satisfied?" she said.

I wasn't. I wasn't sure why, but I wasn't. I asked, "How do you get your food?"

"Mr. Singleton —" She broke off. "Sometimes I walk to the highway and get a lift to Croton and then a lift back. Last week Mr. Singleton brought a lot of food in his car. He's very kind."

"You said you hadn't seen him in weeks," I reminded her.

"Just that one time last week. He drove up in the evening and had a big box of food." Her voice became shrill with complaint. "What do you want from me? I never harmed anybody."

"I'm sorry, ma'am," the trooper told her gently. "I only follow orders. Where's your bathroom?"

"There's an outhouse in back," she said bitterly. "Not even running water. I have to drag it from the pump."

We were through. We went to the door. Rowan was already outside and the trooper was stepping over the threshold when I remembered something.

"Where's your cat?"

"Cat?" Her hands folded. She seemed to be holding herself together. "I guess she ran out when you men came in."

I hadn't seen a cat go out. I hadn't seen a cat at any time.

"Come on," the trooper said. "We saw there was nothing inside."

I followed him out. The door closed. The lock turned.

The bungalow was built on cinder brick piers, the lowest point a foot above the ground and the highest six feet. We searched under the bungalow. Then we looked in the outhouse.

"That's that," the trooper said.

We returned to the two cars on the road. The trooper got into his and removed a radio handset phone from a hook on the dashboard and snapped a button. A red light flashed on. While Rowan and I stood outside his car, he reported over the radio. When he finished that, he described me. Then he hung up and lit a cigarette.

We waited. The bungalow was dark and silent. Not even that thin line of light now showed past the black window shade. Mrs. Beatty was once more in darkness except for the light from the fireplace.

A green light flashed on the dashboard. The trooper picked up the handset. His end of the conversation consisted mainly of grunts.

"Zone headquarters called up the New York police," he told me when he hung up. "They said you were okay."

"What do you do now?"

"Beat it," he said. "They never thought there was a ghost of a chance Singleton would come up here unless he was holding the girl kidnaped. Well, there's no prisoner in that place, so there's nothing else for me."

I said, "I'm staying here. Singleton might still show up."

"From what I heard, that guy could be dangerous."

"I'll stay in the woods. If he shows up, I'll head for the nearest phone."

The trooper shrugged. "This is a free country. If you want to spend the night in the woods, okay. But that guy won't come."

I didn't tell him that I didn't give a damn about Singleton. I stepped off the road, out of the range of their headlights. Mrs. Beatty, peering out at us, wouldn't know that I hadn't driven away with one of them.

When the two cars were gone, I stuck the flashlight into my hip pocket and in total darkness walked up to the side of the bungalow. For long minutes the silence held. Then without warning Mrs. Beatty's voice exploded in the bedroom.

"My God, what have I done?"

Nobody answered her — not even a cat.

"Wake up!" she pleaded. "He'll blame me if anything happens to you. He's a monster, making me stay in this freezing house. How long does he think I can stand it? And now the police —"

I didn't listen to more. I raced around to the porch. On the way I picked up a rock, and I used it to smash in one of the front windows. I reached through the shattered pane and turned the lock and raised the window.

I was through the window when she came at me with the poker. The blow caught me on the side of the arm; I hardly felt it through my overcoat. Then I had my hands on her. She was very strong for a woman, and for a very little while it was a grotesque struggle by flickering firelight. I had never thought I would hit a woman, but when her fingernails raked my cheek I hit her in the face with my fist. She sagged. I grabbed her wrist in both hands and twisted until she dropped the poker and writhed at my feet.

All fight went out of her. Whimpering, she rose unsteadily. She did not resist when I led her into the bedroom.

Judith lay on the floor beside the bed. Her eyes were closed. Her body was as limp and still as death.

21. The Killer's Eyes

Everything stopped, even my reflexes. I did not cry out her name. I did not drop down to her side. As I stared at my wife, the realization came slowly that she was only unconscious.

Her bosom heaved. Her mouth opened and closed laboriously, gulping in air with audible gasps.

I found myself staring down at her legs. She wore no shoes or stockings and around her bare ankles there were curious metal bracelets. The hem of her pale-blue dress was twisted above her thighs, and all of the dress was spotted and soiled and creased. It was torn at the bosom, showing part of her pink rayon brassiere. Her arms were out of sight; she was lying on them. My eyes returned to her face, and all I could keep my mind on was her mouth working like that of a fish out of water.

"She's all right!" Mrs. Beatty wailed. "She's coming out of it!"

Almost, during that long moment, I had forgotten about the woman. My hand was still clamped on her wrist.

"What did you do to her?" I said.

She cowered away from whatever she saw in my eyes. "I had to. She was making those sounds through the gag. Then I saw the policeman outside. I — I held the pillow over her face. I didn't mean to hurt her. He said I shouldn't hurt her. But I had to keep her quiet."

Her voice was wild with terror. Her face was contorted into something hideous.

Retaining my grip on the woman, I moved past Judith. Mrs. Beatty came along without resistance. I left her standing against the window where I would be between her and the door, and I knelt beside Judith.

Those were handcuffs on her ankles. I turned her over on her stomach and saw another pair of handcuffs on her wrists. Straddling her body, I spread my hands above her hips and gave her artificial respiration, the way I had learned to do many years ago as a Boy Scout.

As I rhythmically pumped her lungs, I noticed the pillow which had suffocated her on the floor near her head. Beside it was what looked like a balled-up handkerchief, and also a long crumpled strip of cloth. The gag, I thought. The gag which hadn't been able to choke back her voice completely, through which I had heard her mewling like a weak kitten. Mrs. Beatty had stopped even that small sound with the pillow before I had come into the bungalow the first time. And a few minutes later, when she had seen the state trooper drive up, she had pressed the pillow into Judith's face until she was unconscious. Until she was almost dead.

I raised my head. "She was under the bed when we were looking for her."

Mrs. Beatty stood huddled into herself. "I didn't mean to hurt her. I had to keep her quiet and get her out of sight."

The two small valises had been pulled out from under the bed. I had glanced under there and hadn't seen Judith because the valises had been in the way. Mrs. Beatty hadn't been clever; I had been stupid because I had been sure by then that I had drawn another blank.

Judith moaned. Her head stirred. I dipped my face to her. Her breathing was more regular, though still labored.

I said, "Give me the keys to the handcuffs."

"I haven't got them." Mrs. Beatty had recovered too; the lines of her face were hardening. "Mr. Singleton keeps the keys with him all the time."

She was lying, but this was not the moment to do anything about it. Judith was reviving. I turned her over on her back.

Her eyes were open, staring up at me and not believing what she saw. "Leo," she muttered thickly. "Oh, darling, it's you!"

"I came for you, Judith," I said. "Everything's all right now."

I went to the kitchen for water. From there I could watch the bedroom door. The sink had no tap; I searched for it in bewilderment before I remembered that there was no running water. I found a pot of water on the kerosene range and dipped up a glassful.

"Leo!" Judith shouted hoarsely.

Water sloshed over my coat as I ran into the bedroom. Mrs. Beatty had the window open; her head and shoulders were already through it. I set the glass on the dresser and yanked her back and slammed down the window.

She didn't say anything. With her face like rock, she sat down on the bed and crossed her arms over her sweater.

I lifted Judith to a sitting position and held the glass to her mouth. She drank greedily. She looked thin and wan. The joyful vitality had been drained out of her, and what was left was only a familiar shadow. She couldn't sit without the support of my arm. That was weakness, but mostly it was the handcuffs.

Sitting beside my wife on the floor, I said to Mrs. Beatty, "I want the handcuff key."

"I haven't got it."

"Has she?" I asked Judith.

"I don't know." Judith's voice was unrecognizable with hoarseness. "She never unlocked the handcuffs when she was alone with me." She pressed her face into my chest and started to sob. "The handcuffs were unlocked and I was allowed to walk around only when Eat came."

"My God!" I said. "Do you mean you were chained up all this time?"

Her sobs were her answer.

I looked up at Mrs. Beatty. The murder that I felt in my heart must have shown in my face.

"I only did what Mr. Singleton told me," Mrs. Beatty said quickly. "He came every day and let her have exercise."

So they were fine people, both of them. They let her exercise every day. I had never before wanted to hurt anybody physically. I did now.

Judith was speaking against my chest. "And she kept that awful gag in my mouth. She was afraid I would scream and somebody would hear me."

"I took it out when she had meals, and other times when I was with her in this room," Mrs. Beatty defended herself stolidly. "What could I do? He left me all alone with her."

"Tonight I heard a car," Judith said, her voice barely audible. "I tried to call out through the gag. Was that you, darling?"

"Yes."

I eased Judith down on the floor and stood up. I said to Mrs. Beatty, "I'll kill you if you don't give me the key."

"I haven't got it."

I snatched her right wrist. I twisted it. She screamed. She fell off the bed and writhed on the floor.

I couldn't do it. Even now I couldn't do a thing like that to a woman. I dropped her arm. She sat huddled on the floor, whimpering and rubbing her wrist.

What now? I couldn't carry Judith all the way to the highway. I couldn't leave her here alone while I forced Mrs. Beatty to accompany me to the nearest phone. I had lost Judith once; I wouldn't let her out of my sight until we were home. Singleton would have left the woman a key. If I were more of a man — or less — I would twist her arm off, burn her with matches, beat her. I hadn't had the proper upbringing for this sort of thing.

Suddenly Mrs. Beatty sat straighter on the floor. One cheek dropped to her shoulder. She seemed to be listening to something, and I listened too. A far-off drone grew louder by the second.

A car approaching. The police or Florian Singleton.

Now the car was so close that Judith heard it. She turned her face up to me. "Who is it, darling?"

"Maybe the state trooper coming back," I said slowly, but I didn't believe it. He had had his look.

I went to the window and pulled aside the black shade. Headlights appeared, crawled toward the bungalow, stopped at the fieldstone path leading from the road to the porch. I knew that sedan.

"Singleton," I said.

I should have kept my mouth shut, though it wouldn't have made any difference. As soon as I uttered his name, Mrs. Beatty leaped to her feet.

"Mr. Singleton!" she screamed. "Be careful!" And she bolted out of the bedroom.

I might have been able to stop her, but it didn't matter whether or not she remained in the bedroom. He had been warned. I turned back to the window. In the oblique light from the headlights I saw him stand outside the car, hatless and coatless, and his right hand was against his right hip. I could not see the gun in that hand, but I knew it was there.

I spoke to Judith without turning from the window. "I haven't a chance against his gun, Judith. There's only one thing I can do — get out while he's coming in and run for help."

"Oh, God!"

"I'll be all right," I said tightly. "The darkness will cover me. But I hate to leave you here."

Singleton had come halfway up the path and stopped. Another step would have taken him out of my line of vision. "Who is it?" he asked.

Mrs. Beatty had got the front door open and had told him something while I'd been speaking to Judith. Now I heard her say, "Judy's husband."

He was only a darker splotch in the dark night, but I could imagine him grinning. He stepped forward, and the corner of the bungalow hid him from sight.

"Hurry!" Judith whispered. "Eat won't hurt me. He's — gentle."

I could have laughed at that — at any other time and if I had had a moment to spare for laughter. I slid the window up. The porch steps creaked under his feet. I slipped through the window. This was the high part of the bungalow and I dropped a startling distance, but I fell on my feet. In the bungalow somebody ran.

It would have been safer to plunge directly into the woods, but what was the good of my escape if I gave him a chance to drive away with Judith? I raced toward the headlights he had left on in his car.

There wasn't a chance in the world of turning the car around and driving away in it. Not while he had a gun. I pulled the left front door of the car open.

"Hold it, Leo," he said, "or I'll shoot."

He would be standing on the porch. I didn't take the time to look. My hand was on the light knob. I shoved it all the way in, and the car and I merged with the night.

His gun barked sharply, angrily. He was shooting at where he had last seen me leaning into his car. I was no longer there. I was around at the front of the car, raising the hood, and now I looked at the bungalow a hundred feet or more away. I could see him by the light flowing out from the open door — see him run down the steps and down the path toward me.

My frantically groping fingers found wires, ripped them savagely; got another handful, ripped those too. He had cut the distance in half. If I weren't visible in the starlight, the raised hood of the car surely was. He shot again. There was little of me exposed between the body of the car and the raised hood. What he had hit, if anything, I couldn't tell, but he hadn't hit me. Within a moment he would be too close.

I faded back off the road, ran over stubble, through brush, between trees.

He did not shoot again. After a while I paused to listen. He could not follow me in a hurry without making a lot of noise, and there was no sound. Through the trees I could distinguish a dot of light — the open bungalow door.

Then I heard Mrs. Beatty say shrilly, "Did he get away?"

"Yes." It was more an outraged grunt than a word. "And he tore the guts out of my car."

Good! He would not be able to drive Judith away from there before I brought the police. He and Mrs. Beatty might be able to escape on foot, but they would be foolhardy if they tried to make Judith walk with them.

But would they hurt her before they left? Would they kill her? Why should they? It was a curious thing Judith had said about him just before I'd gone through the window. Eat wouldn't hurt her; he was gentle.

He was gentle. He was ingratiating. He was a killer.

I had been walking parallel to where I imagined the road was. My fingers were over the glass of the flashlight, restricting the spread of its glare. I kept bearing toward the road, and suddenly the brush and stubble were gone and there was mud under my feet and deep car ruts.

How far would I have to walk down the road before I reached the highway? Half a mile or two miles? And how long after I reached the highway before a car came along and stopped for me, or before I reached a house with a phone in it?

Then I found that I wouldn't have to walk any distance. A car was coming from the direction of the highway. Seconds after I heard it I saw its approaching headlights through the leafless trees.

The state trooper returning. Or somebody else who would drive me to a phone. I stood in the middle of the road and waved my flashlight. The car stopped when its headlights covered me. I walked to the driver's door.

Bernard Terhune sat behind the wheel.

He ran a tongue over his thin, firm lips. "Leo, what are you doing here?"

What was *he* doing here? I didn't put my own question into words. I stared at him through the open window.

Then I had it. I started to laugh, but what came out was a nervous giggle. "I guess the New York police told you I'd come up here," I said. "I've found Judith, and I've just escaped from Singleton."

He didn't answer that. The dash light revealed something wrong with his eyes. The pupils were startlingly small, the gray-whites too prominent. He kept licking his lips.

"What's the matter?" I said.

He leaned away from me, as if looking for something on the seat. When he straightened up, I noticed that he had unbuttoned his overcoat. He pushed the door open and swung his legs out, but he did not come all the way out of the car.

A gun was in his hand, and its muzzle was pointed at my heart.

"What the hell!" I said.

He didn't speak, didn't move — sat half in and half out of the car, pointing the gun at me. I lifted my light to his face. He didn't blink. His eyes remained wide, fixed, and I saw now what was wrong with them.

They were the eyes of a man who was going to kill another man.

22. The Gentle Jailer

He didn't kill me. He slid over to the right side of the seat and ordered me to drive the car.

With curious detachment I noticed that his pistol was an army automatic. Captain Bernard Terhune used to pride himself on his marksmanship with a hand gun. I got behind the wheel and drove toward the bungalow.

"I don't understand," I said.

"You don't have to," he snapped in the tone he used at his plant when he was sore about something. "You said you found Judith." He paused and then asked more quietly, "Alive?"

I glanced sideways at him. He sat as far from me as he could get, his torso twisted toward me, his gun very steady.

"You don't seem pleased that she's alive," I said.

That didn't get anything out of him. If we had been driving along a real road, I might have tried to wreck the car in the hope that I could get away alive. On this mud track there was nothing to be done but crawl where it led.

"Edna Runyon died this morning," Terhune said after a minute.

"Was she in pain?"

"I understand they doped her up a lot toward the end."

During the brief moments of that conversation sanity had been restored. An ordinary and anticipated tragedy had occurred: a woman who had been dying of cancer had died, and everybody who knew her was glad that she was through with it. Then the silence between us returned, and we were back in that other world where death was made by man.

The bungalow reappeared out of the night. It was as dark and silent as the first time I had seen it an hour ago. I stopped the car a few feet behind Singleton's car.

"This is Terhune," he called. "I've brought Leo Aikin back."

The bungalow remained silent.

Terhune ordered me out of his car. He and his gun were right behind me. We stood for a moment in the glare of the headlights, then started toward the bungalow.

There was a sound. Terhune had taken my flashlight; he lifted the beam and brought it to rest on Singleton and Mrs. Beatty coming out of the woods.

"Thought you might be the cops and we were going to make a dash for it," Singleton said conversationally. "Leo messed up my car. I was trying to fix it, but I'm a lousy mechanic."

Terhune said crisply, "Who's that woman?"

"Mrs. Beatty, a friend of mine." The grin started to develop on Singleton's face. "I happen to have proof that she murdered her husband, so you needn't worry about her."

Mrs. Beatty's arms crossed over her heavy sweater. She shivered.

"Let's go in," Singleton suggested amiably.

He went first, then Mrs. Beatty, then I, and finally Terhune and his gun. The bedroom door was closed. No sound came from there, not even a mewling.

"Where's Judith?" Terhune demanded.

Singleton had gone to the fire and was leaning indolently against the fieldstone mantle. Mrs. Beatty sat in the reed rocking chair, her shoulders hunched forward, her arms tight about herself.

"Close the door," Singleton said. "It's cold enough in here."

Terhune had stopped on the threshold. He took two steps forward, kicked the door shut and remained where he was. I found myself wondering if his gun was covering the other two in the room as well as myself.

"Where's Judith?" he asked again.

"In the bedroom."

"Alive, I hear."

The grin spread all over Singleton's face, but now there was nothing at all ingratiating about it. "I'm not a killer, Terhune. I leave that to you."

"I suppose you didn't kill Paula?" Terhune sneered.

The grin died. "She killed herself. I've done lots of dirty work for you, Terhune, but I won't kill for you or anybody else or even for myself."

"You let Paula die," Terhune said bitterly. "Through your carelessness you murdered her and caused all this mess."

"*I* caused it!" Singleton turned from the fire, and there was nothing casual and relaxed about the way he stood. "I guess you had nothing to do with it when you murdered Ray Fahn and thought your money could buy you out of anything."

I said, "Didn't Judith kill Ray Fahn?"

Neither of them answered me. I wasn't there. Whatever it was, it was between those two.

Terhune spoke in his brisk business tone. "There's the pond. If we tie rocks to them, they'll never be found."

"So now it's *they*. Not only Judy, but Leo too. That's the way you settle things, Terhune. When Dacia Wilmot became a menace to you, you strangled her."

"You think I did it?"

"I know you did it."

Slowly Terhune dragged his left hand over his face. "What choice did I have when you let Paula get killed? Saturday morning you phoned me that Dacia had a talk with Leo the night before. Then Police Chief Mort Middle came into my office, and I thought that was it, that he'd come for me. But he only wanted me to go to Hartford with him and identify Paula's body. When I met Leo at the Hartford station that afternoon and he didn't say anything about Dacia, I was sure she'd kept my name out of it. While Leo was in the morgue with the police, I phoned Dacia. I reminded her of what she already knew — that I loved Paula. I suggested that I was afraid Judith was involved in her death. She didn't quite believe me, but she believed enough to want to hear more. We arranged to meet in a restaurant in New York. I didn't return to Jorberg with Mort Middle and Mrs. Kloe. After we drove a few blocks, I said I had to see somebody in Bridgeport and got out and hired a car to drive me there and took the train to New York."

"Leaving a trail a mile wide," Singleton commented.

Terhune shrugged. "Only a trail if I were suspected. Nobody even remotely suspects me now."

Nobody, I thought dully, but the people in this bungalow; and of us four he had to fear only Judith and me. And we were completely in his power.

"I met Dacia and persuaded her to drive in my car where we could talk without being overheard," Terhune was saying. "I made the mistake of trying to bribe her. I suppose even a woman like that has an invulnerable spot, and hers was for the two Runyon girls. All I accomplished was to convince her beyond doubt that I was involved. She demanded that I stop the car and let her out."

Terhune's voice became that of a querulous woman. "What could I do? She would tell Leo, which would be the same as telling the police. The whole Coast City mess would come out; and on top of that Paula's death, even if by accident, was legal murder. I had to silence her. We were on the East River Drive. No cars were nearby at the moment. I struck her with a wrench I took out of the glove compartment."

"And strangled her," Singleton finished it for him. "And now you want to murder a couple of more people."

Terhune's tongue moved over his lips. "What else can we do?"

"You figure it out. I've got you out of enough messes."

"The police know about this bungalow," Terhune said. "A few hours ago I came to New York with Mort Middle. We had been told that Dacia Wilmot's body was found this morning. Middle thinks it's his job to continue to look for Judith, and I came along as a friend of the family. We spoke to a detective named Hubbard. He mentioned casually that there was a chance in a hundred that Judith was in this bungalow." He jerked his broad shoulders. "Why are we standing here talking? The police might come any minute."

"A state trooper was here a while ago," Singleton told him. "Mrs. Beatty hid Judy under the bed. The trooper was convinced there was nothing here and went away."

"Suppose he comes back?"

Singleton's reply was a grin.

"And even if the police don't come back," Terhune said, "what are we going to do with Leo and Judith?"

"I don't know."

"Damn you!" Terhune said. "If you'd killed Judith after Paula was killed instead of bringing her here..." His hand moved over his face. "All right, tie them up and put them in my car."

"No."

"Damn you, Singleton, you don't think you'll let them go?"

"No. I don't like to burn in an electric chair any more than you do. We'll work it out some way."

"How?"

"Give me time."

Terhune's mouth curled. "By keeping them here forever, the way you were keeping Judith? Even if that were possible, the police will be back."

"We don't know they'll be back. They had a look and seemed satisfied." Singleton stepped away from the fire. His rugged face was suddenly gray. "We'll work it out. Suppose you drive to Croton and phone Hubbard. He knows you. You're Leo's closest friend and Judy's too; that makes you an interested party. You want to know if they found anything in my bungalow. You'll learn from them how much time we have."

"And if the police come while I'm gone?"

"You won't be here. You'll have time to get away."

"That'll be just fine. I'll have to run from everything I possess — my plant, my home, my position. No, I can't say I like your idea."

"You'd better like it," Singleton said.

I hadn't seen him take his gun out, but there it was in his hand.

Terhune looked at that other gun and then raised his bleak eyes to Singleton's face. His body quivered a little, but the gun in his hand didn't.

Singleton said softly, "This is my house and these are my prisoners. Maybe you'd like to kill all four of us, but I'd object. Do we try to work this out together or don't we?"

"How?" Terhune asked again.

"Find out if the cops are coming back tonight. If they're not, time will be on our side." Singleton raised his gun an inch or two. "There mightn't be much time, so I suggest that you don't waste more of it."

For another moment Terhune stood against the door. Then he turned and went out.

We listened to him walk to the road, start his car, turn it, drive away. After that there was silence except for the crackling of the fire. I looked at the closed bedroom door, then at Florian Singleton.

I said, "Now that you've got rid of Terhune, what do you intend to do with us?"

His grin was as ingratiating as it had ever been. "I wish I knew, Leo." He glanced down at the gun in his hand. "It would be convenient if you tried to jump me and made me shoot you."

"Kill him!" Mrs. Beatty burst out. At that moment her broad face was uglier than anything I had ever seen.

Singleton sighed. "You and Terhune. Kill and eliminate a problem. You ought to know, Mrs. Beatty, that that doesn't do it. You got rid of your husband by mixing arsenic in his soup, but the arsenic remains in his body in his grave. What would happen to your problem if his body were exhumed?"

She shrank back in the rocker. "You wouldn't!"

"Not as long as you leave the decisions to me." He had been speaking to her without taking his eyes from me. "I'm getting tired of holding this gun, Leo. I'm sure you wouldn't mind if I put you in with Judy for a while."

He was so damn pleasant about everything. Gentle, Judith had called him, even after everything he had done to her. If he killed us, it would be regretfully and gently.

He told Mrs. Beatty to come along, and we went into the bedroom. Judith lay on the bed; she was covered by the army blankets to keep her warm. He was very considerate of her comfort, but not so considerate that he hadn't replaced the gag in her mouth.

"You'll be more comfortable if you take off your hat and coat, Leo," he suggested.

I obeyed. Mrs. Beatty pulled down the bed blankets. I saw then that Judith's arms were held extended out from either side of her body by handcuffs attached to each wrist and to the iron rails which ran along the outside of the bed springs. Singleton took two keys out of his vest pocket and handed them to Mrs. Beatty, and she unlocked Judith's left wrist. Then he ordered me to get into the bed. If we had to be manacled at all, that was the way I would want it. I stretched out beside her, and immediately her free hand closed over mine. While Singleton stood at the foot of the bed, covering me with his gun, Mrs. Beatty snapped on my wrist the other half of the handcuff attached to the outside railing of the spring.

"Get something to gag him with," he ordered Mrs. Beatty.

"Please," I said. "I give you my word neither of us will yell out."

He rubbed his cheek with the muzzle of the gun. Gradually his grin reappeared. "Why not? If you make a loud noise, I can come in and shut you up. Take out Judy's gag, Mrs. Beatty."

When the rag was out of Judith's mouth, she coughed and sputtered and worked her lips as if trying to restore sensation to them.

"Cold in here, isn't it?" Singleton said. "This stove doesn't do much."

He stepped around to the side of the bed and spread the blankets over us. He tucked us in as if we were two helpless babies, which in effect we were. When he left the room behind Mrs. Beatty, he considerately closed the door.

I was alone with my wife, where I could touch her again, kiss her again. Where together we could wait helplessly for whatever they decided to do to us.

23. The Bleeding Scissors

After a while Judith told me about the killing of Ray Fahn. She started, "They made me —" and stopped. With her eyes fixed on the ceiling, she said tonelessly, "It goes back before that. At the time I was a strip-teaser in a burlesque show."

"I know all about it," I said. "So what?"

We lay flat on our backs under the blankets, her right arm and my left arm held extended out by the handcuffs, shoulders, hips, thighs touching, the fingers of our free hands entwined.

"Darling, how is Aunt Edna?" she asked abruptly.

I used to be irritated by her habit of leaping from topic to topic without pausing more than a moment on any, but now there was so much to be said, to be asked, to be explained, and so little time.

"Terhune told me that she died this morning," I said.

Her profile remained static. There seemed to be no tears left in her for weeping.

When she spoke again, it was in a listless monotone about how she and Paula had crossed the river to Coast City to work in burlesque. It was a job behind footlights — a way of making a living until they could accumulate enough money to renew their assault on the Broadway stage, somewhat lower in the artistic and social scale of the theater, but still the theater.

"It really wasn't bad," she said. "It certainly wasn't less respectable than getting a fat part in a Broadway production or in Hollywood by becoming the mistress of a big shot."

"Like Luther Hadman."

"So you know about that too, darling?"

"Dacia Wilmot told me."

She kept her gaze on the ceiling. "A woman's on the stage to display herself, whether she wears more clothes or less. It wasn't any different from being a model, from working in a night club. I didn't wear much more in a respectable musical show like *Don't Kid Yourself*."

"You don't have to justify what you did," I said.

"I'm not justifying —" She stopped. Her mouth worked soundlessly before words came again. "There was one thing Paula and I drew the line at, what Luther Hadman wanted — I want you to know that, darling — but the rest, burlesque, was just one phase of show business. You could be decent working at it. Kip Trojan was the kindest and most considerate man I met. Not even Ray

Fahn tried to use the fact that he was stage manager to get anything from me. And burlesque could be the road to better things, especially when I became a star. Other women have gone from burlesque to Broadway or Hollywood. And I became a star. I was afraid and nervous and botched the first time I did a specialty, but I became a star. I'd got somewhere at last on the stage. Between us Paula and I made over two hundred dollars a week. We could buy clothes, anything we wanted. We lived in a furnished apartment in one of the best sections of Coast City."

"It's all right," I said. "I told you it doesn't matter to me."

"But it did matter to me," she burst out. "I didn't think it did. I was one of the wild, reckless Runyon girls. When it didn't come easy for me to do the specialty number, I told myself it was stage fright. But it was my subconscious. You see, deep down inside I was a respectable small-town girl. That's what a psychiatrist told me later. And, after all, we didn't let Aunt Edna know what we were doing. We were supposed to be thoughtless, but we would have died rather than let her know that we were in burlesque. We received our mail from her at Dacia's apartment in New York."

For a long minute there was no sound but her breathing. It was not easy for her to speak; she seemed to be still suffering the effects of having been half-suffocated to death less than an hour ago. As I lay at her side, it struck me that I hadn't heard Singleton and Mrs. Beatty in the other room since they had left us here.

"One night after the show," Judith resumed, "Eat Singleton and Bernard Terhune called for us."

"You and Singleton?"

She turned her face to me. Her eyes were so close to mine that they were a blur. "Darling, that was months before I even met you. I'd met Eat Singleton in New York. He was very handsome, very charming; I liked going out with him. He found out where I worked, and now and then he would come to Coast City to take me out after my act."

"Were he and Terhune friends?"

"I think that that night was the first time they met. Terhune was very fond of Paula, you know; for years he'd been after her. She didn't particularly care for him, but she had known him for so long and he was so persistent that he became a kind of habit. About once a week he would run down from Jorberg to see her. That night, when Paula and I came out of the theater, Eat and Terhune were waiting outside the stage door for us. We went up to our apartment for coffee."

She paused to rest her voice. I watched her profile, lovely as it had always been, but it seemed now to be carved out of something that only resembled flesh. It was too much for her, going over it, reliving that past, better forgotten, and at any other time I would have told her not to. But this was not any time.

She was brewing coffee in the kitchen, she went on, and Eat was keeping her company. Paula and Terhune were in the bedroom, having some sort of private conference. Sometimes his voice rose sharply; whatever the quarrel was about, Paula didn't take the trouble to answer him. The doorbell rang. Eat went to answer it and came back to the kitchen with Ray Fahn.

He really wasn't such a bad sort, she said. Nothing, at any rate, like what was said about him later. It was true he sometimes made it uncomfortable for her at the theater. He was a big, shambling, ugly man who thought that every woman was crazy over him. Judith couldn't make him understand that she didn't want anything to do with him personally, and he kept pestering her, but he had never as much as tried to put a hand on her. He had never before come up to her apartment; probably he came that night because he was drunk. He stood unsteadily in the kitchen doorway and scowled at Singleton. She didn't know what to do with him. She asked him to wait in the living room until the coffee was ready. He shambled unsteadily out of the kitchen.

Meanwhile, the quarrel between Terhune and Paula in the bedroom continued. As usual, he wanted her to quit the stage and marry him. At any rate, marry him. As usual, she turned him down. His rage mounted. He lashed out at her with words. He called her vile names because she worked in burlesque and yet considered herself too good to be touched by him. Paula went to the bedroom door and flung it open and told him that she didn't like him and never had. And Terhune slapped her face.

Judith's fingers dug into my palm, but her voice remained flat. "Eat and I were still in the kitchen. Through the open bedroom door Ray Fahn, who was in the living room, saw Terhune slap Paula. I don't think he would have done anything if he had been sober. But he was very drunk and plunged into the bedroom and hit Terhune in the face. Paula screamed, and Eat and I rushed into the bedroom. Ray kept hitting Terhune. He was much bigger and he seemed crazy."

I saw the picture. Fahn had come there drunk, yearning for Judith, and he had found her with another man. Singleton and Terhune were both strangers, both in Judith's apartment, and perhaps they got mixed up in his sodden mind. Or perhaps it didn't matter which one he used his fists on as long as he could take out his bitter frustration on somebody. Terhune slapping Paula was all the excuse a man in Fahn's state of mind would need.

"I remember telling Eat to stop them, but Eat just stood there grinning, as if it were a prize fight. Paula stood with her hands in front of her face. I knew that I was the only one who could stop Ray, and — and — "

She paused for breath. The words, still uttered without quality, had suddenly started to tumble out as if in a rush to be spoken and done with.

"Before I could reach them, Ray raised his fist and hit Terhune again. Terhune's nose and mouth were bleeding, and I remember that his eyes frightened me more than Ray's madness. I didn't see him snatch the scissors from the dresser. I saw him lunge just as Ray hit him again, and I heard Ray utter the most terrible sound in the world. He stumbled crazily and looked at me. I saw the scissors sticking out of his throat."

Irrelevantly I reflected that she continued to refer to it as his throat when it had been his neck. The carotid artery.

"He was clawing at the scissors and blood spurted past them. I remember that I had a nightmarish impression that the scissors themselves were bleeding. He came right at me, staggering blindly. He reached out a hand. He touched me. All I saw was the scissors and the blood. The blood spurted at me. I felt it on my face. It was so horrible."

Without moving, she seemed to sink back on the bed. "I fainted," she whispered, and then she lay very still.

I couldn't take her in my arms and hold her tight and comfort her. The handcuff on my left wrist held my body away from hers. All I could do was throw my free arm across her.

Time passed. I said nothing. I waited for her to recover, to find the inner strength to go on.

"When I opened my eyes, I was in a strange bed," Judith said presently. "It was in the apartment next door. It wasn't rented at the moment and the superintendent had let Eat carry me in there. Paula and Eat were with me. He sat on the edge of the bed and told me that there would be a terrible scandal. We could avoid it if I did as he said. I looked at Paula. She stood as pale as a ghost by the side of the bed, and wrung her hands, and said, 'I don't know. It doesn't seem right.' And Eat said that all I had to do for the next few hours was to keep quiet till we could talk it over. No matter what the police asked me I was to say I couldn't remember. I looked at Paula. And she told me to follow Eat's advice."

Judith drew in her breath. "Paula stayed with me. I closed my eyes. When I opened them again, a detective was sitting at the side of my bed. He was very kind. He told me not to worry, that nothing would happen to me because I had killed Ray Fahn. I stared at him. 'But I didn't kill him,' I said. 'Bernard Terhune did.' He smiled gently and said I didn't have to put the blame on anybody else. He said it was plain that I had killed Ray Fahn in self-defense. I looked at Paula. She chewed her lips and said nothing. I closed my eyes. I was too tired to think. Then a little later Harold Norman, the district attorney, came in. He too was very kind and told me that it would be all right. This time I didn't say anything. I just closed my eyes."

"I see," I said. "It was murder if Terhune did it. He'd struck Paula and Fahn had gone to her defense. But didn't the detective get suspicious when you told him Terhune was the murderer?"

"He knew the truth. So did some of the other policemen. Paula's screams had been heard and a policeman arrived in a minute or two. Paula blurted out the story; besides, there were the marks on Terhune's face where Ray had hit him. Later I learned what happened. Terhune took Eat aside. He said that Eat, as a private detective, knew all the ropes, and he said that he would spend any amount of money if Eat would get him out of this. I don't know all the details, how Eat arranged it, but he succeeded."

"He bribed them," I said.

"Yes. It must have cost Bernard Terhune a great deal of money."

"Especially for that sanctimonious district attorney."

No, Norman wasn't bribed. He believed what the detective — he was a lieutenant — in charge of the case told him. After all, everything appeared to point to Judith, with only a little dressing up of the facts. They learned of Ray Fahn's reputation with women, and that she had asked Kip Trojan to ask Fahn to let her alone. The post mortem revealed that Fahn had been very drunk. And the weapon, the scissors, was the kind a woman would snatch up to defend herself with. And there was blood on her dress. And the clincher — the fact that she admitted killing Fahn and that all three witnesses agreed.

It was snug under the blankets, but deep inside of me I was cold.

I said, "I don't see why you and Paula let them get away with it."

"What else could we do? In the morning the four of us had a private talk. I was still in that strange bed; I couldn't have endured returning to my bedroom. Eat did nearly all the talking. He said that if Terhune was tried for murder, there would be a sensational trial, and Paula and I would have our pictures in all the newspapers. They would be the pictures taken of us at the theater, in which we wore hardly any clothes, and the papers would call it the Strip Tease Murder. We could very easily imagine what they would say in Jorberg. 'The Runyon girls working in burlesque,' they would say, 'and now involved in a murder. We always said they would come to something like that,' they would say. So you see, darling, it was a matter of pride. But most important, it would pretty nearly kill Aunt Edna. Sometimes we had hurt her, but never deliberately, and never as deeply as that. On the other hand, Eat said, the whole thing would be hushed up if I admitted I'd killed him."

"That was all, merely say you killed a man," I said dryly.

She had been too dazed to make up her mind, she said. She left it to Paula, as usual, and Paula decided that it was the best way out. The district attorney had one more talk with Judith and brought her papers to sign. Then there was nothing else — no trial, no publicity. And she and Paula went back to Jorberg.

"How did Dacia Wilmot find out?" I asked.

"Paula took me to New York from Coast City. I was very sick. We planned to stay in Dacia's apartment till I recovered. I had terrible nightmares and Dacia heard them. In the morning I told her everything. She agreed that we had done the right thing, but she couldn't see why we hadn't made money out of it. She said that everybody else seemed to have. Dacia was a darling, but hardboiled about money matters.

"Not in the end," I said. "Not when she refused to sell out her friendship; and Terhune — " I stopped.

"I heard what he said in the other room. He murdered Dacia. Oh, God, I killed her!"

"Don't say that!"

"A guilt complex, the psychiatrist called it. But that was about the other thing. I let Terhune get away with killing one person, and then he murdered Dacia."

"No," I said. "Blame Singleton. But most of all blame the cops who sold out."

Judith pulled her free hand out from under the blankets and placed three fingers on her mouth. She spoke through them.

She didn't get better at Dacia's. Paula took her home to Jorberg. The nightmares continued, and in all of them she dreamed that she had killed Ray Fahn. Paula slept with her in order to wake her when she started raving so that Aunt Edna wouldn't hear what she said. After a few days of that Paula asked Aunt Edna to call in a psychiatrist. In confidence Judith told him everything except who had really murdered Fahn. He said she had a guilt complex. Her small-town morality was subconsciously outraged because she had worked in burlesque and because she had let a murderer get away with his crime. The two were tied up, he said, and he advised that she appease her subconscious by completely cutting herself off from that part of her past. She and Paula destroyed everything tangible that remained of their attempts to become actresses. Maybe that did it and maybe not, but the fact was that she started to get better.

"And then I met you, darling, and it seemed that everything would be wonderful. And it was until..."

For a long time I had been listening to a rhythmic creaking, a monotonous accompaniment to the monotone in which Judith spoke. Suddenly I remembered the reed rocking chair in front of the fireplace. In that other room Mrs. Beatty was rocking wordlessly while she waited as we waited on this bed. There had been no words between her and Singleton. Had he left? If he was trying again to repair his car, I would hear him, and I didn't.

I heard nothing but Judith's steady breathing. How long would it take Terhune to reach a phone and return? If he would return. He had to. He had too much at stake. He had murdered Dacia Wilmot for less reason than he had to murder us.

I said, "But you and Paula were a constant menace to Terhune. Is that why he had Singleton kidnap you?"

"We brought it on ourself. Paula asked him for money." I lay still, saying nothing.

Judith's free hand slid under the blankets and closed fiercely over mine. "Darling, not blackmail! Please don't think that!"

"I don't."

"Last week Eat suddenly appeared. I hadn't seen him since Coast City. I didn't know why his coming to the house should frighten me, but it did. Mabel Kloe was there. I think I was impolite to her, but I had to get rid of her. Then Eat started to talk about money. I had no idea what he meant until he explained.

Paula had gone to Bernard Terhune and asked him for money. She arrived home in a little while and admitted it. Eat said he would come late at night with the money and left. When Paula and I were alone she insisted that it wasn't — wasn't — "

"Blackmail?" I said.

A little of the old fire came into her voice as she denied it. She said that I had finally impressed on Paula that I was over my head in debt; and she'd bought that Persian rug the day before and was worried about what I'd say when it arrived, even though I had sixty days to pay for it, and —

"My God!" I broke in. "Because of the money you girls were spending on the house! Were a few sticks of furniture worth all that?"

"Darling, it was also Aunt Edna's hospital expenses."

"I could have handled that all right if you girls had kept within my income."

It was downright funny. Here we were in one of our old arguments about her extravagance, when in a little while Terhune would return. I could make another joke: Terhune, by killing us, would never regain the money I owed him. Very funny.

"You've got to understand, darling," Judith was saying. "Paula began to think of what Dacia had said over a year ago, that everybody had got money out of what happened in Coast City but us. She decided that Terhune should at least have paid the expenses for my illness. She went to him and said she wanted only the money for that — two thousand dollars. He'd been responsible for my nervous breakdown, hadn't he?"

"Asked for it fifteen months late," I said, and at once I was sorry I'd brought that up. Paula had had an idea and had acted on it without much thought. The way she and Judith had filled the house with junk and then had hoped that somehow I'd be able to pay for it. Call it a harmless impulse, the kind the irresponsible Runyon sisters had always gone in for.

"At first I objected," Judith said. "Then McCabe brought the Persian rug and you came home and said how poor we were and made him take it back. When you left for the poker game, Paula argued with me again. After all, Eat had come in the afternoon and said that Terhune was giving him the two thousand dollars to give us that night, so it was plain that Terhune was willing to pay for my illness. It seemed to be all right."

"And so Paula phoned McCabe to bring back the rug in the morning. That's what the money was for basically — another piece of junk for the house."

"Darling, I know you despise me."

"Cut it out!" I pressed my face against her smooth, warm neck. "I'll never stop loving you." I uttered a very little laugh. "That Persian rug is spread out on the living room floor, waiting for you."

Saying that was a mistake. Not waiting for Paula now, and probably never for us either.

Softly she started to sob. I couldn't stand it. I had to get her back to talking.

I asked her how Singleton had managed to induce them to meet him on Mill Street.

Between sniffles she told me that at eleven o'clock that night he phoned the house. He said that his car had skidded on the icy road and was stuck on Mill Street. He asked them to drive out there and pick him up.

"And you had no more sense than to meet him on a deserted road at night?"

"We hadn't any idea that he would do anything to us. Paula had asked for money and he was bringing it. Besides, we trusted Eat."

"I know," I said. "He grins and everybody believes that he's the greatest pal on earth."

She was silent. Then, looking up at the ceiling, she went on tonelessly. He was standing beside his car on Mill Street. He took out his gun. He snapped handcuffs on their wrists and made them get into his sedan. He tied their ankles with rope and shoved gags into their mouths. Then he drove away with them.

In the other room the creaking of the rocker stopped. I listened for Terhune to return.

"We lay on the floor of the sedan," Judith said. "It was very cramped. Paula's legs were against my back. Our arms were handcuffed behind us. I could move my fingers, and after a while I started to work on the rope that tied Paula's ankles. I shouldn't have done it. I should have let well enough alone. By untying that rope I killed her."

"Stop it!" I said.

"I killed her!" She screamed those three words. I felt the bed shake with the shaking of her body.

The guilt complex again. I threw my arm over her body, held her tight.

"Singleton and Terhune killed her," I said fiercely. "Don't ever forget that they're her murderers."

Gradually she subsided.

After a long time I said, "And when Paula's legs were free she tried to get out of the car. Is that what happened?"

"Yes." She spoke in a voice I didn't know. "She got up to her knees and opened the car door with her chin. It didn't seem dangerous. Eat was driving very slowly because the road was so very icy. We were passing through woods. She had to go only a few steps and Eat would never find her. Then Eat would have to let me go too because the police would know who kidnaped me. She jumped out. I didn't hear anything after that. Eat had seen or heard her jump; he stopped the car and got out. He was gone a long time. When he came back, he told me that she was — dead."

The bedroom door flew open.

"Mind if I come in?" Singleton said affably.

24. The Damn Fool

He swung the wooden chair closer to the bed and sat astride it, his chest against the back of it, and grinned at us.

"I've been listening to you through the door," he said. "This way is more comfortable. Not that you said anything I didn't know, Judy." His jacket hung open; part of the holster under his left arm was in sight. He rubbed his chin on the top of the chair. "I'm the lad who knows everything but his own mind."

Judith said dully, "You must have heard me tell Leo that I had trusted you."

"You flattered me, Judy," Something wistful came into his eyes. "You were very fond of me once, weren't you?"

She had to move all the way to the right side of the bed before her manacled right wrist permitted her to turn on her left side and face Singleton. "Yes," she said, looking at him over me. "Until you sold me out to Bernard Terhune when he killed Ray Fahn."

"I explained that to you a dozen times." Singleton was mildly annoyed, the way a polite man gets with an obtuse woman. "It was better for you in the long run. The way I managed it, the whole mess was effectively hushed up, and you and Paul were out of what would have been a nasty scandal."

"Except," she said, "that you were the richer."

"Sure, by five thousand bucks." He was a man pleased with a clever bit of business he had turned and didn't care who knew it. "You don't make that kind of dough in a couple of days by being strictly legitimate. Everybody was satisfied. Terhune got out of a murder rap by spending seventeen thousand dollars he could easily afford. A handful of Coast City cops split twelve thousand, and I got what was left. You and Paul were better off than if it had come out in the open. It's true you had a nervous breakdown, Judy, but you would've got that anyway." Suddenly his rugged face set; I'd never before seen him grim. "I'll tell you something I've told you before, Judy: that five grand wouldn't have meant a thing to me if I'd thought you'd be hurt in any way."

I said, "No, you can see she wasn't hurt. And neither were Paula and Dacia."

"A lousy, crummy, stupid break," he said angrily. "If Paula hadn't tried to get out of my car —" His hands, dangling over the back of the chair, clenched hard. "That whole idea was a mistake from the beginning. I knew it when Terhune sent for me and told me that Paula and Judy were trying to blackmail him over the Fahn killing."

"No!" Judith burst out. "It was never blackmail."

"Sure it wasn't. That's what I told Terhune. 'Look, Terhune,' I said to him, 'blackmail is a threat to do something if you don't come across. They can't open up on that Coast City business because they're accessories after the fact.' 'So are you,' Terhune said to me. 'You arranged the bribes.' 'That's how we're all protected from each other,' I said to him. 'We're all in this together.' Terhune said that was okay as far as he and I were concerned, but that those Runyon girls, as he called you and Paula, were irresponsible. 'You don't know them,' he said to me. 'There's no telling what they'll do.' I'm not saying I wasn't also plenty worried. A woman's never too safe with a secret. All that Harold Norman, the Coast City D.A., needed was a hint that some of the local cops had taken a bribe in a homicide, and he'd blow the whole thing wide open. I know Norman — dumb and honest. So I asked Terhune how much Paul wanted. He told me two thousand dollars and that she'd said it was to pay for your illness, Judy. 'Hell, that's not blackmail money,' I said to him. 'They're entitled to that. You should have offered them the money long ago.' 'That's the point,' he said to me. 'It's well over a year since she got better. They didn't ask for it then. Asking for it now means they've decided to exploit what they know.' 'Hell, you've spent seventeen grand already,' I said to him. 'Protect your investment by spending two more.' 'That'll be only a beginning,' he said to me. 'If I give her this money, she'll be back for more and more, always for something else.' Well, he had something there, but that wasn't his real reason. He hated Paul too much to give her a cent."

Judith stirred on the bed. "He loved her," she muttered.

"He loved her, and when his love got him nothing, he hated her. That's the kind of lad Terhune is. He'd show her she couldn't pull anything on him — that is, he'd pay me to show her. It wasn't the money. 'They don't get a cent from me,' he said to me, 'but I'll give you the two thousand dollars to carry out an idea I have.' It wasn't an idea; it was a brainstorm. He wanted me to put such a scare into you two girls that you'd let him alone in the future and forever after be too frightened to let out a peep about the Coast City business. What I was to do was kidnap you two for a few hours, drive you around in my car, then take you home — a sample of what would really happen to you next time. 'That's fine,' I said to Terhune. 'And what happens next day when they squawk?' 'They won't,' he said to me. 'They're accessories to murder, and on top of that blackmailers. While you're driving them around, you can make that clear to them.' Well, I looked at it this way and that. It seemed like a harmless stunt. All the same, though, I didn't like it." He stared at his fists.

"But you liked the two thousand dollar fee," I sneered.

He brought his grin back. "Two grand isn't bad pay for a night's work. That wasn't the first time I'd done something for a client I thought was stupid, as long as I could make a profit out of it. Terhune was laying out cash for his hatred, so why should I pass up the easy dough? The fact is, he was overpaying for a stunt that wouldn't harm anybody. It would've worked out okay if Paul hadn't got her legs free."

Judith drew in her breath in a broken sob. Singleton turned his face to the open bedroom door. In the other room the rocker was again creaking, but outside the night held no sound. Maybe Terhune would not come back.

Singleton went on as if he had plenty of time. "When Paul jumped out of the car, she must've slipped on the icy road. Her head struck some part of the moving car, probably the edge of the rear bumper. She was dead when I reached her, and suddenly what had been just a stunt was murder. An accident, of course, but legally it was murder because she'd been killed during a kidnapping. There wasn't a chance in the world I could prove I hadn't been playing for keeps. I removed the handcuffs and gag and took her handbag and left her body there. The police would think she'd been hit by a hit-run driver. Or they'd think that if Judy didn't tell them differently. She was the problem. I couldn't let her go. I drove into Hartford and left her handcuffed and gagged in the car while I phoned Terhune. At first he tried to shove all the responsibility on me. 'Nuts, Terhune,' I said to him. 'You're in as deep as I am. Deeper, because when this blows up the Coast City mess will blow up too. Judy will have plenty to say now that her sister's been killed.' Terhune was silent for a minute. Then he said that I'd have to take care of Judy. I knew that, but I didn't know how. I told him that I was taking her to my bungalow."

"I suppose it was Terhune who came to my house that night and took their clothes," I said.

"It was his own idea. He told me about it next day when he drove up here. Thought he'd been pretty clever. The cops already believed that Judy had walked out on you and that Paul had gone along. Even if Paul's body was identified in Hartford, it would only mean that she had driven that far and got out and been hit by another car. But there was still the problem of what to do with Judy."

Judith was again lying flat on her back. She told me hoarsely, "Bernard Terhune wanted to kill me. I heard him argue with Eat while I was tied to this bed."

Singleton snorted. "He wanted me to do the job. Nice character. I'd have steady employment if I hung around him. I told him to go to hell. He got kind of pale around the mouth. 'Okay,' he said to me, 'leave her with me.' " Singleton gripped the top of the chair. "I've never hurt anybody in my life, or allowed anybody to be hurt." He looked past me. "Judy, you're the swellest kid I ever knew. Okay, I'm a heel. Maybe I like money more than I like anything else. But I'm not a killer. Not intentionally. You know that what happened to Paul was an accident."

"Go on, whine," I sneered. Sneering was the only weapon I had against him.

He ignored me. He stood up so that he could look down at Judith lying on the other side of me.

"Judy, I tried to treat you all right here."

She didn't answer. But I did. "Sure, you're a gentle, considerate, ingratiating guy."

He shrugged. "What could I do? I couldn't let her go. I finally got rid of Terhune by making him think I'd do the job on Judy. I sent for Mrs. Beatty. But that still wasn't a solution to the problem. I couldn't keep Judy here indefinitely." He shook his head as if arguing with himself. "Maybe I'm too soft for this racket. I should have stuck to making a legitimate living, and starved at it."

"Eat!" Some of the animation flowed back into Judith's face. "You're going to let us go?"

"That would be a damn fool thing to do," he said slowly.

He dipped his face and chewed on his lower lip. After a while his face came up with a sick ghost of a grin. "You know why I came in here to do all this talking? I'm trying to make up my mind. Since I brought you here, Judy, I've been trying to make up my mind. The trouble is that I know what to do to save my skin. I don't even have to do it myself. I can let Terhune do it. He mightn't like to, but he wouldn't hesitate, any more than he hesitated with Dacia Wilmot. Maybe that's why he's a successful business man. He can make decisions and follow them through."

"Eat, you're not really bad," Judith said.

"I half wish I were," he muttered.

He walked to the window and pulled the black shade up. Was he looking to see if Terhune had returned? But Terhune's car would be heard approaching half a minute before it reached the bungalow.

"I've three choices." Singleton spoke as if to himself while looking for something in the darkness outside. "I can do the job on you two kids myself. I can let Terhune do it. I can be a damn fool and let you go."

I said urgently, "We'll promise to keep you out of it."

His grin turned from the window. "Not a chance. The cops are interested in a couple of murders and where Judy fits into them. You'll talk to clear Judy."

The rocker in the other room had stopped creaking. Judith's face was empty. She might have been asleep if her eyes hadn't been open, staring. Singleton stood at the foot of the bed, looking down at us, and his grin was sad.

"Okay, so I'll be a damn fool," he said quietly. And there was an expression of surprise in his eyes, as if at the discovery of what a damn fool he was.

I knew now why I had never been able to hate him.

"Mr. Singleton, you're not going to let him go?" Mrs. Beatty said.

Raising my head, I saw her stand just inside the bedroom.

Indifferently Singleton glanced at her over his shoulder. "Yes," he said.

"You can't! What will become of me?"

"You can beat it now."

She stood swaying there, a short, broad, ugly woman in tight slacks and heavy sweater. "They'll tell the police about my husband. You talked too much."

"They don't know what state he's buried in, or anything about you but your second name." He was hunting through his vest pockets. "Damn it, what did I do with those handcuff keys?"

I remembered. I told him that he'd handed them to Mrs. Beatty to manacle me to the bed while he had covered me with his gun.

"That's right." He turned to the door. She was no longer there. He went into the other room.

Judith's hand was in mine. Our faces were together, and the warm, eager glow of life had returned to her eyes.

"We'll do what we can for him, darling," she said. "The police will go easy with him when we tell them he saved our lives."

I didn't think that the police would ever catch up to him. He would be on his way as soon as he released us.

In the other room he was having trouble getting the keys from Mrs. Beatty. Presently she said savagely, "All right, here they are," and he said dryly, "Thanks," but it didn't end there. She kept pleading with him.

"Please Mr. Singleton, you can't do this to me," she wailed. "They'll tell the police about me. And if the police catch you, they'll ask you and you'll tell them about my husband."

"Get your hands off me. What the —"

Singleton's voice was cut short by a shot.

As one, Judith's body and mine jerked on the bed with the roar of the gun. There was a drawn-out grunt. Something heavy fell to the floor.

"Oh, God, what happened?" Judith said. "Did Terhune come back?"

"No."

I lay waiting for Mrs. Beatty to come into the room with the gun. I heard her feet, but they didn't move toward us. The front door opened. It didn't close. Feet thumped on the porch floor. Then there was no sound anywhere but Judith whimpering.

Mrs. Beatty had not come into the bedroom to kill us, but it would amount to the same thing when Terhune returned and found us still handcuffed to the bed.

25. The Opening Door

There was a sound. An animal moving stealthily in that other room, a part of my brain thought without caring. Maybe the cat I had heard mewling and which had turned out to be Judith, and I felt myself start to laugh the way a madman would laugh.

"Leo, what's that?" Judith said.

She was holding the upper half of her torso propped up on her elbows. I roused myself; I forced myself to concentrate. Somebody seemed to be dragging a heavy weight across the room.

"Eat?" Judith said in a curiously constricted tone.

Something like a breathless gush of wind came through the open bedroom door — something like a long, long moan reluctantly brought to a flickering end.

"Is that you, Eat?" Judith called tightly.

The answer came with surprising clarity. "Sure, but I'm saving my breath." If a voice could grin sardonically, I thought, that voice did.

I sat up in the bed and Judith did too. Never taking our eyes from the door, our nerves quivered to his agonizing approach.

He appeared. He was dragging himself along the floor on his knees and one hand. His other hand was clutched to his belly. He stopped when he saw the bed. He started to sit up. He moved like a rusty automaton, and his grin was a mask of pain.

"Mustn't pass out," he murmured. "Too bad if I pass out."

"Take it easy," I warned him.

"No. Terhune will be back."

He was sitting doubled over, with both hands clutched to his belly. He removed one hand and fumbled with it in his vest pocket. "Lucky she gave me the keys before she plugged me. That was to get me off guard so she could —" He coughed hollowly.

Slowly he straightened. I watched him so intently that my own muscles stained with his agony. Beside me Judith seemed to have stopped breathing.

He pulled his hand behind his hip. His teeth dug into his lower lip as he tossed the key underhand. It landed near the foot of the bed, close enough for me to reach with my free hand. The key didn't fit my handcuffs, but it did Judith's. When she was free, she rolled over me off the bed and went barefooted to where Singleton sat hunched over and got the second key out of his vest pocket and returned to the bed to release me.

Between us we carried him to the divan nearest the fire. While she fetched the pot of water from the kitchen, I bared his belly. There wasn't a river of blood, but there was enough. The set mold of his grin was a measure of his pain.

I told him that in the war I had seen men survive much worse belly wounds.

"Mrs. Beatty knows more about arsenic than about guns," he said, making each word a careful, measured phrase. "She should have stopped to take a second shot at me."

Judith was tearing a sheet into strips. She took my place on the divan and washed his wound. Though she was near the fire, I saw her shiver, and then I realized that I was also cold. A raw breeze was blowing in through the door Mrs. Beatty had left open. I closed it.

"Mrs. Beatty won't be back," Singleton said. "You don't know where she murdered her husband or her full name. There's nothing you can do to her." He winced as Judith touched the wound with the wet cloth. "God, I'm a dope! I let Mrs. Beatty claw at me while she begged me not to let you go. Never trust anybody whose secret you know. I let her get so close to me she could pull my gun out of its shoulder clip. Before I knew it — Easy, Judy!" He twisted his face to the wall.

"I'm sorry." She turned her head to me. "This is all we can do for him, darling. We'll have to get a doctor."

"Sure," Singleton said. "You two kids beat it before Terhune comes back."

"Will he be back?" I asked.

Singleton spoke between his teeth. "He's got to. He's got too much to lose to become a fugitive if it means only a couple of more killings. He'll come back to make sure you're put out of the way, with or without my help."

Judith said, "Perhaps the police..."

"No. They've had their look." With both hands he held the bandage to the wound. "Go on, beat it. And when you get to the cops, tell them to bring along a doctor. I won't be going anywhere."

I said, "I'm going to wait here for Terhune."

"You crazy idiot!" Singleton said. "He's got a gun. Mrs. Beatty went off with mine."

I said, "You go, Judith. I'm going to stay to take Terhune."

She stood at my side, almost as tall as I was, even in her bare feet. In five minutes she had changed, but not back to the Judith I had known. She wouldn't faint or have a nervous breakdown. Death and terror and danger had tempered her, perhaps. Whatever it was, she seemed as sure of what she had to do as I was.

"I'm staying with you, darling," she said.

"What can you do?"

"I'm staying, darling."

Singleton uttered a harsh, cracked sound that was something like a chuckle. "I'm not the only damn fool."

I went to the fireplace. Mrs. Beatty had replaced the fire poker in its stand. There was also a shovel and a pair of tongs. The tongs looked adequate. Hefting them, I returned to the divan.

"Bullets travel," Singleton commented wryly.

"I'll stand at the side of the door," I said. "He won't see me as he comes through."

"Good enough." Singleton's hands became claws on the wet cloth which was soaked with blood. Judith changed it for a fresh one.

I waited at a window from which I could catch the road. I didn't know how long I stood there. Judith sat on the edge of the divan, holding Singleton's hand. I wasn't jealous.

Firelight flickered on her bare legs. Her dress was a crumpled rag, torn at the bodice. Her hair was disheveled and there was a streak of dirt across the bridge of her nose. I thought I had never seen her more beautiful.

Presently Singleton chuckled again. "What a blow-up this will be. I'm going to do plenty of talking. A number of Coast City cops are going to be very unhappy tomorrow. Jorberg will have the juiciest scandal it ever hoped for. Terhune will be headed for the electric chair. And a southern Illinois village is going to learn that the respectable Mrs. Beatty flavored her husband's soup with arsenic."

I waited.

I heard the car before I saw its headlights. My fingers hurt with the tightness of their grip on the tongs.

"He's coming," I said. "Judith, at least wait out in the woods. If he gets me, you'll be safe."

She rose from the divan. She did something at the fireplace with her back to me, and when she turned I saw that the poker was in her hand.

"If he sees you, he won't see me on the other side of the door," she said.

I kissed her. I said something against her mouth about not being a fool, but I knew that that wouldn't change anything. There were three fools in the bungalow.

Around the bend in the road a pair of glaring headlights crawled.

Singleton said reflectively, "At that, it won't be so bad. The cops like all the evidence they can get. They'll be ready to make a deal for me against Terhune. You kids will tell what a damn fool hero I was at the end, and I'll talk my heart out. Maybe I'll get away with ten years. Maybe with a lot less."

Through the window I saw that it was Terhune's car pulling up behind Singleton's disabled car. I saw that it was Terhune getting out.

"That's me," Singleton was saying somewhat wildly. "Florian Singleton, the damn fool who couldn't bring himself to knock off a girl to save his own precious skin."

"Quiet!" I whispered.

Halfway up the fieldstone walk Terhune stopped, an exaggerated shape in starlight. His right hand came out of his coat pocket. That hand held his gun.

I turned from the window. My shoulder touched Judith. Our hands slid in and out of each other. I stepped to the side of the door and lifted the tongs.

The porch shivered under Terhune's step. He stopped. I watched the door. Nothing happened.

"Singleton?" Terhune said from the porch.

Singleton lifted his head from the divan. His grin became a caricature. "What the devil took you so long, Terhune?" he said querulously.

There was another silence. I looked across three feet of space at Judith. The poker was held above her head.

It would be all right, I thought. My wife and I together, always together from now on. I raised the tongs higher.

The door started to open.

THE END

The Evil Days
By Bruno Fischer

Every Man

Wednesday

As on any weekday, I took the 7:52 A.M. to New York City and the 5:27 P.M. home. The train got me back to Mount Birch eleven minutes late, about normal, so that it was around six-thirty when I shuffled with my fellow commuters up the iron stairs to the station plaza. From there I peered up the curving hill road for my car.

It was well up in the string of cars working their way down by fits and starts to pick up those of us hapless husbands who couldn't afford more than one. As I was in other ways a proper suburbanite, it was a station wagon. For a couple of months now it had had a crumpled front fender. I walked up the road to the front of it and opened the left door.

"Hello, dear," Sally said, sliding away from the driver's side of the seat.

Her tawny hair had more gold in it than this morning, and I remembered that she had had a beauty-parlor appointment to have it refurbished.

Brandy reared up behind the seat. "Hi, Dad."

He was alone back there. These days Chuck seldom came along to pick me up. Chuck was eleven, three years older than Brandy, and thus wholly occupied with his own affairs. Which during the middle of the spring was Little League baseball.

I pushed my briefcase in ahead of me as I slipped behind the wheel. Sally and I leaned to each other to brush lips. This done, I cut down the dozen feet that had developed between my car and the one ahead; the only way to reverse direction was at the jammed traffic circle below. I turned my head to ask Brandy how the boy was.

"Miss Fairhoff is a stinker," he said.

"Now, Brandy, that's no way to talk about your teacher," I said by rote.

He mumbled something I couldn't hear because another voice in the car was much louder. The radio was on and we were being screamed at by a woman selling something. I reached to shut her off.

Sally grabbed my arm. "Leave it on."

"Look," I said. "When I come home from work I'd like some quiet to speak with my family."

"It's the six-thirty news. I'm listening to it."

She sounded and looked intense. Normally the things she was intense about were the children's eating habits and new drapes for the living room and the impossibility of attending a P.T.A. meeting in a dress she had worn twice before. They didn't include the world's crises and disasters; she left those to me to worry about. Now there was almost frenzy in the way she clutched my arm to keep my hand from the knob.

"Did something happen?" I asked.

"Happen where?"

"You tell me. In the world. In town. What are you listening for?"

"I merely want to hear the news," she said in the tone she used when scolding the boys or me.

Horns honked angrily. I had again permitted a gap in the line of cars. As I hastened to rectify the lapse, Brandy said in my ear, "Miss Fairhoff *is* a stinker."

He proceeded to explain why—something said or done during a spelling test. I could hear him well enough now because the radio voice following the commercial was reasonably subdued, but I concentrated on it instead of on Brandy. The voice belonged to Mort Reach, editor of the *Mount Birch Weekly Ledger*, who did an evening broadcast of local news on the local station. And Sally, sitting apart from me with hands clasped, listened intently to him telling of accidents and fires, births and deaths, politics and social events.

I achieved the station traffic circle. Willie Jackson was the patrolman on rush-hour duty. When he saw me, he stopped the stream of cars pouring out from the station parking lot to let me go up the hill ahead of everybody else. I gave him a small wave of my hand, though I wished he hadn't done it. I didn't want special privileges. Especially not in the sight of voters who knew me.

Another commercial came on the radio. This time it was Sally who reached forward to turn it off.

In my ear Brandy complained bitterly, "You call that fair, Dad, huh, do you?"

I uttered a noncommittal grunt. That seemed to satisfy him; he took his face from the back of my neck.

The Division Street light turned red as I approached it. Waiting, I took a long look at Sally. Her sweet, small-nosed profile was absolutely static. She sat alone with herself.

"Did you hear it?" I asked her.

"I guess it's too early," she said in that way she had of sometimes speaking to herself rather than to me.

"Sally, what the hell is this about?"

"There's no need to shout." She shifted closer to me and whispered, "Later, dear."

"Why not now?"

"I don't want *him* to hear."

I glanced around at Brandy. He had transferred himself to his favorite position, kneeling at the tailgate window to watch the world go by.

The light changed. As the car moved, I said, also in a whisper, "Is it anything bad?"

"It can wait till we're home!" she snapped. As if she were the one who had reason to be annoyed.

Anyway, we were almost home.

We lived in one of fourteen ranch-type houses lined up on both sides of the street. The houses were not quite identical. Some had garages on the right and some on the left; some had fixed black shutters on off-white shingles and some had white shutters on gray shingles. All had three bedrooms, and a dinette that merged with the living room, and an up-to-date kitchen wide enough for two skinny people, and a cement-block playroom in the basement. In the six years since we had bought it for more than we could afford, taxes had doubled, and in another twenty-four years (when I would be sixty-two), the mortgage would be paid off.

George Huntley, our next-door neighbor on our right, was pushing a power lawn mower behind his substantial belly. When my car swung into my short driveway, he cut the motor and came over.

"That's yours, Caleb," he told me.

"What is?"

"The lawn mower. Mine is being fixed. Nobody was home, so I went in your garage and helped myself. Okay?"

"Sure."

Sally had left the car and was entering the house. Brandy ran to Penny Huntley, who was fussing with a doll in a carriage. She was his age, maybe younger. I got out of the car with my briefcase.

"It's beginning to rust through," George said, critically examining the fender Sally had rammed against a light pole. He taught science in the high school and so could recognize oxidation as well as anybody.

"A hundred and ten bucks just to straighten a fender," I said.

With his thumbnail George flicked off a flake of paint at one of the creases in the metal. "Aren't you insured?"

"One hundred dollars deductible," I said. "And if I try to collect the ten, they'll likely cancel my insurance."

I turned to go and was diverted by the sight of Brandy and Penny peering down into the doll carriage like anxious parents. Against the background of the Huntleys' pink magnolia in full bloom, his shaggy head touched her brown curls.

"That's some hot love affair," George said. If the children had been older, the smirk on his flaccid face would have been downright lewd. "She told me she's going to marry him when they grow up."

"She's got good taste," I said as I started for my front door.

I found Sally in the kitchen. She was bent over the oven, checking on a roast. In that position the spread of her cute rear in her tight slacks was particularly slapable. I slapped it. She straightened up and I put my arms around her from behind to her breasts and nuzzled her hair that smelled of the beauty parlor.

She just stood there, letting my hands have her—stood unresponsive and remote. When I let go of her, she took a pot from the stove and bore it to the sink.

"Tell me now," I said.

"I have to get dinner ready."

"You can tell me while you're doing it."

"I'd rather wait."

At the sink she dumped rice from the pot into a colander, and her face was a stranger's. The tiny nose had somehow sharpened; the softly rounded cheek and chin had acquired angles.

I said, "If it's something like an accident to somebody we know, why can't you simply say so?"

"It's not."

"Then what?"

"It's a long story. I'll tell you after dinner." She ran water over the rice. When she turned from the sink, she frowned at me leaning against the refrigerator. "Dear, I wish you'd find Chuck and bring him home. I'll be ready to serve soon."

"I hate mysteries," I said.

"Dear, I've had a terrible day. Please, dear, for once don't argue."

"All right," I said.

2

I drove the mile to the Little League ball field. Three boys were still there, one of them Chuck, who could be counted on to stay till nobody else was left or somebody came for him. They were peppering the ball around the infield.

"Chuck, it's dinnertime," I called from home plate.

"Aw!" he said.

"Chuck!"

The energy with which he had cavorted around second base seeped out of him. He dragged himself over to me. Like myself at that age, he was mostly bones. I had been well married before I had started to put flesh on my frame, though still not much.

"Chuck," I said as we walked to the road, "did anything unusual happen at home today?"

"What do you mean, unusual?"

"I don't know. Did *anything* happen?"

"I was home just to leave my books and get my glove. We had baseball practice. Hey, Dad, they going to keep your picture all over the place forever?"

My face was plastered around the light pole near which I had parked the car. Above my hairline ran the legend, FOR VILLAGE TRUSTEE, and under my Adam's apple, CALEB B. DAWSON. The photographer had made me look grim, even angry. Portrait of a man who would brook no extravagant nonsense in conducting the affairs of the nine thousand souls in our village.

I said, "Do the posters embarrass you?"

"Well, the election is over and you won. Why do they have to stay up?"

"They're pasted up and nobody has taken the trouble to take them off." We got into the car, and when we were moving I said, "Chuck, who was in the house when you came home from school?"

"Nobody, just Mommy. Hey, Dad, the coach says I have the peg to first down pat."

"That's great," I said. "Did she seem troubled?"

"Who?"

"Mommy. You know, upset in any way?"

"She bawled me out. I didn't do a thing. Honest. All I did, I went to her room to see if she was home. She got mad at me because I didn't knock."

"Was the door closed?"

"Yeah. But nobody ever told me to knock in my own house."

"You're a big boy now and ought to knock when our bedroom door is closed." I turned the car into our street, driving slowly to prolong the trip. "Chuck, what was she doing in the bedroom?"

"Nothing."

"Changing her clothes?"

"She was sitting on the bed. That's all, just sitting and doing something with a pillow. She jumped up like I scared her. Then she bawled me out because I didn't knock and told me to take cookies and milk before I went." He pounded his fist into his glove. "Dad, I still have trouble going to my left."

"Hasn't every shortstop?" I said.

We were back home. I collected Brandy from the Huntley lawn, tearing him away from Penny, and herded both boys inside. Sally told me to see that they washed up. I left them together in the bathroom for maybe twenty seconds and they got into a fight. I yelled at them and she yelled at me for not being able to control them while she got dinner on the table and Brandy was crying because Chuck had pinched his arm and I slapped Chuck, which made me hate myself. Everything quite normal.

At least that part.

Eventually we were all four assembled at the table. The boys bolted down their food and then bore their milk to the television to watch one of their innumerable favorite programs, the usual whining, yelping situation comedy against the invariable background of nerve-rasping canned laughter. As the set was at one end of the living room and the dinette off the other end, Sally and I were left in neither peace nor privacy. We ate dessert and drank coffee without conversation.

Married people don't talk all the time; silences go with intimacies. This silence was one of exclusion, as after a fight. But we hadn't fought, not for weeks. Things had been fine when I had left for work this morning, yet here was an invisible curtain between us. Her eyes, more gray than blue at the moment, were turned in on whatever there was inside her. She began to scare me.

Abruptly, as if roused from a kind of stupor, she jumped up and began to clear the table. She had a phobia about cleaning up as soon as a meal was over. I picked up plates and followed her into the kitchen.

"Now it's after dinner," I said.

"Can't you see I'm busy?"

"The dishes can wait."

"The boys," she said.

"They can't hear us in here with that racket on the television. Or we can go to our room."

Stacking dishes in the dishwasher, Sally ignored me. I had a sense of her hiding from me. Then, as if realizing who I really was, she turned and put her hand on my chest.

"I'm sorry, Caleb." She called me by my name when she wanted to be especially friendly; otherwise I was *dear* and occasionally *darling*. "I didn't intend to mention it at all till the children were asleep. But you guessed there was something—I wasn't exactly subtle in the car, was I?—and if I tell you anything at all, you'll want to see them right away. I mean, it's better not to start till the children are in bed."

"See who, for God's sake?"

"Please, dear, later," she said.

I made a grumbling sound and left her there with the dishes. As she wanted me to. I spent three minutes looking at television with the boys, then went into our bedroom.

I would want to see *them* again, she had said. Had she meant people or things? And Chuck had said she had been doing something with a pillow.

I pulled the bedspread back from the two pillows and looked under them and stuck my hands into the pillowcases. Nothing. I searched under the bedspread and the electric blanket and the top sheet, then under the bottom sheet and the mattress, then under the bed. I looked in the closet and in the drawers of her dresser.

This was ridiculous and I was making myself ridiculous. I straightened the bed, feeling somewhat guilty, and returned to the kitchen, where Sally was scrubbing a pot.

The little white radio over the worktable was on. Normally while she worked in the kitchen she listened to the simpleminded music of adolescents. This time she was tuned in on a New York City station devoted wholly to news; the local station went off the air at seven. Standing in the doorway, I listened for whatever she was waiting to hear. At the moment there was the weather report.

Suddenly, with her back still to me, she said like a mouse squeaking, "Oh, my God!"

She had parted the gauzy curtains on the high window over the sink and was staring at something outside. I leaped to her side. A police car had stopped in front of our house.

"Sally!" I said, putting my hand on her shoulder. I felt her tremble.

Chief of Police Nate Messner got out of the car.

"Are you expecting him?" she said thinly.

"No. But so what?"

"Of course." She let the curtains fall together and reached up to adjust the pleats. "For a moment I forgot who you are these days," she said with a nervous giggle.

But she kept fingering the curtains, keeping her back to me. Then the doorbell rang and I went to answer it.

"Evening, Mr. Dawson," Chief Messner said. "Hope I'm not disturbing you at dinner."

His manner of speaking was to punch out words like jabs to the jaw. Everything about him was brisk and crisp. For a cop close to retirement age, he kept himself slim and wiry. His gold star glistened; so did his uniform buttons and his shoes. I had a feeling he didn't take me quite seriously, but we got along.

Anyway, so far. It was only a month since the new Village Board of Trustees had met to organize itself and I had been persuaded to accept the chairmanship of our fifteen-man police department for no better reason than that the man I had defeated at the polls had held it.

"We've finished eating," I said. "Come in."

"Can't. My missus is waiting with dinner. I'm on my way home."

I closed the door behind me and stepped out on the narrow concrete strip present-day architects (all evidently reared in high-rise city apartments) believed to be a substitute for a front porch.

"What's it about, Chief?"

"I stopped off to give you a copy of the men's proposals for their new contract. Just got it from Sergeant Al Newsome."

As he dug a slim transparent folder out of a manila envelope, I heard behind me a slight creaking. I didn't have to glance around to know the door I had just shut was now slightly open so that she could hear what we said.

I took the folder from him and went through the act of running my eyes over the first of the mimeographed pages. Then I said, "I'll have to study this."

"The main provision is they're asking a thirty percent increase over the next three years—ten percent a year."

I whistled. "They don't want much. Let's see, at present our patrolmen are making around twelve thousand a year."

"After three years on the force, Mr. Dawson."

"Well, that's most of them," I said. "If my arithmetic is right, what they're asking for is well over fifteen thousand in the third year, not counting fringe benefits and overtime, and the higher ranks will be getting proportionate increases. What's your opinion, Chief?"

"It's not my decision, but I'm on their side. The men are hoping you'll be too."

"Within reason," I said, trying to sound like a hard-headed executive instead of a mere intellectual type. "I'll have to study this."

"I brought it so you could, Mr. Dawson. I'm also taking a copy to the mayor."
I walked with him to his car. Neighbors gardening in the predusk watched me being consulted by their resplendent chief of police. Most of them had voted for me; I had done well in my own district. At his car, I said wryly, "And I ran on an economy platform."

"There's no such thing these days," he said. "The men need more money."

"Don't we all?" I said.

When I returned to the front door, I saw it was again closed all the way. And inside, Sally was going through the shrill nightly routine of telling the boys there would be no more television till they finished their homework. She drove them into the room they shared. The third bedroom was a combination study for me and a guest room by virtue of a sofa bed.

Quiet prevailed. She came into the living room, where I was sunk in the wing chair. Without glancing at me, she went to the sofa and flopped down on it and wearily put her head back.

The kitchen radio was still on, turned up loud. Somebody was explaining the machinations of gold speculators.

I said, "Why did the police car frighten you?"

"I wasn't frightened."

"You were."

She looked at me, and I was startled to see her angry. "Fifteen thousand dollars for policemen, but all they pay a trustee is fifteen hundred a year."

"Being a policeman is a livelihood. Being a trustee isn't."

"And what's being an editor? The police come for a tremendous raise to a man who can't get even a small one at the job he calls his livelihood."

"I don't give raises. It's up to the entire board. And I've been with Lakeview only nine months."

"Thirteen thousand a year," she sneered. "Why, an ordinary cop will be making a lot more."

"Maybe cops are more important than editors."

"Oh, yes, be clever. What does your wit get us? And how important are schoolteachers? Everybody is supposed to feel sorry for the poor starving schoolteachers, like for policemen. Look at George Huntley. They say he's the worst teacher in school, but he makes over nineteen thousand and he'll have a marvelous pension and he's home by three o'clock and his summers off and no end of holidays throughout the year. And who was president of the P.T.A. and going around agitating for the teachers to get a lot more money while he had just lost his own job and couldn't find another? You do more for everybody else than for your own family."

"If my family is not exactly rich, we're not exactly destitute."

"We're the poorest people I know," she said. "I've lost count of how many times you were out of work since we were married. Five months last year, living on unemployment insurance and borrowed money it will take years to pay back. We can't afford orthodontia for Chuck. We can't have a second car so I don't have to be your chauffeur as well as your housemaid. All our friends take trips abroad. We haven't been once. I'm sick and tired of not having anything."

"Listen!" I said. "I'm now making fourteen thousand five hundred with my trustee's pay. That's a hell of a lot more than most people make."

"You don't have to shout at me."

She had also been shouting, but it didn't count with her. She was good at putting me on the defensive, usually about money. Deliberately or not, she had switched the subject from herself to me. Whatever I said now would only lead to more bickering about nothing pertinent to what was really bothering her. So I slouched lower in the wing chair and kept my mouth shut.

She went along with the truce. She picked up a magazine from the coffee table and leafed through the pages. In the kitchen the radio spoke of the world's troubles.

After a while I went to the telephone table in the corner of the dinette and dialed Gordon Tripp's number.

In my briefcase was the manuscript he had submitted to me a couple of weeks ago—a paste-up of tearsheets for a proposed volume of his collected poems. He was a friend of sorts. We exchanged literary gossip when we bumped into each other in the village; we now and then found ourselves at the same gatherings; once he had been to our house for dinner. He lived nearby, and I could kill an hour (which badly needed killing) by returning the manuscript to him in person. If he was home.

A busy signal. I hung up.

"Who're you calling?" Sally asked from the living room.

"Gordon Tripp. His line is busy. I want to tell him I'm turning down his book."

Sliding in their sockets, her eyes followed me from the dinette back to the wing chair.

"You're really going to reject it?"

"You know I was never convinced he rated this kind of book."

"Gordon is a very good poet," she said when I was seated.

"Nowadays everybody is a poet who writes uneven lines and uses dirty words for punctuation."

"That's not fair. He's in all the magazines and he's had three books of his poems published. You're prejudiced against him."

"Why would I be prejudiced?"

"You told me you don't like him."

"That was the evening he was here for dinner and used foul language in front of the children. You resented it too." I drew in my breath. "For God's sake, are we going to have another fight, and about a half-assed poet at that?"

"Who's being vulgar now?"

"I'm sorry," I said tartly. "I forgot I'm not a poet."

I went and tried Gordon Tripp's number again, mostly to give myself an excuse to avoid further conversation, if conversation was what it was. Still busy. I hung up and stood in the dinette, not knowing what to do with myself.

Sally was taking her shoes off. If this had been an ordinary evening, she would have done that a lot earlier. Tucking her legs under her, she said, "Dear, don't you usually mail a rejected manuscript back to the author?"

"Usually an author doesn't bring it to my house. I think I owe it to him to return it personally and tell him why to his face."

"Are you going there tonight?"

"Not unless I let him know in advance I'm coming. I'd rather not walk in on him in the sack with one of his playmates."

That at least was nothing she could argue about. She turned a page in the magazine, and I came back to the chair.

Sooner than he should have, Brandy appeared, ready for more television. Chuck was only minutes behind. For once I didn't bother to check their homework; let them make their own mistakes. So on went television, and all four of us watched a drama for the entire family (togetherness) in which any number of people were slugged and tormented and slaughtered. When it was over, Brandy was sent off to bed, and half an hour later Chuck's time was up.

Sally came back from tucking them in and stood in the doorway from the hall looking at me as if deciding who I was. I noticed for the first time that her bangs were shorter, trimmed this morning in the beauty parlor, so that part of her brow was visible in the tawny frame made by her shoulder-length hair.

"Sit down and tell me," I said.

"Come into our room."

I tagged after her. The chattering radio voice became a vague muttering in the house when she closed the bedroom door. I sat down on the bed.

"This better be good," I said.

She slid open the door at her side of the very wide closet. From the top shelf she took down a cardboard hatbox decorated with black lilies. She put it on her dresser and removed two hats. Whatever she was after was under the hats. When she turned, she had a leather pouch in her hand. She sat down on the other side of the bed and pulled open the drawstring and turned the pouch upside down.

The contents spilled out and lay dazzling and incredible between us.

3

There were six pieces—five if you counted the pair of earrings as one. Aside from the three-strand pearl necklace, they consisted mostly of diamonds in platinum and gold settings.

I said, "These can't be real."

"How would you know?" Sally said pugnaciously.

I picked up the bracelet. It had a dozen and more large diamonds, some square and some pear-shaped, and each facet caught the overhead light. It quite dazzled me, but what did that mean? As she had implied, I was anything but an expert.

"Are they real?" I asked her.

"They must be."

I dropped the bracelet as if it had suddenly become too hot to hold. It fell between the brooch and the ring.

"Where did you get them?"

"I found them."

Of course she had found them. What then?

"Where?"

"At Brook Shopping Center. When I came out of the beauty parlor and went to unlock the car. The pouch was right there on the ground."

And all the time as she spoke her eyes were fixed on the jewels with an expression of mingled awe and cupidity.

My heart thumped. I said, "Did you know what you were driving away with?"

"Well, I did look in the pouch when I was in the car."

"And you didn't try to find the owner?"

Sally's head lifted, and her very kissable mouth was sullen. "What was I supposed to do, go all over the shopping center and ask people if they had lost valuable jewels?"

"You know damn well what I mean. You should have taken them to the police. Instead you brought them home and hid them."

"Of course I hid them. I couldn't leave them out on the dinette table, could I?"

"At least you could have told me right away."

"Well, I'm telling you now."

Her voice had grown shrill, and mine loud. We were letting our nerves instead of our heads do the talking for us. I made an effort to control mine.

"All right, let's go back to you finding the pouch," I said almost quietly. "What did you think when you saw what was in it?"

"Think?"

"Jewels like this aren't carried around by somebody going shopping in the Grand Union. Didn't it occur to you that the one place in the shopping center they would be taken to or from was the bank?"

"Of course it occurred to me. A safe-deposit box. I was parked pretty close to the beauty parlor and the bank is two doors from it." Her round little jaw jutted. "I'm not as stupid as you think, dear."

"And so what did you do?"

"I sat in the car waiting."

"Why didn't you go to the bank to try to find out who lost it?"

She folded her legs under her and leaned back against the headboard. Her hair fell over one eye.

"I felt I ought to wait in the car," she said. "If she'd dropped the pouch on the way to the bank, she'd miss it when she went to put it in the safe-deposit box and come right out to look for it. I had found it on the left side of my car and there was a car parked on the next space on my left. That could be hers. Then after about ten minutes a woman with two small children came to it with a shopping cart full of groceries. It was her car and she drove off, so she couldn't be the one, and I was sure then that the woman who had lost it had not been taking it to the bank but from the bank when it had fallen out of her handbag as she—"

"Hold it," I said. "You're way ahead of me. How did you know it was a woman and the pouch had fallen out of her handbag?"

"It stands to reason. Things don't fall out of a man's pocket as easily as out of a woman's handbag. A man has lots of pockets and he wouldn't keep the pouch in the same pocket as his keys. But a woman carries all her things in her bag and it has a wide opening and is often crammed full. Dear, do you remember the time I lost my wallet and hours later you came across it in our driveway?"

"Uh-huh."

"We figured out how it must have happened. Remember? I opened my handbag to take out my keys, and as I bent over to unlock the car door my bag was still open and it tilted and my wallet fell out without my noticing. The identical thing must have happened with the pouch. She had taken it from her safe-deposit box and dropped it in her handbag on top of everything else, and it fell out as she was unlocking the door of her car. Almost always the driver locks and unlocks the front left door, and that was where I found it, near my left door, and that meant I was parked in the same spot as she had been. I must have pulled in after she had driven off. Doesn't that make sense?"

"I guess so. How close to our car was the pouch?"

"Practically under it. I didn't see it when I left the car because I was walking away from it. When I came back, it was in my line of vision. My first impression was that it was just a piece of rag."

"What made you pick it up?"

"I think the drawstring caught my eye. But really, dear, what do the details matter? It got there somehow and I found it."

"But you're full of details."

"There's been little else on my mind," she said, brushing her hair from her eye.

Little else on her mind when earlier in the living room she had brought up my deficiencies as a breadwinner while in her hatbox lay riches. And I stared down at the ring—at the single immense emerald-cut diamond gripped by platinum claws. It made the two-carat engagement ring on Sally's finger (for which I'd blown a good part of my army severance pay fourteen years ago) look like a bauble on a Woolworth tray. I was being probed and tested.

By her? By myself?

I said, "The important details are what you did, not what you thought. You were up to where the woman in the next car drove away with her children and her groceries, and that convinced you that the owner of the pouch was long gone. What did you do then?"

"I drove home."

"Just like that?"

"There was no sense waiting any longer, was there?"

"And no sense going a quarter of a mile out of your way to the police station. That was what you should have done, and you damn well know it."

"And you're acting just like a policeman," she flared up. "What are you doing, practicing the third degree on me just because you've been put in charge of them? Are you trying to make me feel like a criminal?"

"I don't have to make you feel like one. You felt like one when Chief Messner pulled up to the house. You thought you had been seen picking up the pouch and that he was coming after you."

Huddled against the headboard, she watched one of her fingers stroke the smooth brown leather of the pouch. Like a lover's caress. And said nothing.

"Sally! Why not the police?"

"I... well..." Lifting her head and giving me another thrust of her jaw, she said firmly, "I'm human. I couldn't resist taking them home for a real good look at them."

"And two or three hours later you were still looking at them here on this bed when Chuck barged in and you stuffed them under the pillow and bawled him out."

"Oh, he told you."

"I questioned him. That's right, just like a cop. I had to find out from somebody what the hell was going on."

The hair was back over her face. Her breath tossed a tendril as she said, "Chuck startled me by opening the door so suddenly. I nearly jumped out of my skin."

"Like somebody surprised at counting the loot," I said.

Sally shrank into herself, and I thought she was going to burst into tears, and my heart went out to her. Here on the bedspread was the stuff of dreams—the pot of gold, the buried treasure, the winning lottery ticket—and wouldn't that dream have possessed anybody at that stunning moment in the car when she had opened the pouch? And how immune from it was I?

"I'm sorry, honey, I shouldn't have said that." Leaning over the glittering things causing this trouble, I stroked her ankle. "The police will have lots of questions, so let's go over the facts as you know them. Okay?"

Solemnly she nodded.

"Do you know the exact time you found the pouch?" I asked.

"I can't say exactly. I had a ten o'clock appointment at the beauty parlor and arrived on time. I was there about an hour."

"Did you go straight to the car?"

"I stopped off at the drugstore. No more than five minutes."

"From there you went to the car and found the pouch?"

"Yes."

"And then sat in the car ten minutes, you said?"

"Maybe a bit longer."

"So it was about eleven-thirty when you got home."

"Just about."

"Then what did you do?"

"Nothing, really. I kept taking them out of the pouch and looking at them. I tried them on. Every piece. I imagined myself a grand lady at a ball. Caleb, try to understand. I had never even been close to anything like these."

I could understand. Maybe I understood more than was good for us. I found myself wiping sweaty hands on my shirt.

"And all the time the radio on," I said, "to find out who the owner was and how valuable they were."

"Yes."

"What would you have done if the radio had mentioned the owner?"

"What I had been doing, I suppose. Waiting for you to come home. I needed you, darling."

"So then I was home and you didn't tell me."

"I couldn't in the car with Brandy there, could I?" she said earnestly. "And then I did have to get dinner on the table. And then I thought it best to wait till the boys were asleep. I knew you'd argue and yell. We needed privacy and time to discuss it and decide what to do."

Excuses, I thought, to put off disruption of the dream.

"Do?" I said like a delayed echo. "Is there anything but one thing to do?"

She had nothing to say to that. Bending from the hips, she scooped the jewels together in a heap with her hands.

I stood up and took two steps from the bed and turned. "It's over ten hours since you found them. What reason can we give for having taken that long to return them?"

"You're the boss of the police," she said without looking up. "They come to you for raises."

"That's right, and it makes me especially vulnerable. Nobody will believe your explanation for the delay."

"You don't either." Her shoulders remained hunched over that glittering heap; she spoke down to it. "Why do we have to explain anything to anybody? I mean..."

Her voice dribbled off without saying what she meant. She didn't have to say it.

I turned away. I went to the side window to give me something to do with myself, and looked out at the evergreen growing close to the window. The previous owner had planted it as a seedling. I had trimmed the top to keep it from blocking the window, but what that had done was thicken and widen it. Again it was blocking part of the window. Some day I would have to convince myself to cut it down completely.

At my back was Sally with her dream, and I had a physical sense of being drawn into it.

"Probably there will be a reward," I said, turning from the window. "If they're real."

"Oh, they must be real." She had pulled open the mouth of the pouch; she shifted herself closer to that overwhelming display of possible wealth. "Would she keep them in a bank vault if they weren't?"

"We don't actually know if she did. Or if it's a woman. Or if they're not glass and paste. Why hadn't there been anything on the local radio news if they're worth very much?"

"She may not have missed them yet."

One by one she was dropping them back into the pouch—the brooch shaped like a thistle with a gold stem, the pendant earrings, the bracelet, the ring. Her fingers lingered on each before letting go. Then only the pearl necklace was left. She let the triple strand writhe like snakes from one hand to the other, where it ended up curled on her palm.

"I wonder if they're natural or cultured," she said.

"Or paste," I said. Hoping that after all they were.

"No, you can see they're not. Even if they're cultured, they're worth thousands of dollars. Look at their size and how perfectly they're matched. And if they are natural..." She looked up at me standing over her. As if the touch of the pearls effected a miraculous cure, the lines of strain were gone. Her blue-gray eyes glistened as when we made love. "Dear, how much would a reward be?"

"I don't know. A hundred dollars. A thousand. It depends on what they're worth and how generous the owner is."

"It could be nothing at all."

"That's right."

The necklace slithered into the pouch. She pulled the drawstring tight and got off the bed and replaced the pouch under the hats in the hatbox and the hatbox on the closet shelf.

Then we went into the kitchen to hear if the radio had anything to say. It hadn't.

4

I walked the mile and a half to police headquarters. Going there not with what Sally had found but to use my position as an elected public servant to find out if the loss had been reported and by whom.

"No matter what you hear, don't tell anybody anything," she had said when I had been leaving the house. "Come home and let's discuss it first." And I had nodded and had gone out into the night.

I was walking instead of driving because I had to be alone with myself to think. But as I followed the beam of my flashlight along the side of the black road, all I could think about was what Sally had been thinking about since noon. How nice and cozy it would be for once in our lives to be ahead on money instead of behind.

I reached the center of the village where there were lights and sidewalks. And the shopping center. Not a car in the huge parking area. Nobody searching for something lost this morning; that had been done already or not yet done. I looked at the dark bank, at the dark beauty parlor close to it, at the dark everything, and I hurried by as if past a graveyard where ghosts lurked.

We were haunted tonight, Sally who was waiting at home and I who was passing the scene of the—the what?

Cross the road, turn a corner, go another three blocks, and there was the sixty-year-old red-brick municipal building.

Police headquarters occupied a section of the ground floor and a good part of the basement. In the main room, behind the railing and the high counter dividing the reception part from the working part, Sergeant Andy Swan sat at one of the three desks pecking at a typewriter with two thick fingers. The radio cackled in the way of police radios, and the teletype clicked for a line or two and stopped.

"Good evening, Andy," I said.

He glanced up lazily, saw who I was, and jumped to his feet. It was pleasant to be given that kind of respect. I wasn't used to it anywhere else.

"Evening, Mr. Dawson." He was a lumbering, heavy-faced man who could have been typecast for what he was, a small-town police sergeant. He came to the counter and noticed the flashlight in my hand. "Trouble with your car, sir?"

"No. I was taking a walk and stopped in."

"You walked all the way from your house?"

"It's not over three miles both ways."

I could sense him wondering if the new chairman of the department was some kind of nut. In the suburbs you walked only if by chance you didn't have wheels available.

"Come in and take a rest, Mr. Dawson."

"I'm staying only a minute. It seems pretty quiet here tonight."

"Most nights are."

At his left the squawking radio produced an articulate voice. "Andy, the streetlight on Pine and Ledge is broken again."

Swan turned to it. "Okay, Bill." He wrote on a pad. "Those kids with their rocks," he told me. "It goes in streaks, like a rampage. Last month sixteen were broken in one night. This is another one of those weeks—eleven lights since Sunday."

"Has that been the most dramatic thing tonight, a broken light?"

"Dramatic, sir? It depends on what you call dramatic. A speeder. Two cars smacked on the highway, but nobody hurt bad. A complaint about a dog barking. Some high school kids having a noisy party. In the middle of the week and parents off somewhere. Ralph Caruso answered that one. He thinks they were smoking pot, but don't they all? First thing, they flush it down the john." His eyes mocked me. "It's seldom—ah—dramatic like on the TV."

And no lost jewels. If not since he had gone on duty, what about before that? How could I ask him?

I said, "Would you mind letting me take a look at the report book?"

Sergeant Swan's heavy face froze into a deadpan. He was putting me down as the busybody kind of chairman.

"Sure thing, sir." He brought the book to the counter and opened it and turned it around to me.

I pretended to study each of that day's entries, though I could see at a glance there had been no report today of anything lost. When I thought I had spent enough time on it, I looked up with a forced grin. "I suppose you're wondering why I'm curious."

"It's your right, sir."

"Chief Messner complains we're understaffed. I want to see how busy the department is during a typical day."

"We sure can use one more man," he said, warming up to me. "The blotter doesn't tell half the story. Like traffic, which is a big part of our job."

"Pretty routine stuff, though."

"That's what police work is, sir—routine. We don't have all the violence and robberies like in the cities. We're peaceful—most of the time. You have to give the department credit for a lot of that. Of course, sometimes somebody gets killed or—"

"Murder?" I said. "I don't remember any murder in Mount Birch."

"Who said murder? Last one was seven years ago. We don't kill each other in this town except with cars, and we do plenty of that, especially the young ones. A drowning now and then and that suicide last year. But like what I was saying, traffic is our big headache. What with vacations and sickness and all, one more patrolman..."

Sergeant Swan had turned positively voluble. Also amiable; the road to popularity was lined with cash. Needless to say, pretty soon he got around to the new contract, and how reasonable the men's proposals were compared to what policemen in the cities all around were demanding and getting. And I listened with only half an ear and nodded and grunted as required and thought of how everything began and ended with money.

Money for everybody, as Sally would say, but us.

5

Sally was in bed when I returned home. She lay flat on her back, not sleeping and not reading, just lying there like somebody in a sickbed.

"The police haven't heard a thing," I told her.

She sighed and closed her eyes. With relief? Could she be so foolish as to hope nobody would claim the jewels?

"You were gone a long time," she said.

"I walked."

"So that's it. I thought something had happened."

I was hanging up my jacket in my part of the closet. I looked at her over my shoulder. She hadn't opened her eyes; her voice sounded as if she were muttering in her sleep.

"You mean something happened like me telling them we had the jewels?" I said.

"I waited and waited. All kinds of things ran through my head." Her voice roused. "Caleb, I hope you were very careful about what you did say."

"Uh-huh."

She pulled the cover to her chin and curled up on her side.

As for me, there was the preparing for bed routine. Lock the front and side doors. Turn off the lights she had left on all over the house. Look in on the boys. Get out of my clothes and into my pajama bottoms (I never wore the tops). Wash up and brush my teeth. Wind the alarm clock. Switch on the baseboard night light and switch off the bedside table lamp. Then at last in bed with her.

Usually Sally turned immediately to me, to snuggle in the curve of my arm with her head on my chest and her thigh across my middle. Not tonight. She was again on her back, but she stayed where she was, keeping distance between us as when we quarreled and didn't make up for a while and spent the night in bed divided by a kind of sword.

And I didn't move to her. I lay by myself with my jitters, and I knew she was doing the same.

After a while I said, "I suppose she hasn't looked in her handbag yet. She must be taking for granted the pouch is in it."

"That's likely," Sally murmured in the semi-darkness.

"Odd, though. Why would she have gone to take them from the vault this morning if she didn't intend to wear them tonight?"

"I can think of a number of reasons," she said. "The affair was called off or she's taking them on a trip, or anything. I think we ought to stop thinking and go to sleep."

"Right."

The refrigerator went on in the kitchen. It was irritatingly noisy; I hadn't called in a repairman to quiet it because whether he could or couldn't he would charge an arm and a leg. Out in the street a car door slammed and a girl shouted, "See you, Stanley," and the damn-fool kid driver peeled off with a roar.

"Caleb," Sally said.

"Yes?"

"How much do you think they're worth?"

"Forget it for tonight."

"Fifty thousand dollars? Maybe more?"

"Maybe a lot less," I said. "Weren't you the one who said we should sleep?"

"I can't."

I shifted closer to her and put my hand on her. As always, her shorty nightgown was up about her waist. I moved my hand. She began to quiver, a sign that she was ready and eager.

But what she said was, "No, don't."

"Why not? We're not falling asleep."

"I don't want to."

"It will do us good. It relaxes us."

"No!" She grasped my wrist with both hands and clamped her legs together. "I'm not in the mood tonight. I'm too much on edge."

"Oh, all right," I said huffily.

I turned my back to her, hating her a little for her rebuff. It was what we needed—anyway, what I needed—and it was the easiest thing for her to give.

The refrigerator cut off. No sound left in the house and in the bed. Outside, insects hummed.

Sally got out of bed. By the dim night light I saw her float out of the room like a wraith in her scant white nightgown. She came back with water in a paper cup.

"I took a phenobarbital," she said. "I brought you one."

"What's mine for, to quiet down my libido?"

"It's better than staying up all night worrying."

"I'm not worrying," I snapped at her.

"Please take it." She sat down on the bed, holding out the cup and the tiny pill.

I popped it into my mouth and washed it down. Then she bent over and kissed me. A brief, chaste kiss—the kind she gave her other boys when she put them to bed. I groped for her breasts tumbling out of the low neckline. She pulled back and stood up and went around to her side of the bed.

But at least, when she was again under the cover with me, she cuddled her body to mine. I felt myself both accepted and rejected. Eventually the pills took effect.

Thursday

When the alarm clock woke us, we lay silently for those few minutes before it was time to get up and start the day. Sally kept her back curled to me as if avoiding me, and I had nothing new to say or that now in the morning I was prepared to say. Silence had its own eloquence.

We got out of bed at the same time. We stood on opposite sides, I yawning from a restless night and she putting on a robe. She looked no more refreshed than I felt. She pulled up the blind of the window beside the headboard and stared out at the back yard and spoke at last. "It's going to be another nice day." I grunted agreement and went into the bathroom to shave.

Fully dressed, I came into the dinette to find the boys at the table and Sally pouring their orange juice. In the kitchen the radio was turned on loud to the news. We looked at each other and she shook her head. The boys did most of the talking during breakfast.

I gulped down my second cup of coffee and went to take the car out of the garage. I had to honk the horn twice before she came dashing out in slippers and a lightweight coat over her robe. She would rush back, after she had dropped me off at the station, to see that the boys were properly dressed and send them off to school. A second car would come in mighty handy.

Alone together again as we drove through the awakening village, we clung to silence like a shield. Till we were on the station plaza and had pecked at each other's lips and my hand was on the door handle.

"Call me at the office if you hear anything," I said.

"I will."

I got out of the car and paused at the open door. "Be careful what you say on the line. Lucille listens to everything."

"I know." Sally wore almost no make-up, and when she was pale with strain, as she was this morning, she was very pale. "Good-bye, dear."

"Good-bye, honey."

I closed the door and went down to the station tracks.

2

Lakeview Press was a venerable and respected book publishing house. Some fifteen months ago it had been taken over by Paragon Materials, Inc., to become a division of that glamorous conglomerate of drugstores, trade magazines, parking lots, radio stations, real estate holdings, and what all not. About the first act of the new management had been to fire most of the editorial staff, beginning with the old-timers, for what was called an infusion of fresh blood. Which fresh blood had included mine.

I had gotten the job nine months ago because I had been somewhat acquainted with Edward Martaine, president of the whole Paragon shebang. Nothing like influence. I was taken on as an associate editor at fifteen hundred dollars less than my previous job. Big deal.

The 7:57 A.M. arrived at Grand Central on or about 8:44. This morning I had escaped most of my daily quota of brain-washing by the *Times* (it was the only game in town) by spending less than ten minutes on it. For the rest I looked out of the window and thought about having some real money for the first time in my life.

Maybe.

The train lurched and we were there. I plucked my briefcase from the overhead rack and drifted on the tide of nine-to-five mankind out of the train and up the ramp and out of the station and along skyscraper-lined streets. After a number of minutes, normally thirteen, I looked up and there was the Paragon Building. A glass monolith glittering in the morning sun like a gigantic jewel.

A jewel. Even my cliché figure of speech.

This morning there was a picket line, the first in several weeks. The window washers this time. Their placards didn't say what they wanted; it would be more of whatever they had. Everybody wanted more. Like the Mount Birch police. Like Sally.

Like me.

Careful not to look any picket in the face, I slipped through the line into the lobby's buzzing swarm and jammed myself into the express elevator.

Among the things that had been done to Lakeview Press by Paragon had been to move it to these sterilized quarters from the moldering dignity of the three-story brick building it had occupied since the turn of the century. We had most of the thirty-third floor to ourselves, with me squeezed into a tiny bit of it.

At least, though, my office was on a window side. More minor editorial workers had interior walls, and office workers were dumped into the huge center room. Not that I had a whole window to myself. A frosted glass partition running two-thirds of the way to the ceiling cut it in two; another editor, Stu Stitchman, was in possession of the other half. A senior editor at that, but in our company the main distinction between a senior editor and an associate editor was a couple of thousand dollars a year. We shared not only a window but a secretary.

Her name was Lucille Treacher. At her desk, which stood outside and between Stu's door and mine, she was opening a container of coffee. Since it was only a few minutes after nine, she needed it to sustain her till the official coffee break at ten.

She was in her mid-twenties, married last year and this year separated from her husband, chubbily pretty and given to bodices which were pleasantly distracting as she leaned over her pad when taking dictation. Her shorthand was adequate if one spoke slowly and spelled out the hard words, and she could type a letter with no more than three or four errors to a page. Because of her, Stu and I were the envy of the other editors.

"Oh, Caleb, can I get you coffee?" she said when I paused to say good morning. "I found the wagon on the thirty-first floor."

Normally my breakfast coffee held me till ten, but this was not a normal morning. "All right, thanks."

I entered my office. The efficiency boys had come and measured the length of my legs and the extent of my reach (all right, if not literally, virtually) and had determined the maximum number of square inches required for me and my desk and my swivel chair, plus a typewriter table, two bookcases, a filing cabinet, two side chairs. I took off my jacket and loosened my necktie and scowled down at the jumble of manuscripts and proofs and memos and such completely covering my desk. On top of all that I had put my briefcase, and it was only then I realized that with my mind very much otherwise occupied, I had lugged Gordon Tripp's manuscript back with me.

When Lucille brought in my coffee—with a Danish I didn't particularly want—I told her to get Gordon Tripp on the phone.

"Did you return his manuscript to him last night like"—she caught herself, remembering that she no longer worked in advertising but in book publishing—"*as* you said you would?"

"It's here in my briefcase."

"Then you changed your mind about it?"

"I did not. I called him from my house to tell him I was coming over, but his line was busy. It was, in fact, busy twice and I didn't try again. By mistake I brought it back. It weighs a ton and I don't intend to keep dragging it back and forth. We'll return it the usual way, by mail, but I'd like to tell him in person I'm turning it down." I leaned back in my chair. "Have I anticipated all your questions?"

"I have to know what's going on for my manuscript record, don't I?"

"Now that you know, would you mind getting him on the phone for me?"

"Isn't it too early?" she said. "I mean, you know these writers. He's probably still asleep."

"Then wake him up. I get a kick out of starting a poet's day for him with bad news."

Lucille pulled strands of long loose hair from her face to give me the full benefit of her frown. "Caleb, you're in a rotten mood today."

"You're not my wife. You're being paid to bear with it."

"Don't I know. You owe me forty-five cents for the coffee and cake."

"Take it off the five bucks you borrowed from me last week."

"You *are* in a rotten mood," she said.

She didn't close the door after her. I got up and closed it. I had no end of urgent work, but all I did was sit and drink coffee and nibble Danish and wonder how long it would be before Sally heard anything.

My phone rang. Not Sally. Not Gordon Tripp either. One of my authors with the standard complaints. Why couldn't she or any of her friends find her recently published book in the bookstores? Why wasn't it being reviewed except in some papers down South she had never heard of? Where was the advertising she had been led to expect? I explained and appeased for a good fifteen minutes before I could induce her to say good-bye. Authors!

I licked up the crumbs of the Danish. A genuine pearl necklace that size could be ten, twenty thousand dollars. Even more. The brooch...

I heard Stu Stitchman arrive, singing out his hearty good mornings to Lucille and others and then noisily settling himself in his office next door. Unlike me, he adhered to an editor's prerogative to ignore regular office hours.

"Caleb, are you there?" he called over the partition.

"Yes."

"Last night I spent a little time on that Carlton novel you asked me to look over. By all means take it on."

"Don't tell me you liked it!"

"What's that got to do with it? It's up to his usual standard—incredibly bad. What's to the point is that he sells."

"I know. That's why I hesitate to turn it down. If only he knew a bit about writing."

"If he learned how to write, he'd rise to mediocrity and lose his public."

"Well, I'll see."

Soon after that the coffee break. I lined up at the wagon in the center room. With plastic cup in hand, I joined an editorial discussion on the chances of the Mets this year. I cited an expert, my son Chuck, who contended that once again they had traded themselves out of a pennant. Eventually we broke up to straggle back to work. At her desk Lucille said, "Mr. Tripp's line has been busy for practically an hour."

"At least that means he's home and awake," I said.

I stopped in my office long enough to pick up a magazine. I took it with me to my sanctum, the end booth in the men's room. Another fifteen minutes. When I returned, Lucille told me that Mr. Tripp's line was still busy.

I said, "No man talks that long. One of his broads must have spent the night with him." I moved on to my door and stopped. This wasn't one of my be-kind-to-authors days. "The hell with me talking to him, Lucille. I tried. He's not that special I can't do it by letter. Bring your book."

I dictated the routine empty words: "...afraid that for all its merit this collection of your poems does not fit in with our current publishing program... deeply regret... hope you'll be able to place it elsewhere... with best wishes..."

It was close to eleven when she brought in the letter for my signature. She took the manuscript out of my briefcase and bore it away.

Production called. The color separations for a travel book I was handling had come in. Though there was no urgency, I said I'd be right over. After I had okayed them, I sat with the production manager exchanging gripes about the idiots who ran the company. The morning was slipping by. On the way back I met Lucille looking for me.

Sally, I thought, urgently wanting me to call back.

"Mr. Martaine wants to see you right away," she said in a voice of awe. "He's in Mr. Atkinson's office."

The boss of bosses himself. Edward Martaine seldom came down to the thirty-third floor from the Paragon executive offices on the thirty-seventh floor. When he did, it wasn't for contact with associate editors. Now here he was waiting for me with Harve Atkinson, Lakeview's editorial director.

Was that good or bad? Publishing was in one of its business slumps—when wasn't it?—and there were rumors of impending cuts of the staff.

"Any idea what it's about?" I asked Lucille uneasily as we walked together down an aisle between desks.

"I asked Joy—Mr. Atkinson's secretary, you know—and she hasn't the faintest."

In my office I adjusted my tie and put on my jacket. My stomach was queasy with fear. There was nothing more insecure than the world of the written word. Seven jobs since I was out of college—magazine, book, radio, book, television, advertising, book. Musical chairs, we grimly called it, and between this chair and the previous one had been a gap of five awful months.

Though possibly a promotion, I told myself with a small lift in spirit as I set out for the front of the building where the offices of the Lakeview big shots were. But why in that case would Edward Martaine involve himself? I wasn't that important. Or that much of an acquaintance.

We were fellow villagers of Mount Birch, which would hardly have brought us together socially if not for the fact that his wife and I were fellow local activists. With lots of time and scads of money on her hands, Norma Martaine was perennial president of the Mount Birch Library Association, and I had been secretary for a couple of years before I had resigned the post to run for village trustee. As a result, Sally and I had been invited to several intimate (no more than twenty guests) cocktail parties at her home, and of course, we were always included among the couple of hundred guests at the annual affair the Martaines threw every summer on their sumptuous lawn for the local who's who.

For days before the one held last August, Sally had prodded me and rehearsed me to take advantage of the occasion to hit up the host for a job we so desperately needed at the time. He would be more amenable to a guest, she had insisted, than to somebody his wife merely knew who tried to get to see him at his place of business. So I had hovered near the great man till I had had a chance to get him alone as he came from the liquor table with a tall glass in each hand.

"Mr. Martaine, may I have a word with you?"

"Certainly, Carl."

"Caleb."

"I'm sorry. Caleb." He smiled affably. "Caleb Dawson," he said to make amends by showing he correctly recalled my second name.

He had a world-weary, well-conditioned face on a lean, well-conditioned body. Tennis and boating and all that. White jacket and dark ascot. A dozen years older than I. Master of all these acres and, hopefully, of my destiny.

"I realize this isn't the time and place, Mr. Martaine, but it's only for a minute. I hear Lakeview Press is taking on editors, and I'm a good one."

His smile remained, but it had become a different smile, the set smile of a host too polite to show annoyance with a guest. He glanced at the glasses in his hands, then said, "Our divisions run themselves in such matters. I suggest you make out an application with the Lakeview Personnel Department."

"I did months ago. Nothing happened, not even an interview. I thought that if you..."

My voice sounded wheedling to myself. Standing there humbly before him amid the sun-drenched gayety on the manicured lawn, I hated the son-of-a-bitch.

"Where are you working at present, Caleb?"

"I'm not. That's the point."

He nodded. "Send me your résumé with a covering letter. I have heard my wife speak highly of you. I will see what I can do."

"Thank you, Mr. Martaine."

I watched him head for a red maple under which stood a sinuous redhead (not his wife) with hair to the base of her spine. He gave her one of the two glasses and she gave him a peck on the cheek. She was a lot younger than his wife, though no more attractive. I hunted up Sally to tell her there was hope.

Since that August afternoon, there had been no occasion for Edward Martaine and me to say a word to each other, professionally or otherwise, except for good-mornings and how-are-yous when now and then we came face to face on the train or in the elevator. Now, in May, I was at the door on the other side of which he was waiting for me. Resenting my pounding heart, I knocked, then discreetly opened the door a bit and stuck my head in.

3

Behind his desk, twice the size of mine, Harve Atkinson, in a striped short-sleeved shirt, sat bald and plump as a Buddha. He said, "Come in, Caleb, and close the door."

His undersized mouth amid flaccid folds was tight as a gumdrop, a sign of discomfort that didn't make me feel any better. Here on the thirty-third floor he was definitely somebody, editorial director of the trade department and a Lakeview vice-president, but in the presence of the lean, precisely tailored man lounging on the leather sofa, he was not very much. I said good morning.

Edward Martaine nodded without cracking his face. He was one of the few men off television or a movie screen who wore a breast-pocket handkerchief to work. He looked at me as if he couldn't decide what to do with me.

I sat down on a padded wooden armchair and crossed my legs. Portrait of a man at ease among equals.

"Well, now," Harve said. "Caleb, Mr. Martaine questions one of your decisions."

"Please. I simply wish to discuss it." Martaine gave me a tired smile of reassurance. "Harve has explained to me the procedures concerning submitted manuscripts—that his approval is required to accept, but that an editor can reject on his own."

"This is true in theory, Mr. Martaine," Harve put in, "but let me make my own responsibility clear. I hold a weekly conference with each of my editors to review all he is doing so that I can keep on top of our entire editorial operation. In all fairness to Caleb, during our last discussion, held as recently as yesterday afternoon, he did mention he was rejecting Tripp's manuscript, and I saw no reason to disagree with his judgment."

Was this all it was about? I began to relax.

"There's no reason for anybody to be on the defensive," Martaine said. "It's not my policy to interfere in the routine decisions of responsible persons in any of our divisions. I merely said I would like to discuss this particular matter."

His voice almost died on that last sentence. He sounded bored with what he was saying. But I knew that sure as hell he was going to interfere or he wouldn't have had me in here in the first place.

I said, "I can't see any kind of market for the collected works of a third-rate poet."

"Yet knowing this, you took the manuscript from him for consideration."

"I didn't expect what I got. He's had three books of his poems published by Dean and Knight, and he's appeared in magazines from popular to esoteric. It was possible, just possible, that we would go for one of those slim volumes with low production costs and a high enough price to maybe break even. But what did he give me? Four hundred pages of everything he's ever had published in his books and magazines or both. Who does he think he is? He has to be either very good or have a big following. Neither is true. Who'll buy it?"

"I admire your devotion to the interest of the company rather than to that of a friend." Was there mockery in Martaine's voice? "But look at it this way. There's also Lakeview's image to be considered. Lakeview used to be a leading publisher of poetry. Our fall list has none."

"Our fall list hasn't a decent novel either." I was getting sore. Nobody, not even the Great God Martaine, was going to play games with me. I plunged on. "Talk about our image! We editors have been bombarded with memos bawling us out for thinking in terms of a dirty word like literature instead of an exalted word like sales. Right now I have on my desk an awful novel by Earl B. Carlton. I'm going to recommend it because it's the kind of garbage we've been panting for. Now all of a sudden I'm blamed because—"

"Caleb, try to understand Mr. Martaine," Harve broke in. Chiding me like an intemperate child. Next thing he would tell me (like Sally) not to shout. "Nobody is criticizing you. He is simply suggesting a sense of proportion. We want money-makers, of course we do. But publishing is a matter of prestige as well as dollars and cents."

"Some prestige Gordon Tripp will bring us!"

"I would differ with that," Martaine said. Voice low and listless, as if he couldn't care less. "Gordon may not be a major poet—how many are there?—but in my opinion he's a good minor poet."

In his opinion, my eye! But why was I getting myself in a sweat? I knew and he knew that nothing being said was to the point. The point was that I was not the only fellow villager and acquaintance of Gordon Tripp in this room. That was one reality. Another reality was that it wasn't any of my money, merely my critical judgment. All there was for me to do was say yes, Mr. Martaine, as you wish, Mr. Martaine.

He was staring blankly at me. His blue eyes were weary and drab in the healthy tan of his face. He was waiting for me to be a proper wage-slave and say those words.

I didn't. I wouldn't. Let the son-of-a-bitch overrule me.

The phone rang. Like the bell ending a round in which I had been bruised if not battered. I uncrossed my legs.

"Yes?" Harve barked into the phone. His manner changed. "It's your wife, Mr. Martaine."

Languidly Martaine rose and took the phone from him and spoke half-leaning against the desk. "Yes, Norma... Have the police searched the parking lot yet?... What about the bank?... I see... Has Maxwell looked at the insurance policy?... I was aware of that... For God's sake, Norma, stop upsetting yourself."

There was more of the same, but I heard it as a mumbling from a distance. I recrossed my legs the other way and held myself together. The worst of it was that he was looking directly at me as he spoke to his wife. I turned my head to a window as if something had caught my attention on top of the high building across the street.

I shouldn't have been surprised. Few women in Mount Birch were rich enough to own such a pouchful of jewels, and Norma Martaine was certainly one of them.

He hung up. Our eyes met. Scowling, he said, "Dawson, do you know about this?"

Something inside me jumped. "Know about what?"

"My wife's jewelry."

"Jewelry?" I said. "What about it?"

"It's been lost or stolen."

He was standing over me. I almost cringed.

"Why do you expect me to know?" I said.

"You're our police commissioner." Tiredly he shook his head. "No, I'm not thinking. I had almost no sleep last night. The police weren't informed till this morning, and of course, your real job is here." He returned to the sofa and dropped down on it.

I had to fill the silence. "I'm not police commissioner."

"You're not? I'm sure I read in our local paper you were appointed after your election to the Village Board last month."

"My title is Committee Chairman of the Police Department. Every trustee has general supervision over a department, and I was given the police because the man I defeated had had it. Actually, the chief of police runs it." Enough of this chatter; I had killed time, I was in possession of myself. "You said lost or stolen. Doesn't your wife know?"

"She dropped them into her handbag when she took them from the bank vault yesterday. Her bag could have been picked, but she doesn't think it's possible. She went directly home from the bank; she wasn't near anybody. Knowing how careless she is, it's a reasonable assumption they fell out of her bag between the bank and the car." He snorted. "She'd lose her head if it weren't screwed on."

Harve spoke up then. "Were they very valuable?"

"Worth a quarter of a million, that's all."

Harve gasped. It would have been perfectly natural for me to have gasped too, but I was being very careful with my reactions. There was no blood in my fingertips.

"I suppose they're insured," I said.

"There's a policy for a quarter of a million. It is likely they have increased in value since the policy was taken out. I expect to take a substantial loss." Martaine took out his breast-pocket handkerchief and dabbed at his lips. "It's not only the money. It's the damn stupidity."

"A shame," Harve muttered appropriately. Then he cleared his throat. "Getting back to Tripp's book..."

What could be more unimportant now?

Briskly I said, "There's nothing to get back to. If it makes anybody feel any better to have me agree to doing it, sure, what the hell." I stood up. My legs were stiff, the muscles bunched with tension. "There's one thing. I mailed the manuscript back this morning with a rejection letter."

"It could still be in the mailroom," Harve said. "Use my phone."

I dialed my office code number. Lucille's voice. As I told her to hurry to the mailroom and retrieve the manuscript, Edward Martaine rose and said he was leaving. I gave him a small wave of my hand and he gave me a really bright smile. I was a good boy. *A quarter of a million dollars!* The door closed behind him.

4

Harve Atkinson heaved a sigh that jiggled his jowls. "Whee! That was really something."

"Yeah," I said. "I've never had my arm twisted so affably."

"Don't brood about it. I'm the one who'll be held responsible for an expensive clinker on my list. This won't do my budget any good."

"I saw the fight you put up," I said.

"What was there to fight about, for heaven's sake? If you want a pat on the back for standing up to Ed Martaine, you won't get it from me. I'm not so foolish as to fight for lost causes when a cause isn't worth fighting for in the first place. And don't give me that tired line about your critical integrity."

"All right then, I won't."

"There's one thing I don't understand," he said. "I recognize leverage when I see it. What's Gordon Tripp's?"

"He's a neighbor or a friend or something. The few times Sally and I were at parties at the Martaines', he was there."

"Exactly. So when he wasn't getting anywhere with you, he went running to—"

"Wait a minute," I said. "Gordon didn't know I was turning down his book. I hadn't spoken to him for a week, and the rejection letter was written only this morning."

"He got impatient. I don't have to tell you about authors. His leverage with you didn't seem to be doing it, so he used a bigger lever. Half an hour ago Ed Martaine phoned down and asked me what was being done about Gordon Tripp's book. I didn't know what he was talking about. In effect I said, 'Gordon who?' Then he said you were the editor, and I recalled that during our conference yesterday afternoon you'd mentioned in passing that this was one of the things you were turning down. When he heard that, he said he'd be right down to talk it over with both of us."

"Instead of summoning us up to his sanctum sanctorum?"

"Of course I said we'd come up to his office, but he said he was leaving the building and would stop off here."

"How very democratic of him," I said. "Noblesse oblige."

"Caleb, you give me a swift pain in the rear." Harve blew air out of his fat cheeks. "How do you think you got your job here? I never told you the details. Listen. Last summer I'd weeded down a long list of applicants to five. I was making up my mind which one I'd hire when I received a memo from Ed Martaine with your resumé attached to it. Just a few lines to the effect that I might want to consider one Caleb Dawson for an opening when there was one. Nothing else. Leaving it strictly up to me. Oh, yeah? You weren't any better qualified than any of the others, but guess who got the job? You know who, and in exactly the same way as Gordon Tripp is getting his book published. So do me a favor and stop acting morally superior."

A quarter of a million dollars in Norma Martaine's jewels in Sally's hatbox. "You're right, Harve," I said tonelessly and turned to leave.

"Before you go, Caleb, what's this about an Earl B. Carlton novel? You said something about it to Ed Martaine, but never to me. He's a Wisdom Brothers author, isn't he?"

"He's unhappy with them and wants to change. I had lunch last week with May Dortle. She's his agent and offered it to us. He'd just finished it."

"Why didn't you let me know?"

"I wanted to read it before discussing it. It's as bad as anything he's done."

"Is it worse?"

"I don't believe that's possible. I gave Stu the manuscript for his opinion. He let me have it this morning. He agrees on its quality and recommends we take it on."

"Earl B. Carlton," he said, pinching one of his chins. "I understand he does very well in paperback. What does he ask?"

"That's the rub. May insists on an advance of fifty thousand dollars."

Harve didn't turn a hair. "The paperback rights alone could cover that. Offer twenty-five thousand. If they balk, let me in on the bargaining."

"You haven't even read it."

"Spare me. I have confidence in you and Stu."

"It'll require a hell of a lot of editing."

"You're the editor, so edit."

"While Carlton takes the fifty thousand."

"What's the matter with you today? Everything gets your back up." The loose folds of his cheeks contorted into a sardonic grin. "We'll have something to make up our loss on Gordon Tripp." The grin broadened. "Speaking of losses, how can a woman simply lose a king's ransom in jewels?"

"To begin with, she has to have a husband who can afford to buy them for her."

"That she certainly has. I met her only once. Aside from being attractive, what kind of woman is she?"

"Very nice. Not unintelligent."

"But very, very careless."

"It would seem so," I said. "Anything else you want me for?"

He shook his head and I went.

I stopped off in the men's room. And as I stood there, Edward Martaine entered. Just as if he were anybody.

He must have dropped in briefly on somebody else on this floor after he had left Harve's office, and then, not having a key to the Lakeview executive washroom, had come in here to do his thing with us common folk. Of whom at the time I was the only one present, since it was past noon and most of the staff had gone to lunch. He gave me his weary greeting nod and placed himself at the urinal next to mine.

"What did you call your position with our police department?" he said as he unzipped. "Chairman, I believe. Whatever your modesty, I would think it carries considerable authority."

"I didn't say it didn't carry some."

"Then I wish you would see to it that those Keystone Kops make a real effort to locate my wife's jewels."

Standing shoulder to shoulder with him, I was as nervous as any thief. Or had been till he had said that. Where the hell did he come off giving me orders about something outside my job with Lakeview Press?

"They're not Keystone Kops," I said crisply. "It's a good small-town department, better than our taxpayers are willing to pay for."

His head came up from watching what he was doing, and his mouth smiled at the corners. "That's telling me off."

"Mr. Martaine, all I meant—"

"No, you were perfectly right." He stepped away from the urinal. "I mustn't try to spread the blame for the consequences of my wife's stupidity."

Though he had finished, he continued to stand close to me. We could have touched each other as I zipped up. His eyes rested on me, pale and steady and expressionless, and a fantastic notion popped into my head. That he knew who had the jewels and had hung around after leaving Harve's office to get me off by myself. Which had to be impossible on every score—and anyway, without another word on the subject he was moving to the washbasins.

It was I, after all, who knew who had them and should grasp this opportunity to learn more. I joined him at the basins, as he had joined me at the urinals, taking the one next to his, and as I turned on the water I said, "Why didn't you call the police at the time the jewels were lost?"

A familiar question. Last night I had asked it of Sally when she had told me about finding them, instead of with her I had said *found* instead of *lost*.

Edward Martaine gave me a sidelong frown. "You said you weren't in touch with the police. How do you know when they were lost?"

"You said in Harve Atkinson's office she had taken them from a bank safe-deposit box."

"Did I?"

I thought I remembered he had. I had to be very careful in my probing. The water ran over my hands.

"You said something like it, Mr. Martaine. Maybe I'm mistaken."

"No. She did keep them in the bank."

"So it must have been yesterday during banking hours that she went for them, and she must have lost them before last night, since you had also said you hadn't had much sleep because of them."

Abruptly he laughed. More of a snort, actually. "I see you are in fact acting like a policeman."

"You asked me to, Mr. Martaine."

"So I did. You're right. I've explained it all to the police chief. She didn't discover their loss till after eleven last night." He yanked a couple of paper towels from the holder. "We were to attend a charity ball last evening here in the city—at the Pierre. Don't ask me why a woman finds it necessary to buy a dress for eight hundred dollars and bedeck herself in hundreds of thousands of dollars in jewels in order to dance for the poor, but that's the way they all are. Yesterday at about noon she went to the bank for them."

"Which bank?" I asked, playing the role of cop to the hilt.

"The County National at the Brook Shopping Center. When she came home she developed one of her sick headaches. She got into bed. By dinnertime she felt somewhat better, but not well enough to dress and drive to the city and attend the ball. Instead we spent the evening at home watching television. At eleven she went to her room to prepare for bed. I stayed to watch the news. A few minutes later she reappeared quite agitated. She had looked in her bag for the first time since she had left the bank, and the pouch containing the jewels was gone."

"What about servants?" I asked routinely.

"I went through all that with your policemen. We have an elderly couple I have known most of my life. They worked for my mother; when she died, they came to work for me. I would stake everything I possess on their absolute honesty. A cleaning woman comes in three days a week, but yesterday was not one of her days. There is a part-time gardener, but he hasn't been in since Monday—I suspect off on a drunk. No, they could not have been stolen." He tossed the crumpled paper towels into the bin. "This was one reason I delayed calling the police. I knew they would immediately suspect the servants and badger them. I wished to avoid that."

"If that was one reason, was there also another?"

"Publicity. It would hit the papers, and it did make my wife look ridiculous. There was a chance we could find them ourselves. I roused the servants to help us. The four of us covered every inch of our parking circle, the walk to the house, the downstairs and upstairs halls, and of course, her room—everywhere she had been when she had carried the bag from the car to her room. Though it seemed useless, she and I and Joseph drove to the shopping center and searched the area where she remembered having parked. It was after two when we returned home. Norma in particular didn't feel up to being questioned by the police. Her headache had returned. I decided that whatever could be done that night had been done and I would wait till morning before reporting the loss to the police. At seven this morning I called them. A patrolman showed up and shortly afterward the chief himself. This is where it stands."

I said, "Why isn't it possible that her handbag was picked while she was in the bank?"

"It's possible, but she doesn't think so. Does it matter? Stolen or lost, they're gone." He passed a hand over his face. "I shouldn't have let it disturb me so much. I am insured. But I couldn't sleep when I finally got to bed. Stupidity annoys me, and Norma..."

He left the rest of that dangling. A gentleman didn't discuss his wife's stupidity with an outsider. Or shouldn't.

"Why don't you go home, Mr. Martaine?" I said as if I were the big boss.

"I am about to. Though they're insured, Norma is devastated by their loss. Such possessions mean more to her than..." He didn't finish that either. "You're her friend. For her sake, Caleb, see that the police are—ah—diligent."

"I certainly will," I said with a straight face.

Minutes ago we had both finished what we had come in here for. Now he moved to the door, and I kept pace with him. And when we were outside the men's room I said, "Are you announcing a reward for their recovery?"

"Why the devil should I?" he said. "That's the insurance company's problem, not mine. I expect service for the huge premiums I've been paying." He gave me a friendly touch on the shoulder. "About Gordon's book, I hope I wasn't rough on you."

"That's all right."

"Yes. Well, good-bye now."

"Good-bye, Mr. Martaine."

He paused at the water cooler for a drink. I stood where I was a moment longer. The insurance company. Thanks for the idea, Mr. Martaine.

5

Lucille was almost the only worker in the center office who hadn't gone out to lunch. She jumped up from her typewriter when I appeared.

"It's too late," she said. "The morning mail had already gone to the post office."

I didn't immediately realize what she was talking about. Tripp's manuscript was not the thing uppermost on my mind. I nodded vaguely and went into my office.

She tagged after me. "Was it very important that it not go out?"

"What's the difference, it can't be helped. Did my wife call?"

"Yes, some time ago. She wants you to call her right back."

So Sally had heard on the radio. Heard to whom they belonged and that they were valuable beyond her wildest dream. I sank into my desk chair.

"Should I get her for you?" Lucille said.

"Not just yet." This was a call that had to be made on the outside.

"What about Gordon Tripp?"

Spare me a nagging secretary. "Shove Gordon Tripp!"

"You wish you could," Stu Stitchman's voice said over our partition. Naturally he had been listening.

Then he came through my door. A short man with the shoulders of a bull and the beard of a college kid and a pipe seldom out of his mouth. A man of culture and casual women and never a wife, though he was pushing forty. One of my favorite people.

"Let me guess," he said. "Lucille told me that Martaine had descended among the proletariat and summoned you to an audience in Harve's office, the result of which was that you sent her scurrying to keep Tripp's rejected manuscript from being mailed. Am I right in assuming a ukase from on high?"

"In a way."

"Norma's doing, I'll bet anything," he said.

"You know her better than I do."

"Not better, I think, but well enough. A fervent collector of culture like Norma Martaine wouldn't overlook a poet who lives in her back yard." Stu took his pipe out of his beard. "Am I right that we are going to publish Tripp after all?"

"Yes."

"Aha," he said. "With a friend like Norma, who needs talent?"

I wished he would let me alone. Gordon Tripp and his manuscript had ceased to be anything personal, and the only interest I had in Norma Martaine was as the owner of what Sally had in her hatbox.

"If it's ruffled pride that's bothering you," Stu was saying, "console yourself with the fact that you'll be the one who's taking Lakeview back to poetry. And it isn't as if Tripp isn't a pro of some small merit."

"Frankly, I don't give a damn one way or the other."

"Something's eating you," he said. "Did Martaine give you a bad time?"

"He's always a perfect gentleman," I growled.

"Caleb has been moody all morning," Lucille explained to him. "Even before he saw Mr. Martaine."

There was a welcome interruption. Bob Roth, our managing editor, stuck his head in to remind Stu they had a date to lunch together. They asked me to join them. I said no, thanks and they left. But Lucille continued to stand at my desk.

"What is it now?" I demanded.

"It's still Gordon Tripp. I sent the manuscript with your rejection letter first-class registered, so he may receive it first thing tomorrow. Oughtn't you tell him before he has it that you're taking his book after all. I mean, it would be thoughtful and kind."

"Thanks for keeping me thoughtful and kind. All right, get him for me."

She dialed his number on my phone. I could hear the busy signal.

"Funny," she said. "Unless his phone is off the hook. If you write him right away, he'll get the letter at the same time as the manuscript."

"Forget him. I might drop in to see him this evening."

She sighed. "I had a husband like you. A sweet man, but he also got into those moods."

I got rid of her by sending her to lunch. I sat in my office, practically alone on the floor. Nearby an unattended phone rang interminably; at long last it stopped. Bob Roth had sent around an angry memo that secretaries stagger their lunch hour so that they could cover each other's phones, but as usual they were ignoring him.

Stu had returned Earl B. Carlton's manuscript. It filled my In-box. Fifty thousand dollars advance, and likely a lot more in eventual earnings, for a novel I would to a large extent have to rewrite. Policemen, window washers, third-rate poets, fourth-rate novelists—everybody was getting his. Sally was right. It was time we came in on it.

I made a note on my desk calendar to call Carlton's agent this afternoon and went out. I walked three blocks in heady May weather (the kind of day which makes New York endurable) and in a supermarket-type drugstore I stood on line at the phonebooths. When eventually I got into one, Sally answered at the first ring. Probably sitting at the phone waiting for my call.

"Dear," she blurted, "why did Edward Martaine want to see you? Lucille told me you were with him when I called."

"So you heard who owns them?"

"I heard it on the local station at twelve o'clock. Dear, can you talk?"

"I'm in a booth."

"Why did he send for you?"

"Don't worry, it was a business conference. He merely wanted me to change my mind about turning down Gordon Tripp's collection."

"Oh." I could hear her breathe over the wire. "Did he say anything about... *it?*"

"He mentioned that his wife had lost a quarter of a million dollars' worth of jewels."

"Was that all?"

"He said if there's any reward, it will have to come from the insurance company."

"Caleb, that will be hardly anything. They're worth so much."

I had no answer to that. There was a painful pause before her voice filled the void.

"Caleb, what are you going to do?"

"Nothing for the time being. There's no hurry. We'll sit tight."

"For how long?"

"I don't know. We have a lot to think through."

"Yes." She sounded greatly relieved that I was not about to do anything unreasonable. "Well..."

There seemed to be nothing else we had to say to each other, so we said goodbye.

6

Sally came alone to pick me up at the station at the usual time. She greeted me as if I had returned from a long journey (which in a way I had), grabbing me as soon as I had replaced her behind the wheel. There was something besides ardor in her kiss. There was a clutching frenzy. The *nouveau riche* also had their troubles.

"This was such a long day waiting for you," she said.

The inevitable horns reminded me that I was holding up the line of cars crawling down for the turn at the plaza. She shifted away from me, leaving my hands free for driving.

Mort Reach's voice on the car radio with the local news. A brush fire this afternoon in the hollow, a bazaar next week at the Temple. That kind of thing.

I said, "I suppose Mort started his program with the Martaine jewels. It would be the big news in town."

"He had nothing new to say."

"What can be new except that they've been recovered?" I turned off the radio. "Did you see the *Post*?"

"No."

"It's in my briefcase. A couple of paragraphs on the third page. Quite sketchy, but enough to make it the topic of conversation for Mount Birch commuters. Wisecracks flew all over the train."

"I can't see what's funny."

"Not funny to us or to the Martaines. But how often do people have cause to laugh at the very rich? The idea of the grand lady of the grandest family in the village blithely dropping those jewels into her handbag and then losing them—well, I'd laugh too if I weren't on the way to being a crook."

"Dear, don't talk like that."

"How then should I talk?"

We reached the plaza circle. Patrolman Jackson called "Evening, Mr. Dawson" as I rolled by him. I wished I hadn't run for trustee.

Sally spoke when we were free of the heavy traffic. "What did Edward Martaine say when you were with him? You told me hardly anything on the phone. Why did he talk to you about the jewels?"

I told her of the phone call from his wife while we had been in Harve Atkinson's office and what he had said to us after he had hung up. By then we were almost home, and there at the dinner hour, with the boys under foot and at the table, would be no place for talking. I pulled the car off the road and turned to her.

For the first time since I had gotten into the car I found myself looking at—really seeing—more of her than her face. She was all dressed up in her beige suit and a flowered blouse. Even her amber beads. Not her usual outfit of the busy housewife who in the midst of preparing dinner rushed off to pick up her husband at the station.

I said, "Where were you?"

"What do you mean, where was I?"

"You're dressed for going out."

"Oh." Sally folded her hands on her lap. "I went to a meeting of the League of Women Voters. Why did you stop the car?"

"How could you go off to a meeting today?"

"You went to work, didn't you?"

"That was different."

"Why was it? I got terribly jumpy when I heard how valuable they are. I had to do something to take my mind off things. Be with people. I came home late and I had so much to do preparing dinner, I didn't have time to change." Her eyes searched my face; they were wide and frightened. "You stopped the car because there's more Edward Martaine said to you."

"Just the details about how she'd lost them. I met him again after I left Harve's office. In the men's room. I got him into a further conversation about the jewels." I paused and added wryly, "After all, I am connected with the police."

As I reported on the conversation in the men's room, she sat with her head back and her eyes half closed, limp and drained after the emotional explosion when I had gotten into the car.

"So your reconstruction of how the pouch was lost was pretty much on the mark," I said at the end.

She stirred then. She stretched her legs and unclasped her hands and gave me that wide-eyed stare of hers. "But, dear, it was so obvious. It couldn't have happened any other way."

"I guess not." I started up the engine.

"Let's not go yet," she said. "I want to talk some more."

"About what?"

"How much do you think we can get for them?"

"That's a good question. Just because they're worth a quarter of a million doesn't mean we can get anywhere near that. I don't even know how to go about finding a fence. We've been moving in the wrong social circle. But there may be another way. I've read that insurance companies are willing to make deals. They'd rather lose a good part of it than the whole amount. They might settle for fifty thousand dollars."

"Oh, for more, I'm sure. We should insist on at least one hundred thousand."

"All right, we'll insist. Besides, don't forget that ill-gotten gains are tax-free."

I was trying to be a bit flippant about it all, but her reaction was to nod gravely. "A hundred thousand dollars," she mused, already having dismissed the thought of a mere fifty thousand dollars. "But we can't just go to the insurance company and say, 'Let's make a deal,' can we?"

"I suppose it will have to be worked like a ransom. Exchange the jewels for small bills without their ever knowing who we are. It'll be dangerous and tricky. It will need plenty of thinking about. As yet we don't even know the name of the insurance company. Now let's go home."

Sally sat silent and huddled till we reached the turn-off to our development. Then she burst out, "We're not taking anything from the Martaines. They won't lose a cent by it."

"The insurance company will."

"That's what they're in business for. They take in much more money than they pay out. We've been paying premiums since we were married and we've never collected on anything."

Said like any upright citizen out to bilk an insurance company. The easiest part of being a crook was to find excuses. I swung the car into our driveway.

Down the alley formed by our two houses, George Huntley in a soiled underwear shirt lumbered behind my lawn mower. He left it against the wall of my garage and came to my car as I got out.

"I borrowed it again to mow in back," he said.

"Any time."

"Caleb, can I talk to you?"

"Sure."

Sally went on to the house. In the warm predusk shad flies reared up from the grass to assault us.

"Marie got a ticket this morning for passing a red light," George said. "It was right in the village, the light on Division and Emerson. Can you do anything about it?"

"I'm not the judge."

"Before it comes to him." He swatted a shad fly on his meaty bare forearm and studied the corpse. "It was Officer Rinaldi who gave it to her. If you'll say a word to him..."

"Pay the ten dollars."

"It may be more. This is Marie's third moving violation in less than a year. They could suspend her license. As a personal favor, Caleb."

Over nineteen thousand a year and no end of extras and holidays and another raise in the works. Standing there, fleshy and sweaty and a tasty dish for the shad flies, George was everybody for whom I was expected to make or save money while all I could do for myself and my family was turn crook.

"George, you've got a hell of a nerve."

His face reddened at the jowls. "I'm not asking anything that's not done all the time. Every politician in town does favors for friends. You barely beat out Gelber—what was it, forty votes?—and I got half that many for you myself at my school."

"Why did you, so I would be able to fix traffic tickets for you?"

He just looked at me. Then he sputtered, "You s-s-sanctimonious bastard!" and strode off with outraged rumblings in his throat.

I laughed. He heard me and swung around in astonishment. "Are you laughing at me?"

He couldn't know I was laughing at myself. I turned and went to my house. The shad flies accompanied me to the door.

7

After dinner I climbed up to Gordon Tripp's cottage. His phone had continued to give off busy signals—it had to be out of order—and I was anxious to let him know that the rejection had been a mistake before he received it in tomorrow's mail. If he wasn't home, I would leave a note.

"Dear, don't be long," Sally said as she stood at the sink scraping off the dinner dishes into the garbage disposal. "I've been without you all day, and the way I feel, I need you with me."

"I'll be back very soon."

I kissed the back of her neck and went.

By car it was some two miles; by foot a quarter of the distance on a footpath that ran along the edge of the woods behind the houses on my side of the street and then rose steeply through brush-clogged private land to the road on which he lived. Being a walker, I walked. I took along a flashlight for the return trip.

Gordon Tripp's cottage was fixed high on the hill, giving him even in summer a magnificent view over the tops of trees. A poet's aerie, he liked to call it. Humph! In my opinion, far and away the most attractive thing about it to him was that it was owned by a brother of his who let him live in it rent-free and tax-free.

Below, lights were going on all over the village in the dusk, but all his windows were dark. And there was no answer to my knock. The shad flies were up here too, buzzing about my head.

His Volkswagen was in the dirt driveway. That didn't necessarily mean he had to be in, but it did induce me to try the door. It opened.

No significance in that either. Mount Birch was as yet free from the depredations and terrors of the cities; we tended to leave our doors unlocked when we were away for only a short time. I pushed the door all the way in and stepped over the threshold directly into the living room.

Before me in the deeper dusk of the interior a pale shape lay on the floor.

I snapped on my flashlight. It was Gordon Tripp in an agonized sprawl on his back. One eye stared up at me—a dead man's eye. Blood like dried paint covered his other eye, matted his flowing blond hair, lay in splotches on his bare chest.

For a second or a hundred seconds I stood regaining power over myself. Then I turned and flipped the light switch beside the entrance door. A light went on against the floor—a standing lamp that had been knocked over and still worked. It was like a spotlight on him.

He was stark naked. As grotesquely and obscenely naked as only the dead can be.

I hated to touch him. I knew his flesh would be terribly cold, but I had to make myself do it. I touched him where there was no blood, under the right side of his collarbone. Not so cold as clammy cool. I snatched my hand away.

There had been a struggle. A chair knocked over as well as a lamp. And a small table on its side; the telephone had fallen from it, the handset a foot or two from its cradle. And patches of dried blood on the floor and streaks of it swished across part of a papered wall. He had wanted desperately to live.

I started toward the phone and checked myself. "Touch nothing," I heard myself say aloud. I was something of a policeman these days. I had responsibilities.

There were three other rooms—kitchen, bedroom, bathroom. The kitchen had no door and the doors to the other two rooms were wide open. Careful to avoid everything, especially blood, I moved this way and that, shining my light into each room. Kitchen clean and orderly. Bathroom the same. In the bedroom the bed was unmade, a chaos of pillows and top sheet and blanket.

I got out of there.

8

A narrow tarred road weaved down the hill. The first house below Gordon Tripp's showed lights. I knocked.

A girl in her mid-teens came to the door. Streaming hair and bare thighs. I was almost bowled over by a blast of sound from a record player or radio or television turned up beyond the endurance of any but juvenile ears. I asked her if her parents were in.

"I'm the baby-sitter." Round eye lay flatly on me. "You're Mr. Dawson. You know my dad. I'm Cathy Ryan."

"Then you won't mind my coming in and using the phone, Cathy. It's an emergency."

"There's one in the kitchen."

Without taking me to the kitchen or telling me where it was, she hurried through a doorway to the source of the house-shaking clamor. Passing the doorway, I saw a boy her age lounging on the sofa. Nice work at a dollar an hour.

I located the kitchen and called police headquarters. Johnny Burke, our one lieutenant and second in command, was at the desk. His voice got excited when I told him.

"You're sure it's murder, Mr. Dawson?"

"It's a fair assumption. I suppose the district attorney and the state police have to be notified, and of course Chief Messner."

"I know what to do," Burke said dryly. Then he paid me back for my amateur officiousness by adding, "You ought to go back to the house and wait. Be sure to wait outside and not touch a thing."

I hung up. Dishes were piled in the sink and pots were on the stove. Sally would never go off leaving her kitchen like that. Sally, having cleaned up, was waiting for me to come back home as she sat on a quarter of a million dollars. I dialed my number.

"Don't expect me home for some time," I told her.

"Why not?"

"Gordon Tripp is dead. I found his body in his house."

"Oh, God!" she said. "How did he die?"

"He was murdered."

"Oh, no! Do they know who did it?"

"I found the body only a few minutes ago. The police haven't come yet."

"It's incredible," she said. "Where are you? I hear music."

"I'm calling from a nearby house. I have to wait for the police and then I'll have to hang around. I don't know when I'll be home."

"Dear, I'm afraid."

"Of what?"

"If he was killed by a madman prowling about..."

"There's nothing for you to worry about. I think it happened last night or before. Lock the doors if that will make you feel safer."

"I will. Dear, don't be too long."

"I'll be home as soon as I can."

I was back on the road when the first police car appeared. Patrolman Ralph Caruso stopped to pick me up.

9

When Chief Nate Messner arrived fifteen minutes later, I went back into the cottage with him. I would as soon have stayed outside, but I had a position to uphold.

On the floor the eye that wasn't covered with blood stared up at me. At Messner, too, but I had an unreasonable sensation of its staring at me in particular.

"An unholy mess," he grunted. Gingerly avoiding blood and knocked-over furniture, he moved about the room.

I didn't budge from my position near the door. My legs were tired. Too much was happening. I would have liked to sit down, but not in this room. I turned to the window on my right so I would not have to look at the dead eye.

Night had fallen. From here I could see strung-out headlights on the curving hill road below. The shouts and whistles of our valiant cops laboring to keep it open drifted up. The word had already spread of a major event in the village and the gawkers were on their way. It seemed that the main job of our department in a murder was the same as at a high school graduation or a concert sponsored by the Mount Birch Friends of Music—traffic control.

"Dead for hours, I'd guess," Messner said in his staccato voice. He had returned to the naked battered thing on the floor.

I said, "At least twenty-four hours. Maybe longer."

"How's that?" He threw me a sharp glance. "You know something about it?"

"I'd been trying to get him on the phone since about this time last evening. There were always busy signals."

"And it looks like the phone was knocked over in the struggle which killed him. Go on, Mr. Dawson."

"That's practically all of it. I had to speak to him about a book of his my company is publishing. When I couldn't get him on the phone, I took a walk up here. There was no answer to my knock, so I tried the door. It was unlocked."

"Was this lamp on?"

"No. I put it on. It's controlled by the wall switch."

"And you just walked in?"

"What then? A constant busy signal and his car in the driveway. Something could be wrong."

"Like what?"

"Like anything, Chief." He was beginning to annoy me with his questioning about the obvious. "A person living alone can get sick or break a leg or drop dead and nobody would know."

"Or be murdered." Messner scratched his jutting jaw. "You were a good friend of his, Mr. Dawson."

Not a question. A flat statement, and I was startled to realize that I had to be the first—and so far only—suspect.

"An acquaintance," I corrected him.

"All right. But you know the same people in town he knew."

"Some of them."

"Know anybody who had it in for him?"

"You will have to ask people who were more intimate with him. What you called friends."

"I will, Mr. Dawson, you can depend on it."

"I would hope so."

For the first time since I had taken office we weren't making an effort to get along with each other. Put it down to the tension caused by the thing at our feet. This was one hell of a place for a discussion.

"Look, Chief, can't we talk outside?"

He didn't seem to hear me. Staring down at what had been Gordon Tripp, he said, "If this was a woman, all naked and beaten, the first thing we'd think of was rape. But a man..."

The door was opened by Patrolman Rinaldi, who was stationed on the other side of it. A burly man in a business suit stepped in past him. The door closed.

The newcomer's eyes impassively swept the room, taking in the dead man, the blood on the floor and the wall, the chair and the lamp and the table on their sides, the telephone in two pieces. Then he said, "Got anything, Nate?"

"So far just what you see," Messner said. "Dan, this is Mr. Dawson. He's a trustee—our new department chairman. Mr. Dawson, this is State Police Investigator Dan Kibble."

"Not pleasant, is it?" Kibble said affably as we shook hands practically across those bare legs.

"Not very," I said.

"It's all in a day's work," he said. "I see a lot worse. Like the other week a killing with a shotgun over in Apple Valley. This is nice and clean by comparison."

So I had to linger on in there lest they think the new chairman had a weak stomach.

Messner and Kibble moved about the cottage, turning on lights, attending to business, while I stayed near the door. I became aware of a musty smell. The smell of death in warmish weather. I turned again to the window—and there like a wavering ghost was Mort Reach's pinched face on the other side of the pane.

He grinned at me, so help me!

"Get away from there!" Rinaldi's voice burst out.

The face vanished, but I could hear Mort protest, "Give me a break, Vito. I have a story to write."

"You're trampling evidence."

"You've found evidence out here?"

"Never mind. I've orders to keep everybody away."

Mort reappeared. The outside light was on, and spotlights from two patrol cars added to it. Notebook in hand, he headed for Sergeant Swan on the road. As editor of a suburban weekly, Mort was also its star reporter.

The voices behind me were now in the bedroom. Through the open door I saw them standing at the foot of the disordered bed.

"No struggle in here," Kibble said. "No blood. Nate, did you see anything could be a weapon?"

"Not a thing. But I took only a quick look. Didn't want to disturb a thing before the lab men came."

"Are you questioning neighbors?"

"We'll get to it. My off-duty men are being rounded up."

The small cottage got smaller and smaller; it stifled me with the smell and presence of Gordon Tripp. They, the experts, weren't doing anything, and I was doing less. I wasn't needed here or wanted. I went out into the clean air.

At my appearance on the pebble walk, Mort Reach abandoned Sergeant Swan to come running to me.

"Caleb, what's going on inside?"

He was a round-shouldered little man burdened by a sense of being trapped in a small town. He had a fat wife, five notoriously wild children, and seventy pages of a novel he had been working on for years and threatened to have me read some day.

I said, "You saw through the window what's in there."

"I'll say! What a day in our town! Nothing worthwhile happens for months, then on one day—bingo! And it's just my luck the *Ledger* went to press last night and I missed out on both stories. But all is not lost. Do you know I also cover area news for the AP?"

"Is that so?"

"Well, I do. I have no idea how many afternoon papers picked up my story of Mrs. Martaine's jewels. I bet quite a few did—in the metropolitan area at least and possibly all over the country. Terrific human interest. It makes a reader's mouth water to think of all that wealth lying on the ground for anybody to come along and pick up. Now this. It's even better."

Close by, a police car radio squawked with its usual incoherence. Into my head popped a question: To what extent would today's crime distract attention from yesterday's crime?

I said, "What makes you think outside newspapers will be interested in our little murder? They have plenty of their own they don't bother to mention."

"A poet," Mort said. "Poets are the epitome of romance in the public mind. Never mind how good he was or if many people ever heard of him. Who reads poetry anyway? I'll make him out to be a more romantic figure than Shelley and Byron put together. You have to admit he did have their genius as far as the bedroom is concerned." He leered up at me through cigarette smoke. "That's the reason he was knocked off. Right, Caleb?"

"I wouldn't know."

"Come off it. You know what everybody knows about Gordon. You saw more in there than I did, and I saw he was naked and his bed in a shambles. He had to have been in the sack with a woman when somebody like a husband or a boy friend of hers caught them at it. You agree, don't you?"

"I agree it's the only angle to get the papers to pick up the story and maybe give you a byline."

"So why not? I can use a good quote for the lead."

"Chief Messner speaks for the department in matters like this."

"I prefer you. You're not only an official. You found the body, you were his friend, you were his editor. I'll give you a big play."

"What do you mean, I was his editor?"

"Of his book you're going to publish, what do you think I mean?"

"Who told you that?"

"Gordon."

"When?"

"I don't know, some days ago."

"The decision to accept it was made only this morning, and Gordon never knew it."

"So he anticipated you would accept it. Look at all the free publicity for the book if the murder is played up right. We'll be helping each other."

"Sorry, Mort. You'll have to do your own mongering of rumors."

"You won't give me a break?"

"No."

At that he lost all interest in me. A snappy white sports car had rolled right up on the lawn, and out stepped a snappy young man in a checked blazer over a fawn turtleneck shirt. He was Dave Bernstein, an assistant district attorney I had met a time or two at political functions. Mort dashed over to him. Talking all the time, he accompanied Bernstein to the cottage. But only to the door; it closed in his face. A reporter's life was full of frustrations.

Left to myself, I took up a position beside a dogwood tree in full bloom. If I had nothing to do, at least the citizens could see me on the scene, right on top of the crime of the year or the decade. A couple of our cops, reinforced by a couple of state troopers, kept them on the other side of the road—murmuring, shifting, shadowy shapes among whom the murderer might well be. One shape yelled, "Hi, Caleb," and without knowing who it was, I waved to it.

The laboratory van arrived. Shortly after that a man carrying a doctor's bag entered the cottage; I assumed he was from the medical examiner's office. Was I shirking my duty by not going back in there?

Fred Lytoon, our mayor, spotted me from the walk and came over. Everybody was out tonight. He was a heavy man who walked and spoke with the pretentious dignity of his office. The job at which he made a living was vice-president of a public relations firm in New York City.

"I phoned you at your house," he said. "It was your wife who told me what had happened here. A terrible thing for the village."

"Also for Gordon Tripp."

"Yes. Well. Caleb, we've got to discuss those ridiculous demands of the policemen before Saturday's board meeting."

"Are they ridiculous?"

"A thirty percent raise!" he said. "You're not shocked?"

It was only at that moment that I definitely made up my mind to go all the way with the men. Who was I to object to anybody sharing the wealth?

"I see no reason to be shocked," I said.

"Do you realize what such a pay raise would amount to in the third year?"

"A decent wage."

"You're new on the board," he said. "You don't understand the full implication. All the other village employees will ask for equivalent raises. It will kill us. We have an obligation to our taxpayers."

"The taxpayers have an obligation to the people who work for them."

"Sure, sure. I'm not against a raise. I suggest three percent a year on a three-year contract. I don't know how we'll squeeze even that in, but we'll have to. It's going to be a sweat to hold the tax rate down to sixty-two dollars a thousand even as is."

Lieutenant Burke entered the cottage. It must be getting crowded in there. I said, "Fred, let's discuss it some other time. Somebody I knew well has been murdered, and I was the one who walked in on his body."

"Yes, I heard. It must have been a nasty experience." The mayor assumed a funereal expression. "Are there clues?"

"Not a thing up to a few minutes ago."

"You know, the board will never give in to any such terms," he said, getting back to the important business. "I hope you haven't a closed mind."

"I hope the same for you, Fred."

The cottage door opened. Out came Chief Messner and Investigator Kibble and Assistant D.A. Bernstein. Mort Reach pounced on them. So did a man I knew from the County Press Association and a third from the daily which covered this corner of the county. An impromptu news conference formed on the lawn. Bernstein was the spokesman.

The mayor and I joined the conference, he at Bernstein's side and I, being a novice politician, at the edge.

After Bernstein had described the scene inside the cottage, he said, "I'm afraid that's all we have. The lab boys have just begun, and Assistant M.E. Dr. O'Neill has had time for only a preliminary examination of the body."

"How long has he been dead?" the County Press man asked.

"A considerable time. I have been told that Mr. Dawson had tried since last evening to reach him on the phone without success." Bernstein looked about; his eyes swept past me. "Has Mr. Dawson left?"

"I'm here," I said.

"Sorry, I didn't recognize you in this light." He addressed the reporters. "As you may know, Mr. Dawson is a village trustee. Since I heard his story only at second-hand from Chief Messner, I'll let him speak for himself. Okay, Mr. Dawson?"

I thought him a bit patronizing; it was necessary for his ego to assert his jurisdiction. Like editors. Without frills I told of my phone calls and my secretary's and why I had come up here.

When I finished, Bernstein took over again, "It is Dr. O'Neill's tentative opinion that Gordon Tripp may have been dead as long as twenty-four hours and not many hours less. The autopsy may pinpoint it more definitely. At present we are assuming that the murder occurred during last night."

"Why last night," Mort Reach said, "if Dawson says he got the first busy signal around eight o'clock?"

"That busy signal could have been quite legitimate," Bernstein said. "He could in fact have been speaking on the phone; this will be checked out. I have mentioned that the bed was unmade and disheveled. This would indicate that he was in it when he heard somebody in the other room and jumped out naked as he was to grapple with the intruder. In short, during the time when a person normally sleeps—at night."

"Bullshit!" Mort said.

Bernstein looked startled. "Beg pardon?" he said.

"When you're in bed with a woman whose husband is off at work, during the day is the time for it," Mort said. "I'll bet anything Tripp wasn't the only one naked in his bed when the killer barged in."

"That possibility is being considered," Bernstein said smoothly. "As well as other possibilities, such as that the murderer was a burglar. At this moment the neighbors are being questioned by Mount Birch policemen to learn if they heard anything unusual or saw a stranger lurking—"

"Bullshit!" Mort said. "Why would anybody want to rob this dump when there are fancy houses all about? That was no stranger. That was a respectable matron's commuter husband."

Chief Messner spoke up irritably. "If you have any information, Mort, come out with it."

"Me, I'm merely a newspaper reporter asking questions," Mort said. "Dave, would you care to give me a direct answer to one question?"

"If I can," Bernstein said.

"It's this. In view of Gordon Tripp's reputation as a womanizer, is consideration being given to the fact that he could have been in bed with a woman during the day yesterday when her irate husband burst into the house?"

"The answer is yes, of course, this is definitely being considered."

Grinning, Mort Reach wrote on his pad. He had his lead. The newspaper racket was like any other.

Soon afterward the gathering at the cottage drifted apart. It was after ten; I had left my house two hours ago. I plucked at Messner's sleeve and said I saw no reason for hanging around.

"That's up to you," he said.

"See you," I said.

Behind my flashlight beam I walked down the path to the scene of my own crime. Mine and Sally's, back home.

10

The path down the hill took me to my back yard. Light showed in our bedroom windows.

Usually when I was out at night, to a meeting or a poker game, Sally went to bed early with a book, and as often as not I would come home to find her fast asleep sitting propped up against the headboard with the lamplight in her eyes and the book on her legs. At the side corner window, the one pretty much covered by the evergreen, I stopped and parted some branches to take a look. Sally was in there, awake and out of bed.

She stood at the full-length door mirror bedecked in Norma Martaine's jewels. And wore absolutely nothing else.

She looked at her image and I looked at her. The diamond earrings dangled a good three inches from her earlobes. The magnificent bracelet sparkled like fireworks on her tanned forearm. The huge emerald-cut diamond was like a brass knuckle on the middle finger of her right hand. The three-strand pearl necklace lay on her luscious breasts with her pale nipples caught between the strands. Only the thistle-shaped brooch was not on her because clearly there was nothing to pin it to.

Or so I thought. The brooch was held between two fingers. Smiling down at it, she brought it to her navel, and I had a mad notion she was going to pin it to her skin. Of course she didn't; with a naughty giggle she tried to pin it to her pubic hair. The short curls couldn't hold it; it fell to the floor. She picked it up and clipped it to the hair of her head, rakishly behind her ear.

Then she began to move and turn and undulate like a belly dancer, watching herself all the time in the mirror. There was something quite unfamiliar about the familiar body, a hothouse lushness that seemed to have changed it in subtle ways—something unfamiliar about the sensuous smile directed at her naked image. And she was different. She had never before had a quarter of a million dollars in jewels on her flesh, and the erotic effect they had on her in the mirror reached out to me at the window.

I, her husband, felt like a Peeping Tom. I moved on to the side door.

She must have heard me unlock and then lock it and turn off the lights she had left on. She would be tearing off the jewels and putting on a robe. I was eager to get to her before she could. But when I was in the inner hall, Brandy called out, "Dad!" and so I had to go into his room.

I said, "What is it, son?" He sat up. In the dimness of the night bulb he blinked up at me, rubbed his eyes, and complained, "Lemme sleep." I could have slapped him or kissed him. I arranged him on his back and adjusted the blanket and kissed him on the cheek. Sally had had plenty of time to get back to normal.

But tonight wasn't like any other night. When I entered our room, she was exactly as I had seen her through the window. Naked adorned, she stood at the foot of the bed facing me, one hand at the pearls on her breasts, the other on her thigh with ringed finger crooked. And her eyes shone and her lips were parted moistly, and I knew that the jewels on her flesh were as much a preparation for me as for herself.

We grabbed each other.

In no time we were on the bed. We were like brand-new lovers. As we rolled together she helped me off with my clothes. The earrings swung against my chest. Pearls on the necklace popped into my mouth along with her nipples. The brooch scratched my cheek, and I felt the bracelet fiercely caress my back. It was as if each jewel had become an additional erogenous zone of her body. It was stupendous.

Presently we lay on our backs, holding hands. Both the lamp and the overhead light were on; for once Sally hadn't insisted on darkness. Tonight the aftermath was particularly sweet.

"Poor Gordon!" she said suddenly.

"Yes," I said.

"You were gone very long. Did they find out anything?"

"Not yet. Only that he was beaten to death last night or earlier."

"Oh." There was a silence, then she said, "Let's not talk about it tonight."

"You were the one brought it up."

"I know. But let's not talk about it."

"Sure."

I moved to kiss her—her mouth, her body. Something hard pressed the hip on which I leaned. I plucked the brooch out from under me. It must have fallen from her hair during her wild tossing.

Sally took it from me, examining it as if she had not done it many times since yesterday noon.

"It was silly," she said with a small giggle. "But waiting for you to come home, I got the idea of putting them on without clothes. It excited me very much."

"You and me both," I said, nuzzling the pearls. "At least they've been of some practical use to us."

"There'll be more. You'll see, darling. They'll make life easier and better." She kissed me with more than usual wifely ardor. "I love you, Caleb," she said. Then she got out of bed to put the jewels away.

Ordinarily on the brief occasions when she was not wearing a nightgown in bed, she would snatch on a robe as soon as she got out of it. Not tonight. I lay with hands behind my head watching her, so very lovely as one by one she took off the jewels and put them into the pouch.

"I decided the hatbox isn't safe," she said as she unclasped the necklace. "It's the first place they'll look."

"They? Who are they?"

"Burglars, who do you think? Now that we have something valuable, we have to worry about it. We have a better hiding place."

"Where?"

"Your secret drawer."

A couple of years ago she had picked up at a garage sale a marble-top Victorian dresser, what she called an antique and I called second-hand. A gift for me, so I couldn't protest vehemently even though it held considerably less than my good old up-to-date chest of drawers had. Sally had been especially impressed by a secret drawer that looked like the two-inch bottom molding. The drawer was too shallow for clothes and I had no secrets, so I had almost forgotten about it.

One could never tell when something like this would be useful, could one?

Sally flattened out the pouch and stuck it all the way to the back of the drawer and turned off the lights and came back to bed, still without a nightgown. She got on top of me.

Even without the jewels on her, the night had hardly begun for us. We had not had one quite like it since before Chuck was born.

Friday

It was a good day for Mort Reach in the two New York City morning papers. I picked up both at the station newsstand and looked through them as I waited for the train.

The *News* had picked up his AP story with its emphasis on poet-cum-sex. It was on page six, LOVE TRIANGLE BELIEVED IN BLUDGEON MURDER OF POET, with a two-column publicity photo of him looking soulful in the frame of his flowing blond hair.

In the *Times*, Mort had achieved a byline by writing a special slanted to its awe of men of letters. It was stuck in between the chess column and a book ad on the page opposite the book review, GORDON TRIPP, POET, SLAIN IN SUBURB, and quoted appropriate, if not memorable, lines from one of his poems:

> Where is the light? The switch
> eludes me.
> I am stricken by the soothing dark. I
> reject its comfort.
> Please god restore the violent light.

In each story I received brief mention as editor of his forthcoming book of collected poems who had found his nude (newspaperese for naked) body.

When I was settled on the train, I hunted through the papers for the really important news. In each there were a very few inches about Norma Martaine's jewels. Both stories probably Mort's. Since the news had broken for the evening papers and newscasts, the follow-up in the morning papers consisted mostly of mouth-watering descriptions of the pieces.

For me nothing else that had happened in the rest of the world, not even the baseball scores, was worth reading this morning. I folded the paper and put my head back and luxuriated in the memory of how Sally had looked last night wearing the jewels on her flesh. And the aphrodisiac effect on both of us.

2

Two blocks from the Paragon Building, I heard my name called. With pipe jutting from his beard, Stu Stitchman was dodging cars as he crossed the street against the light to get to me. He lived not a dozen blocks away, on the East Side, yet I could not recall his ever having been much less than an hour behind me.

"What are you doing out this early with the hoi polloi?" I said when he reached me.

"I had no choice." Stu fell into step with me. "I spent the night with a chesty high school teacher at her place in Queens. Could a gentleman do less than rise with her when she did before seven and take her out to breakfast and walk her to her school? Then there I was with nothing to do but hop the subway and go to work myself. During rush hour yet! Though the ordeal was somewhat mitigated by all this intriguing reading about us."

He tapped the two morning newspapers under his arm. Like me, he had also bought the *News*, which normally we snobs wouldn't be found dead with.

I said, "What do you mean, us?"

"Lakeview Press, what then? Our alter ego till we're fired or find a better job. I read that the spouse of our biggest boss is more careless with a pouch of jewels beyond the dream of avarice than I am with my tobacco pouch. I also read that in the same town and within a period of a day, if not less, our newest author is knocked off, and it's one of our editors who strolls in on his gory remains. It gives one pause."

"Does it?"

"There's more. All three of you were acquainted."

"So?"

"So I asked myself how many coincidences are required before they stop being coincidences."

"No matter how tenuous?"

"Well, how tenuous are they? My problem is that I'm like Will Rogers. All I know is what I read in the papers. You must have inside dope."

I had dope so far inside, it was limited to Sally and me, the only ones who knew who had found the pouch and where it was stashed and why it couldn't be related to anything else that had happened in Mount Birch. I didn't mind freely discussing murder, but I had no taste for the other subject.

I said, "Your problem, Stu? I thought your games were double-crostics and seducing women with big boobs."

"Speculating about murder is anybody's game, the more so when it concerns people one knows." He tossed me a sidelong grin. "Okay, I understand. You have to be close-mouthed about whatever your cops aren't telling the public."

"I've been told nothing to be close-mouthed about."

We were at the entrance to our building. The window washers' picket line separated us. When Stu and I came together again in the lobby, he said, "Don't your cops report to you?"

"Sure. When they want a raise or a new patrol car."

"Ah, cryptic," he said. "That's significant."

I let him play his game without me. Anyway, an elevator was waiting. We jammed ourselves into it.

On the editorial side of the thirty-third floor, clock-punching office workers and such editors who showed up on time were abuzz in the open space at the Xerox machine. This morning they had not one but two conversational tidbits about "us." As I approached with Stu, I heard an elderly copyeditor argue, "How can you stand there and talk about honesty if you have never been tempted by anything more than receiving too much change from a cashier?" and in another group an earnest assistant editor recently out of Vassar earnestly declare, "What a waste for such an authentic poetic voice to be cut off!" and then Bob Roth, our managing editor, spotted me and yelled, "Caleb!" and I had to stop. So did Stu, sticking to me like a bodyguard.

Bob came out to the aisle to confront me. "How come I had to learn from the newspaper that this Gordon Tripp was our author and you his editor?"

"He wasn't quite. Hadn't been signed yet. Talk to Harve."

"You bet I will. I've got to know who's going to be on our list." He turned solemn. "That must have been some experience for you."

I said, "It wasn't pleasant," and moved on, Stu with me.

As he was about to part from me at his office, Lucille came out of it with some file folders. Today she wasn't wearing one of her low necklines; she wore a green body shirt up to her throat, with spectacular effect. Ignoring the good morning of her other boss, she jounced wide-eyed to me.

"Caleb, I didn't think you'd be in today. How horrible for you!"

"That's nothing to what it was for Tripp," Stu said.

"Everything's a joke to you," she snapped at him. "Caleb, I get the shivers thinking he was lying there dead all the time I was trying to get him on the phone yesterday. Do you think he was?"

"Probably. The phone was knocked over in the struggle."

"It gives me the shivers," she said. "Would you men like coffee?"

We both would. She went in search of the wagon and returned with three plastic cups of coffee and three jelly doughnuts on a plastic tray. We assembled in my office for the repast, and from behind my desk I told them about going up to the cottage and what followed. It had been an interesting experience, and we had fallen into the habit of telling each other our interesting experiences—up to a point. I was regaling them with my colloquy with the mayor outside the cottage last night when he had been more concerned with taxes than with death, when my phone rang.

Lucille, being an efficient secretary, rose and grabbed it, though it was two feet from my good right hand. "It's Mr. Atkinson," she told me.

Stu lowered his coffee cup and licked jelly from his fingertips. Lucille returned to her chair and crossed her legs. Both devoted themselves to listening.

"I read about Gordon Tripp at breakfast," Harve said. "A terrible thing."

"I was going to go to your office for a talk," I said. "Where do we stand on the book now?"

"I don't see where anything has changed."

I said, "Maybe now Mr. Martaine doesn't care one way or the other about doing the book."

"Well, I do. The decision is mine as editorial director. It would be absurd not to cash in on all this publicity."

"Uh-huh."

"Wouldn't it be something if the murderer is caught and the book would be out before the trial? Do you think you can rush it through in three months?"

"No chance, Harve. I'll try for five. Even then there'll be no lead time."

"Make it four months. Get up a jacket at once and we'll give it to sales to push the book well in advance. Caleb, have you a copy of the manuscript?"

"I suspect the one I sent back yesterday is the only one in existence, since it's a paste-up of his published stuff. It was sent first-class, so it should arrive today or tomorrow. I'll get it. But, Harve, there's a serious problem. We have no contract."

"What about the estate?"

"I've heard of a brother. He owns the cottage Gordon lived in. I'll find out what has to be done to get a valid signature on a contract."

"Do that. But don't wait for it to be signed before editing the book." Harve remembered to sigh. "It's a shame about him. I'm really sorry."

I grunted and hung up after he did. Stu and Lucille looked at me expectantly.

"Harve is sorry Gordon is dead," I told them. "He's also sorry we can't exploit his murder at this time, but he will be very happy if the murderer is caught and brought to a sensational trial when the book is in print."

"He's absolutely right, you know," Stu said. "At least now there's a valid reason for bringing out the book. We should cut the killer in on the royalties."

"Stu, you're disgusting!" Lucille said. "It's no joking matter. I don't care what you high and mighty editors think, he was a fine poet and a real sweet man."

"How would you know?" Stu drawled.

"I met him and read his manuscript, that's how. He was charming, which is more than you are with your stupid wisecracks." Indignantly she was gathering up the cups and napkins. At the door she said, "Don't think I'm a moron just because I can type and take shorthand," and she bounced (literally) out of my office.

Stu whistled. "I had no idea they were palsy."

"I wouldn't know about palsy," I said. "They got acquainted when Gordon came here last month. I asked him to lunch to discuss a possible book. He had an idea for a novel, but a couple of weeks later he came to my house one evening and handed in the poetry manuscript. Anyway, the day we had lunch I was busy in advertising when he arrived and Lucille kept him company."

"And that juicy build of hers inspired him to turn on the dreamy-eyed personality," Stu said. "A footloose girl with the intellectual pretensions of a semihighbrow would be quite vulnerable to a professional poet. The way she carried on just now could have some deep meaning."

I tilted back in my swivelchair. "Another connection of Gordon's with Lakeview Press to give you pause in your detective game."

"She could be if they got together after the time they met here. Did they?"

"You're asking the wrong person."

"And she wouldn't tell me if there's any reason not to." Stu stood up. "Seriously, though, I'd better go make my peace with her."

"You'd better if we want a contented secretary."

Left to myself, I tackled the most routine job around, checking page proofs against corrected galley proofs, while the best part of my mind devoted itself to working on safe techniques to convert useless jewelry into useful cash.

I was getting well into the swing of the thing when Lucille buzzed my phone and told me that Chief of Police Messner was on the line. My guilty heart lurched.

"Hope you don't mind me calling you on your job," his crisp voice said.

"Not at all. What's up?"

"About your statement, Mr. Dawson. I got it verbally from you last night, but I need it written out and signed by you."

"Right away?"

"I'm not in such a big rush. Your story is in my report. But the state police, they're not happy till they have it in triplicate in your own words and signed by you. I figured you could stop off on the way home from the station."

"Right. To save us all time and trouble, is it okay to have my secretary type it up?"

"Don't see why not. Have her make four—no, five copies. We need two for our own files."

"Chief, are there any developments?"

"We're digging. I have three men on it. Will cost us overtime. Also, there's a state police investigator. You know, you met him yesterday. Dan Kibble. I'm waiting for a preliminary report from the county medical examiner. Then there's the murder weapon. We can't find it."

"The murderer must have taken it with him because it can be traced to him," I said profoundly.

"What I figure. Like a gun registered in his name. He didn't want a shot to be heard, so he used it like a club. Another idea I have, it was a cane. Say somebody with a bum leg or back. The M.E. might be able to give us something to go on from the wounds."

"Chief, what happens to the mail Gordon Tripp receives from today on?"

"Naturally we're interested in who writes him and all. Why, you have something in mind?"

"Yesterday my secretary mailed out to him the manuscript of his book my company is publishing. It may be the only copy in existence, so I want to make sure it's not lost. It could arrive in today's mail."

"I'll see it's taken care of."

"I'll appreciate it. There's something else. I have to know with whom to do business on the book. Have you been in touch with his family?"

"His brother. He owns the house and I got his present address from the tax rolls. I used to know him when he lived in Mount Birch. Better than I knew the poet. Moved to Denver a couple years ago. I phoned him there this morning and broke the news. He's flying out tomorrow."

"Please ask him to get in touch with me when you see him. It's urgent."

"I'll make a note of it."

"Thanks, Chief."

"Any time for you, Mr. Dawson."

In a moment he would hang up. I said deviously, "I can imagine how busy you are with so much happening in town."

"Got only three hours' sleep last night because of the murder."

"And on top of that there are the lost Martaine jewels," I said.

"That was yesterday. Isn't much the department can do. Somebody picking up a lost pouch isn't like a burglary or this here murder. There can't be any leads. Who can you question? An ordinary citizen bends down and picks something up. Could be a dozen people see it, but who would pay attention and remember? People are all the time dropping things and picking them up. So you can't blame us, Mr. Dawson, if we don't get anywhere on this."

"I'm certainly not blaming anybody."

"The best chance they'll be recovered is if who has them tries to sell them. Descriptions of the jewels have already been sent out. We do our best, Mr. Dawson."

"I know you do. Well, good-bye, Chief."

"I'll see you later on, Mr. Dawson."

I hung up in a glow of reassurance. It was nice getting it from the chief of police himself.

THE EVIL DAYS

I called in Lucille and dictated the statement for the police. It was brief; it covered a page and a half, double space, and I could have edited it down to a page if I had bothered. Six copies, I told her, the sixth for myself. She was impressed by the whole thing, especially as her own name was in it as the one who had made the unanswered phone calls yesterday morning.

That took care of more of the morning. Then it was noon, and I went out to lunch earlier than was my habit. I was beginning to feel good. I felt so good that after I had had a hot pastrami sandwich on rye and coffee I didn't return to the office.

It was another bland spring day and it was a Friday, and I wouldn't be the only one in the higher echelons (which began with associate editors) who would slip away today for an early start on the weekend. From the restaurant I walked down to Grand Central and took the 1:22 local home.

3

In the past I would have phoned Sally from the station that I had taken an early train and to come and pick me up. Only if she hadn't been home would I have blown the dollar, plus a quarter tip, on a taxi. But today, what the hell, why bother her? The rich didn't give a thought to the cost of a taxi ride. They just got in. Which I did.

A second car was in my driveway, parked behind mine. One of those snappy little red Opal two-seaters. I knew nobody who owned one.

The street was quieter than I, who was almost never home on a weekday early afternoon, was used to. No children; they were still at school. And the nonworking wives were napping or shopping or socializing. Or like Marie Huntley, reading under the red maple on her lawn. She looked up from her book to watch me pay the taxi driver.

"Caleb," she called when I started up the walk to my house. "Caleb, have you a minute?"

What could I do? I shifted direction. She rose from her redwood rocker and we came together at the edge of her lawn.

Marie Huntley was a bit of a thing, half the size of her overblown husband. Looking pleasantly girlish in short shorts and sleeveless jersey and hair streaming down her back. About the only thing I disliked about her was that a couple of drinks at any kind of get-together made her nerve-jarringly jolly and affectionate.

She said, "Caleb, about the ticket I got for passing a red light."

"What about it?" I said, my face going stiff.

"George shouldn't have asked you to fix it. A ticket isn't worth bad feeling among friends."

"I agree."

Marie had in her hand the book she had been reading, a finger stuck between pages to secure her place. Professionally I noted the title. A current moneymaker on the female orgasm, of which, I had gathered from skimming reviews, the author, a female, heartily approved.

"I told George it was an imposition to ask you." Marie sounded a bit breathless. She tilted her head to peer up into my eyes. "But he did and got very upset when you refused. I wish you would make up."

"He's the one who's sore."

She had stopped looking at me. And listening to me, I felt. Something behind me had captured her attention. I turned my head. A man had come out of my house.

A complete stranger. Young. In his low twenties. No hips and broad shoulders in a black T-shirt and a yellow windbreaker. Shaggy sideburns and a pirate's mustache taking up much of his face. Sunglasses he apparently had worn indoors as well. That sort.

He headed for the Opal. On the way around it to the driver's side he gave me an impassive glance. He knew me no more than I knew him; he wouldn't know I belonged to the house he had just left. He got into his car, backed out of my driveway, drove down the street.

For those twenty or thirty seconds between his appearance and departure Marie Huntley and I had stood in a kind of suspension, like people waiting for somebody to pass out of earshot before continuing a private conversation. Now he was gone, and turning back to her, I found myself looking down at her long loose hair because she was looking down at the ground.

I thought I could see into her mind. From her rocker on her lawn she had observed him arrive; some time later (how much later?) I had come home by taxi, meaning probably unexpectedly; within a couple of minutes thereafter Sally's male visitor had scooted out of the house. A simple matter of dirty arithmetic.

"Well," she said, shifting her book from one hand to the other and thus losing her place, "I do wish you and George would make peace."

"There's no war as far as I'm concerned." A sanctimonious bastard, he had called me. Who was I these days to resent the adjective along with the noun? On impulse I said, "Let me have the ticket, Marie, and I'll see what can be done about it."

"Will you, Caleb?" Her head went back again, and her eyes were aglow with admiration for an officeholder who was, after all, no more constrained by ethics than any other upright citizen. "Stay here, I'll bring it out."

Nuts, I assured myself as I waited. If it were credible that Sally would engage in that kind of hanky-panky, would the guy park right in our driveway for Marie and other neighbors to see? And if she had sent him hurrying off after she had noticed my homecoming through a window or had heard Marie call my name, would she have let him out through the front door right in my face? Let's be logical, shall we?

Marie Huntley emerged from her house and came running diagonally across her lawn as if afraid I would get away. "Caleb, you're a doll," she said as I took the traffic ticket from her.

Was a doll better than a bastard? I put the ticket in my wallet and resumed my circuitous route to my front door.

Sally heard me enter. "Who's there?" her voice came from beyond the living room. "Chuck? Brandy?"

"It's me."

She appeared in the inner-hall doorway. She was wearing her Roman-striped housecoat and her furry slippers.

"Dear, is anything the matter?" she said.

"I didn't feel like working. There's too much on my mind."

"I know. Like me."

Her mouth was tired; she didn't look well. Maybe even frightened.

"How did you come from the station?"

"By taxi."

Nothing wrong with the dialogue. The usual when a husband came home earlier than expected. Yet our words sounded as if they were filling empty space.

I went to her where she stood to give her the delayed hello kiss. She threw her arms about me, but didn't put her head back for my mouth. She had either forgotten she was supposed to be kissed or didn't want to be. All the same, the way she clung to me reminded me of our passionate night last night.

My hands ran over her body. They felt nothing under her housecoat.

"Haven't you dressed today?" I said.

"What a question! I came home from marketing and took a shower." Sally's grip on me loosened; her voice became businesslike. "Dear, have you gotten in touch with the insurance company?"

"I told you I wasn't going to rush it. Besides, I don't know which it is."

"You were going to find out."

"I will. You didn't expect me to ask Edward Martaine when I saw him."

"Wouldn't the police know? I imagine the insurance company will be in touch with them. And you have a perfect right to ask what your police are doing about things, haven't you?"

"I guess I should have broached the subject when Nate Messner phoned me this morning."

"He phoned you? What about?"

"Don't let it scare you. It was about Gordon's murder. He wants a signed statement from me about finding the body."

"Have they any clues yet?"

"Nothing, as far as I know."

"You fool!" Sally burst out. "He called you up, you're his chairman, yet it didn't occur to you to ask the name of the insurance company."

I said tonelessly, "I'm afraid our problem is going to be my lack of experience as a crook."

"Don't talk like that." She returned to me, snuggling. "Darling, I'm sorry for what I said. I'm all nerves. We should get this over with as quickly as possible. You don't know what this waiting does to me."

"You're right, we won't delay," I said, stroking her head. "I'm going over now to give Messner the statement. I'll see what I can find out about the insurance company."

She put her face against my shoulder like a child needing to be comforted. My mouth tasted her hair. It was dry; of course she had worn a shower cap. My hands roamed her back and buttocks, feeling her skin warm and so very smooth in its nakedness through the thin material. There was a hollow in the pit of my stomach.

"Sally, what did that man want?"

"What man?" she said against my shoulder.

"I saw a young man in a yellow windbreaker come out of the house."

"Oh, him." Was that a significant pause before her answer? "He sells magazine subscriptions. If you subscribe to any five of a number of different magazines, all you have to pay is the postage."

"I hope you didn't bite. It's a racket."

"Is it? Anyway, I told him I would have to consult my husband."

She eased herself out of my arms and said she was going to dress. I went into the bathroom to wash up.

The nylon bathmat was damp; wet feet had recently been on it. I had a sickening picture of her taking the shower *afterward*, or even not alone. Goddamn it, stop it! But why hadn't he carried a briefcase or something in which to keep his forms and other papers and maybe some sample magazines? Stop it, stop it!

In our bedroom Sally had her underwear on and was stepping into a skirt. I told her I would be back soon. She nodded. I gave her behind an affectionate pat and went.

The red Opal wasn't anywhere on our street. I drove up the two other streets of our development to see if he was peddling his magazines at other houses. He and his car were definitely gone.

4

Sergeant Alvin Newsome was on desk duty. A college graduate and still in his twenties. Slim-hipped, mustached, hair as long as the chief would permit. Secretary and brains of the Mount Birch Police Protective Association. Lecturer at the local schools on the theme of love your cop. One of the new breed.

He acted delighted with me. He came from behind the high desk to stand at his side of the rail, and he said he had heard I was backing the men one hundred percent in their contract demands. In the drowsy afternoon nobody else was around.

"Who told you this?"

"Vito Rinaldi. Last night at the murder scene he saw you and the mayor talking. Then later he heard the mayor bitching to some people about how you want to give us everything we ask for."

"I never said everything. There will have to be give and take at the bargaining table."

"We're ready to negotiate any time. But the mayor is crazy if he thinks we'll let ourselves be conned like the last contract."

"You won't be if I can help it."

"That's what we like to hear, sir." Sergeant Newsome leaned against the rail to make a confidential statement. "The men are very pleased that for a change there's a chairman sympathetic to them."

In this aura of good feeling I remembered my chore for Marie Huntley.

"By the way, Sergeant, my next-door neighbor got a ticket for passing the Division Street light. She's quite upset. She put me in a position where I had to say that if anything can be done about it..."

The teletype clicked and the radio said something unintelligible. I didn't care for the way I had sounded. Too defensive.

"Have you the ticket?" Newsome hardly glanced at it when I handed it to him. "Tell the lady to forget it."

"Thanks, Sergeant." Which was all there was to it—as simple as picking up a pouch in a parking lot. To cover a residue of embarrassment, I said, "The reason I came is to see the chief. Is he in?"

"Somebody's with him in his office."

"I'll wait."

"Let me tell him you're here." Newsome spoke on one of half a dozen phones hooked to the side of the high desk. "He says to go right in."

Nate Messner's office was no bigger than mine at Lakeview Press, though a lot neater, like the man himself. Even in here he didn't let go. He sat quite upright behind his desk, every shiny button of his uniform buttoned.

State Police Investigator Dan Kibble was with him. He rose from a side chair to pump my hand. His hand was as big and hard as everything else about him, gulping up mine and crushing it.

"I didn't expect you till after six-thirty," Messner said.

"I came down with a case of spring fever," I said, "and your request for a statement gave me a reason for cutting out after lunch. Here are five copies."

"Thanks a lot. Mind signing them?"

I wrote standing over his well-ordered desk. Near my writing hand was a very large, very thick padded mailing envelope with a Lakeside Press sticker on it.

"I see you've picked up Gordon Tripp's manuscript," I said.

"It was at the post office. Why don't you sit down, Mr. Dawson? We were talking about the murder."

I sat and crossed my legs and asked the proper question. "Anything new to talk about since I spoke to you last?"

"Some," Messner said. "We know a soda bottle killed him. One of those twenty-eight-ounce bottles. Hit over the head two, three times. The last blow broke the bottle. Tiny bits of glass were found in the wound."

"Then why weren't there pieces on the floor?" I said. With the next breath I answered myself. "I see. The murderer gathered them up because he thought his fingerprints might be on them."

Investigator Kibble joined the conversation by saying, "I figure him as a cool, careful character. He took no chances. He went through the house wiping everything. When he got through, there wasn't even a decent set of Tripp's own prints left in the house. It was easier and quicker to take the broken glass away with him. Did you ever break a glass in the kitchen? You're sure you've found all the pieces and then a few days later you walk barefoot and cut yourself on one. That's how it was with him. He missed a couple of pieces which were against the wall."

"Were there prints on those?" I asked.

"Too small," Kibble said. "Still, the lab boys were able to tell they were from a bottle exactly like two bottles of cherry soda in the refrigerator. They were unopened, but the one did the killing had been empty. No sticky soda on the floor or in the victim's hair or on his skin."

"Murdered with a bottle of cherry soda," Messner said. "Now I've seen everything."

"It's not exactly the kind of weapon you take along to kill somebody with," Kibble said. "It's something you'd snatch up from the table where it had been left after it was drunk empty."

"The phone," I said. "Did he also wipe the phone?"

"Absolutely clean," Messner said.

"Then he must have used it," I said, "either before or after the murder."

"We've already checked with the phone company," Messner said. "No toll calls made these last few days. If a call was made, it was a local call, which the company doesn't record."

"There's something else about the phone," I said. "Why didn't he replace it on the cradle and pick up the furniture if he went to all that trouble to clean up?"

Chief Messner smiled like a parent at a precocious offspring. "You're on your toes, Mr. Dawson. You ask the right questions. Dan and I were belting that very thing around when you came in. What's your opinion?"

I was flattered. I, merely the chairman of the department, was being treated practically as an equal by these pros. I worked at living up to the role. "I suppose to make it look like a struggle when there hadn't been one."

"Maybe that," Messner said. "Or if there had been a struggle, to keep it looking like that so we'd think Tripp had caught a burglar in his house."

"Or still another reason," Kibble said. "Say he was thinking ahead to maybe being caught. A struggle would make the difference between premeditated and unpremeditated murder. A real cool customer. You have to have good nerves to hang around and clean up while all the time that bloody thing is on the floor."

"With all that blood spurting from his wound," Messner said, "spraying the wall and all, the killer would've gotten some blood on him. We're looking for somebody who might have seen somebody with blood on their clothes."

"I don't know, Nate," Kibble said. "A cool one like that, he wouldn't go running around town with blood on him." The chief said to Kibble, "Likely you're right, Dan," and then to me, "You must be thinking nearly everything we do in an investigation is a waste of time. You're right, but we have to do it. You never know where a break will come from. The big break I'm hoping for is finding the lady who was with Tripp when it happened."

I said, "So you've bought Mort Reach's sex angle?"

"His angle!" Messner snorted. "Reach can write anything makes a good story. News doesn't have to be true. He's written downright lies about my department in the *Ledger*. Anyway, exaggerations. Police have to deal with true facts. Evidence. From the beginning last night I never had a bit of use for it being a burglar. Even a crazy hopped-up kid wouldn't pick a little house like that while it's occupied. But where was the sex angle last night? There were rumors he liked the ladies. Is that any kind of evidence? This afternoon we have a few facts. Like semen stains on the bed sheet. Three separate big splotches looking like countries in a map. And all the same age."

"He had himself a time," Kibble said.

"And then his pajamas," Messner said. "He was a man wore pajamas in bed. Two clean pairs in his chest of drawers. Another pair in the hamper for dirty clothes in the bathroom. Why wouldn't he be wearing them when he got out of bed and went into his living room, where he was killed?"

"He could have been coming from the shower," I said, playing my role to the hilt.

"Yeah, could've," Messner said. "Then what about the semen stains? Not one but three! Like Dan said, that's like an orgy. A lady in bed with him, all right, and in bed with her he wouldn't be wearing his pajamas. These days even in movies for kids you see couples in bed together stark naked."

"My wife and I always sleep raw," Kibble said smugly.

"That so?" Messner said blankly. "Then, Mr. Dawson, there was what we found in an ashtray on the table beside the bed. Three stubs of marijuana cigarettes. We found nine more sticks in a drawer and some cubes of LSD in the refrigerator. Would you know if Tripp was a heavy drug user?"

"He didn't seem to be," I said, "but I wasn't that close to him. Did you find any hard stuff?"

"Just the pot and acid," Messner said. "Sometimes I think these days you can find the same in half the houses in Mount Birch. Not just kids and poets. Parents."

"You see, Mr. Dawson, how a picture begins to develop?" Kibble said. "We were growing partial to this one when you came in. Wednesday morning Tripp has a lady visitor and they—"

"Wednesday morning?" I broke in. "You have evidence it was in the morning?"

Kibble opened his mouth to answer, but Messner beat him to it. "I have a preliminary report from the medical examiner. Tentative, he calls it."

"If you ask me, as close as they'll ever get in the final report," Kibble said. "Those babies give themselves plenty of leeway."

"The interesting thing, the leeway is all in the daytime Wednesday," Messner said. "The M.E. puts the time of death between approximately nine in the morning and three in the afternoon."

"Sounds like business hours," Kibble said. "When a husband would be off at work. Being Tripp was a poet and writing at home, he could receive the lady any time convenient for her."

I thought of the stranger in sunglasses I had seen come out of my house while I was supposed to be at work, and it was like a kick in the stomach.

Messner had said something I hadn't listened to, and then Kibble was saying, "I started to give you my reconstruction. Nate agrees with it."

"Speculative," Messner grunted.

"It's the best we have so far and it hangs together," Kibble said. "The lady comes to Tripp's cottage. They have a drink of cherry soda together and leave the empty bottle on the living-room table. Then they go to bed. If he's dressed, he undresses along with her. If he's still in his pajamas, he takes them off and puts them in the hamper. They lay in bed smoking pot between doing the other thing she came to do. In the middle of it the killer comes in and finds them together."

"Why in the middle of it?" I said. "She could already have left."

"Whatever way, she's the motive," Kibble said. "He found her there with Tripp or he saw her leave or he knew she'd been there. It led to a fight, and during the fight the husband grabbed the bottle which—"

"Or her boy friend," Messner said. "Or her father or brother."

"Let me finish, Nate, okay?" Kibble said. "Whoever he was, he was killing mad. Maybe there wasn't even a quarrel. Not even a fight. Say through the window he saw them rolling in bed, and he slipped into the house and grabbed the bottle because it was the only thing around like a weapon, and he waited beside the bedroom door for Tripp to come out and then let him have it. The details don't matter in this case. Find the lady and you have the key to the case."

"That's right," Messner said. "Find her and prove she was there and get her to testify. Simple."

There was a silence. They seemed to have run out of anything more to tell me. They looked at me as if expecting me to come up with some brilliant observation. I couldn't think of a single one.

A lot more important to me, I couldn't think of how to bring up at this time in the most offhanded way the subject of Edward Martaine's insurance company.

Then Kibble spoke. "I was telling Nate there could be something in that book of Tripp's poems."

Messner had shifted the Lakeview envelope from the side to the middle of his desk. Putting his hands on either side of the envelope, he said, "The newspapers called it his collected work. Dan says this means it contains all the poems he ever wrote."

"Not all," I said. "Only those that appeared in print—in publications or his previous books or both."

"Anyway, I have this idea," Kibble said. "Poets write love poems. Right, Mr. Dawson? Do you follow me?"

"Completely," I said. "Find a poem by Gordon Tripp to a lady love, with her name conveniently in the title, and, ergo, you have your mystery woman."

"I'm serious," Kibble said a bit huffily. "Poets turn themselves inside out in their poems. That's something I wrote in a term paper in English when I was in college. I still remember it. And I used to write poetry when I was a kid." He shifted his bulk in his chair—like, in a way, a shy schoolboy. "The reason I tell you this, I know a little about poetry. I'm not an expert like you, of course. You're the editor, Mr. Dawson. You read the poems thoroughly. Was there any kind of clue? A hint?"

"I doubt it," I said. "And bear in mind that few are anywhere near current, since they'd all been previously published."

"Could be we have to go back years in this investigation," Kibble said. "Who can tell? Mr. Dawson, I'd like to take these poems home and read them carefully."

"I think you'd be wasting your time," I said. "But it's your time. I'll have a Xerox copy made for you at my office first thing Monday morning."

"Monday's three days off," Kibble said. "I'd like to read it this evening."

"It's the only copy in existence," I said. "I can't risk its being lost."

"I guarantee you I won't let it out of my sight," Kibble said. "Okay, Mr. Dawson?"

With anybody else, I supposed, they would simply have taken as evidence anything mailed to a murder victim. They had either the legal right or could obtain it. I was being handled with kid gloves, but I was being handled.

"If you insist," I said.

I hadn't meant that anybody but me should open the mailing envelope, but that was what Chief Messner at once proceeded to do. He took a staple remover from a drawer in his desk and extracted the staples. He slipped out the bulky manuscript of paste-ups on bond paper held together between cardboard by thick rubberbands. Clipped to the top cardboard was the long business envelope containing my covering letter.

He didn't ask permission if he could take out the letter and read it, but he did that, too. I waited. Without comment he reached diagonally across his desk to extend the letter to Kibble, who leaned for it. Kibble chewed his lower lip as he read. Finished, he rose and placed the letter on the desk and sat down again.

It struck me that from the first it wasn't so much the manuscript they had wanted to see as my letter to the man who had been dead for perhaps twenty-four hours when I had written it. Because of a hunch or whatever, they had come up with a fascinating item. I prepared myself for the attack.

"Mr. Dawson," the chief said in what amounted to a measured tone for a man who normally barked his words, "you told me you went to see Tripp last evening about a book of his you're publishing. This morning's newspapers said the same, and nobody denied it. But this letter is dated yesterday, and in it you say you're rejecting the book."

"My mind was changed for me shortly after I dictated the letter," I said. "Wednesday I brought the manuscript home with the intention to tell him in person I was turning it down and give it back to him. I tried to get him on the phone to see if he was in, and if he was, to go see him. You know what happened. Busy signals; he was already dead. Next morning, yesterday, I tried again to get him on the phone, but of course I couldn't. I then took the customary steps with a rejection. I had my secretary mail it back. Later in the morning there was a meeting of higher-ups and I was persuaded to reverse my decision. By then the manuscript and the letter were at the post office. Again my secretary tried to get him on the phone, this time so I could tell him the rejection was a mistake. I was in a highly embarrassing position. I had to speak to him or at least leave a note on his door before he received today's mail. That was why I went to his house last night."

Messner dipped his head to read the top copy of my statement. He seemed to take a long time. Kibble rose and tugged one of the carbons out from under the original Messner was reading, then they were both reading. If I had been a smoker, I would have lit a cigarette in order to have something to do with my hands.

Messner lifted his head and said what I expected him to say. "You didn't mention this in your signed statement either. Just that the reason you went to see Tripp was to discuss his book."

"I saw no point in going into the complexities of the publishing business," I said. Which was true. Also, that I had had no wish to broadcast how my arm had been delicately twisted by my bosses.

"In a serious case like this," Messner said, "we like to have the whole story."

"You can never tell what will be of help," Kibble put in. "A phrase. A word."

I felt hemmed in. Why this fuss over something so unimportant? And why were my armpits sweating? I had no cause to have any guilt feelings about anything connected with the murder. All my guilt feelings were concentrated elsewhere. I worked at being wholly relaxed.

"Look," I said, "I am aware that rule number one is to suspect first of all the person who reports a murder, and on top of that I fit into the theory that the murderer could be a working husband whose wife stays at home. All right, you have a job to do, and I certainly don't object to you men doing it. But please don't think me so stupid that if I had killed him I would deliberately have withheld information which can easily be checked out at my office, and which anyway doesn't matter one way or the other."

Messner looked sincerely shocked. "Whoever said anything like that, Mr. Dawson? You shouldn't get mad because I try to clear something up by asking a few questions."

"I'm not mad," I said.

"I'm glad to hear it," Messner said.

The soft soap was being laid on thickly. But there was Messner's head again dipped over his desk, rereading my rejection letter to Tripp. What was he looking for now?

"Paragon Materials," he said abruptly. He had a finger fixed to the bottom of the letterhead. "It says here Lakeview Press is a division of Paragon Materials. Isn't that Mr. Martaine's company?"

"He's president of the corporation," I said.

"I didn't know Mr. Martaine was in the book business too," Messner said.

"You name it and Paragon is in it," I said.

"Hey," Kibble said, "is that the Martaine whose wife lost the jewels?"

The turn of the conversation gave me the opening I had been looking for. "That's right, he is," I said to Kibble. Then to Messner, "This makes him my top boss. Yesterday at the office he spoke to me about the jewels. He had a notion my position with the department is something like police commissioner, and I had to put him straight." I uttered a deprecating laugh; it came out sounding inane to me. "He asked if our police could be counted on to do a thorough job on locating the jewels. I said everything possible was being done, though it won't be easy." Now for the subtle business. "I also told him I thought his insurance company would have an ace investigator on the job. Chief, was I right about that?"

"Sure thing, with all that money involved," Messner said. "He was here yesterday and again today. Took me out to lunch. The expense accounts these boys have!" He spoke to Kibble. "Gridley of Arco Mutual. Ever hear of him, Dan?"

"Hal Gridley," Kibble said. "A good man. Did Martaine carry full insurance?"

"He told me he's probably underinsured."

"My heart bleeds for him," Messner said. "He has that huge company and that great big house on Fiddle Hill and all that expensive property up there and I don't know what else. I'll tell you what a real loss is. When it happens to a poor man and he carries no insurance. A few weeks back my missus lost her engagement ring. I paid twelve hundred for it thirty-eight years ago. Worth lots more now. My gosh, the different kinds of insurance I carry, but for that I didn't have a nickel's worth."

"Tough," Kibble said.

I had what I needed. "Well, gentlemen," I said, "I'll be going if there's nothing else to keep me here." As I shook their hands, I kept repeating to myself Arco Mutual and Hal Gridley like somebody keeping in mind a couple of items his wife was sending him out to buy.

We had no Manhattan phone directory at home, so I stopped off at the drugstore in the shopping center, where there was one chained to the side of the end booth. Arco Mutual of Hartford, I found was the full name, and there was a midtown New York office. It was likely that Hal Gridley worked out of this office, though he wouldn't necessarily be the one I would have to do business with. I wrote down the phone number in my little memo book. The names I would remember.

I returned to my car (parked two aisles from where Sally had made her find) and drove home. It had been a not unfruitful hour in the police chief's office. Sally would be pleased.

5

My street had livened up greatly now that school was out. It was noisy with children and lawn mowers, and all my family was in sight outside the house.

My car passed within a yard of a white-haired woman I did not know standing with Chuck at the side of the driveway. He was telling her something in that fidgety way of his with adults, continually pounding a baseball into his glove as he spoke. On my left Sally knelt at the narrow flower bed up against the front wall of the house. She looked around at me—rather at the car—and dug her trowel into dirt. On the Huntley lawn Brandy and Penny squatted beside her bike. He had a screwdriver between his teeth and he was working on a wheel with a pair of pliers.

My world—and why did I have to envy any man?

I got out of the car, and I could hear Chuck say, "So we're two and two in our league, and if we beat them tomorrow we'll be tied for the lead."

"I hope you win," the woman said.

She wasn't white-haired, not in the sense of being old and gray; she couldn't have been out of her thirties. Her hair was one of those streaky platinum beauty-parlor jobs piled on her head in a couple of layers. Otherwise, a matronly type chubby in a flowered dress. Under her arm she carried a plastic portfolio.

I said, "Hi, Chuck," and he said, "Hi, Dad," and tossed the ball in the air and caught it with a swipe of his glove. The woman gave me a rather nice smile. I nodded to her, but she didn't introduce herself. I went over to see what Brandy was doing to Penny's bike.

"Brandy's fixing it for me," Penny informed me proudly. "The gears stick."

"Do you need help?" I asked him.

"Naw," he said.

Marie Huntley was coming to me; she must have seen me from the house. I went to meet her so we would be out of earshot of our innocent children. I told her that the ticket was being taken care of.

"Caleb, you're a doll."

Chuck was running up the street, no doubt to the ball field to practice for tomorrow morning's big game. The woman was walking off in the opposite direction.

"Do you know who she is?" I asked Marie.

"She's making a survey for the school district. You know, how many children are in the family and their ages. Caleb, I'm awfully grateful. George is out right now, but he'll come over and thank you."

"It's not necessary," I said.

Sally had gone into the house. I found her washing her hands in the bathroom. She didn't look around at me standing in the doorway.

"What's wrong?" I said.

"Wrong?" she said, bent over the basin. "What makes you think something's wrong?"

"The remote way you've acted since I came home from work."

"I don't know what you mean by remote."

"By remote I mean remote," I said. "We had a perfect night last night. This afternoon I seem to have lost contact with you."

"What nonsense!" Pause while she turned to take a towel from the bar. Then she said, "Did you find out the name of the insurance company?"

"Yes, from Nate Messner. Also the name of their investigator. He was in Mount Birch yesterday and today."

"What kind of an investigator?"

"Like a detective, I suppose. The big companies have them on their staffs. His name is Hal Gridley. Next week I'll call the company and speak either to him or somebody with authority to make decisions."

"Why wait till next week?"

"Because now it's past four on Friday and businesses close for the weekend."

"You don't have to speak to me as if I were a moron."

"You asked a moronic question and I answered it."

"And you—you're always so smart!"

She had finished drying her hands, but she continued to hold the towel. There were lines at the corners of her mouth I had never noticed before. Suddenly I wanted to take her in my arms, but I felt that if I did, it would be like grabbing hold of a stranger.

I said, "Sally, let's not let our nerves get the best of us."

"Yes, nerves!" she said. "How I wish this were over! Dear, you said you'll contact the insurance people next week. I hope you mean the first thing Monday morning."

"All right, Monday morning. I'll call them from a phone booth in the city and find out if they're willing to do business."

"Oh, they will be. They'd rather lose part of it than all of it. You said so yourself."

"That's what I think, not what I know. I'll have to find out."

"You said a hundred thousand dollars. Don't settle for a cent less."

"There may be haggling. If I can't get more than fifty thousand—"

"No! Don't be your usual foolish self about money. Don't give in to them. Hold out for a hundred thousand."

There in the cramped bathroom we stood confronting each other. Her eyes blazed. She looked feverish. With greed? With fear? If she was like me, with both.

"Let's not get into a stew about it now," I said. "Monday I'll find out how they'll react. It's not going to be settled in a matter of hours. And I've not yet come up with a plan for making the transfer."

"Transfer?"

"How do we exchange jewels for money without their ever finding out who we are?"

"You said it would be like collecting a ransom."

"It's a ransom, but not like a ransom in a kidnapping. There's no pressure of a human life at stake, where ransom is paid in the desperate hope that the victim will be released. The insurance company isn't going to leave money for me to pick up and trust me to send the jewels to them. There has to be a personal exchange on the spot, the jewels for the money, and how can I do that without showing myself and be around for the police to nab me?"

"Dear, you're clever. You'll think of a way."

"A minute ago I was a fool. Now I'm clever."

With a cry like a sob she threw herself at me. "Let's love each other," she said. "Now of all times."

And she clung to me, my poor sweetheart, lovely wife of my bosom, mother of my children. We stood in the bathroom holding each other.

6

After dinner Sally and I went to the movies. Chuck was now old enough to be the sitter for both himself and Brandy. We left them watching television.

In the theater we sat holding hands. We had come to relax, and I for one relaxed so well that during the picture I whispered in her ear, "Wear the jewels on your skin the way you did last night."

"Pay attention to the picture."

"I'd rather anticipate how you'll look in them naked and the effect that has on you. Not to mention me. Okay, honey?"

"Maybe," she said, squeezing my hand.

We returned home in good spirits. After we had looked in on the sleeping children, she took first crack at the bathroom. When I came out, she was already in bed. In her nightgown. And the jewels not on her.

I wound the clock and climbed in with her and gathered her to me for a passionate kiss. The passion was all on my part. When I started to pull down her nightgown, she said, "No, don't." And turned her back to me, curled in a ball.

The sexual moods of wives. But this I hadn't been led to expect.

"Is that it?" I said. "Turn your back and go to sleep."

"Dear, I'm tired."

Lying flat on her back beside her, my hip against her buttock, I could hardly breathe with sexual tension. Tired? Tired of what? Usually a night like last night whetted our appetites, hers as well as mine, but what if her appetite had been sated by a kid in yellow windbreaker and dark glasses who had beat it from my house when I had arrived and had left her naked under her housecoat? Hell, was I at that again? But why would a door-to-door magazine salesman drive out of the area as soon as he had left her? Wouldn't his next stop that early in the afternoon have been the house on either side of ours or across the street or around the corner?

Questions with a choice of answers, and if tonight in my need for sex I wanted to titillate myself with far-fetched answers, I was having my fun. I was no jealous-husband type, and she had never given me reason to be. Why now?

I knew why now. I knew the glib Freudian explanations. I was by-passing my sense of guilt at being a crook by tormenting myself with wild images of magazine salesmen, of all things!

I sat up, fuzzy-headed. In the light from the hall I looked down at Sally. Sleeping, she was at peace. We had a very good marriage. I kissed her cheek and lay down, covering her to the neck with the blanket and then myself.

I wouldn't kid around when I got to speaking on the phone with a big shot from the insurance company. Listen, bud, one hundred grand, take it or leave it, and they being hard-headed businessmen would take it. All right, they would say, bring over the jewels at such and such a time and we will have the cash waiting for you in small, unmarked bills. But I'd be too smart. I'd say... I'd say... not in this bed, our bed, her Roman-striped housecoat still in the closet and the yellow windbreaker and black T-shirt and the rest of his clothes on the floor... disguise myself for the exchange, a beard and a mustache, a shaggy wig... childish... not our bed, the niceties maintained, the sofa bed in the study, not bothering to open it because they wouldn't need much room... an exchange of keys to two lockers in Grand Central Terminal, the jewels in one and the money in the other, but of course the police would be waiting for me at the one with the money in it... she would never... my lovely devoted wife against whose back I was snuggling... tomorrow I would work out a foolproof exchange... tomorrow and tomorrow...

Saturday

The Little League game between Chuck's team, the Royals (sponsored by Berman's Hardware), and the Titans (sponsored by the County National Bank) was scheduled to start at ten o'clock and the meeting of the Village Board of Trustees at ten-thirty. Since ball games almost always started on time and meetings almost never, I figured I could get in a couple of innings. Brandy and I went together. Sally preferred to stay home to give the kitchen and stove a thorough cleaning.

Chuck's Royals were up first and he batted second in the lineup. With one out he walked and took second on an infield out. The next batter grounded to the first baseman, who had trouble coming up with the ball; he threw too late to the pitcher covering first to get the runner. Meanwhile Chuck had rounded third. This was no play to score on, but Chuck, all arms and legs, kept going. I screamed, Brandy screamed, a couple of hundred children and adults screamed. Chuck slid and beat the throw home.

When the uproar had subsided, somebody said to the back of my head, "Your son can fly, Mr. Dawson. Anybody else would have been out by a mile."

I turned. Brandy and I were sitting in the second row of the four-row open stand. The speaker was a vaguely familiar blond woman seated directly behind me. She smiled a cozy, round-faced smile.

"You don't remember me, Mr. Dawson. I was speaking with Chuck yesterday in your driveway when you drove up. I heard him call you Dad."

"You were making a survey for the school," I said.

"That's right. It's just a temporary job."

She had let her streaked platinum hair down. Literally. It hung girlishly loose past her shoulders. The matronly flowered dress had given way to white sweater and black pants, both of which she more than adequately filled. Loads of eye make-up. Far from the matronly type she had looked yesterday when she had been representing the dignity of the school district.

"I'm an ardent baseball fan," she told me, leaning forward with her arms on her knees. "I die every time the Yankees lose. But I like to watch these children as much as the pros. They're so intense." She stood up. The benches were backless; she stepped over our bench and sat down beside Brandy and enveloped him with her chubby smile. "Let's see, you're Brant Dawson. I remember your name from the survey. You were working on that darling little girl's bicycle. Remember me?"

"I guess so," he muttered.

"Would you like some popcorn, Brant?"

She had a box of the hot popcorn high school girls were making and selling behind the stand for the benefit of the school band. Brandy said, "Sure, thanks," and dug in. Then reaching past him she offered the box to me. I took a handful. The boy at bat looked at a third strike and the top of the first inning was over with one run scored.

The only dramatic event in the bottom of the inning was that Chuck caught an easy pop fly. While the Trojans were going down in order the survey lady was making herself perfectly at home with us, especially with Brandy, who as he munched her popcorn briefed her on the batting and fielding ability of every boy on both teams.

I spoke to her only once, when the Royals were taking the field after having failed to score in the second. "You know my name, but I'm afraid I don't know yours."

"Kelly," she said.

"Any connection with the Greg Kellys on Ridge Drive?"

"I'm afraid not. I'm rather new in town. I know hardly anybody as yet."

There was a roar. The Royals' right fielder had played a line single into a triple. The next boy up hit a grounder to Chuck. I held my breath. He handled it well, faked the runner back to third, and tossed out the batter. I had seen it done worse at Shea Stadium. The woman named Kelly stood with Brandy and me to applaud Chuck.

The second inning passed with the score one to nothing in favor of the Royals. I would have liked the game to end that way so that Chuck would get the headline. But it was time for me to leave. I told Brandy I was going and I told Miss or Mrs. Kelly I was glad to have met her.

"The pleasure was all mine, Mr. Dawson." She patted Brandy's knee. "I've found a friend and an authority on the game."

I lingered a while longer at my car parked on the road. In the third inning Chuck was again the second man up. He lifted a high fly to left. Unfortunately the fielder was right there and the ball stayed in his glove. I drove to the Municipal Building and got to the meeting fifteen minutes late, which was five minutes before it started.

The courtroom where we met was jammed with the inevitable indignant public. Today the indignation was both pro and con over the big thing on the agenda—the report of the Planning Commission opposing the rezoning of the lovely Greeley property on Notch Lake for an industrial park. For two hours the courtroom was filled with cheers and boos, charges and countercharges, innuendos and open insults. Participatory democracy in action. Mayor Lytoon and one other trustee were for the industrial park because it would greatly increase the assessed valuation of the property; the other three of us backed the Planning Commission and ecology. When the mayor saw how the vote would go, he maneuvered the entire matter back to the commission for further study.

What with other business, it was past one o'clock before the matter of the police contract came up. The mayor wanted to appoint a committee of three to negotiate with the Mount Birch Police Protective Association. A standard ploy. He would have to name me to the committee, but he would also put himself on it and most likely Doc Birdwell, who was ardently economy-minded about everything but doctors' fees. I countered with a motion to request the State Public Employment Relations Board to send in a fact finder. The trustees were hungry and weary and had things they wanted to do on a sunny Saturday afternoon. My motion carried, three to one, Doc Birdwell against and the mayor abstaining because he hated to be in a minority. Quickly we adjourned.

It was around two o'clock when I returned home. And the little red Opal was there. Not in my driveway, as yesterday afternoon. Parked on the street, directly in front of my house.

The magazine salesman was back. What the hell for?

He and Sally were in the living room. Another man was there, too, sitting placidly with legs crossed in the wing chair.

Sally rushed to my arms. Her face was ravished by tears.

"Caleb," she wailed, "they've got Brandy."

2

Over her tawny hair I looked at those two.

The one I had seen come out of the house yesterday stood against the wall, shoulders against the Modigliani print, stolidly watching me from behind his dark glasses. The other was considerably older, by contrast a picture of disarming ease in my chair. As our eyes met, he gave me the tentative nod of a visitor who had not yet been formally introduced to his host. Then he brought to his mouth one of the squat amber juice glasses from the kitchen cabinet.

I said, "Sally, what are you talking about? Who's got Brandy?"

"They kidnapped him," she sobbed against my chest.

"Kidnapped?" It didn't penetrate. "Who are these men?"

"The kidnappers."

On the end table beside the wing chair stood a bottle of my Scotch. What the man was drinking like any guest.

"The kidnappers?" I was too stunned to say anything which wasn't an echo of her words.

"Your wife exaggerates," the older one said. He had a thin, gray face. Bags under his eyes in puffy layers. "Your son is on an outing with a lady. Every now and then she phones here to find out if it is time to bring him home. Whether or not she does depends entirely on you."

Against me Sally shuddered.

"What do you want from us?" I said.

What else could there be? Except that how could anybody possibly know? "Please, Dawson, let's omit that act." He had a voice that sounded bored with itself. "Your wife's story is that she doesn't know where you have hidden the jewels. I am inclined to doubt her, since two days ago she did have the brooch, and yesterday she attempted to make a bargain with my young friend here. The lady who is with your son already has phoned twice. Now that you are home, I expect to have them before she phones again." He drank and added matter-of-factly, "If you care for your son."

If some of his words didn't make sense, the important ones did. Sally bored her face deeper into my chest, like a distressed child trying to hide herself there. She had managed to hold them off till I came home. Now here I was, the man of the family, the stalwart husband, and it was up to me to come up with a stroke of genius to retain for us our wealth without endangering our son.

"Sally!" Grasping her by the shoulders, I held her away from me so I could look into her anguished face. "Sally, what have you been holding out on me?"

"Dear, I was such a fool. I thought... all I did..." Her voice fell apart.

I let go of her. I stood in the middle of the living room, facing the man in the chair. "*You* tell me!"

"Are you saying you don't know about the brooch business?"

"Not a thing."

"I do believe you. I understand that you are not an unworldly man—an editor, an official of this town. You would have shown a modicum of sense. Greed clouds one's mind—I find I must sometimes struggle for rationality when sorely tempted—and this is especially so with the female of the species."

"I didn't ask for a lecture," I said.

"No. But we must deal with one another, and it is essential that you understand I hold all the cards." He sipped my Scotch. "Your wife threatened me with the fact that you are head of the local police force. This was supposed to terrify me. A rational person—like you, I trust—would realize that your very respectability is to your disadvantage in this situation. Any move you make to counter me will expose you and your wife."

"And expose you as a kidnapper," I said, "which is a far worse crime."

"Who says I am? A lady with whom you were friendly at a baseball game took your son on an outing. He went eagerly with her. She was attentive and generous, and in his eyes she was a friend of his father. Mr. and Mrs. Dawson are the only criminals in this room. Otherwise, would I and my friends reveal ourselves? I concede that if you compel us to retain him for a length of time, our status will change. But tell me, sir, are you willing to engage in a war of nerves with your son's well-being at stake? I do not think so."

"Brandy never came home from the game," Sally said. She had dropped limply down on the hassock when I let go of her. "Chuck came home without him. He didn't know where Brandy was. I began to worry. Then these awful men came and told me."

"Where's Chuck now?"

"I couldn't give him lunch. I couldn't have him in the house while they are here. I gave him money to buy a hamburger. Oh, Caleb!"

On the other side of me the older one had taken my bottle of Scotch from the end table and was refilling the juice glass.

"A fair Scotch," he said, raising the glass to me. "I acquired a thirst waiting for you. During our search of the house I came across your liquor cabinet. Since your wife did not offer me a drink, I helped myself. Yes, we conducted a search, though only in the obvious places. I saw no point in letting my young friend take this charming place apart. This entire matter can be kept simple and orderly. I must warn you, however, that my patience is not endless."

Meanwhile, in his smug confidence he was content to sit there and enjoy my whiskey along with the drone of his voice. And not telling me anything much but the obvious. I turned from him to my wife.

"Sally, what about the brooch?" I stood over her huddled on the hassock. "What crazy thing did you do yesterday when this kid came to the house?"

Her head tilted back. She had a facial tissue at her chin. "It wasn't yesterday. It was Thursday. I mean when I went to the pawnshop in the city."

"You *what?*"

"I know," she said. "But that was the day after I found them, and at the time you were so unsure about what we ought to do. You were talking about a reward from the owner. A very small reward, if anything at all. Remember? You went off to work. I was home alone, all the time listening to the radio. Then there was the news about them having been lost and how much they were worth. Then during your lunch hour you called me, and you were still vague about doing anything. Remember? It wasn't till you came home from the city that you told me you had this idea about making a deal with the insurance company. By then I'd already been at the pawnshop, where—"

"Couldn't you have waited?" I broke in. "No, you couldn't wait because you couldn't trust me to keep them. You went to sell them so you could hand me an accomplished fact."

"Only one piece."

She looked up at me with soft face and humid blue-gray eyes absolutely earnest. Our audience was silent, listening, probably amused. The hell with them. They knew all this. I didn't.

"Go on," I told her.

"I thought at least I would find out what I could get for the brooch. I drove to the city and looked and looked till I found a small pawnshop. It was rather seedy and looked like they'd not ask too many questions."

The man in the chair chuckled. She stared past me at him.

"Never mind him," I said.

"I thought there was no risk. There'd been no description of the pieces on the radio." She sat forward on the hassock, her hands clasped as if in prayer. "The pawnshop was empty except for the man behind the counter. I told him a boy friend had given me the brooch and we had split up and I wanted to sell it before he could take it back. He looked at it and said yes, he was interested. He went into the back room and I heard him on the phone. I was frightened. I would have left if he hadn't taken the brooch with him. He came back all smiles. He said he wasn't the boss, the boss was out, and he couldn't take it on himself to offer a price on a piece that valuable. He said if I left my name and phone number, his boss would call me when he got back."

"You didn't!"

"I certainly did not. I told him I'd be back next day and took the brooch and drove home."

"And you were still dressed in your beige suit when you picked me up at the station," I said. "And you told me you'd been at a meeting of the League of Women Voters, and that was all you told me."

"You would have been angry. There had been so much fighting about the jewels already. I realized I'd made a mistake. The pawnbroker suspected something. And soon he'd see a description of the jewels and he would know where they had come from." Her hands kept unfolding and folding. "But he could have no idea who I was. How could I be found? I decided not to bother you with it. Just to forget it."

The man in the chair chuckled some more.

I swung around to him. "Are you the pawnbroker?"

"I? Heaven forbid."

"A fence then?"

"You may call me an expert merchandiser of such items as your wife tried to sell."

"How did you locate her?"

"A simple matter. The pawnbroker followed her to her car and took down the plate number. He is not a man who considers himself dishonest. On the other hand, when an opportunity presents itself to pick up an extra buck, he seizes it, even as you and I. He relayed the information to me and thenceforth was completely out of it but for an honorarium I will be obliged to send him. Next morning the papers carried a description of the brooch as one of the pieces Mrs. Martaine had lost. I had only a license number, but it so happens I have a connection who, also for an honorarium, can obtain the name and address to match a license number with—"

"Gab, gab, gab!" the young one burst out. It was the first time I heard his voice. "Where's all this crapping around getting us?"

"Would you very much mind letting me handle this?" the older one said.

"Yeah, I see how you're handling it." The young one had stepped away from the wall; within the frame of his pirate's mustache his mouth twitched. "Like we was at a party, you sitting and lapping up the booze and gabbing about how smart you are. Jesus Christ, you want free liquor, I'll buy you some. In a minute I can make them do the kind of talking we want to hear."

"You could," the older one said. "But it's not my way, and we're doing this my way, so kindly do me a favor and shut up."

Those dark glasses focused on the other for a long moment before their wearer returned his shoulders to the wall. In a gray suit complete with dress shirt and tie he could more easily have passed for a door-to-door salesman than yesterday in black T-shirt and yellow windbreaker. I wondered if he had a gun in a holster under that buttoned jacket.

"Left to himself, my young friend would bull his way to the jewels," the older one droned at me. "He would concentrate on your lovely wife, to his immense enjoyment. It would be nasty and quick and effective. In no time you would both break. However, I abhor violence, if for no other reason than that its consequences tend to get out of control. I have survived in a hazardous profession because I rely solely on this." He tapped his temple. "I would have been happy to have been able to avoid taking your son, though her acceptance of my offer would have added considerably to my expense. She is a quite obdurate—"

The phone rang. Everything else stopped—his voice, our breathing. I had never heard a bell so jarringly shrill.

"You answer it, Dawson," the older one said. "If it is my lady friend, I'll speak to her. Otherwise, I advise extreme caution in whatever you say."

I went into the dinette and picked up the phone. It was a man's voice.

"Is this Mr. Dawson who was Gordon Tripp's editor at Lakeview Press?"

"That's right."

"I'm his brother Christopher. Nate Messner said you were anxious to speak to me."

"Gordon never got the chance to sign a contract for a book we'd like to do. It's his collected work."

"I read about it in the paper. I am very pleased. It will be like a memorial to him."

The stillness in the living room behind me weighed down on me.

"Look, Mr. Tripp, I can't discuss this with you right now. I understand you flew out from Denver. How long are you staying?"

"We plan on a full week. Mrs. Tripp is with me. We used to be New Yorkers ourselves, you know. That was how come we bought the cottage here in Mount Birch as a summer place. Having had to come back for this tragic occasion, we thought we might as well make a week of it. There is no place like New York."

"Can we get together first thing next week and settle the matter of the contract?"

"I'll be glad to. It so happens I'm Gordon's executor. Last year I finally persuaded him to draw up a will. He said it was pointless because he owned nothing but his car and his typewriter, and I had bought him those. There is one thing I learned from having a brother a poet. No matter how good a poet he is, he can't make the living of a common laborer on his poetry alone."

"Mr. Tripp," I said desperately, "an emergency has come up and I can't speak with you any longer. Will you call me at Lakeview Press on Monday?"

"I sure will. I am anxious to have that book as a most fitting memorial to Gordon."

"Good-bye for now, Mr. Tripp."

I hung up before he could say more. In the living room nobody seemed to have stirred. I resumed my position in front of the wing chair, like an actor who had the placement for his feet chalked out for a particular scene.

"You mentioned an offer to my wife," I said. "What kind of offer?"

"She did not tell you that either? Ah, women! I surmise she feared you would have the good sense to take the five thousand dollars and consider yourself fortunate to get it. As indeed you would have been."

I couldn't see Sally's face. Her head was bowed.

"Let me get this straight," I said to the older one. "You sent this kid here yesterday to offer five thousand for the jewels?"

"I did. And I must say it was quite generous in view of what my other expenses will be disposing of them. She began by denying she had them. When it became clear that my friend knew about the brooch, she demanded one hundred thousand dollars, no less!"

"They're worth a quarter of a million," I said.

"Legitimately perhaps. Their disposal will not be legitimate. The inflated idea you amateurs have of the fruits of crime!"

I said, "All right, we'll take the five thousand dollars."

The young one snorted. The older one smirked and took a long drink, leaving little in the glass when his mouth came away.

"I am certain you will," he droned. "Now that you have the entire picture, you are trying to salvage what you can. But that was yesterday's offer. Five thousand dollars was for a safe and simple transaction. Since then I have had to go to some trouble and, unfortunately, a certain amount of risk. I always plan for contingencies. In a matter like this, time is of the essence. Yesterday I sent my lady friend along with my young friend here. She was waiting in the wings, as it were. When he came out empty-handed, as I had anticipated he might, she went into action. In a short time she learned a good bit about the Dawson family by pretending to be taking a survey for the school, speaking not only with Mrs. Dawson but with talkative neighbors, and being lucky enough to have the opportunity to become friendly with your sons. Then this morning at the baseball game—"

"For God's sake!" Sally was on her feet, trembling. "Give us the five thousand dollars and you can have the jewels."

"Madam, you shock me." He downed whatever was left in the glass and smacked his lips. "How can you people think of money at a time like this? I said the situation has changed since yesterday. I offer you something infinitely more precious than money. I offer your son."

"They're in the bedroom," I said. "I'll get them."

"We will go with you."

The older one rose from the wing chair. The young one took his shoulders from the wall. Sally stepped to my side. All four of us were in motion when the phone rang. We stopped dead.

"You answer it this time," the older one told the young one. "If it's her, tell her to hold the line."

The young one went into the dinette. From where I stood I couldn't see him, but I could hear him say, "Yeah?... Yeah, me... Yeah, they're getting them this minute... Hang on till we make sure." He reappeared.

"Is my son with her?" Sally asked him.

"Where then?"

We resumed our trek into the bedroom, I leading the way. They crowded in after me. I pulled open the secret drawer at the bottom molding of the dresser.

It was absolutely empty.

3

Squatting at the dresser, I looked up at Sally staring open-mouthed down into the drawer. "Did you take them out?"

"They have to be in there," she said. "I don't understand."

"When was the last time you saw them?"

"Yesterday afternoon. If was right after you left to see Chief Messner." She had to clear her throat. "This man had been here with his offer, and the jewels were on my mind, and I took them out for another look at them. But I put them back."

I straightened up. Between the bed and the dresser I was hemmed in by those two men. My heart was choking me.

"You heard her," I said. "They were in there and they are gone."

"Jesus Christ, is that the best you can dream up?" The young one poked a finger into the joint of my shoulder. His dark lenses were like the eyes of some nightmare creature. "No more crap, mister. Where are they?"

I stepped backward away from his finger; my ankles struck the open drawer. Sally whimpered as she chewed on her knuckles.

"There's only one place they can be," I said to his face close to mine. "You found them when you searched this room and you're keeping them for yourself."

"Why, you son-of-a-bitch!" he said, leaning on me.

"I'll handle this." The older one shoved himself between us. "Dawson, for your information I was the one who searched this room while he was searching the others. Assuming he would be so stupid as to try to double-cross me—

which I have very good reason to doubt he would—the fact is he was never in this room."

"Did he go to the bathroom while you were in another part of the house? It's next to this. He could have slipped in then."

"I see no purpose in debating the matter." He seemed bored to death with me. "But I will humor you for one more minute. That is as much longer as I will keep my lady friend waiting on the phone. If he did have an opportunity to come into this room, it was after I had searched it. I had neither the time nor the inclination to do a thorough job of it, since you were expected home at any moment anyway, but I did go through every drawer."

"Including this secret drawer?"

"My dear man, secret only to babes in the woods. One of my experience begins by looking for such a drawer." He shook his head. "This is the end of my patience. If you are leveling with me, your wife isn't. I have learned that she does not tell you everything."

"I swear!" Sally said. "They were in there. I want my son. I don't know where they are."

"One of you had better know," he said in a suddenly brisk voice. "Come with me, all of you."

We followed him back into the living room. Sally was weeping against the back of her hand. In the hall I put my arm about her waist. Sagging against me, she blubbered, "Caleb, they disappeared. They really did. I don't care about them any more. I want Brandy."

"Yes. I know."

The younger one brought up the rear, and in the living room he stayed behind us. Like a guard. Did he have a gun? Would he stop me if I dashed out to call the police? Did I dare leave Sally alone with them?

The older one was in the dinette, picking up the phone. We listened to him speak to the woman who had Brandy.

"Hello?... Sorry to keep you waiting... No, not yet. They're still giving me the runaround... Take him where we arranged and lock him up in the—"

"No!" Sally shrieked. "You can't!"

Over his shoulder he looked at her. Then he said into the phone, "Listen, I think she's breaking. I'll give them one last chance. Hang around for another ten minutes, then call again before you do anything drastic to the boy."

His words were to the woman, but they were meant for us.

He was coming out of the dinette when a bell rang. He looked around at the phone he had hung up and took a step back to it.

"It's the doorbell," the young man told him.

Sally stiffened in the circle of my arm. I let go of her; I felt myself poised like a sprinter waiting for the starting gun. The doorbell rang again. By then the young one was at the triple windows, peering out past an open drape.

"Cops," he whispered. "Two of 'em."

The older one came all the way out of the dinette. "Dawson, if you let on... if you say one word..."

I went to the door. Almost I ran. I flung it open.

Sergeant Newsome and Patrolman Jackson stood there. Both in uniform. Guns on their hips. I could have hugged them. "Have you a minute?" Newsome said. "The men are confused about the board's decision. We're on duty, but Lieutenant Burke knows we're here. Okay?"

"Come in, come in," I said.

Sally gaped at them entering. The knuckles of both her thumbs were at her teeth. I hoped she would have the control to keep quiet and follow my lead.

"You have company," Newsome said when he saw those two in the living room. "We can come back later."

"No, no!" I said. "My business with these gentlemen is practically over. They're waiting for a phone call. They'll stay in the study while we talk in this room." I had regained my ability to smile; I smiled at the other two standing very still, very watchful. "Will you gentlemen come with me?"

The older one said, "I guess we'll leave."

"I wouldn't think of letting you go before you receive your phone call," I said. "It's as important to me as to you. Sally, offer the officers refreshments. I'll be right back. Gentlemen, this way."

I conducted them into the hall and into the study. I closed the door and stood with my back against it.

"Dawson," the older one said in a tone I had not heard him use before, "if you think—"

"I'll tell you what I think," I cut him off. "Your threats are no longer worth a damn. You lost your power when I ran out of choices. I would have given you the jewels if I had had them. I don't know what happened to them, but they're gone, and you don't believe me. What's left for me? It's either my son or my standing in the community and maybe a short jail term. Is that a choice? If you're as smart as you boast you are, you know it isn't."

"The son-of-a-bitch is bluffing," the young one said.

"Am I? Then try me. Try leaving this house past the officers in the living room. You've heard I'm chairman of their department. One word from me and they'll arrest you for any reason they can think of and take you to the station house for questioning, and you'll have my son brought back pronto to save yourself from a kidnapping rap. Sure, that'll expose me and my wife, but what else can we do? A while ago you spoke of a safe and simple transaction. You meant the jewels, now I mean my son. Have him brought back and you two can walk out of here. No explanation to anybody. No harm done to any of us."

"Agreed," the older one said. "At the same time let's be practical. I'll go higher than five thousand dollars. This will cut greatly into my share, but I'm willing to give you ten thousand."

"I won't tell you again I haven't got them."

"You may think you haven't. But your wife—"

"My wife is a mother. If you don't know what that means, there's no use telling you. We want our son back as soon as that woman can get him here after she calls. There's a phone jack in this room. I'll bring the phone from my bedroom."

When I returned in half a minute with the phone, the younger one swung away from one of the two screened windows as if caught in a guilty act. The older one was on my desk chair—not lounging now, not bored now. The bags under his eyes seemed to possess all his face. Like me, like Sally, he had seen the glimmer of wealth fade away. Both silently watched me plug the phone into the jack in the baseboard beside the desk.

They had run out of words, but I had a few left. At the door I said, "I'll keep the cops occupied between here and the exits till my son comes home. You can get out through the windows, but all that will do for you is make you fugitives as well as kidnappers. I can provide perfect descriptions of all three of you. Let's none of us have to expose ourselves. Okay?"

The older one nodded, and I left them there.

In the living room Sergeant Newsome and Patrolman Jackson were seated side by side on the sofa in that unbending way of officers in uniform. Sally was serving them Coke and cookies from a tray on the coffee table. She raised her head when I came in. Apparently she had washed her face.

"I expect Brandy home very soon," I told her.

Her eyes came alive. She sniffled as if with a cold and resumed pouring Coke into glasses. I needn't have worried about her control. She handed each man a glass, then filled one for me. The Coke stung my constricted throat. As I stood drinking, she took her favorite seat when we had guests, the hassock, and hugged her knees. I think we both wanted to scream.

"...doesn't look like an advantage for us," Sergeant Newsome was saying.

I hadn't been listening closely. My ears were waiting for a bell. The ten minutes since her phone call must surely have passed.

"It would have been definitely to your disadvantage if the mayor had had his way and put it into the hands of a stacked committee," I said.

"The men feel a state fact finder will never give us everything we're asking for."

"The men are learning the way of the prosperous," I said. "The more they'll get the more they'll want. One of the top labor mediators in the East is one of my authors. He told me it's almost always to the union's advantage to have a fact finder. Management, in this case the board, is content to maintain the status quo, and the worst a fact finder will do is effect a compromise. Nobody in life ever gets all he wants."

"He only recommends, doesn't he?" Jackson said. "We're not bound by his decision."

"That's right," I said. "His recommendation will be the floor. From there you can go on and demand the moon."

While we now were poor again—or what Sally called poor. Good. Let us have Brandy back unharmed. Please God, let us be poor and have Brandy back.

Then it rang. My insides jumped. Sally bit her lower lip. "Pardon me," I said, putting down my glass. I touched her head when I passed her on the way to the dinette. I picked up the phone.

"For us?" Sergeant Newsome asked.

I shook my head. The voice of the chubby platinum blonde was saying, "But did you get them?"

"I'll tell you later," the older one replied. "Dawson, are you on the line?"

"Yes."

He said, "Honey, bring the boy home at once. How long will it take?"

"Ten, fifteen minutes. Listen, did it go okay?"

"We will discuss that later. Don't drive up to the house. Leave him off a block from the house and then go to our place. I'll meet you there."

"You sound like something is wrong."

"Do as I say."

I waited till they had hung up, then I did. Sally had her tense face turned to me. I made a V-for-Victory sign with my fingers and moved past her to the wing chair.

The bottle of Scotch was at hand on the end table. It was almost empty; the bastard had guzzled quite a bit of it. I offered some to the officers. Properly they refused. Jackson carefully explained that he never drank while on duty, which was not what I had heard. I poured a stiff one for myself in the glass from which I had drunk my Coke.

They became uneasy about staying so long while on duty.

They said they'd come back in the evening. I said I wouldn't be home tonight (not true); it was all right, they had my permission to stay and discuss what was after all department business; headquarters knew where to reach them if an emergency arose. Lounging back, I let my mouth run, pausing only for sips of Scotch (much like the man who had sat in the same chair not so long ago), holding them in their seats by expounding on the differences between fact-finding and arbitration and mediation. While Sally, as if bored with my long-windedness, went to fuss in the kitchen as an excuse to watch the street from the window over the sink.

All of a sudden she ran to the front door and out of the house. I said, "Excuse me," and put down my glass and followed her with as much dignity as I could manage. Brandy was running toward the house laden with toys.

He was startled and embarrassed by his mother's hugging and kissing him and sobbing right out there in the street where everybody could see. I hovered over him. A doll dressed like a fashion model fell from his arms. I picked it up. He had had the lucky number on a wheel at the fair. What fair? The firemen's fair in a nearby town the lady who was my friend had taken him to after the Little

League game. She bought him anything he wanted. Gosh, he had a bellyache from all the stuff he ate. "Look at the airplane kit, Dad, it flies with a real motor." And he had three potholders she had given him the money to buy for Mommy, and a pen for me which wrote in six different colors, and he'd saved a candy bar for Chuck, and Clara had also bought him—

"Clara?" I said.

"Hey, Dad, don't you know your friend's name even?"

"Oh, yes. Clara."

Of such had been the nature of terror.

Sergeant Newsome and Patrolman Jackson were coming out of my house. I joined them. I accompanied them to their car. Shaking my hand in turn, they said they guessed I had done the right thing for them at the board meeting.

After they had driven off I went back inside to tell those two in the study to get the hell out of my house.

4

Chuck came banging into the house. "Where's Mommy? I'm starved."

"She's lying down."

"What's the matter, is she sick?"

"Just tired. Brandy told me your team won five-three and you got two hits after I left."

"You should've stayed, Dad, and seen me slam a double with two on and two out. They both scored and then I scored on an error, and that was the ball game. And you know what, Dad? I handled every chance at short cleanly."

"That's great."

Outside the house Penny Huntley squealed. She had been off somewhere with her parents; when Brandy heard their car return, he had rushed out to give her the doll he had won at the fair. I patted Chuck's head because he was also my son.

"I'm dying of hunger," he said. "When will we eat?"

"It's only five o'clock. Make yourself a peanut butter and jelly sandwich."

He went into the kitchen. I decided to look in on Sally. Quietly I opened our bedroom door. She was lying on the bedspread in bra and panties.

"Did you sleep?"

"No. Not really."

"How do you feel?"

"Headachy. I'll take a couple of aspirins. Dear, I've been lying here thinking. It must have been the pawnbroker. He came last evening when we were at the movies and the children had gone to bed. You've always said a thief could open our locks easily."

"If he had intended to do that, why didn't he keep to himself the knowledge that you had the jewels?"

"He needed that horrid man to find out who I was from the license-plate number. People like that, they always double-cross each other. Either the pawnbroker or somebody else in the gang."

"My candidate is the kid. He came back after he had spoken to you yesterday afternoon, then he had to go through the act of pretending today he didn't have them."

"Or he and that woman working together against their boss."

"What's the difference who?" I said. "There's nothing we can do, so let's stop thinking about it."

"Oh, Caleb, how I messed it up! And to think what could have happened to Brandy!"

"Well, he for one had a fine time." I sat down on the bed and put my hand on her bare thigh. "Honey, let's face it. We weren't cut out to be crooks. I would have messed it up if you hadn't. Worse than you did, because I might have landed in jail. I kidded both of us. How could I know the insurance company would give us a hundred thousand dollars? Or fifty thousand? Or a red cent? It was wishful thinking. And how would I have worked the transfer without being caught? Even real crooks don't know how; that's why they have to deal with fences for a pittance. We're babes in the woods, as the guy said. Like believing that drawer was secret when it was about the first place anybody who knew the ropes would look. All in all, we got off lucky. We're no worse off than before you found them."

"That's sour grapes," she said.

"It could be. But honestly, I'm able to breathe. I don't know what we'd do if we came across those jewels again. Hell, I do know. We'd take up where we left off. But I'd hate it."

"You enjoy being poor," she said.

I took my hand from her thigh. I stood up. A nerve throbbed in my cheek. "You're starting that again," I said. "My God, didn't you learn this afternoon we're rich in the only way that counts?"

"Darling, darling." She reached both arms up for me. "I know, I have two wonderful sons and the sweetest husband of anybody. Come lie down here with me."

I took off my shoes and got on the bed.

"I love you," she said, snuggling to me. "It was all such a mess. I'm glad it's over. Say you love me."

"I love you very much."

After a while we heard both children in the house. They were yelling at each other about something.

Sally untangled herself from me. "I'd better think of starting dinner."

We got off the bed. We were back to normal.

Sunday

What did one do on a rainy Sunday afternoon when Sally (in the hangover from her shattered dream) occupied herself in the kitchen with Marie Huntley on one of their mutual health kicks, the baking of whole-wheat bread, and when neighborhood boys had descended out of the storm to help Chuck help Brandy assemble the airplane from the kit the kind lady had bought Brandy yesterday at the firemen's fair, a cooperative play activity which inevitably turned into shrill horseplay spilling up the steps from the basement playroom to the rest of the house, and when I had read more of the Sunday *Times* than I cared to and there was nothing on television worthwhile, the Mets at San Francisco not due to start for another hour and a half and the Yankees rained out at home? What I did was shut myself in the study with the crossword puzzle.

There Sally brought Chief Messner to me. He had come to return Gordon Tripp's manuscript.

He was out of uniform, but he was the same man—that wiry body erect and flat-bellied in a snappy checked sports jacket. Over his arm his raincoat hung in precise folds. Under his other arm was the thick manuscript in its mailing envelope wrapped in a plastic bag to protect it from the rain.

He refused to surrender his raincoat to Sally to be hung up. "Only staying a minute." He beamed at her rear as she left us. "That's a pretty lady," he informed me when we were alone. "And that Mrs. Huntley, cute as a button. I was talking to them. Took me into the kitchen to give me a taste of their bread just out of the oven. Baking their own bread like my mother used to fifty years ago. What I mean is wholesome."

"The bread or the women?"

"About the bread I can't say. It was kind of heavy and gritty. Mrs. Huntley said my taste buds have been corrupted by the packaged library paste Americans think is bread. Her words. She could be right, but I'm used to it." Messner chuckled. "I mean those ladies are wholesome. Making fine homes for their husbands and raising fine families and having fun in the kitchen instead of running around with men and booze and drugs like so many do these days. That's a word you don't hear any more about people. Wholesome."

"Come to think of it, you don't," I said. While thinking that yes, indeed, here Sally and I were wholesome people again through none of our doing or desire. I took the manuscript from him. "Well, Chief, did Kibble find a vital clue in here?"

"You never expected him to, Mr. Dawson."

"Was I wrong?"

"There's a poem," he said. "It's about a girl."

"Aren't many of them?"

"This one's not like any of the others. Dan Kibble pointed out to me the way it's different when he gave the manuscript back to me yesterday, and this morning my daughter Agnes spotted it without me telling her."

"How does your daughter come into this?"

"Agnes, she's the one lives out on Long Island. Her husband's in real estate and she teaches English at Stony Brook. They're visiting this weekend with their four children and I asked her to take a look at these poems. Being she's a college English professor, you can say she qualifies as an expert."

"And I don't?"

"I'm not saying an editor doesn't know as much as a college professor. I guess he has to. But what's the harm of another opinion?"

"From somebody who's not a suspect," I said.

"Another opinion," he repeated firmly and evasively. "Like, you know, with doctors. Dan Kibble is a smart detective, but I don't think he knows as much about this here highbrow poetry as he claims. As much as admitted he had to give it up—except for this one poem even I can make sense of. Agnes even taught some of his poems in her classes. Thinks he's very good. That's where she disagrees with you."

"What has his ability as a poet got to do with his murder?"

"You're right. Fact is, the poem I'm talking about Agnes didn't think much of."

"Which one is it, for God's sake?"

"It's called 'On the Occasion of February 14.' That's St. Valentine's Day, you know, so it's a valentine love poem. Remember it?"

"I'm not sure. I didn't give the manuscript the thorough reading I will when I edit it."

"Page 217," he said.

At the desk I extracted the mailing envelope from the plastic bag and the manuscript from the envelope and removed the rubber bands. The unusual thing about that poem, aside from its short length, was that it was one of the very few in typescript instead of a tearsheet from a magazine or a book or a photocopy from either. I read:

ON THE OCCASION OF FEBRUARY 14

Sweet, your minstrel plucks his lyre
    Ardently for you his lay.
Let concupiscence inspire
    Loving deeds on Cupid's day.
You who beatify my bed
Do so not uncomforted.

"Not bad," I commented, replacing the sheet on top of page 218. "Especially the couplet."

"Agnes didn't like it. She said the pun is vulgar. Did you catch onto the pun?"

"I should hope so."

"Agnes explained it to me. A lay is a song the minstrels used to sing in the olden days, but in the poem it also means what I thought it did. A pun. Vulgar, she said. I guess it is, but you know what? A lot of those poems have real dirty words in them, right there in print, words I wouldn't say in front of my own wife, but Agnes didn't think those poems were vulgar. Can you figure her out, Mr. Dawson? I can't."

"I doubt that the woman he wrote it to would consider vulgar a poem that said she beatified his bed. That may be the loveliest line he ever wrote."

"Well, at least in this poem I know what he's talking about," Messner said. "He was having an affair with this here lady. Called her his lay. Talked about her in his bed. Could be she's the one was with him Wednesday morning."

"If she exists at all. Poets tend to write love poems about imaginary women."

"From what I hear about him, he didn't have to imagine them," Messner said. "He had them. And why does a man write a valentine poem? For the same reason you go out and buy a valentine card. To send to a person you're sweet on. This is more literary, I guess, than you buy in a store, but it's written in rhyme just like them, which he never did in his other poems, and this one you don't have to be a college professor or an editor to make head or tail of. Well, how come? Because if a man, I don't care how he writes his other poems, sends a valentine to a sweetheart, he wants her to know what he's saying. Right, Mr. Dawson?"

"I agree. But so what? All this tells us is that he had a bedmate at one time or another. Which is hardly news. Too bad he didn't make it easy for you by putting in the year along with the day. He could have written it this year or ten years ago. He could have run through a number of bedmates since this one."

"Look, Mr. Dawson. This is the only poem in the book was never published."

"How do you know? Oh, your daughter Agnes. I suppose she checked the credit pages."

"I'm getting an education," Messner said. "I didn't know what concupiscence meant till Agnes told me. Agnes explained about the credits, which they tell where each poem in the book was published before. The valentine is the only one in the book not mentioned. Agnes says because a magazine would print a valentine only in its February issue. He wrote it to the lady for last St. Valentine's Day, three months ago, and so it couldn't be published till next winter. Agnes says."

"Agnes has an inflated idea of his standing as a poet. He would have had a lot of rejections. This may have been one of them."

"You're an editor. Would you have rejected it?"

"It would depend on the kind of magazine I was editing. This wouldn't be proper for most. Also, there's the possibility that he simply didn't want it in print."

"He wanted it printed in this here book."

"So he did." Standing at the desk, I read the verse again. *Do so not uncomforted.* Very nice. I said, "All right, assuming he wrote it this year, I don't see how it can be the least help."

"Maybe yes, maybe no." Messner had wandered to another part of the room; his brisk voice was behind me. "How does an investigation work? You dig up other things, a letter, a note, a bit of gossip, somebody has seen somebody somewhere—who knows what?—and you put it together with a valentine poem, and you have two or three things add up to a little something. That's the way it goes. The poem is useless now, but you never know. Dan Kibble had copies of the valentine made."

I turned. Chief Messner was standing at the bookcase. On top of it, shoulder high, was the *Times* magazine section opened to the crossword puzzle I had been working at when he arrived.

"In addition to the valentine," I said, "have you dug up any of those other things?"

He seemed more interested in the crossword puzzle. Eyes fixed on it, he muttered, "It's not easy to tell what means what. Dan Kibble is busy as a beaver." His voice rose. "Upper berth!"

"Huh?"

"I have a word for you. Forty-three across. Ten letters. Part of a Pullman section. It has to be upper berth."

I went to his side and looked at where his finger pointed. "I thought of that, but it doesn't fit in with the down words I already have. I didn't know you went in for crossword puzzles."

"Sometimes I take a stab at the easy ones." He looked some more at the puzzle. "It ought to be upper berth, but you say it isn't. Like a lot of the things you think you have when you investigate a crime."

"Chief, now that we've considered valentines and other puzzles, how about sitting down and having a drink?" But he had stayed longer than he had intended. He wanted to be home in time to say good-bye to his daughter Agnes and his four grandchildren. I accompanied him to the front door. I stopped off in the kitchen, where Marie cut off a slice of the warm whole-wheat bread for me and Sally covered it with healthy, wholesome (unhomogenized, of course) peanut butter. Munching it, I returned to the crossword puzzle.

Eventually I realized that the puzzle maker had been cute. The ten-letter word for Pullman section turned out to be *birthplace.* Gordon Tripp hadn't been the only goddamn punster around.

Monday

The first thing Lucille Treacher told me when I came in Monday morning (breathlessly, she had been holding it in over the weekend) was that a man from the state police had phoned her Friday afternoon to ask her questions about me.

"Dan Kibble?" I said.

"That's his name. He told me he was a state police inspector."

"Investigator. What time did he call?"

"It was around four-thirty. You didn't come back at all from lunch on Friday, you remember."

That would have been shortly after I left the confab with him and Messner in the chief's office. I had told them, with a bit of asperity, that my story of the rejection and then the acceptance of Tripp's book could be easily checked at my office—and, by God, Kibble had gone and done so without delay.

"It was like being cross-examined," Lucille said. "Like he tried to punch holes in every answer I gave him. I don't mean he was unpleasant. Every other word was please and thank you. Caleb, why all those questions about you?"

We were standing at her desk in the center office, at the edge of the nine o'-clock bustle of arriving workers, and with her juicy body quite close to mine (today she was back to one of her low necklines) she whispered like a conspirator.

"He's investigating Gordon's murder," I said, "and the job of an investigator is to investigate."

"I can understand his asking about my calls to Gordon Tripp Thursday morning—about what time it was I started to get the busy signals and when I made the last call to him. But why so many questions about the manuscript? When he had given it to you and when you had decided to reject it and things like that."

"What things like that?"

"Why you changed your mind after you'd rejected it. I told him I didn't know, he should ask you." She leaned even closer, like a spy passing on information in a crowded street. We could have gone into my office, but apparently she was too excited to take the time. "Caleb, talking to him on the phone, I couldn't think of what I ought not tell him."

"Why not whatever you knew? I've no need to be protected."

"Oh, I'm sure you don't. Anyway, he already knew about your meeting Thursday morning with Mr. Atkinson and Mr. Martaine."

"He knew because I'd told him."

"Then why did he ask me?"

"Cops are skeptics. Specifically, what did he ask about the Thursday morning meeting?"

"Where it was held and who was there. Then he asked first name and his questions about Mr. Atkinson, like his position. I don't understand it."

"Anything else?"

"He wanted to know when you'd gotten in Wednesday morning and how long you were out to lunch and when you left for home. It sounded like you needed an alibi."

"I happen to have a pretty good one. The medical examiner believes he was murdered Wednesday during the period when I was here at work. You should be relieved to know you're not the secretary of a killer."

"What a horrid thing to say! I never for a moment thought anything of the kind."

"Don't tell me you didn't spend your time since then titillated by the idea."

"Oh, you! I never know when you're joking. I was going to call you at home Friday and tell you about Inspector Kibble's call—"

"*Investigator* Kibble."

"All right, investigator. I went straight from the office for my weekend in the Catskills with two girl friends and I never got the chance to call you. Did it matter?"

"Not in the least, since I am pure of heart."

Anyway, where murder was concerned. I was nothing worse than a jewel thief whose purity of heart, if not of deed, had been restored by another jewel thief. My only problem with the life and death of Gordon Tripp was with the publication of his collected work, and that manuscript was in my briefcase. I gave it to Lucille and told her to make two Xerox copies, one for production to design the book and jacket and one for the copyeditor, and to put the original in the file.

"I am glad," she said, holding the manuscript on her two hands like an offering to a god, "that at least this part of him will live on."

"Uh-huh," I said, and headed for my office.

A short time later Christopher Tripp's lawyer phoned. I made an appointment to be at his office next morning with a contract.

I was saying good-bye when Harve Atkinson dropped in. He lowered his massive rear on a chair and looked out of my half of the window. He didn't often bestir himself to visit one of his editors; he maintained his figure, along with his status, by having them come to him.

"That was Gordon Tripp's brother's lawyer," I told him. "They're eager to do business."

"In that case, don't go higher than two thousand advance, and as it's poetry, don't go higher than a straight eight percent." Harve dragged both himself and his chair closer to my desk without rising from it. "A state policeman in plainclothes with the absurd name of Kibble came to see me yesterday at my home. He said he knows you well."

Messner had been right about Kibble. He had been—no doubt still was—as busy as a beaver, and I didn't know the half of it.

"I assume it was about the Tripp murder," I said.

"What then? He had called here Friday. It was after four and I had left. He obtained my address from Joy. Why, then, he drove to my home in a downpour on a Sunday morning to ask a few pointless questions is beyond me. From the tenor of his questions one would have gathered that the crime he was investigating was the publication of Tripp's book. He wanted to know absolutely everything that occurred in that conference you and I had with Ed Martaine. I withheld nothing."

"There was no reason why you should have," I said.

In the next office Stu Stitchman had arrived; he was on the phone bawling out an artist. We both paused to listen, as if there were something new or significant in his words.

"I can advise you what to do with your concept of art," Stu said. "This is a book jacket, in case you've forgotten, and the least we can do for the buying public is to let them in on the title and the name of the author. Try reading type in your anemic red on your muddy black."

Then, briefly, there was a silence next door as Stu democratically let the artist have his say, and Harve leaned still closer and whispered, "But why? Why was this man Kibble interested in your handling of the manuscript and in our conference about it with Ed Martaine?" He cleared his throat. "Caleb, are you under—ah—suspicion?"

"Sure. I make a habit of knocking off very minor poets to keep from having to publish their collected works."

"But seriously."

"Seriously, I have a pretty good alibi. I was here at work during the period they calculate the deed was done."

"Is Kibble aware of this?"

"He checked it out with Lucille by phone."

"Then what can he be after?"

"It doesn't follow that he himself knows," I said. "Likely he's just browsing."

He put his hands on his knees as a preliminary to pushing his weight up to his feet. "Anyway, Caleb, I thought you would want to know."

"It's interesting, Harve. Thanks."

He departed and I tilted back. Next door Stu had production on the phone and he was yelling that he wanted another goddamn artist on the book jacket. I looked at the ceiling.

Something was going on.

2

Most of the work I did that day was at lunch in a plush restaurant on my expense account with Earl B. Carlton, author of tripe, and May Dortle, his tough-minded agent. Which was the way of the publishing business, and in the way of the publishing business a good part of the lunch came out of cocktail shakers. High on gin, we haggled amiably over their demand of fifty thousand dollars' advance on his novel and a sixty-forty split on reprint rights. By two o'clock our only agreement was to meet again later in the week—same place, same martinis—with the addition of Harve Atkinson, decision maker. I signed the tab and floated back to my office.

Lucille advanced to meet me in the center office. That and the size of her eyes told me she had big news.

"Mrs. Martaine is here to see you. She's in Stu's office."

"Norma Martaine?" My head wasn't on any too firmly because of the three martinis.

"I recognized her the moment she appeared, before she told me who she was. I've never seen her in the flesh, but I've seen pictures of her in magazines." Lucille breathed deeply. "In the flesh she's even more stunning."

"She asked for me?" I said, sounding hazily stupid to myself.

"Yes. I was telling her you weren't back from lunch, when Stu saw her. He came out and took her into his office. He said to tell you to go in as soon as you return."

His door was closed. I opened it. The grand lady of Paragon and Mount Birch sat at the side of his desk. Legs in pants crossed, a cigarette hovering at her chin.

"Hello, Caleb," she said in her low-pitched voice. "Stu has been so kind as to keep me company while I waited for you. I have a frightful headache."

I had heard about her headaches. Her husband had mentioned them last week in the men's room. She had had one the day they were to attend the charity ball.

"That's too bad," I said automatically. While thinking: *So?*

Norma Martaine took a drag on her cigarette. I had seldom seen her without one clamped in her fingers. For once in his life Stu had nothing to say.

Flicking the filter end of her cigarette with her thumbnail, she went on to explain. "I drove in this morning to spend the day in the city shopping and visiting. Edward and I planned to have dinner out and then drive home together. But I got this headache and I want to go right home. I don't feel up to driving and Edward can't get away till later. Caleb, it won't be at all out of your way to drive me home."

"Now?" I said. "I can't leave till five."

It wasn't so much the gin that was making me dull-witted, though that helped. It was my total lack of ease in the presence of the woman whose jewelry Sally and I had stolen.

"I hoped you would right away," she said. "My head is killing me. If you need permission to leave, I'll ask Edward to give it to you."

Stu cackled in his beard. That was all. He simply cackled. I felt an utter fool.

"I'll be delighted," I blurted. "I can go any time you're ready."

Norma Martaine rose. She wore a woven-silk pants suit with that youthful chic of the middle-aged rich. Jacket of mosaic squares, pants of varicolored stripes. Rather tall, she had that bony-shouldered, emaciated look of fashion models in the swank women's magazines.

"Good-bye, Stu," she said as she destroyed her cigarette in the mess of pipe tobacco in his ashtray. "Thank you for keeping me company."

"It was a pleasure, Norma."

Her car was in a parking garage several blocks away. Walking there, she took my arm, but we hardly spoke. She seemed to be preoccupied with her headache. As for me, what do you say to a lady you've robbed?

The parking fee was five bucks. She opened her wide-mouthed handbag (the one out of which the pouch had fallen?) and gave me the ticket to give to the garage attendant, but she didn't take out the cash to cover it. Rich women can't be bothered with money. And when the attendant brought down her sumptuous white Lincoln, I could not demean myself in his eyes by tipping him less than two whole quarters.

I sent her car laboring through crosstown traffic. She sat a mile away from me on the incredibly wide seat, her head all the way back, her eyes closed. Her face was oval, cheekbones prominent. Stunning? Lucille's word for her, a woman's word. A man would say not pretty, even ugly at certain moments, but never unattractive.

When I had at long last achieved the FDR Drive and I could let the powerful engine have some head (traffic at that time comparatively light), I broke the silence. "Are you asleep, Norma?"

"Just resting."

"How's your headache now?"

"It feels better." She unbuckled her seat belt so she could reach an extra pack of cigarettes on the dashboard shelf. "Do you smoke?"

"I quit years ago."

"I wish I could." She pushed in the dashboard lighter. This brought her closer to me and I could smell her heady perfume. "Do you have any bad habits, Caleb?"

Well, for one thing I was a failed jewel thief. What I said was, "Hasn't everybody?"

"You've always struck me as being a very solid citizen."

"Is that supposed to be good?"

"It is the way I mean it. Solid but not stuffy." Then she added, "To the limited extent I know you."

Chitchat with a personal overlay. She didn't shift back to her end of the seat, staying where she was, her head back again, her eyes closed again as she nursed her headache. I had a sense of our shoulders and hips touching, but when I looked sidelong, there were a good twelve inches between us. Smoke flowed from her mouth past my face to my open window.

She didn't speak again till her cigarette was gone, and she had to have another immediately. After she had it going, she said, "How is your wife? Let me see—Sally."

"Fine," I said.

"She's very pretty."

"Yes."

"You have children, I believe."

"Two boys. Eleven and eight."

"I wish I had a family," she said.

"You have a husband. That's family."

"I suppose so. Edward is very kind. Even that thing with my jewelry last week, the way I lost it, he was quite tolerant. Do you know about my jewelry, Caleb?"

Her face had turned to me, cheek against the back of the seat, and her eyes, dark and quiet in deep sockets, watched my profile. As if she knew or guessed or wondered.

Which had to be nothing but my nagging conscience. People looked at people they spoke to, didn't they?

I said, "I've read and heard what everybody else has. Why wouldn't your husband be tolerant? It's easy to be when one is both rich and insured."

"That's true. What I was trying to say is that Edward is my very best friend. I don't think many married couples can say that of each other."

"You may be right."

"We should have had children," she said. "He wanted to have two or three more, but I could never carry through. He has a daughter. My stepdaughter. He was married once before, you know."

"I didn't know," I said. Who cared?

"We seldom see her since she went off to college. That was five years ago. She dropped out of school three years ago. Edward misses her very much. So do I. I came from a large family. Our home feels empty."

She could be close to fifty, I thought. Though why fifty? Why not closer to forty, only half a dozen years older than I? It was difficult to tell with a woman who had the time and money to do all the right things to herself. At any rate, the lonely rich watching life pass them by. I had no patience for clichés.

Another cigarette had burned itself up in her lungs. She got rid of the stub and sank back. "You're a fortunate man, Caleb. There's no substitute for a happy family."

There were clichés and there were clichés. This one I could heartily endorse, what I had been trying to convince Sally of.

Another long silence. The Lincoln glided on the highway as on air. Mount Birch. Norma sat erect when she realized we had entered our village.

"How do you feel now?" I asked.

"So much better. The drive has done me a world of good."

"Do you want to drop me off at my house and drive the short distance from there?"

"I wish you'd take me to my door," she said. "I'll have Joseph drive you home."

We skimmed by within a thousand feet of my house, then weaved up Fiddle Hill and rolled through a fieldstone arch and along the Martaine blacktop road to the parking circle at the side of the double-winged Tudor house.

I stopped the car and we sat. We both seemed possessed by inertia. Then Norma said, "Come in for a drink."

"Thanks, but I had too many at lunch."

"Then coffee." She put her hand on my knee. "Please do." My knee tingled. Her eyes fixed on my face were very dark, very deep. The tingling spread.

"All right," I said.

But when we were out of the car she didn't take me to the house. She took me up a paved walk angling away from it, past the swimming pool and through immaculate shrubbery to a grove. When I asked, "Where are we going?" she replied gayly, "You'll see," and grabbed hold of my hand.

The grove consisted of an acre or two of pines, trimmed high and spaced like the pillars of an ancient temple. Cool and hushed and—yes, the word was romantic. She continued to hold me by the hand, tightly, warmly, and I half expected her to make me flit with her between the trees like the standard pair of exuberant young lovers in slushy art movies, bounding in slow motion. I felt myself light-headed enough to do it, too.

You'll see, Norma had said, and very soon I saw. It was a log cabin beyond the grove, nestled against a knoll. Made of honest-to-goodness logs and all.

"Our guest house," she said. "We call it the lodge. It's cozier than the big house."

Cozier? That could make a man wonder.

She pushed the door open with the hand not clinging to mine. When we were over the threshold she pulled my hand and the arm it was attached to about her waist. She had a slim girl's waist. My hand spread on her hip.

"Isn't it charming?" she said.

There was the requisite massive fieldstone fireplace and close to it the requisite bar. For the rest, a divan smothered in pillows, a deep sofa at an angle to the fireplace, chairs to be sunk into. But charming? What I was charmed by was the exciting snugness of Norma Martaine in the circle of my arm.

"Past that door there's a small kitchen," she said. "I can put up a pot of coffee. Should I?"

She turned her face to me with the question, head tilted back, high-cheeked face possessing a beauty I had never before noticed, dark eyes quietly welcoming me. As she had said, I wasn't stuffy. I kissed her.

During the kiss she swung herself hard against me. When I pushed my hands between us to her breasts, she said as if choking, "Oh, yes!" and then she said, holding my head, "Caleb, Caleb, you will make love to me, won't you?"

"I'd like that very much," I said.

She gave me a quick kiss and slipped away from me. She locked the door and then went from window to window to close the blinds.

3

Afterward Norma Martaine wept softly on my chest. Who would have thought that such a poised and sophisticated lady would have tears in her for having made love with a man not her husband? If that was the reason.

"Are you sorry?" I said into her hair.

"It was beautiful, darling. That's why I'm crying. Hold me." She needed comforting.

We had tossed pillows from the divan to the floor to make room for us. They lay like strewn boulders on an uncleared field. The cabin had a bedroom, but she had not taken me into it. The divan served, and in the warm afternoon in the shade-drawn room we had no need for a cover.

Stroking her back, I said, *"You who beatify my bed/Do so not uncomforted."*

She sniffled on my skin; her weeping was about over. "How lovely, darling. Say it again."

I repeated the couplet. "Is it familiar, Norma?"

"I don't think so. Who wrote it?"

"Gordon Tripp. They're from a valentine poem he wrote to somebody."

She didn't stir. My hand ran up and down her back, up and down.

"Somebody?" she said like a delayed echo. "Do you know who?"

"No. It was included in the manuscript of his collected poems. I assume you know we're doing the book."

"Edward told me."

"Did you make him make me accept it?"

"Why do you put it that way? Edward is the president. He has every right to make final decisions."

"And you're the president's lady. I merely asked if you made him throw his weight."

"I didn't *make* him." As she spoke, her breath brushed my skin. "This is what happened. Early last week Gordon phoned me."

"What day?"

"It certainly had to be before Wednesday, the day the police say he was"— her voice dipped to a whisper on the next word—"killed. Tuesday it must have been. Tuesday was the last normal day I've had. He told me on the phone he had submitted to you a book of his collected poems and he had heard you were going to reject it."

"How could he have heard?"

"From you, I supposed."

"He didn't," I said. "On Tuesday the only ones who knew I was about to turn it down were my secretary and Stu Stitchman, with whom I discuss everything like that."

"Then Gordon must have had a feeling you were going to reject it. I don't exactly remember how he put it. Anyway, he asked me to speak to Edward. It wasn't as if I didn't admire his work. I have all three of his books and I do think highly of them."

"Of them or of him?"

"What are you implying?" she said, lifting her head.

"Only that there's an advantage to knowing the right people. Everybody uses it, including editors." I pushed her head back where it belonged. "Go on, Norma."

"That's it. I said I'd be glad to speak to Edward, and that evening at dinner I did. Edward said he'd discuss it with you when he had a chance. Poor Gordon, lying dead while you were talking over whether to publish his book." A pause as if in respect for the late departed. "Edward told me he admired you for standing up for your opinion."

"That's me, a fighter for lost causes."

We had another of our silences. Her skin was velvety and tight, sensuous to the touch and tasty to the mouth.

"How's your headache?" I asked presently.

"You cured it for me some time ago." She wriggled higher on me to reach my mouth with hers. "Darling, I could fall in love with you."

That scared the hell out of me. Me, solid citizen, who could at one and the same time have a roll on a divan with the woman I had robbed and cheat on the wife I loved. It had happened and I had let it happen, but the last thing I needed was to involve myself in a protracted affair with her.

But you couldn't tell that to a naked woman in your arms. I couldn't. Holding her, I kept my mouth shut.

Nearby an engine started up. Too raucous to be a car. I decided it was a chain saw; I changed my mind in favor of a tractor mower. The gardener was doing his job on the great expanse of lawn at the front of the house. He could have seen us arrive and go toward the cabin; the house servants could have seen us. The whole world could find out. It was bad enough I knew.

"I ought to be going," I said.

"Please, not yet. What time are you expected home?"

"Sally picks me up at the station at six-thirty."

She pulled my left arm around for a look at the only thing I wore, my watch.

"It's not yet five." She snuggled. Who could resist that? She said, "Darling, what do you know about the police bothering Edward?"

"Are they? In what way?"

"You're chairman of the police. You must know."

"Is it about your jewels?"

"That was my first thought when a Lieutenant Burke came here to see us on Saturday. Since Thursday morning I'd been constantly questioned about them by the police and the insurance people and reporters. But it was about Gordon. Lieutenant Burke wanted to know everything we knew about him."

"That's routine in a murder. All his friends and neighbors are being questioned."

"We understood that. We were anxious to cooperate, though there was little we could tell him. Then yesterday morning shortly after breakfast Chief Messner came with a man in plainclothes from the state police."

"Dan Kibble."

"Yes. Then you know about it."

"I know Kibble and that he's working with our police on the case."

"He did practically all the talking. It seems somebody saw Edward near Gordon's house on Wednesday afternoon."

"Was he?"

"He probably was. You see, he did take a walk. That was the day we were supposed to go to a ball at the Pierre and I went to the bank for my jewelry. Edward came home early in the afternoon so he could relax and have a leisurely dinner at home and dress and then we'd drive to the city. He found me in bed with a severe headache, even worse than the one I had today."

"I heard about that headache from him."

"I get so many. We decided I wasn't feeling well enough to go to the ball. I was in bed and Edward went for a walk. It was a nice day and he's a great walker. He walked through our property and down the other side of the hill, but where he was seen wasn't so very close to Gordon's house. Anyway, suppose it had been?"

"What time was that?"

"Four o'clock or a bit later. He took a local from Grand Central and was in the house before three-thirty."

"The medical examiner thinks Gordon was murdered between nine in the morning and three in the afternoon."

"So you see!"

"Though that time span is flexible," I said. "Gordon was dead so long before he was found that it can be expanded at either end."

"Surely they can't believe Edward could have done such a thing?"

"I don't know what they believe. The state police don't take me into their confidence."

"But Chief Messner would have to."

"Not necessarily. And he didn't."

"Are you sure?"

"Don't you believe me?"

"It's not that." Norma had raised herself on an elbow. Her face hovered over mine, and I had a startling impression of her high-cheeked face and deep-set eyes having turned into a living skull. "There could be something you're not supposed to tell me," she said.

If there was something, I hadn't been told either. When yesterday afternoon Nate Messner had come to my house to return the manuscript, he had spoken of home-baked bread and poetry and crossword puzzles, but not a word of that morning's visit to the Martaines.

I said, "They have a theory that the murderer may be a husband who caught his wife in bed with Gordon. There's some evidence to back it up."

"I gathered as much from Kibble's questions, though he didn't come right out and say it. So he thinks I am the woman and Edward the husband!"

I lay on my back looking up at her face. The skull effect had definitely passed. Her mouth went crooked as she said, "Well, darling lover, no comment?"

"I don't know what Kibble thinks, but I suppose he thinks you might be."

"What do *you* think? If I am like this with you, why wouldn't I have been with Gordon?"

"If you were, he was a lucky man. Anyway, till Wednesday."

A cloud came between us. "Caleb, I don't sleep around. I don't!"

"That's your business, not mine."

"Kibble seems to be making it his business."

"Okay," I said, "let's see what he might have. I often meet your husband on the train I take in the morning—the 7:52. Do you know if he took it Wednesday morning?"

"He definitely did. This was one of the questions he was asked. Edward could prove it by Joseph, who drives him to the station, and of course the time he arrived at his office can be verified by people on his staff. Also the time he left to make the early train back, and exactly when he arrived home from the station because he took a taxi and all the drivers know him."

"Can you prove you were in bed at the time he was seen at Gordon's place?"

"I can and I did," she said vigorously. "Kathy came into my room several times. Once she brought me coffee. Caffeine is the best thing for my headaches. I had her tell that to Kibble." She sank down on her back and took my hand. "Why is all this important?"

"If you and your husband couldn't have been in Gordon's cottage at the same time Wednesday morning, there goes the theory that he was the jealous husband who caught his wife with Gordon."

"Is that their only theory?"

"It's the best they had, unless they've come up with a better. You can play all sorts of variations on the theme. My guess is that they were only trying you and your husband out for size to see if you fit into it. I wouldn't worry."

"I'm not worried. It's just annoying to have to be harassed because of a theory. Edward was quite patient with them. Then he grew testy and said he wished they would be as diligent about recovering my jewelry."

As we lay side by side holding hands, I was afraid that mine would begin to sweat in hers. I said, "Now that that's off your mind, I really must be going."

"No, you mustn't." She swung to me; her weight pinned me down. "There's time yet, and here we've been wasting it with this chatter." She was suddenly gay, and gayly she kissed me. "Stay where you are, darling. I'll be back in a minute."

The first thing Norma did when she got off the divan was light a cigarette. Then she padded off to the bathroom. If she had a robe in the cabin, she didn't put it on, going and coming. She reappeared and stood smiling at me. I thought her beautiful.

"Would you like a drink, darling?"

"A Coke if you have it."

"I'll see what's in the refrigerator."

She went into the kitchen and returned with a large bottle in one hand, holding it by the neck, and two water glasses in the other. "All we have is ginger ale."

"Swell."

It was a delight to watch her move, slender and elegant, without that mincing self-consciousness of most women (of Sally) when walking about naked. She set the glasses down on the bar and poured.

I said, "It may have been something like this Wednesday in Gordon's cottage."

She frowned at me past her shoulder. "What?"

"Except that it was cherry soda," I said. "They had a drink together from a bottle that size. Maybe it was before they went into the bedroom together; maybe later he or she got out of bed to bring the drinks. Anyway, the empty bottle was left in the living room—there for the murderer to use."

She set the ginger ale bottle down. It was still half full.

"Is that the way it was?" she said.

"The bottle killed him. That's known. The rest is part of the theory."

"I thought we were finished talking about morbid things."

"I'm sorry. The theory was still on my mind."

She picked up the glasses. I swung my legs off the divan, sitting up. She handed me a glass and sat down beside me.

"I never talk about this," she said. "But I must tell you. Edward and I haven't slept together at all in over three years."

"Oh?"

She drank and ran her tongue over her lower lip and said, "He knows I go with other men. I don't do it often, but sometimes. Like I'm with you now. All he asks is that I don't be crude and obvious. If he came home now and knew you were here, he would simply stay away. His attitude toward you would not change."

"Is he impotent?"

"Not in the least."

"Should I keep guessing?"

"I wish you wouldn't. We have made our accommodation. We're fond of each other and live in the same house. There's just no sex. That may be why we have a better marriage than most people I know."

"Is it a marriage?"

"In every way but one. So you see, the theory about a jealous husband can't apply to Edward."

"But it applies to why I'm here. You need a man."

"Not any man. You."

She took the glass from my hand and put it and hers on the floor. She sat up and her body bore me down on the divan.

"Comfort me," she said. "Once more, darling."

This time, afterward, there were no tears. Norma Martaine smoked a cigarette, still on the divan, as she watched me dress. We had run out of words. She got rid of the cigarette when I bent to kiss her good-bye. I unlocked the door and slipped out into the open.

4

Being a walker (like Edward Martaine), I knew the paths through the woods and fields which covered a good part of the high ground in Mount Birch. I headed away from the sound of the tractor mower, away from the house and the road. If I had been seen arriving with Norma Martaine and seen going with her to the guest house, I did not care to be seen leaving a couple of hours later. She might not care, her husband might not care, but I did.

I ducked into brush above the knoll behind the cabin. I blundered through briers and undergrowth and dead branches before I hit the path running through the Martaine wooded acres—the path Edward Martaine would have taken in his walk over the hill Wednesday afternoon. I climbed a fieldstone boundary fence to somebody else's property, and pretty soon I reached the fork I was looking for, one branch leading to the road that ran past Gordon Tripp's cottage and the other curling down steeply to the back of my street.

It was two minutes after six when I approached the rear of my house. Plenty of time. Sally did not leave to pick me up at the station till twenty after.

Electric light glinted in the rear corner window of our bedroom. Though outside there was full daylight, inside that room was always dim because of the two dogwoods in the back yard and the evergreen at the side window. I parted branches of the evergreen to see if Sally was in there, changing her clothes or combing her hair before she set out for the station. She wasn't. The light was on because she had a way of leaving a blaze of lights behind her wherever she had been in the house.

I stepped back and saw George Huntley watching me. From where he stood in his back yard he had an angled view of me past the corner of his house. He was in his gardening clothes, his underwear pasted to his belly sagging over his belt, and he was leaning on a rake.

The instant my head turned he looked away from me. He resumed raking grass cuttings. And all at once it struck me.

I went to where he stood. He stopped raking. The shad flies had been roused by his raking; they buzzed about his sweaty meat. He said uneasily, "Hello, Caleb."

"Hi. Marie said you'd come over to shake and make up."

"I intended to. I appreciate what you did about Marie's ticket. I really do. I've been too busy to thank you."

"What you've been," I said, "was afraid to look me in the face. You're scared, George. I can understand the feeling. I felt the same way till you relieved me of them."

"I don't know what you're talking about."

He knew, all right. I was sure now. His eyes gave him away. Sally and I had been better at it.

I said, "To begin with, my being a sanctimonious bastard. In case you've forgotten, that was what you called me when I refused to do anything about Marie's traffic ticket. Why sanctimonious? You were in a rage; the adjective came out by itself. That didn't have any significance till now, when it fell into place. I was sanctimonious because you knew what we had in our bedroom while I was standing there morally indignant over being asked merely to fix a ticket."

"I'm sorry I insulted you, Caleb. I say things I don't mean. Let me apologize."

He stuck out his hand. I ignored it.

"You must have been having your kicks at our bedroom window for quite a while now," I said. "It was too tempting. Because of the evergreen we don't bother to close the blind of that window. It never occurred to us that our next-door neighbor would fall into the habit of standing close against the tree and part branches and have a perfect view into our bedroom while he was covered by darkness. You must be quite an authority on our sex life."

"I won't stand here and listen to such nonsense."

"Sure you will, George. You have to know how much I know about the rest. It all falls together. Something was stolen from our bedroom, and who would know we had it and exactly where we had hidden it and when we would be out of the house so he could come and get it? Who but our Peeping Tom?"

"You must be crazy," he said. But he mumbled the words, meaningless sounds to fill a gap.

I felt somewhat giddy—maybe from what gin lingered in me, maybe from illicit sex, certainly from a sense of power over a fellow crook. I still had a few minutes, and there in his back yard we were pretty much alone.

"Let's see," I said, "it was Thursday, when I came home from work, that you called me a sanctimonious bastard. The night before that Sally had shown them to me in our bedroom and told me about them, and when the news broke next day you knew whose they were and how valuable. That night you were again at your post at the window—the night I found Gordon Tripp's body, and probably you were already there when I came down the hill. You would hear me approach in the night. You would duck out of sight and watch me pause at the window to take my own look at Sally putting them on her skin. That was quite a sight, George, wasn't it? And later we put on a prime show for you, didn't we? I ought to break your neck."

He said nothing.

"You had to be at the window Thursday," I said, "because that was the night Sally transferred them from her hatbox to the secret drawer in my dresser. Your chance came Friday evening when we went to the movies. Sally may have told Marie we were going or you saw us drive off without the boys. That side door is nothing; I've opened it myself with a credit card once when I locked myself out. You waited till the boys were asleep, then in less than a minute you slipped in and out of the house."

The upright rake fell from his hand; part of the handle buried itself in the heap of grass cuttings. He waved feebly at the shad flies. They didn't much bother me.

"Is Marie in on this?" I asked.

He spoke up then. "She knows absolutely nothing about it."

"It's better so. Wives can be a nuisance."

"You got me so mad," he said bitterly. "Just a traffic ticket and you sneered at me like I was trying to corrupt you. You! I had to show you."

"Who's being sanctimonious now, George? You're as greedy as any of us."

"I don't want to talk to you."

He turned to go away. I grabbed him by his bare, sweaty upper arm.

"I want them back, George."

"They're not yours."

"I haven't heard that you've returned them to their rightful owner. You'll give them to me."

"Why should I?" he said.

But there was no spirit in his voice. He was a man too weary and frightened to fight. I knew all about the emotional stress on people like us who went in for this kind of thing. I let go his arm.

"You will," I said, "because it's to your best interest."

His face revived; his eyes got crafty. "Are you offering a split?"

"I'm offering to take them off your hands."

"In return for nothing?"

"I wouldn't call safety and peace of mind nothing. You'll never draw a real breath till you get rid of them. But that wouldn't impress you. We're all the same; we know it and don't want to know it. You'll give them to me because you're not sure of me. Who can tell with a guy like me, I might have an attack of morality? Or sheer vindictiveness. I can say we intended to return them—we were simply waiting for a large reward to be offered—but you stole them. Both thief and Peeping Tom. That'll be a fine thing for a local schoolteacher who on the new contract will be making over twenty thousand a year, plus fringe benefits. Think, George, are they worth anything like what you've already got?"

All that rhetoric wasn't required. I could think of good arguments on his side, but he didn't give them. He just stood there, a lump of sweaty blubber, food for the shad flies.

"Where are they, George?"

"In my garage," he murmured.

Together we walked between our houses toward the street. Children flitted by, running or on bikes; I heard the voices of others unseen, probably my own children's among them. All of a sudden a reaction set in; I was not proud of the pounding I had given George. I had little to be proud of these days, and I had an impulse to chuck the jewels. But it is harder to let go of things than to take hold of them in the first place.

My car was still in the driveway. Any minute now Sally would be leaving.

"They're in here," George said.

I followed him into the garage. He reached up to pull down the door, a movement that yanked his underwear out of his pants and exposed his potbelly. The door came down and we were shut out from the street.

He didn't put on a light. In the dimness he went to the rear of the garage and crouched at his narrow workbench. Under it he had tin cans and rags and tools and whatever else one keeps in a garage. He fumbled at something; what it was I couldn't see past his body and I wasn't interested. Then he rose with the pouch.

"There," he said. "Go to hell."

"Thanks," I said. "I know the direction."

I dropped the pouch into my jacket pocket. We hadn't once mentioned the nasty word jewels.

5

Sally was getting into the station wagon when I came out of George Huntley's garage. I shouted to her. She withdrew her foot from inside the car. The jewels rattled in my pocket as I hurried to her.

"I was just about to go for you," she said when I reached her.

In a trim white square-necked dress she looked as fresh and youthful as the day I had first met her. All the same, I would rather not have kissed her so soon after having come from that divan. But it was the thing I always did when I came home, so I pecked at her mouth. Then I explained, "Mrs. Martaine gave me a ride home from the city."

"Norma Martaine?" she said as if to make sure I didn't mean somebody else.

"Why not? It isn't as if she knows about the jewels, and I have to act normal with her, don't I? She was in the city with her car and expected her husband to drive her home, but he was tied up and she had a bad headache, so she came down to my office to ask me to."

"How nice of her!" Sally said.

Why the sarcasm? It couldn't be that she doubted my story. It had the ring of truth because it was true. As far as it went.

She started to take my arm as we moved to the front door. Wrong arm! If she brushed against the pouch in my pocket on that side, she would want to know what I had in it. I slipped to the other side of her, put my arm about her waist, and like that we went the remaining fifty feet to the door. She had a better waist than Norma, slim without being skinny.

Oh, hell!

The boys were in the house, both flopped in front of the television. I was pleased to note, though, that while Chuck had one eye on the screen, his other was on a book. I paused to say hello to them (Brandy still kissed me except in public), after which I made for the bathroom.

Nobody in the family locked the bathroom door unless outsiders were in the house. I locked it and then checked the contents of the pouch. All the pieces were there. I removed the lid of the toilet tank and pulled up the right sleeves of my jacket and shirt and placed the pouch on the bottom, in a rear corner. Over the years minerals in the water had stained the inside of the tank, especially the bottom, so that the pouch lay on a kind of protective coloration unless one peered in. An obvious hiding place, even more obvious than a secret drawer, but Sally never lifted the lid even when the toilet stopped running (she yelled for me) and I didn't think anybody would come again to look for it.

I had no wish to be badgered any more about the jewels. When they came out of the tank, it would be my decision, whatever it would be.

I replaced the lid and washed up and went to have dinner with my family.

Tuesday

At ten in the morning I met with Christopher Tripp and his lawyer in the office of our company lawyer. I had had Lucille fill in our standard contract form. The terms were less than generous, but Christopher Tripp didn't know or care. He would have paid to have his brother's book published.

He was a soft-spoken, low-keyed man, something or other in electronics in Denver. "I always watched over Gordon," he told me. "He was an impractical dreamer, you know. He never worried where his next cent was coming from. Most of it came from me. When you have a poet like Gordon for a brother, a man who makes a great contribution to the culture of the country, you are happy to help him make that contribution. And now this memorial to him."

"Uh-huh," I said.

Meanwhile his lawyer was quibbling with the Lakeview lawyer about every second clause in the contract. Over the wrong ones; he was a lot more familiar with the real estate business than with the book business. Finally, when it got down to signing, I learned what the lawyers should have revealed in the first place, that Christopher Tripp's signature wouldn't be valid till the will was probated. This matter was kicked around for some time—at two lawyers' fees at a fortune per hour—till they agreed on a formula. A clause was typed into the contract to the effect that he was signing it subject to his appointment by the court as executor.

So I had the book signed up after a fashion, though I couldn't feel a sense of accomplishment. I had not wanted it, Norma Martaine didn't care any more, which meant that her husband didn't either, and when the book came out, Harve Atkinson would growl about it because by then Gordon Tripp would have been forgotten, as already he was pretty much forgotten by everybody but his brother and the police and his murderer.

A memorial, Christopher Tripp had said over and over. Well, I couldn't begrudge anybody a memorial.

When I returned to my office, the morning pretty well shot, Lucille had a piece of breathless information. Mrs. Martaine had phoned me from her home, twice, and I was to call her back immediately.

"Should I get her for you?" Lucille said.

"All right."

I went into my office and sat. I was annoyed with Norma. She had hardly given me a chance to catch my breath. I should have made it clear to her yesterday that once had been too much. I was having some difficulty making it clear to myself.

Lucille buzzed my phone. "Here's Mrs. Martaine," she said. And then there was Norma saying, "Caleb, I've been waiting and waiting for your call. You have to help us."

"Hang up, Lucille." I heard the click. "What is it, Norma?"

"Edward has been arrested."

"For Gordon's murder?"

"Yes. But I shouldn't have said he was arrested. He hasn't been yet. But they made him go to the police station. I mean he went willingly, but they did come for him."

"Take it easy, Norma. Try to be coherent."

I realized I had spoken too loud. I didn't hear Stu in his office, but that didn't mean he wasn't quietly at his desk on the other side of the partition.

"It was Lieutenant Burke," Norma was saying. "He phoned very early in the morning, before Edward left for the station, and asked Edward to wait for him. I was still asleep in my room when Lieutenant Burke arrived. Edward woke me and said not to worry, he'd be back soon. He didn't come back. Finally I called the police and they let me speak to him. It's ridiculous. Just because he was seen near Gordon's house that afternoon."

"There must be more than that if they took him to headquarters," I whispered into the phone.

"I don't know what. Edward told me almost nothing on the phone. You must know."

"How would I?"

"I can't hear you, Caleb."

"I don't know a thing," I said, raising my voice a bit. "It seems to me what he needs is one of his big-shot lawyers."

"He was trying to contact Maxwell Gerhardt when I spoke to him. Maxwell has been his lawyer for years. He's not in. His office is trying to locate him, and when they do, he has to come all the way from the city. Caleb, you have to do something."

"The lawyer will do whatever needs doing."

"You can do more. You're in a position to with the police. Caleb, we need your help."

If she had been less of a lady, she could have said I had an obligation. I had an obligation to her for a pleasant couple of hours in her guest house, and to my boss for being my boss, and then there was the one she didn't know about in the form of her jewels in the tank of my toilet.

I said irritably, "What do you expect me to do, call up Chief Messner and tell him to lay off your husband no matter what he has on him? And if I did, do you think he would listen to me?"

Her tone also had an edge to it. "All I ask is for you to find out. Is that too much to ask?"

"They have to tell him, and he'll tell you."

"But when will that be? Meanwhile I'm sitting here going out of my mind."

"All right, Norma. I'll call you back in a few minutes."

"I knew I could count on you, darling," she said in a voice like a caress.

I wished she hadn't said that on an open line.

2

After I had said good-bye to Norma Martaine, I waited some ten seconds. Then I picked up the phone again and dialed.

Sergeant Swan answered. He said the chief was very busy on an important matter and couldn't be disturbed.

For the first time since I had been named chairman I employed the tone of authority. "I want to speak to him at once."

That got action. In less than a minute Nate Messner's staccato voice came on.

"Chief, why is Edward Martaine being held?" I said briskly in my no-nonsense mood.

"He's not being held. He was asked to come in and answer some questions."

"Why couldn't he have answered them at home?"

"Will you hold on?" I heard voices in the background, then the hum of an empty line. It was a while before there was the rattle of a phone being lifted. "Mr. Dawson. I was in the general room with the others, where I couldn't speak freely. Now I'm in my office. It's an unpleasant business. I understand how you feel, being you work for him."

"Have you reason to believe he murdered Gordon Tripp?"

"If I didn't have some reason, I wouldn't be bothering him. Did you know Mr. Martaine is a homosexual?"

Since yesterday afternoon I was less than startled by the news. "What if he is?" I said.

"Dan Kibble found it out. He's been digging these last few days."

"I heard about some of that. For a time I thought he was hot on my neck."

"Well..." Messner said. "Anyway, about Mr. Martaine. You wouldn't think it to look at him, but it turns out he's what they call a closet queen. He's married and all, this one his second wife, but it seems he likes boys better than girls. I guess you knew."

"Sort of. But what does it prove?"

"You know how those gay people are. More jealous than straight people. More excitable."

"That's evidence, Chief?"

"I'm not saying it is by itself. But if it fits. Killing with a soda bottle, that's an act of excitement. Caused by jealousy at finding somebody with Tripp. It wasn't Mrs. Martaine. At first Dan and I thought it likely was her. You can just see it. A pansy finds his wife fooling with his boy friend. He's jealous not because his wife is being had but because she's having him. Kind of funny, huh?"

"Not very."

"Anyway, we dropped it being Mrs. Martaine when her alibi checked out. Mr. Martaine left his house around seven-thirty and got to his office around nine. She never gets up with him. She was in bed more than an hour after he left. Later she went to the bank. Do you remember that was the day she lost her jewels?"

"I remember."

"Funny, all the things happened that day. Well, they couldn't have been in Tripp's house at the same time that day. At two she was back in bed with a headache and didn't get up till it was time for dinner. Her two servants swear to this. So unless the servants lied, when her husband was seen coming out of Tripp's house at four o'clock—"

"Hold it, Chief. I heard he was seen taking a walk near there. Was he actually seen coming out of the cottage?"

"As good as. He was seen coming from it on the walk from the front door to the road. Do you know Tony Powell who runs the Triangle Garage?"

"I should. He's taken enough of my money."

"Tony knows Mr. Martaine very well. Mr. Martaine has three cars and he wouldn't let anybody but Tony touch them. Wednesday afternoon Tony came around the bend above Tripp's house in his tow truck and saw somebody suddenly come up the walk and dive out of sight in some bushes. It was Mr. Martaine. When he first heard of the murder, he couldn't make up his mind if he should tell, being Mr. Martaine was his best customer and he liked him. But he told his wife and she kept after him about his duty, and Saturday he came in and told me."

"What's Mr. Martaine's explanation?"

"Claims he was taking a walk in the woods and lost the path and found himself behind Tripp's house. Claims he had come around to the front to look for the path and Tony saw him going back into the woods."

"What's wrong with that?"

"There's no path that side of the road, that's what's wrong with it. Anybody would know who does as much walking in that area as he says he does. And why would he start running when he heard a car coming around the bend?"

"I wouldn't call that conclusive evidence."

"Mr. Dawson, if I had conclusive evidence I'd arrest him. Then there's the money. How much would you say Tripp earned writing poetry?"

"Very little."

"Including his books?"

"Even less. And the public-appearance market was pretty much closed to him, he was such a lousy lecturer and reader of his poetry. What are you getting at?"

"I had a long talk with his brother Christopher. He practically supported his brother like a father does a son who can't make a living for himself. Sent him a regular check every month. Then last September, Gordon Tripp sent back that month's check and wrote thanks, he didn't need them any more, he was doing very well on his own at last. But there's nothing to show he made any more money on his poems than before or on anything else. Magazines and publishers and such, they always pay by check, don't they?"

"Always."

"He had a checking account at the County National. The checks he deposited in recent months wouldn't have paid for the gas in his car. The girls in the bank all knew him. Sounds like most of them had a crush on him. They remember that since last fall—when he wrote his brother about being able to support himself—he made deposits in cash. Two or three hundred dollars at a time in twenties and fifties. And last month he bought a stereo in Bill Sanhurst's place. Paid over four hundred dollars for it. In cash. Bill remembers it was in fifties. And in his wallet we found one hundred and seventy-two dollars, including two of those fifty-dollar bills. What does it look like?"

"You tell me."

"It looks like a rich boy friend who wouldn't want the nosy workers at the bank to know he was giving Gordon Tripp big sums of money, so instead of a check he peeled a few fifties and twenties off his bankroll every time he came to visit."

Lucille opened the door and stuck her head in. I waved her away and she withdrew.

I recalled how fascinated Gordon had been by Lucille's bosom, even as the rest of us, and I said, "All right, you have one fairy, but it takes two to tango. Gordon Tripp's eye was strictly for the ladies."

"You're sure of it?"

"Chief, you asked me the same thing when you came to my house Sunday. You knew what Kibble was digging into and that Martaine had been seen at the Tripp cottage Wednesday afternoon, but you kept it from me."

"Mr. Dawson," he said stiffly, "we never had a chairman who asked for a blow-by-blow account of an investigation."

"It could be you have one now. But that's not the point. In my house we were discussing the case. We discussed a valentine poem and when it had been written and all that. You didn't once mention Edward Martaine."

"You work for him. We weren't ready to make a move."

"Look. I have two different jobs and I owe different loyalties to each. All you had to tell me was to keep it to myself."

"I'm sorry you're getting so excited, Mr. Dawson."

I drew in my breath. As with Sally when she told me I was shouting at her.

"Getting back to Tripp," I said, "have you found any indication he was a homo too?"

"So far, no. Lots of them swing both ways, and they're not all swishy. Say, to Tripp, a man or a lady, they were all the same. And Mr. Martaine is very rich. The thing with these rich fags, you can always hold them up for money."

"You think Tripp blackmailed him?"

"No. Mr. Martaine doesn't go around shouting he's gay, but he doesn't keep it such a secret either. Dan had no trouble getting a line on him. I mean Tripp became Mr. Martaine's boy friend—or whatever it is they call each other—because Mr. Martaine was generous with him. It's one way for a poet to make a living."

"A couple of questions bother me, Chief."

"Such as?"

"If on Wednesday afternoon Martaine killed Tripp, why on Thursday morning did he insist I accept Tripp's book?"

"That's an easy one. Dan learned that was a very unusual thing for Mr. Martaine to do in his business. The answer is he did it to cover himself before the body was found. He knew he'd been seen coming out of the house. If he would need a defense, he could raise that same question. Matter of fact, in my opinion, that's a count against him."

"Possibly," I said. "I've another question. If Tripp was Martaine's lover, why did he give the manuscript to me instead of to him? That would have been a surer way to get it accepted."

"Exactly what I asked Dan. And you know what he answered? Tripp was proud. Look at how he stopped taking money from his brother as soon as he didn't need it any more to live on. He figured a big-shot poet like himself didn't need influence to get his book published. He'd do it strictly on his own. Dan's opinion, and I buy it."

"All of which may be true, but I still don't see where you have a case."

"Well, now." He cleared his throat. "A man of Mr. Martaine's standing, we have to be careful how we handle him. We could've questioned him in his own house this morning, like we did before, but I find when they're in the station house they get very nervous and open up easier. We didn't make him come. We asked him and he came. He's being very cooperative except for one thing. He won't talk."

"I understand that he's waiting for his lawyer."

"It's his right. But why does he need a lawyer if he has nothing to hide? Why couldn't we get a yes or no out of him this morning about anything, even if we asked was the sun shining? He made I don't know how many calls to New York to get hold of his lawyer. Finally he did. The lawyer is on his way."

"Where is Mr. Martaine now?"

"He went home. He was leaving when you called me. He said he'd be back at three this afternoon with his lawyer."

"So that's all?"

"For the time being, that's all, Mr. Dawson."

I hung up and at once called Norma Martaine. Joseph answered. It took her quite a while to come to the phone.

"Edward just came home," she said so listlessly I could hardly recognize her voice.

"I know. I've been speaking with the chief. He didn't tell me anything your husband can't tell you."

"Is it serious, do you think?"

"I doubt it." Then I added, "Unless he did do it."

She responded with one of her pauses. When she spoke, her voice trailed to me as if it had come a weary distance in time. "Thank you, Caleb."

A wife in name only, to coin an apt phrase. But a friend, she had said. Her husband's very good friend, and very frightened.

3

I was fed up with Gordon Tripp—with his poetry, his love life, his death. Yet there was no getting away from him. As soon as I had finished speaking to Norma Martaine for the second time, Lucille called out beyond my closed door, "Mr. Dawson is free now, Miss Bosworth," and an elderly woman I didn't know entered with one of the copies of Tripp's manuscript.

She wouldn't sit down. Standing somewhat timidly before my desk, Miss Bosworth told me she had joined our copyediting department only yesterday, and as her first assignment our chief copyeditor had given her this to rush through. Her specialty was science, she said, though she was at ease with poetry. Owlish glasses dominated her rather sweet face. She found a clear spot on my desk on which to place the manuscript.

"I worked on it yesterday afternoon and this morning," she said. "Needless to say, I didn't presume to change as much as a comma in the verse, but you will find several queries to the author. I was unaware that he was dead—so recently, so appallingly!—till Miss Treacher told me ten minutes ago."

"I'll take care of the queries."

Suddenly Stu Stitchman was in my office. Miss Bosworth had left the door open; I looked up to see him standing beside it, sucking his pipe like a baby bottle as he waited for her to leave.

"One of my queries concerns the short verse which apparently is a valentine," she was saying. "Do you recall it?"

"Very well."

"It is out of place where it is, stuck in the midst of—ah—more serious pieces. I have suggested in a note that it be placed elsewhere, though I could not find a proper spot for it. Perhaps it should be deleted."

"I'll think about it. Thank you, Miss Bosworth."

Stu closed the door behind her. He pulled one of the chairs close to the desk and dropped into it. "How about lunch, if you're free?"

"Sure," I said. "I'm ready any time you are."

"It's early. In half an hour. I've a couple of things to do first."

But he didn't go and do them. He reloaded his pipe. He hadn't had to come and sit to make a lunch date. Usually he yelled that or whatever else was on his mind over our partition. I waited him out.

"I listened," he confessed when he had the pipe drawing. "You kept your voice down when you spoke to Norma and your police chief, but I got some of it by putting my ear to the partition. I'm an incurable snoop."

"Did it help your detective game any?"

"Have they actually got the goods on Ed Martaine?"

"It was your intention to feel me out on the subject during lunch," I said.

"Why not wait till then?"

Stu's grin appeared. Though not his Grade-A, open-faced grin. It scarcely penetrated his beard.

"You're right," he said. "But as long as we're talking about it..."

I saw no reason not to tell him—anyway, as much as Messner had told me this morning. He relit his pipe twice before I finished.

"That doesn't have the feel of Ed Martaine being in deep trouble," he commented at the end. "If he killed anybody, it would be in cold blood. No losing his temper. Certainly not with a bottle. I never knew anybody so controlled."

"You've known him a long time."

"Five or six years. Like you, I know her better than him. I must have told you about Norma's literary soirees. That was when they had an apartment in the city as well as that house in Mount Birch. She needed Manhattan to indulge her penchant for collecting people in the arts. I rated not as an editor but because my one novel had recently come out, with some critical success if a commercial disaster. So about once a month for a couple of years I spent an evening in their apartment with fifty other supposedly glamorous people."

"Were you aware of Martaine's sexual proclivity?"

"I have an eye for such things. Small mannerisms and attitude. Besides, it was an open secret."

"I never heard it from you."

"I may be a snoop, but I'm not much of a gossip."

"Did he ever make a pass at you?"

"That's right, you're playing cop—and you sneer at my detective game! No, he didn't. Probably I didn't appeal to him. Or he was aware of my total dedication to heterosexuality."

"Did Norma?"

"Make a pass at me? Again, no. Nor I at her. It wouldn't occur to me, and that's not because she's a bit too insubstantial above the waist for my taste. She's a very elegant lady, and I still bear the burden of being the son of Saul Stitchman who eked out a crummy living in a candy store in Brooklyn. And have you noticed that at her parties she is one hostess who never kisses anybody hello or good-bye, male or female? She's strictly a handshaker. I have a theory she is frigid, which is why she can be on such good terms with her faggot husband."

I said nothing.

Stu struck a match. Over the flame he looked at me. He blew it out without putting it to his pipe, and stood up.

"What the hell," he said. "Lunch in half an hour. Okay?"

I nodded and he went. I heard him enter his office.

I had a hundred things to do. I had spent a good part of the week on Gordon Tripp and his manuscript, in one way or another. Here it was again before me, ready to be put into production after I had okayed the copyediting. In half an hour I could get rid of it. I opened the manuscript.

Two notes from Miss Bosworth were clipped to the title page. One was an explanation of how she had reorganized and reduced the credit pages to a single page. The other gave the opinion I had already heard from her about the valentine. Page 217.

Miss Bosworth had made a notation next to the second line to the author she had thought was alive: "Awk." Penciled in lightly, as if hardly daring to make a comment.

Well as I knew the verse, I read it again. Twice.

> Sweet, your minstrel plucks his lyre
>   Ardently for you his lay.
> Let concupiscence inspire
>   Loving deeds on Cupid's day.
> You who beatify my bed
> Do so not uncomforted.

Did a homo send a valentine to his lover? I had no idea. Would he call his lover his lay even as a pun? I doubted it. Anatomically it didn't seem...

Miss Bosworth was right, if only somewhat. The second line tended to be a bit awkward on the tongue with that *for you* between *ardently* and *his lay*. His problem had been to get in both the pun and the rhyme, and he had not been facile in the choice of the adverb with which he had started the line. *Ardently* was unmusical in that spot, and anyway, pedestrian.

And then I saw it. There it was under my eyes where it had been all along.

Distantly in the center office a persistently ringing phone was not being answered. It was well after twelve; the secretaries were out. In the next office Stu coughed once. Bob Roth yelled, "Damn it, isn't anybody around to answer that?" The heels of a running girl clicked. The ringing stopped abruptly, somebody said, "Jean Heller speaking," and then there was nothing to listen to.

Stu moved noisily about. His door opened and then my door opened, and he was saying cheerfully, "It isn't half an hour, but I can go now."

I wet my lips. I didn't know what to say.

He frowned. He came close to my desk. He looked down at the manuscript spread open to page 217, he looked up at my face, he looked again at the manuscript. Then he sat down and fumbled with his pipe.

"So you know," I said.

He nodded glumly. "I spotted it yesterday. After you and Norma left. Thoughts ran through my head about the possibility of a feigned headache and hanky-panky and what not. Caleb, don't bother to protest. I've had a bellyful of the detective game; I've stopped playing it. But yesterday I was still at it. I can't resist any kind of puzzle or problem. I got this idea for a fling at literary detection. You know, like the scholars who claim they can find proof in Shakespeare's sonnets that his dark lady was actually a man. I asked Lucille if there was a copy of Tripp's manuscript around, and she brought me the original from your file. I browsed in it for a clue."

"The police were ahead of you. They had the manuscript over the weekend for the same reason. The chief had his daughter, who's an English professor, go through it."

"And nobody saw it?"

"Everybody wondered what the valentine was doing in this collection, but that was all. I didn't see it myself till a few minutes ago."

"I was hoping you never would." Stu scowled at the empty air. "I've the kind of mind that feeds on puzzles. I spotted this one right off and realized what a nasty game I was playing. From that minute on I wanted no more of it."

"What game were you playing a short time ago when you heard that Martaine was being questioned by the police?"

"That was no game," he said. "You're my very good friend, Caleb. Ed Martaine means nothing to me."

"Therefore you'd rather have him the murderer than I. Stu, I'm deeply touched."

"I'm glad to hear the good old Dawson sarcasm. I hope it means you're going to let this whole rotten business be buried with Gordon Tripp." His hand slammed down on my desk, completely covering those six lines on page 217. "To include this with the rest! That taunting, smirking son-of-a-bitch got what was coming to him!"

"Stu, I didn't kill him."

"I don't give a damn."

"I didn't kill him."

"I know you didn't. You wouldn't have left that page in the manuscript. You wouldn't have had copies made of it. Besides, it appears that Ed Martaine is the most likely candidate."

"He didn't kill him either."

"Caleb, why don't you drop it? What's the difference who did it? He's no loss, not even to poetry. For God's sake, don't get righteous!"

"Me righteous?" I said, and laughed.

He looked at me as if I had gone off my rocker. Then he said, "Let's go out to lunch and get potted."

"Yes," I said. "Let's."

4

I didn't get potted. I had one bourbon-and-water and then found I had no taste for more.

I was glad that in the overcrowded restaurant Stu and I had to share a table with two strangers, that we had to speak loudly to be heard in the lunch-hour bedlam, so that whatever we talked about in public couldn't be the one thing on our minds. I followed the drink with a hot pastrami sandwich and two cups of coffee, and amid all that chatter and clatter and with my very good friend Stu Stitchman across the table from me, I was very much alone with myself.

How many coincidences were needed before they stopped being coincidences?

Stu had said something like that a long time ago, Friday morning when we had met on the street on the way to work. Of course I didn't remind him of it. I didn't mention that now on Tuesday there were no more coincidences.

When we were out on the street, I told him I was not returning to the office.

"Where are you going?" He seemed worried about me.

"Home."

"And there?"

"I have some urgent responsibilities in Mount Birch."

"Caleb, I'm no good at dishing out sentiment. Don't let this throw you. Keep in mind you have more to hold onto than anybody I know."

"Have I?" I said.

"Don't be an idiot. Think about it and you'll see."

All I was doing was thinking. Stu might be a whiz at puzzles, but he didn't have anywhere near the facts I did. Such as the one in the tank of my toilet at home.

Having plenty of time till the next train, I walked with him back to the Paragon Building. There I left him.

This was the third afternoon in a row I was taking off from work. I didn't know if I would ever be back.

5

Mort Reach was on the steps of the municipal building when I stepped out of the taxi. He scurried down to meet me.

"He must be in a tight spot if he sent out a frantic call for you," he said.

"Nobody sent for me."

"Then why in the middle of the afternoon aren't you at your job in the city? You're wearing a jacket and tie and got out of a cab. You must have come directly from the station."

"You amaze me, Holmes."

I started up the steps. The avid little newsman kept pace with me. He demanded, "What's going on inside?"

"I was about to ask you."

"You're a great kidder, Caleb. Edward Martaine being such a big wheel, they've been trying to keep it from the press. But I damn well know he was brought in this morning for grilling and that half an hour ago he returned with a lawyer in tow. And Dave Bernstein is in there with them for the D.A.'s office. And now here's the department chairman who just so happens to be one of Martaine's wage slaves."

"Is that innuendo going to appear in your story?"

"It depends. The citizens of Mount Birch have the right to know if one of their trustees is looking out for their interest or that of the man who heads the company he works for."

I stopped at the double entrance doors. "Tell them I am dedicated to truth and justice."

"Caleb, I'm serious. Something big is cooking, but nobody will say what. This is connected with him being a pansy. Right?"

"Is he?"

"You're getting to be like the others," Mort said. "Too bad. You were a nice guy, now you're a politician. What gripes me, they owe me plenty. I was the one who gave Nate the line on Martaine being queer. Then when they followed that lead they wouldn't tell me where it led to. It must lead to Tripp's murder—but how? I've a glimmering. They wouldn't tell me, but they don't mind picking my brain. Dan Kibble came to me and asked me if Tripp was that way too."

This was more important than whatever was going on inside. "Well, was he?" I asked.

"In no way. I saw a lot of Gordon this past year. When I couldn't stand my home—try relaxing with five barbarian kids and their mother constantly screaming at them—I'd go to his place with a bottle of booze, and in peace and quiet we'd sit and talk and get pleasantly plastered."

Except for traffic in the street it was remarkably quiet outside the building. Nobody came or went. I was afraid to ask the question, but I had to.

"Did he talk about his sex life?"

"I've been asked that a dozen times these last few days," Mort said. "It was Gordon's favorite topic. When he was in his cups he loved to tell me the erotic details. I think that was what he liked most about our drinking sessions. I was a good audience. I admit it, I got a vicarious charge out of listening. Maybe he exaggerated, but probably he didn't have to." He cocked his head. "But there were no names. That's what Nate wanted to hear and what you're waiting to hear. In that, Gordon was the perfect gentleman. Kiss and tell, but no names."

No names except one in a valentine.

"All I can say definitely," he was saying, "is that he had two steady pieces going at the same time. He was amused by the problem of keeping them from knowing about each other. There were others now and then, usually one-timers; his main interest was in those two. What a man! There's no money in being a poet, but it has other compensations."

Audibly Mort smacked his lips. I could have strangled him where he stood.

"No man in his life?" I asked.

"That way? Meaning Martaine, of course. I tell you what I've been telling the police—I would have known. It's not because he never once gave any sign of trying to make me. I realize I'm not the most appealing hunk of flesh on earth, and that goes for both sexes. When he was really crocked and rambling about his bedroom activities, he would have given me some idea. And then there's the fact that in homo affairs, at least one of the partners is more or less effeminate. Martaine isn't—unless you think about it and then you notice small signs—and Tripp was as masculine as they come in both mind and manner. You can take my word for it."

"I do," I said.

"Damn it, Caleb, here I've been doing the talking when a reporter's job is to listen. One good turn deserves another. Come on, what gives?"

"I came to find out."

I entered the building. Mort stuck to my side.

They were all in the hall at the police headquarters end of the building. It was over; they had come out of the room they had been in, but they were still hanging around in an altogether amiable way. Edward Martaine wore his courtly smile as he stood in a group consisting of himself and Chief Messner and Assistant D.A. Bernstein. Investigator Kibble was nodding his head in agreement at something being said to him by a squat man I didn't know, probably the lawyer. One would think they had come from a tea party.

"Why, Caleb," Martaine said. He left Messner and Bernstein to come and pump my hand. He wore a turtleneck pullover and a tweed jacket; he could have passed for the kind of aging actor young girls adore. "Norma told me she spoke to you on the phone. It was good of you to come. But unnecessary."

"I felt I had to," I said, looking him in the eye. "How did it go?"

"Very well. I appreciate your concern. I believe I have convinced them I could not have been involved."

"That's good."

"Caleb, I would like you to meet Maxwell Gerhardt, my attorney." With hand on my shoulder, he took me to the squat man in conversation with Kibble. "Max, this is my good friend Caleb Dawson. He is one of our more brilliant editors at Lakeview and also a village trustee here."

Such a build-up rated a promotion at least. And all of a sudden I had become a good friend. Everybody was good friends.

Then they left, Martaine and his lawyer, pestered all the way down the hall by Mort Reach clamoring for a statement. He got none, of course. He disappeared with them, and I was left alone with the law and order of the village, the county, and the state. I asked them if they had gotten anything out of Martaine worth the trouble.

"There is no conclusive evidence," Bernstein said, "other than that he was seen apparently leaving the house. Whatever else there is, is sheer speculation. In my opinion he should not have been brought in at this time."

"He might have broken," Kibble said. "Lots do when you lean on them."

"Come into my office, Mr. Dawson, and I'll fill you in," Messner said.

"Thanks, but not now," I said. "I'm going home."

I knew a lot more than he could tell me. I knew most of everything. I wished to hell I didn't.

6

Half a mile from my house a station wagon like mine flitted by me walking on the left side of the road. It stopped with a squeal of brakes; it was in fact mine, and through the tailgate window I saw Sally's tawny head. She was alone. I broke into a trot.

When I opened the right door she looked, incredibly, the same Sally as always—the soft-faced, trim freshness that today twisted my heart.

"I couldn't believe it was you," she said as I got in. "Did you walk all the way from the station?"

"I'm coming from police headquarters." I closed the door. She didn't start the car; she was watching me with her reaction suspended. I said, "The police have been questioning Edward Martaine about the murder. They think he might have done it."

"He couldn't have," she blurted.

"Why not?"

She recovered quickly. "He doesn't strike me as the type."

"Who would be the type?"

She let the question slide over her. I was sorry I had asked it. There was no point to it.

On the two-lane road cars coming up behind us at considerable speed had to swing out to the opposite lane to pass us. Our standing there created a dangerous situation, but she seemed to have forgotten that she was the one behind the wheel. She had an urgent question of her own. "What makes them think he did it?"

"Bits of this and that. Mostly because he was seen coming out of Gordon's cottage Wednesday afternoon."

Sally put the car into motion then. We hadn't kissed hello.

"Why did you have to leave work to go there?" she said.

"I didn't have to. It was strictly my idea. I wanted to make sure they didn't pin it on the wrong person."

"How do you know he's the wrong person?"

Within two minutes of our home wasn't the right time. I couldn't make up my mind if there should ever be the right time.

"You're the one who said he's not the type," I said. Which was no answer, of course.

Then we were home. George and Marie Huntley were sitting under their red maple, she knitting, he reading a newspaper. She waved to us when our car turned into our driveway; he glanced up and quickly stuck his head behind the paper. There weren't many innocents around.

Sally had been marketing. I carried the two bags of food into the kitchen. Normally I would have helped her put away the groceries, and while doing so I would have touched her here and there, given her a hug and kissed the back of her neck. Today it hurt to be near her. I told her I was going to take a shower.

I let the water run cold. That changed nothing. I dressed in my at-home outfit—cotton pants, polo shirt, soft shoes. The boys were nowhere about. I went into the study to read submitted manuscripts I had brought home over a week ago. One was probably publishable, on consumer fraud, but when I had finished it I realized I had been reading words without absorbing them.

I came out when Sally called me for dinner. The chatter of the boys swirled around us, dominating the meal even more than usual. Every now and then I caught Sally giving me a worried look. Once she asked tentatively, "Dear, don't you feel well?" I shrugged and she didn't pursue the subject. As soon as we finished eating I returned to the study.

Dusk seeped in. I didn't turn on the standing lamp beside the armchair in which I did my serious reading. Another manuscript was on my lap. I hadn't gone past the first page; it was there as a prop. Night entered the room, merging with the night in my soul.

The door opened. Sally was closing it again without entering when, by the light from the hall behind her, she caught my outline on the chair.

"Dear, why are you sitting in the dark?"

I turned on the lamp. "Where are the boys?"

"They've finished their homework. They're in their room playing Monopoly."

"Close the door and sit down," I said.

She closed the door and sat on the desk chair. Her legs were straight down and her feet were together, like a schoolgirl apprehensively waiting in the principal's office to be disciplined. I imagined that her insides were as constricted as mine.

I said, "I suppose you realize that I know."

"Know what?" she said automatically, and caught her lower lip between her teeth.

"I've been sitting here telling myself I ought to let it alone. What was done was done, and mostly we did it to ourselves. But I can't. Sally, I can't let myself be manipulated any more."

At least she didn't say she didn't know what I was talking about. Her lip stayed between her teeth. Her eyes were very wide, watching me as if I were a snake about to strike.

But I didn't want it to be like that. I couldn't hate her. What I felt was a kind of weary sadness for all of us.

"That valentine Gordon wrote to you," I said, "were you aware that he included it in the manuscript of his collected poems?"

"Wrote to *me*? A poem to me?"

"Sally, for God's sake! He must have sent it to you. That's the purpose of a valentine. It's an acrostic verse. The first letters of the six lines spell S-A-L-L-Y-D. Sally D. He would have told you it was an acrostic. Otherwise there would have been no point in writing it in that form."

She was silent.

"It was only today at noon I caught on it was an acrostic," I said. "When I saw that, other things fell into place."

She spoke listlessly. "It doesn't mean what you think. Yes, he tried to make love to me, but I wouldn't let him. He sent it to me last St. Valentine's Day and I promptly burned it."

"I can believe you burned it. You wouldn't have wanted me to come across it. Nothing else is true. You were in his bed with him Wednesday morning."

"No! You mustn't say that."

"That's the point, I must say it all. So must you if there's to be any hope for us. That poem couldn't have been more explicit. You were his lay. You beatified his bed, and in it you were not uncomforted. Sally, why did you have to go to him to be comforted? What had I done to you?"

"That wasn't it!" The words rushed from her throat like a scream. "They're a poet's words. I guess he liked the sound of them. They rhymed, that was all. It had nothing to do with being comforted."

"Then what? Was he better in the sack than I? Merely that?"

"Caleb, I love you." She subsided. Her voice took on a remote quality. "I don't know why I did it. I really don't. I suppose I was a—a bored housewife. He was after me for a long time. I wouldn't. Then one morning—" She stopped.

"Go on."

"One morning I walked up to his place."

"When was that?"

"Last January. There was snow on the path. It was after the Christmas vacation. The children were back at school. I had driven you to the station. I had sent the children off to school. I had made the beds and straightened up the house." Again she stopped.

"Then, having nothing else to do with yourself, you went up there."

"I suppose it was something like that," she muttered. "He called me on the phone, and instead of saying no, as always before, I said yes. I liked him very much. I admit it. He had an animal appeal. He was very charming. But, Caleb, you have to believe me. I never stopped loving you."

"He was so very charming that he couldn't resist taunting me over possessing my wife by including the valentine in the manuscript he submitted to me. And in his charming way he used to get drunk with Mort Reach and tell him in detail the things you did together. Did you know that?"

"Oh, God, he didn't!"

"What could you have expected? But don't worry, he never mentioned your name to Mort, or that of any of his women. And he thought the chances were I wouldn't spot the acrostic. He took care to indent the second and fourth lines to make it more obscure. Though he must have had a good laugh to himself at the private joke he was playing on me when he handed me the manuscript. The bastard's charm was positively overwhelming."

Elsewhere in the house voices were suddenly raised. Chuck shouted, "All right, be a baby!" and silence returned. She sat quite erect, skirt well above her pretty knees, hands folded on her lap in an attitude of indrawn waiting.

"Did you go up there often?" I asked her.

"Once or twice a month."

"Or two or three or half a dozen times a month?"

"Not that often."

"When did you see him last week?"

"I didn't see him at all last week."

"Stop lying, Sally. Somebody told him I was thinking of turning down his manuscript. I had mentioned that to only two people in the office before he was killed, Stu and Lucille, and I was becoming convinced it had been Lucille because she was another female who had found him charming. But you also knew. When I come home from work I tell you what happened at the office, what decisions I had made or was thinking of making. Tuesday evening I told you and Wednesday morning you told him."

"I may have mentioned it." She caught herself. "But it wasn't on Wednesday."

"When then could it have been if I told you Tuesday evening and he was dead on Wednesday?"

She flared up. "Caleb, you're playing cat-and-mouse with me!"

My God, was I actually enjoying this in my bitterness?

"I don't mean to, Sally. But I'm set on getting at the truth."

"All right. I forgot I spoke to him on the phone Wednesday morning."

"You spoke to him, but not on the phone. You told him as you lay"—a lump in my throat momentarily gagged me—"in his arms."

"I wasn't there Wednesday. I was in the beauty parlor. You can ask Mrs. Simon and look in her appointment book."

"That changes nothing. From the beauty parlor you drove to his cottage. No, you wouldn't have driven. You said you'd walked up the first time, and you would always walk because you wouldn't want your car seen there. You came home from the beauty parlor and walked up the path. The walk made you thirsty. He gave you a drink of cherry soda. He also gave you pot to smoke with him in bed." I frowned, for the first time a bit uncertain, though that part was not essential. "You've never smoked even a cigarette. I suppose marijuana fitted the setting. LSD too. Some was in his refrigerator."

"I wouldn't touch LSD."

"But you smoked marijuana with him."

"He made me try it and it made me feel good. I never smoked it anywhere but in his place." She looked angry, not with herself but with me. "I've admitted I used to go there, but I wasn't there Wednesday."

"You were in his cottage at noon," I said, "which was about when he was killed."

"Caleb, are you saying I killed him?"

"I'm saying you saw him killed. That evening when you picked me up at the station you were listening intently to Mort Reach's newscast, and when we got home you kept the kitchen radio on. When you finally showed me the jewels, you led me to believe it was news about them you were listening for. But you knew all about the jewels. What you were listening for was whether the murder had yet been discovered. It wasn't till the next evening I found the body. You knew what I would find when I went up there to see him."

Her head was bowed. She had nothing to say.

"You didn't have to be very good at playing the role," I said, "except to have your lines prepared. Your tenseness, your fears, your irritability with me could be blamed on the jewels. It must have been partly that, but also you had seen your lover lying dead. No wonder you wouldn't let me touch you that night—anyway, hardly—or the other nights. You're not insensitive; you'd just brutally lost a lover. If Thursday night was an exception, the night you put the jewels on your bare skin and we had ourselves an orgy, I think even that was done to manipulate me, using sex the way you used lies and your discontent to get me to do what you wanted me to do about the jewels."

"Caleb, please!"

"Please what?"

"The jewels were for you as well as for me. Because I love you."

"There's nobody else around to love, with Gordon dead."

"How can you say such an awful thing? I am sorry he's dead, but I never loved him. I love you. I wanted a nice life for us and the children. And you wanted to keep them. You did. You would have tried to get a lot of money for them if they hadn't been stolen. And about Gordon—I'd beg you to forgive me, but I know you, you'd make one of your sarcastic cracks."

"Don't for a moment think I feel morally superior," I said, "That's not what I'm talking about at all. Let me tell you something about me you don't know. It hurts like hell every time I think of you rutting with him, but I'm not entitled to throw stones at you. Yesterday I drove home with Norma from the city a couple of hours earlier than I let on to you. They have a log cabin on their grounds, a guest house, and I tumbled her a couple of times on a divan they have there."

"Not her," she whispered.

"Funny, isn't it? It could be said she was the aggressor, but I didn't exactly put up a struggle. Probably less than you did with Gordon. For whatever it can mean any more, I feel rotten about it."

"I know. I hate myself because of Gordon."

"I want to believe that," I said. "I'll believe it when you tell me what happened in his cabin Wednesday."

"I wasn't there."

"How did you get Norma Martaine's jewels?"

"You know very well how. I found them." That little jaw of hers was set. "You said you had wanted to let it alone. Let it alone! The jewels are gone. Perhaps our marriage is gone. Do you have to destroy the children too?"

I had a sudden urge to drop to my knees and put my face in her lap and let the past bury itself. Except that when it came down to doing it, I couldn't.

"Wait here," I said. "I'll be right back."

In passing the boys' room, I looked through the open door. They were stretched out on the floor with the Monopoly board between them. I moved on to the bathroom and took the pouch out of the toilet tank. It was sopping wet. I squeezed as much water from the pouch as I could (the diamonds and such inside felt like pebbles) and returned to the study.

Sally hadn't stirred; she sat fixed to the desk chair, erect but drawn into herself. Her mouth fell open when she saw the pouch. I held it dangling from its drawstring.

"You had them all along," she said hoarsely.

"George Huntley helped himself to them while we were in the movies Friday."

"George?" she said incredulously.

"He got into the habit of peeping in our bedroom at night from behind the evergreen. His interest was in watching you, but while he was at it last week he saw what we had and where we hid them. First chance he had he came and took them."

"How did you guess?"

"I've been in a figuring-things-out stage lately. I had to lean on him to get it back. It was easy. He hasn't your strength of character, Sally." I swung the pouch by its drawstring. "This is the key, and of the outsiders, only I have it. So maybe I didn't have to be very smart. But I know, Sally. There are a few things that happened in the cottage Wednesday I'm not sure of, but I know the essentials. I think it's better for what's left between us, if anything, if you will willingly open up to me."

She just sat. The way she held her jaw told me it was no use.

I stuck the pouch into the right pocket of my pants. She watched me blankly. The pouch wet the pocket and through it my shorts.

"What are you going to do with them?" she asked as if afraid of the answer.

"Return them."

"Caleb... if..."

"Don't you ever give up?" I said. "We're returning them tonight. Now."

"Do I have to go with you?"

"You sure do. I suggest you get a coat. It's turning chilly out."

We stopped off in the boys' room. She told them it was past their bedtime, and that we were going out for a short while.

"Aw, we've almost finished the game," Brandy said. "Can't we stay up, Mommy, and finish?"

She had too much to fight to fight them. "Very well, but both of you get into your pajamas."

When they had their pajamas on, she kissed each of the boys as if she were going on a journey. In a way she was. I kissed Brandy and ran my hand affectionately through Chuck's hair. Then she put on her black suede coat and I put on my tweed jacket. Water from the pouch ran down my leg and into my shoe.

7

Joseph admitted us. He was an elderly, powerful man, too big and awkward-looking for a house servant. He said both Mr. and Mrs. Martaine were in. He ushered us into the entrance hall the size of our living room and dinette combined, and he went up the wide curved staircase to inform them that Mr. and Mrs. Dawson were here to see them.

There were places to sit in the hall—a long upholstered bench, heavily carved chairs on either side of a marble table beneath an ornate gold mirror—but we remained standing. Sally held her coat wrapped around her like a black magician's cloak in which she could hide.

Edward Martaine came down the stairs. He wore a casual corduroy jacket; as always, there was an inch of handkerchief showing from his breast pocket. He must have known why we had come here together at this hour, but you couldn't tell it from the quietly affable way he shook our hands.

"My wife will be down shortly," he said. "Mrs. Dawson, may I have your coat?"

She shook her head, clinging to it as if she expected the place to turn cold. She hadn't said a word since we left our house, and here she didn't either.

He conducted us into the library. It was all oak and leather, and some of the books on the ceiling-high shelves had a look of having been read.

"Won't you sit down?" Sally dropped into a deep chair; I stayed on my feet. "Would you care for a drink?" I said no, thanks; Sally didn't seem to have heard him. The right side of my cotton pants was wet from the pouch in my pocket.

Norma entered. In denim pants and a loose pullover, like a teenager. She had a cigarette in her mouth and a pack of them in her hand. I said, "Hello, Norma." She looked at me impassively and nodded; she acted as if Sally weren't there. She sat down on the leather sofa. Her husband came and sat down beside her and took her hand. Friends.

"All right," I said like a committee chairman opening a meeting. "I know most of it. You're thinking my wife told me. She didn't. She didn't trust me at the beginning to cover up murder and go in for blackmail, not to mention shrugging off her bedroom antics with Gordon Tripp, and now she trusts me even less. She knows that if I bring it all out into the open, it will be impossible to keep her out of it. So she keeps denying the obvious even to me in the hope that the mess will go away."

"As it will," Martaine said. "She is smarter than you." He glanced at her and added wryly, "At least in this instance."

Sally found her voice, speaking not to me but to him. "He doesn't realize what a scandal there will be and how it will hurt us." She turned her crumpled face to me. "Caleb, I know you despise me. But think of the children. They won't be able to hold their heads up in the community. They'll never get over it."

"Children have to learn to endure their parents," I said. "I'm not going to let you hide behind them."

"You're a fool," she said. "You always were in some ways. I did it for them. And for you."

"Does that include your hanky-panky with Gordon?"

Her eyes lowered; her spurt of indignation had left her limp. "I wasn't talking about that," she mumbled.

"We're going to talk about it because that's why he's dead." I turned to the Martaines. Standing as they sat, I felt like a prosecutor at a trial at which I myself was one of the guilty. "I would apologize for having a family squabble in front of you, but it's not private. Since last Wednesday there have been you three against me. Well, I'm goddamn tired of being manipulated—in bed and out of bed. I've been a thief—or I thought I was and I accepted it. I've been an accessory to blackmail without knowing it. And now, if you have your way, I'm to be a party to cover up a murder. No, thanks, on all counts."

"It wasn't murder," Martaine said. "At the worst it was a minor degree of manslaughter. It would probably be considered accidental or temporary insanity."

"Then why didn't you have Norma call the police when you came home that afternoon and she told you she had killed him?"

"It wasn't the police we feared," he said. "It was the news media, the scandalmongers. People like us, a man in my position, Norma's social standing, a well-known poet, a suburban housewife—you can imagine the obscenely sensational way that would be treated throughout the country and even abroad. Every aspect of our lives, in particular the—ah—sexual, would be in newspapers and magazines, on television, the vulgar gossip of millions of people. Can't you see, my dear man, how unnecessary that was?"

I said, "Sally for one didn't believe I would see how unnecessary it was. As she mentioned, I'm a fool, and the three of you conspired to make a fool of me. That's over. For a starter, take these back."

I took the wet pouch from my pocket. I stepped to the oak library table near which I had been standing and opened the drawstring and shook out the contents of the pouch. The jewelry fell to the table with small tinklings. The two Martaines stared at them as if they had never before seen them.

"These tie it all together," I said. "Earlier today I learned that Sally was his mistress. One of his two steady mistresses, it turned out. I discovered it through a verse he—" I didn't bother finishing the sentence. "Never mind that now. The thing is, I found out. She refuses to admit she was the woman in his bed Wednesday, for then she would have to admit what happened when she was there, and she doesn't trust me not to take it to the police."

Norma said past her hand holding the cigarette at her mouth, "Do you intend to, Caleb?"

"You called me a solid citizen. Remember?"

"Then she is right, we must admit nothing. You are merely guessing."

"Your husband has already admitted you killed Gordon."

"Did he?" Norma said. "I am sure none of us heard him."

I said, "Sally, what have you to say to that?"

She had not a word to say as she sat huddled in her black suede coat in the warm house.

"All right, then, I'll lay it out." I moved backward against the wall of bookshelves so I could face all three at once. "It was obvious, Mr. Martaine, that you couldn't have killed him, and that wasn't because I'd been told you were a man who was neither bothered by his wife's extramarital affairs nor were having one of your own with Gordon. Probably so, but not proven. The existence of the jewels, though, was a fact, and it was too far-fetched a coincidence that they were lost in a shopping-center parking lot about the same time he was killed—lost by a woman who knew him well and found by a woman I learned had been his mistress. Likely they hadn't been lost at all—or if they had been lost, not in the parking lot. And since Sally had had them when our son came home from school at three o'clock Wednesday afternoon and since you hadn't returned from the city till three-thirty, you had to be out of it as the actual killer."

He gave me his weary, courtly smile. "Then that was your reason for rushing to police headquarters this afternoon? You did not wish to see an innocent man blamed."

"Not innocent. Only an accessory after the fact." I tugged my wet pants from my skin. "We begin with a pair of acknowledged facts Wednesday morning. Sally went to the beauty parlor and Norma went to the bank to take her jewels from the vault. That much was true, but only that much. Norma didn't lose her jewels in the parking lot. I think Sally drove off some time before Norma came from the bank. Sally drove home and left her car there and walked up the path to Gordon's cottage. Norma also went there and found them together."

I had the total attention of my audience—the Martaines holding hands on the sofa, Sally buried in her coat.

"I'm not sure of the time sequence," I went on. "I think Norma must have gone directly from the bank if she still had the pouch in her handbag. If she had gone home first, she would have left it at home instead of carrying it around with her. It bothers me because of the manuscript business. Sally had to have told him that morning while with him that I was turning it down, and it had to be that he then told Norma by phone before she arrived. Probably Norma left for the bank later than she said she did, and she was still at home when Sally, smoking pot in bed with him or doing whatever, mentioned that I had decided to reject—"

"No! Not then!"

Sally had moved to the edge of her chair. Her coat was open; she was trembling. I had thought she would give in, but not so soon. I must have touched a very raw nerve.

"I wouldn't have talked about you at such a time," she said wildly. "I never mentioned your name when I was with him. I always felt so guilty." She glared at Norma. "I don't care. You can see he knows everything. I don't think he wants me any more, but I love him and I need him and I'm going to be honest with him."

Norma put a fresh cigarette between her lips. Her husband held a match for her. They were remarkable people, both of them, for good or ill.

"Go on, Sally," I said.

"He phoned me early Wednesday morning. He asked me to come over. I said I had a beauty-parlor appointment at ten, so I'd be there at eleven. While we were talking on the phone he asked me if you had said anything about his book. That was when I told him."

I nodded. "And he promptly called up his other mistress and said I'd had the abominable judgment to reject his deathless verse and would she be a grateful bedmate and persuade her husband to overrule me. She said she would, and inspired by the sound of his voice on the phone she decided to stop off on the way home from the bank for a tumble before lunch."

"You're vulgar," Norma said without passion.

"Pardon me. I forgot that when a poet copulates it's an ethereal act on a cloud with angels singing. He might at least have locked the door."

"There you're wrong, he did lock it," Sally said. "I mean I locked it myself." Now that she was no longer holding back, she was being mighty fussy about minor points. "He kept an extra key under a flower pot on the ledge of a back window. I knew it was there and she must have known. I had also drawn the shades in the bedroom, but the windows were open and I guess she heard us and got the key from under the flower pot. We didn't hear her enter the house. All of a sudden the bedroom door was flung open. I had never seen anybody so furious."

"And then?"

"She told him she never wanted to have anything to do with him again. He jumped out of bed and just as he was, ran after her. I was so embarrassed I could have died. She was screaming at him in the living room and he was trying to placate her."

"I can appreciate how each of them felt," I said. "This afternoon Mort Reach told me Gordon used to joke about his problem of keeping his two regular women from knowing about each other. I imagine his main worry was you, Norma. You gave him some nice sex, but he could and did get plenty of that elsewhere. What made you of primary importance was that you freed him from having to depend on his brother for a steady income by feeding him a steady diet of fifty-dollar bills. As for your side of it, you'd arrived all on fire to pop into his bed, only to find another woman already in it. Yesterday you kept bringing up the subject of how young and fresh and pretty Sally is. You're by no means bad-looking yourself, but I don't suppose you feel particularly young and fresh any more. And you were paying him for his love, and you'd told him a short time before on the phone you'd be happy, darling, to make your husband make me accept his manuscript. Nobody is going to blame you very much for having clobbered him over the head with a soda bottle."

"I hit him with my bag," Norma said quietly. Deciding what the hell, there was no use any longer maintaining silence now that Sally had opened up. "The first few times I lashed out at him with the bag. I couldn't stand him grabbing at me while he was naked from another woman and begging me to be reasonable. I wanted to get out of there and he wouldn't let me. I don't remember how the bottle got in my hand. I didn't even know what it was. It was something else to strike out with. Then he fell away from me. I bent over him and saw he was dead. I rushed home."

"Unaware that your pouch had fallen out of your handbag when you were swinging it at him," I said. "And then you, Sally, came out of the bedroom and saw your lover dead on the floor and a pouch filled with jewels. You picked up the pouch and also beat it home."

"You make it sound so cold-blooded," Sally said. "It was a nightmare. But the jewels were there, and why should I have left them for somebody else to come and take?"

How did you counter such reasonableness? They were all nice people, really. Sally loved her children very much, loved her husband well enough, had liked her lover who had relieved the tedium of ordinary days; she wouldn't knowingly harm anybody. Norma and Edward Martaine were about the same. Standing here before them, I was not only an impractical fool. I was a bad guy for raising such a needless fuss.

"So much for the death of a poet," I said, again speaking to none of them in particular. "Enter the husbands. When Norma was back home she discovered the pouch was gone. She knew exactly when she had lost it. Besides being valuable, the jewels would be evidence against her, but she couldn't bring herself to go back and get them. She turned to her best friend—her husband. She phoned him at his office and he hurried home. She had taken to her bed—with a genuine headache, I would think—and told him all. He walked to the cottage. The pouch was gone, but he had other things to do. He cleaned up after his wife, wiping everything in the place that could hold fingerprints, because she had been a frequent visitor there, and picking up the pieces of the bottle. The signs of the struggle were left as they were to give the impression of an intruder. A job well done, coolly and efficiently, but there was still the matter of the jewels. He could have no doubt who had them." I addressed him directly. "Mr. Martaine, did you phone my wife or go to see her?"

"I phoned her when I returned home." He smiled sourly. "It was quite a conversation."

"I can imagine," I said. "She had had several hours to prepare for your call. She can be quite glib when she's had a chance to rehearse. She told you she intended to keep them."

"Blackmail," he said. "What could I do? I agreed."

"Especially as it wouldn't come out of your pocket," I said. "The insurance company would reimburse you. Fine and dandy. Everybody would be happy. But there was one complication—the other husband. Me. And she knew me to be untrustworthy—a plodding fellow of some wit but no ambition as far as doing right financially by his family went. She thought that if handled properly she could induce me to retain the jewels—finders keepers, you know—but that I would surely balk at blackmail and covering up a murder. She may have overestimated my moral fiber. Anyway, that was how she handed it to you, and your acceptance meant that the three of you had to agree on a couple of stories—yours and your wife's for the police and the insurance company, hers for me on where and how she had found them. So manipulation began last Wednesday afternoon before I came home from work, and it's ending here and now tonight."

Edward Martaine slammed his fist against the palm of his other hand. Coming from him, the gesture startled us.

"What a tasteless charade I had to play!" he said in a voice suddenly feminine-shrill. "Waking my servants in the middle of the night to make a search they took seriously. Next day waylaying you in the men's room after that meeting in Atkinson's office—I cared not one whit about his book being published when he was alive and less when he was dead—to have a private talk with you to make sure in the most devious manner that you knew no more about how your wife had gotten hold of the jewels than you were supposed to."

I said, "And don't overlook your wife's charade. Hers was a beauty, and I flatter myself there was some fun in it for her. Do you swap stories about the men you each seduce? Did she tell you about yesterday in your guest house, Mr. Martaine? Maybe it was even your suggestion. Tony Powell had seen you come out of Gordon's cottage, and by Sunday it became clear to you he had told the police and they were focusing on you. Getting me to make love to her was supposed to put me in the mood to spill all the inside police dope on the murder. It could even be she didn't dislike me, but all the same it seems to me she went to a lot of trouble for very little."

"Caleb, why don't you ask *me*?" Norma said in her quiet way.

"It's not important. I should have striven to be a gentleman and not mentioned it."

"You've mentioned everything else." She mangled her cigarette in an ashtray balanced on her thigh. "I liked you very much or I wouldn't have. But if you must know, I really did it to get back at that bitch of a wife of yours. She took my lover, she made a murderer out of me, she took my jewelry. I wanted something precious of hers in return, and I got it."

Yet in my arms she had wept, I remembered.

The room had become very quiet. Sally was staring at Norma, and Norma was staring back at her. By their expressions they could have been poised to jump for each other's hair. I wondered if it was because of Gordon Tripp or because of me or because he and I had merged with each other.

Then Sally stood up and wrapped her black coat around her. "I'm going home," she said.

"One minute more," I said. "There's still the matter of calling Chief Messner. It will look better for you, Norma, if you call him yourself."

"This is sheer nonsense," Edward Martaine said. He was also on his feet now. "Dawson—Caleb—the jewels are yours. Take them."

"You're still bargain-hunting, Mr. Martaine. Let your insurance company pay. Thanks, but I've gone through that already."

"Then what do you want?" he said. "Name it. You are a bright young man. There is no telling how high you can go in the Lakeview organization. Indeed, in the Paragon organization. You have nothing to gain by calling the police and everything to gain by not calling them."

Sally was at the closed door. Her face revived with expectancy. She waited. Everybody waited.

I said, "Norma, if you're not going to call the chief, I will."

She stood up. She moved to the phone on a bookshelf. She picked it up and said to me, "Do you have the number?"

"He'll be at home at this hour. The number is 5738."

She dialed. Edward Martaine, her friend, went and stood at her side. On the oak table the scattered jewelry lay glinting under the light.

8

Side by side without touching Sally and I walked to our station wagon in the Martaine parking circle. She said with her head down, "I suppose I'll have to testify at the trial."

"You're the only witness for the defense. But it won't come to a trial. I doubt that the D.A. will seek an indictment when he hears from you how it happened."

"But it will all come out into the open."

"Probably. We'll have to live with it."

We got into the car.

"You said we," she said. "Do you mean all four of us still—you and me and the children?"

"It's all we have and we ought to hang onto it. But remember, I'll never be rich."

"Yes, I know."

I started the engine. The soft May night was cheery with the chatter of insects. We drove home.

THE END

CPSIA information can be obtained
at www.ICGtesting.com
Printed in the USA
LVOW10s1333041217
558575LV00024B/727/P

9 781933 586809